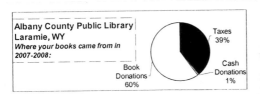

THE SON OF HEAVEN

THE SON OF HEAVEN

Philip Boast

severn
House

This first world edition published in Great Britain 2007 by
SEVERN HOUSE PUBLISHERS LTD of
9–15 High Street, Sutton, Surrey SM1 1DF.
This first world edition published in the USA 2007 by
SEVERN HOUSE PUBLISHERS INC of
595 Madison Avenue, New York, N.Y. 10022.

Copyright © 2007 by Philip Boast.

British Library Cataloguing in Publication Data

Boast, Philip
    The Son of Heaven
    1.   Rome - History - Nero, 54-68 - Fiction
    2.   Detective and mystery stories
    3.   Historical fiction
    I.   Title
    823.9' 14 [F]

    ISBN-13: 978-0-7278-6498-7

All Severn House titles are printed on acid-free paper.

Printed and bound in Great Britain by
MPG Books Ltd., Bodmin, Cornwall.

Prologus

Rome, the Villa Paria
Year 2762, month xin-wei, *day* jia-zi

The girl lay stretched on her back in darkness, too thirsty to sleep. Hours had passed (at least, it felt to her like they had). By now the stuffed leather pouches pressed heavily on her eyes. Her bed was hard as stone, her sheets scratchy linen not soft cannabis. Her long silk nightdresses were scented with jasmine, fabulously rare here so far from civilization, but the foreign air smelt dull and heavy. She lay with her arms crossed over her breasts and her feet together, as if she were dead, yet her heart fluttered like a bird's. She held her breath, listening.

The sound that had woken her did not return.

The barbarians called this Monday, Moon's Day, but the dark was never-ending. She untied the silk cord and pulled the leather sand pouches from her eyes, seeing from the moon's angle in the courtyard the hour was still *ban ye*, deepest night. Foreign spirits haunted a girl awake at such a time, yet sleep was impossible.

She called again in her calmest voice, 'Who's there?'

No one. Silence.

No cough. No body turning over. No strange echoing rhythm, *clop-clop-clop*. No cry in the dark.

'Is it you, An?' she whispered, sitting up. 'Chong, is that you?'

The house held its breath, silent. She stood in her bedroom doorway holding high a white porcelain lamp, intricately carved, in her right hand. The little flame from the dragon's snout cast more shadow than light, throwing the room and pillars around her into deeper darkness, yet to anyone watching illuminated her from head to toe.

She was eighteen years old, already a widow. Her name was Zhao.

Anyone could see Zhao was much too tall, her face not round enough; no one called her beautiful. Everyone agreed Zhao's nose was too long for perfection, and the crease on each eyelid had a touch of barbarian about it. A face with far too much personality. A sensible man wouldn't give this one a second glance.

Zhao's eyes, wide open as she peered into the dark, were deep as night.

The whole household-family slept. The pagan villa sprawled breathless, muffled, stifled in the night heat. The strange sound – *clop-clop-clop* – was too soft to enter most dreams. But she slept lightly.

Thirst is no excuse for a sip of water. Temptation is resisted. Her head ached. Just one sip. One cup, no more.

Plenty of cool water in the kitchen.

She'd heard something, hadn't she? *Clop-clop-clop*. That couldn't be ignored. 'Dutifully I investigated as far as the kitchen but found nothing,' she'd excuse herself if Manas discovered her. Yet discovery was unlikely. The oversize bodyguard slept curled at his master's door, dozing like a mountain cat, but the Forbidden Quarters were hidden at the back of the house. The kitchen and water cistern, fed from the public water supply, were downstairs at the front, and the walls were thick. Captain Lo's guards were few and weary; a gamble, no more.

Odds-on in her favour.

She moved gracefully past the pillars of the peristyle garden, her toes flashing busily beneath the hems of her satin over-gowns. The lamp-flame, slanted by her swift movement, gleamed in her eyes. She left the private rooms behind her, bowed low to the empty Mian chair in the family audience chamber, then glided through the moonlit atrium – the traditional cooking area, no longer used for that purpose, but left open to the sky – past the locked side door, to the public rooms at the front of the house. Faintly came the sweet scent of opium, then it was gone.

The circle of the lamp-flame flickered around her busy, satin-slippered feet. The floor stopped, going downstairs into deeper darkness. She teetered on the top step. Down there, hidden below her in the dark, lay the broad entrance hall. Beyond it, the narrow vestibule and the heavy outside door, the single entrance to the house.

What if the doorman were awake? The Roman was called

an *ostiarius* and was said never to sleep, like one of their gods. He had two faces, one to look back into the house, guarding, while the other looked out, protecting. Perhaps it was true. He'd been friendly to her and she'd snatched glances at the back of his head, wondering if a second face was concealed by that crescent of white hair. You never knew with barbarians.

She heard no snoring, but his lamp was out. So, obviously, he was a quiet sleeper. No doubt a most useful skill for an ostiarius at his post all day and night.

Her slippers made no sound going down the cold marble steps. She turned smoothly to her left into the kitchen corridor, and if anyone was looking, was gone almost at once from sight.

Zhao leant back against the kitchen door until it creaked, almost closed. So far, so good. She held up her lamp and looked around. The flame burned steady and straight. Naturally she always took the closest interest in cooking and household matters, so the kitchen held no ghosts or spirits to frighten her. Pots and pans gleamed in the shadows. She made out shiny knives, cleavers, a cutting block, the heavy work table, ropes of onions and garlic. A row of feathered carcasses hung by their necks from hooks. The long brick range still felt warm from the evening meal, making the night hotter than ever. Her mouth was dry as dust.

The lamp-flame quivered, catching her eye. She watched the flame bend slowly until it lay almost level, then stand straight again.

It was as if the house, alive with unseen forces, had drawn a breath, and then exhaled. She shook the lamp.

The flame burned steady and tall, pretending it had never moved.

Behind the chimney that divided the kitchen were the women's latrines, four sociably-facing holes in all; various storerooms and larders locked at night to prevent pilfering; and service stairs to the dining room. She noticed the last woman to leave had knocked the table slightly out of place, affronting the kitchen's harmonious spirit. The tabletop was cluttered with pots, too. Another slight to house and family spirits that must be remedied before cooking began.

Thirst cracked her tongue. A small brown jug lay on the floor. She picked it up. It would do.

The water pipe came through the outside wall to a heavy

stone cistern set on bricks. The cistern was two feet deep and three long, covered by a lid. Kneeling, holding the lamp high in her right hand, she stood the jug under the wooden spigot low on one end of the cistern, and twisted the valve.

Not a drip. Her lips tightened. She had a temper.

She turned the spigot off, then on again. Rattled the jug. A single drop. Then a few more, then nothing.

She tilted the jug to her mouth, thirstily drained what little there was, made a sour face. She turned to the cistern lid, mostly used as a shelf for pots and jugs because so rarely opened. But tonight the lid was bare, everything piled on the table instead.

She looked around as a brief, greenish glow flickered down the chimney. A moment later a blood-red flash came around the kitchen door, printing its shape on her eyes. She waited for the roll of thunder. The sound came almost at once, sounding less like thunder than a single, echoing clap of great hands. One of the barbarian gods. She thought no more of it, raising the cistern lid with her thumbs.

The lid felt heavy at first, then lighter as she lifted on tiptoe, and finally it fell back on its hinges against the wall. Her lamp doubled in brightness, reflecting her face on the black surface. The cistern wasn't empty; it was full to overflowing.

She dipped the jug. Her reflection shattered. Stiff, cold fingers touched her hand underwater.

Zhao disgraced herself. She screamed.

She dropped the jug. The lamp went out. Darkness fell.

I

Luca's Taberna

Rome
Monday 16 July, AD64

Ex-Senator Septimus Quistus, no longer dead drunk, lay on his face where he'd passed out, his legs higher than his head, bare feet splayed soles-up on the cellar's fifth step, arms cradling the wine jug like a sleeping woman. His tight-closed eyelids twitched from side to side, up and down, mimicking his darting eyes as he dreamt. Wine's kindly stupor had given way to something much worse: sleep.

The dream took him as it always did, with the terrible cruelty of truth. His children were alive. His wife was beautiful. He heard their laughter from the *therma*, the hot pool at the heart of the villa. He knew what would happen.

'Don't . . .' he murmured. But for them it was always the first time. The corridor of the Villa Marcia grew longer as he ran to save them. Their laughter turned to screams. He tried to shout for help but the door, decorated with mother-of-pearl dolphins, slammed shut in his face. Locked from the inside, barred with iron. His fists beat on the heavy mahogany panels, dark drops of his blood smeared mother-of-pearl. He shouted their names, his eight lovely children. Lyra, his only daughter. His wife, Marcia. Shouting out their names over and over.

One by one their screams stopped.

'Marcia,' he whispered. He couldn't open the door. He never could.

An annoying voice spoke. Quistus tried to wake up. One eye peeled open, staring. He tried to look around but couldn't, paralysed by cheap drink. Underground somewhere. Absolutely no memory of being here. A dim, dirty place, upside down, with upside-down tables. Even the yawning girl who watched him seemed, because of his own position, upside down.

Horror stole over Quistus. He'd died and fallen to Hades, the cavern of eternal dullness, worse in its way than the Hell of Christians.

'He looks like a baby.' The girl spoke to someone he couldn't see. 'A big ugly baby. Not cute at all. If he was mine, I'd dump him.'

'He's been dumped already.' A man's voice grunted like the pigs grunting outside the light-vents. 'My dear Ertola, our name-less, unwanted guest has been dumped by everyone from Nero on down. He's the biggest piece of shit in Rome, and that's official. Everything he owned's been sold by imperial order, his house, slaves, even Princess Omba. Everything except his life. Still got that. So where's the only fucking place that takes our untouchable, no good, dead-but-living lodger, thanks to my dear sentimental *pater*? Here, the lowest orifice in Rome. Luca's.'

Luca? Quistus thought frantically. Who's Luca?

His mouth tasted of rotten wine, brain swelling fit to burst. 'Omba,' he whispered, trying to hold on to the name.

'I'm sorry for him,' the girl lilted. 'He was a great man once.' She scratched her wig for lice. She had long legs. Quistus had seen those legs dance. He'd spoken to her. He tried to remember last night. He had the dreadful feeling that he was adrift, that he might never remember who he was, that he'd lost himself, his own identity, as well as his family.

'Great man.' Luca hawked, spitting noisily. 'Finished.'

'Maybe that's what the strange star meant,' the dancing girl said. 'Death of a great man.'

Quistus tried to remember a strange star. His mind blanked. He'd seen something, hadn't he? He tried to remember what he'd said to the girl.

Ertola was a British name, or rather nickname. Her voice still lilted like a Brit's. She crossed Quistus's fixed, inverted field of vision and sat on one of the tables beneath the roof arch, pulling off her tall black wig and letting her wispy red hair hang, too tired to sleep. She lifted her legs as the pigs grunted at her toes, let in by Luca from the garden above to clean the stinking floor of the night's trade. Their wet snouts snuffled Quistus's neck for spilt wine. Luca One-Knee hopped after them whacking with his stick. Dawn showed up Quistus's tunic, once cream, now filthy as the rest of him. One of his eyes was stuck open, grey-green. Luca pissed on him, grinning. No reaction.

'Who cares about this shit, eh? Anyway, that was no star, just lightning.' Luca was heavy and clumsy, his whiskery face set hard with dirt. He licked his filthy fingers, squeezing the flames from the candles as he limped between the tables. A couple of hayseeds woke blearily, country pagans, pockets turned out, every penny stolen not already drunk. 'Out, out, you worthless shits.' Luca whacked their thick heads and they fell over the body on the steps.

'Who's that?' one said blurrily.

'No one,' Luca growled. The ex-Senator's eye had closed. He slept. Perhaps he dreamed.

Ertola studied her bitten nails. While the top door opened she briefly heard cries from the busy street above, shoppers making the most of the cool hour before dawn. The door slammed behind the hayseeds. Luca shot the bolts and thumped back down.

'There were no clouds last night,' Ertola said. 'Not one. It's the heat. There wasn't a storm. I saw a noisy new star burst like a flower in a clear, windless sky.'

'Stars make a noise? They look like flowers?'

'This one did.' Ertola found a fingernail long enough to be nibbled. Just her luck to end up at Luca's. Everyone knew Luca wasn't a patch on his brothers, which was why Luca Patella Unum rotted down here in the Subura in his father's meanest, lowest, dirtiest whorehouse while old man Vitellius – who owned no house but, it was said, possessed many homes – enjoyed his prolonged retirement by shuttling between the soft beds and sunny dinner tables of his many beloved wives and sweethearts, with the mothers of his children to spoil him with exotic spices, pastries and calves' brains, and their hardworking sons to keep him rich. Ertola stuck with Luca because Vitellius (whatever he looked like) might drop by and notice her, and she'd have a son by him, and escape drudgery to a wonderful new life.

'I don't pay you to dream at the sky,' Luca grunted.

'I know, you pay us to lie on our backs. I'm different, Luca.'

'You're no different.'

'I want to look up at something better than ugly faces. The stars look pretty.'

Luca hobbled awkwardly after the pigs, which brought him back to Quistus.

'The only thing our ex-noble, nameless, disgraced ex-Senator has looked at in the two months since Nero cursed him,' he snorted, 'is the bottom of a wine jug.'

'He saw the special star,' she said wistfully. 'Quistus would've been interested if he wasn't such a drunk. A star that was born and bloomed and died in a flash. He'd have known what god it was, what it means, if he was sober. Signs in the sky bring death. Quistus would've known.'

'Don't say that name,' Luca warned. 'That name's dangerous, he's an official nonentity. He don't exist, he's nobody now. Nobody. My father's a fool to let him stay here, the man who double-crossed Nero. Double-crossed Nero in the Circus Maximus in front of everyone, just to save a few slaves.' He grinned unpleasantly. 'Serves him right.'

She shook her head. Word was, the Emperor had sworn some sort of oath not to harm Quistus – had been tricked into swearing it on his honour – and that was the only reason Quistus was still alive. Not that Nero had much honour, but an Emperor had to pretend.

'You didn't see the star, Luca,' she said. 'You'll never know how amazing it was.'

'Look at him. He's paralytic. He disgusts me. He's a broken man.'

'It was beautiful.'

'You heard it, Master?'

Princess Omba stumbled barefoot behind her new owner, Vulpus the spice-seller with his showy red cloak and slimy gold teeth. Her coverings – hardly clothes – were greasy, rough-sewn sacks barely stuck to her breasts and thighs. She staggered under the heavy load of salt across her shoulders, long limbs bent, dragged through the Subura slums by Vulpus's heavy chain at her neck. The gold bracelets and bangles she'd worn for Quistus were long gone, her heavy gold belt replaced by knotted string, her golden skull tattoos hidden by tight new curls.

'Silence!' Vulpus, hawk-nosed, weak-chinned, stunted by childhood diseases, jerked her chain in his small white fist. 'Heard? Heard what? I heard nothing in the night.'

He lied. Vulpus always lied. He'd heard the strange thunder all right. Omba slept on bare boards outside his door, securely padlocked to a joist. He didn't fart without her knowing, the walls were so thin. His room was a miserable wooden shack tacked by speculators on to the *insula Fortuna*'s roof. Cracked tiles let in the rain when it rained and the sun when it shone, and when the lightning flash struck close by over the Viminalis Hill she'd heard him wake screaming he was on fire. Vulpus dreaded fire. He slept fully clothed, wedged in a filthy corner among spice bales more precious than his life, ready to run with all he could carry. Three times streets on which he lived – different streets at that, and different *insulae*, in different wards of Rome – had been pulverized by fire. When Omba called out, 'Don't be afraid,' there'd been a moment of embarrassed silence, then he'd cursed her for waking him for no reason. What a liar.

He'd been afraid all right. A man, her *owner*, scared witless by thunder. It made her laugh.

'Stop laughing!' Vulpus jerked the chain so hard he broke the first rule of ownership. He damaged his property. A thread of slow, dark blood leaked under the iron neck-fetter, trickling from Omba's throat almost invisibly down her skin.

'You made me do that,' he lied. The chain hung limply between them. He stood lower than her shoulder, and very pale. Then Vulpus said something perfectly incredible. 'Sorry.'

Gods preserve us, she thought, appalled, he's infatuated. I thought I had problems enough.

Spicers were always liars, everyone knew that, but Vulpus lied to himself if he dreamed of having her just because he owned her. His father and grandfather had both been *condimentes*, so he was a third generation *condimentus*, a born liar, a seller of dreams, and now he'd sold a dream to himself: her. A clever *condimentus* exaggerated and confabulated, talked up the price of goods already overpriced. His silver-tongued patter made priceless rare spices, herbs, fungi, scents, cures, venoms, poisons, aphrodisiacs and hallucinogens, hauled step by step on years-long journeys through unimaginable hardships to Rome's warehouses from the lands of the Far Beyond. Lands of the fabled East so remote and exotic that their very names reeked of myth and legend: Ecbatana, Charax, Kashgar, India. Whether these places at the Spice Road's rainbow end (if they truly existed) were islands, towns, peoples or whole countries, nobody cared. Rome was the centre of the world; wholesale prices were all that mattered. From any of these stalls doing business along Pepper Street a single peppercorn, the emperor of spices, cost more than a meal. Business had never been better, prices never higher, customers more eager. Competition was fierce. A *condimentus* put on a show to stand out and Omba was part of Vulpus's show, his African princess dragged at his heel like a monkey. A woman to publicly humiliate and secretly adore.

She noticed how tattered Vulpus's cloak was, despite its expensive colour. Obviously a new cloak of cinnabar-red was more than he could afford. He'd paid too much for her. Infatuated, and broke.

'You didn't buy my heart, Vulpus,' she murmured in her deep, slow voice. 'You understand, my master? My heart won't ever be yours.'

He looked up. 'You think I give a fig for what you say, slave?'

He let the chain go. He'd always win in this relationship. He knew she'd follow, she had nowhere else. Omba watched him push out of sight through the crowd, setting up his stall on the street corner where he – like his father and his grand-father had before him – rented their patch from the Spicers' Guild. She had no choice but to obey, and quick.

Omba looked back yearningly, steadying the heavy sacks of salt on her shoulders. To one side the Viminalis Hill climbed steeply to rich white houses already bright in the rising sun. Below lay the dark, stinking, swarming Subura. In the shadows of the valley people lived in *insulae* piled up like anthills. Beyond Triton's fountain, where the poor stood like ragged crows and quarrelling women scooped weedy water with broken pots, tumbledown apartment blocks carried on worse than before, red-brown, flaking, leaning together like drunks holding each other up. Luca's tavern was down there in the warren, in one of those twisting alleys. Quistus was there, maybe. Three weeks ago Cook's lad, running an errand, saw him, or someone who looked like him, slumped over a table at Luca's. The lad had asked cheekily if he was dead, and a dancing girl said he was dead all right, dead drunk.

The lad, sold by imperial order like everyone else at the Villa Marcia, including Cook, had been whipped away by his new owner. But from the corner, the lad had looked back at Omba, and he'd nodded to her. One big, slow nod.

Quistus was alive. She was sure of it.

Drunk? Impossible. Quistus was a Stoic, and Stoics didn't get drunk. But these were strange times, and strange times did strange things to men. Fate came from the gods. What could she, a mere slave, do to change Quistus's fate, or her own? She turned to follow Vulpus to the stall, then, slowly, turned back to Triton's fountain. Her eyes narrowed.

A plump-bellied man, strangely and fabulously dressed in shimmering garb, stood near the entrance to the alley. Although the sun touched only the tallest rooftops in the valley, he wore a broad-brimmed straw sun hat that hid his face.

The hat turned from side to side. He was searching.

Ertola sat on the table swinging her legs, watching Luca drove the pigs up the back steps to the garden. As soon as she was alone she opened her knife, knelt by Quistus on the front stair, parted his legs, and reached up his tunic with professional skill. Luca had already robbed him of whatever he hadn't drunk, naturally, but there were places a man hid money where even Luca didn't like to put his hand. Ertola wasn't squeamish. She cut the leather thong holding the bag of coins next to the ex-Senator's ball bag, tossed it in her palm to gauge the weight – heavy gold *aurei* – and dropped it neatly down her bosom. Quistus's fingers closed on her wrist. She wriggled.

He whispered with foul breath, 'Who am I?'

'Luca's coming,' she hissed. 'He'll give you a good kicking. Let go!'

'*Who am I?*'

Ertola jerked her hand free. 'Who cares?' He didn't shout for his money or beat her. Too drunk. She looked at him with contempt. He didn't even know she'd stolen all he had.

He slumped. 'Last night, Ertola, did I say I loved you?'

'Who doesn't when it's dark and you're drunk?'

'Did *I* say it?'

'Who cares what you said?'

'*Did I say I love you?*'

She rubbed her wrist, sulking.

'No,' she said, 'you didn't, Septimus Quistus.'

He closed his eyes. He repeated his name, trying to remember. 'I'm Quistus. Yes . . .'

She spat at him. His clothes stank. He tried to sit on the steps and slithered down, no better than a hundred she'd known.

'Useless, you are,' she said. 'Drunk.'

His eyes opened, grey-green as old lead. 'Did I go into the

garden with you, Ertola? Did we look at the stars? I remember a shooting star. I remember you looking at the sky.'

'You didn't pay,' she complained. 'You talked.'

He held his head. Luca's wine was flavoured with lead, then stirred with a red-hot lead stick to heat it.

'You asked me what my name was, that's all,' she sighed. 'Nothing happened. Where I come from, how I got here, all about me. I thought you were trying to get it for free, at first. I mean, who talks?'

'Did I talk about myself?'

'Yes.' She looked bored. 'Marcia. The right name?'

'Yes.'

'How much you love her. Still married to her. You'll never look at another woman. All that stuff.'

'And Lyra? Did I talk about Lyra?'

Ertola yawned. 'Your daughter. Beautiful. The usual.'

He pushed back, sitting against the wall. 'Four years. Four years, seven months. You know what happened?'

'Everybody in Rome knows. Your wife, seven sons, Lyra your only daughter . . . it was at your house.'

'The Villa Marcia.'

'They were hacked to death.'

'I found their bodies. Did you know that? All that was left of them. The pool was full of blood. It *was* blood.'

'No one knows why they were murdered or who did it.' Ertola touched his hand. 'It could have been anyone.' The gold coins clinked between her breasts and she was ashamed of herself, but he didn't notice.

He blurted, 'When their bodies were prepared for burial . . .' Even a Stoic didn't have perfect control of his emotions. He started again. 'You see, Ertola, when they, the pieces of them, were put back together ready for burial, then . . . we discovered that two bodies were not there. Septimus, my eldest son and namesake, fifteen years old, and his twin sister Lyra, were missing. They survived.'

She stared. 'Quistus, everyone knows they're dead.' Stolen to be sold, she thought, the boy for his muscle, the girl for her virginity. Something went wrong, their throats were cut, the bodies thrown in a ditch, or buried under manure, or fed to pigs, that's how it went.

'They're alive,' Quistus said. 'Ransom demands, I paid them

all. Maybe they were sold as slaves. The gladiators' arena. Whorehouse. Anything, anywhere. Maybe my two children escaped, maybe they *will* escape. They're walking the earth, Ertola.'

'Then why don't they come back?' she murmured.

'I don't know.'

'They say you went mad.'

'No, hardly mad, no. I searched. Rome, the Italian provinces. Slave markets. Arabia. Africa, the Nile, Gondar. In the land of the Oromos I found Princess Omba staked naked over a hill of fire ants, honey smeared on her tongue. I saved her. I, who couldn't save my children. Together we never stopped searching. The north, Ultima Thule. Deserts, hot and cold. The west, to India's coast. Septimus and Lyra are alive.'

She said gently, 'You have to believe that.'

'No, Ertola, it's true. Five months ago, in Gaul, I saw Lyra. In Lugdunum, between the bridges over the two rivers. She ate a lobster. I saw her face as close as I see yours.'

'Lugdunum.' Ertola's Brit lilt softened the town's name to *Lyon*. 'Did she see you?'

'She rode away like the wind.'

'You made a mistake. She was someone else.'

'No. She was Lyra. Lyra grown up, a woman, twenty years old. More beautiful than ever.'

'Then why did she ride off? Why didn't she know you, her own father?'

'She knew me. I saw it in her eyes. She ran, she hid, she rode away.'

Ertola asked quietly, 'Why?'

'I don't know,' Quistus said.

Slowly, thoughtfully, Omba climbed Pepper Street towards Vulpus's stall. Sunlight slid down the filthy walls and the bright heat of dawn struck her. Salt leaking from the shoulder bags mingled with her sweat, drawing white lines down her muscular limbs. Women talked high-voiced. 'You heard it? Like this!' A girl clapped her hands. Last night's storm had been a warning from Rome's gods. Nothing happened by accident. Some big man would die, some tragedy befall the city. Priests cut the head from a chicken and watched the body run in circles, reading the future in the bloody scrawl.

Omba pushed uphill, eyes squinted in the glare. She thought about the man behind her in the shadows, wearing a sun hat where there was no sun.

'What storm?' grumbled the toothless patchouli-woman who lived down by the river. 'We heard no storm.' The shy girl from the Caelian called, 'I saw a flash, that's all.' But an apple-seller shook her head. 'I rested by the Appian road, I heard and saw nothing, you're imagining it.' But the Subura urchin who clapped her hands shouted excitedly, 'It was louder and brighter than anything!' She pointed at the fine houses on the hill. 'It was up there, I saw it grow. Lightning grew from the earth. The rich people are going to die.'

'No one's died,' the toothless woman said. 'We'd know by now, they'd be crying, wailing, mourners running—'

'What do you think, Omba?' the Caelian girl called.

'What does it matter?' Omba said irritably. 'Haven't you got more important things to worry about?'

The women gave each other knowing looks. Something's up with that one, their looks said, and they turned back to their business.

Omba thought about the foreigner in the straw hat. He wasn't right. An honest Roman stood with his gnarled brown feet braced apart, head up, ready for trouble. He didn't hang about with his fat head meekly bowed and smooth white ankles pressed together like that, like some fancy lady, not unless he wanted to get robbed, mocked, shoved over. A Roman's baggy woollens were woven, patched and darned by the women in his life to be hard-wearing and manly, not shiny, fluttering, effeminate. A Roman tied the loose ends confidently over his belly, not primly in the small of his back. Even a lady never wore shiny slippers in the street.

Omba dropped the salt bags behind Vulpus's stall while he honey-talked a favoured customer demanding nutmeg. She held out her hand for the room key. 'My master, a thousand apologies, I forgot to bring the cardamoms. I could fetch nutmeg too.'

'Be quick!' Vulpus fumbled the key from the heavy iron ring on his belt, flustered. 'See if there's nutmeg in the bag in the corner. Go!'

'Yes, my master.'

'Silvanus says he has nutmeg,' the customer complained.

'His is rotten, mine's fresh.' Vulpus called after Omba, 'Don't delay!'

Omba looped the neck-chain around her arm to stop it rattling as she ran. She paused at Triton's fountain but there was nothing to see, only crowds. The man in the straw hat was gone. She watched until she was surrounded by beggars and children. No one had seen him. They drifted away because she was penniless.

She sighed, knowing Vulpus's impatient temper, and crossed the street to the *Fortuna*. Rickety wooden stairs crisscrossed the light-well to the fifth floor. Vulpus's shack was on the sixth floor, its crooked wooden walls legal as long as its roof was tiled. She clambered up a ladder, used the key, and ducked inside. The roof creaked loudly as the thin tiles heated in the sun.

What a mess. Only dust came from the nutmeg bag. Vulpus's stock was empty bags, mostly. She reached deep into the sack that once contained cardamoms, finding just half a dozen caught in the seam, thin, dry, and worth their weight in gold. She held them gently in her fist, locked the door, and returned downstairs. For a moment, moving from shadows into the street, she was blinded by sunlight. Someone bumped into her. She blinked, seeing the man in the straw hat. The broad-brimmed hat fell from his head, rolling in a circle on the ground.

He snatched it up at once, but she'd seen his plump round face, brown almond-shaped eyes, long black hair knotted on top of his head. More hair, carefully twisted and oiled, hung from his temples and chin. His mouth was small and round. He looked . . . *different*. All the world came to Rome. She'd seen every race, tribe and type on these streets. She'd never seen anyone so completely strange.

'Hey, you,' she growled. He ran. The crowd hid him. She stood on a step and at last made out his hat. He was headed back to Triton's fountain. She followed some poor fellow tottering under baskets of wool. The hatted stranger looked round as the crowd thinned but the wool baskets concealed her. He halted at Luca's alley. This was the place he'd searched for earlier, Omba realized, the alley he'd found, left, and now so soon returned to. Why? Why would a man do that? She thought of only one reason.

He was a scout, leading someone here.

She moved around the fountain until Triton's statue stood between them, and peered between the sea monsters.

The plump man stared back along the street, hands folded in loose sleeves, waiting for it to fall quiet. A rich builder strutted, hangers-on fawning, guards tramping. Now some veiled lady in a sedan chair swaying on the shoulders of scented slaves. A moment of emptiness, his chance. At once the man beckoned someone Omba couldn't see. His sleeve slipped, revealing a hand like a claw, shining talons for fingers. He hid them instantly, looking round in case he'd been seen – straight at her, in fact – but saw only the monsters and splashing water.

A low whistle acknowledged his signal.

Omba stared in amazement. A giant crossed the road. He was seven feet tall. On his shoulder he carried a coffin, a child's coffin, but like none she'd ever seen, painted and mirror-lacquered, a work of art showing amazing landscapes of hills, rivers, bare trees. Behind the giant shuffled a man who seemed small because he was of only normal size, dressed to blend in like a Roman, at which he failed as utterly as the man in the straw hat, for his clothes, too, were of shimmering satin. The giant nodded and the plump man ran to join them. The three disappeared together into the shadows towards Luca's tavern.

Luca shut the pigs in the garden. Ertola watched his shadow moving in the light-vents. Soon he'd come thumping down the back steps. Time to make up her mind. No one as drunk, sick and in pain as Quistus, his head sunk in his hands, would remember the theft of his money, or even notice it was missing until he was sober and she was long gone. But that wasn't the point. She sighed, lifting the bag of gold coins from her tunic. The money was her freedom. Quistus would just drink it. She knew he meant to drink himself to death. I must be mad, she thought. Just because we talked in the garden and saw the star together.

She swung the bag. It clinked. 'You dropped this. I found it.'

'No.' Quistus spoke without looking. His voice was slurred but his hearing worked just fine. 'You stole it.'

She shrugged.

He said, 'It's yours. Go on. I won't touch it.'

'There's fifty *aurei* here, more. It's a fortune. Think about it, Quistus. You won't get drunk tonight.'

He said, 'Exactly.' He winced as Luca slammed the garden door.

Ertola stared at him, amazed, then quickly stuffed the bag down her cleavage.

'Awake, is he, the old bastard,' Luca said. 'I know him. He'll need a cup of our best house, then another.' He pushed past Quistus at a knock on the top door. 'Closed!' he shouted up the steps.

'Quistus doesn't want wine,' Ertola said protectively. 'He doesn't want you keeping him drunk. I know what you're up to, even if he doesn't.'

'Shut up.' Luca hit her face with his open palm so she wouldn't bruise. 'I told you not to say his name.' The knock came again. 'Closed!' he bellowed.

'Your father, Vitellius, ordered you to keep him drunk,' Ertola accused. 'I swear it's true, Quistus. Luca talks in his sleep.' Luca struck her with his knuckles. She fell with her hands to her mouth.

Quistus stood.

Luca raised his stick. 'Try me, you filthy drunk.' Above them the door banged open, pouring light and heat down the stairs. One of the iron bolts, broken, clattered down the steps. Everyone stared without moving. Then Quistus put out his foot and stopped it, listening.

'Vulcan's arse!' Luca swore, wishing his stick was a sword. He thought it was the usual business, Dorca's mob knocking the place apart, or not, in return for a small fee. Quistus squeezed his shoulder. Luca shut his mouth.

Above them a harsh, impatient voice spoke Greek. 'Manas doesn't know his own strength, An! He broke it.' A shadow stretched down the steps. 'I see them. Barbarians, *yi*. We've interrupted their barbaric ritual, fighting over the woman.'

'What's he say?' hissed Luca. Quistus held his finger to his lips.

A second voice spoke, mild-mannered, oily. 'Is Heaven safe here?' Two silhouettes moved forward, peering into the gloomy cellar.

'Is anywhere safe, An?' The first man pulled off his broad hat with relief, as though discarding a disguise. Quistus saw a honed, intelligent face, sharp as a hatchet beneath a handle of knotted hair. 'You really think the street's safe, An? Be logical. I warned you, Manas attracts attention.'

'We should never have come, Chong,' whispered the plump,

sweating man. 'We should have kept running. There are places even farther away to hide—'

'How much farther?' Chong demanded fiercely. 'How much farther must we fall, An? Heaven commands us to stay. Besides, I want to know what a Stoic looks like close up. Oh. Not too impressive, look at his gums.' He turned. 'Manas!'

Quistus stared quietly. Luca gave a low moan of fear. A third man, gigantic, his face round and flat, with shaven skull and swinging moustaches, his torso bound with thick leather straps, padded swiftly and silently downstairs. His slitted eyes were blue as mountain sky. On one shoulder he carried a child's coffin. He ducked, placing the coffin on a table so gently and effortlessly that it seemed empty. The table creaked, settling. There was a body inside.

The giant stood back a half pace, nerves twitching in his hard-muscled bare legs, alert as a stalking cat. He crossed his arms lightly over his chest, waiting.

They stared at the coffin.

'Not another dead child,' Ertola whispered. Dead children over a year old were meant to be buried outside the city wall, but it was inconvenient and floors were cheap. Any whorehouse stood on a discreet cemetery of very small bones, a factory obliged to bury unwanted by-products beneath its premises.

Luca smiled, thinking he understood. 'Certainly, gentlemen,' he welcomed them in Latin. 'How much will you pay for a discreet disposal?'

The giant ignored him. Luca did not exist. Ertola, being female, never had. His pale blue eyes stared at Quistus like splinters of ice.

'You're not Greeks,' Quistus said. No response. In Greek he said, 'What do you want with me? Are you my death?' Still no reply. Quistus struggled to speak clearly, but he couldn't stop his hands trembling from drink. He called to the two men by the steps. 'There's only one other reason why gentlemen like you – I see even the impatient Chong pretends to be a gentleman – trouble to seek out a man like me in a place like this.'

Chong said coolly, 'What reason's that?'

'Desperation. If you aren't sent here by powerful people to murder me – you've already taken your time – you're here because you need my help. Desperately. You don't come to a place like this unless you're at your wits' end.'

Chong and An exchanged looks.

'The common people say your name, Quistus,' Chong admitted. 'Our doorman spoke highly of you. Until last night we convinced ourselves we were safe at last. Now that's changed. There's been a . . . slightly unfortunate accident.'

'A *confidential* incident,' An said smoothly. 'We rely on your discretion.'

Chong went up the steps, shot the one bolt intact on the door, wedged furniture against it, and returned.

'*Slightly* unfortunate?' Quistus asked.

'Delicate,' An whispered.

'Delicate.'

'Secrecy is essential.'

Quistus asked, 'Why come to me, gentlemen? Why not choose a Roman who retains his power and influence?'

They bowed their heads, but not to him. Quistus turned.

The coffin lid creaked open, and a boy sat up. He was a boy like no other, his knotted hair pinned high, dressed not as a corpse but in a loose-sleeved smock of shining gold. His eyes snapped wide open, full of life. His teeth were white as pearls. He gave a squeal of delighted laughter at their surprise.

'Because you are Quistus!'

Omba waited across the alley from the broken door. The men who'd gone in hadn't come out.

She forgot about Vulpus and the cardamoms crushed in her hand.

She thought, What if Quistus is in there? He *is* in there.

After a few moments the door was pushed closed. Wood squeaked on wood as it was wedged shut from the inside. The strangers had closed the place off. No witnesses. Luca would get visits like this when he was late with rent or forgot to make the right donations to the right people. But these visitors didn't look like thugs.

Quistus's enemies were worse than thugs. People like Stigmus, for example, the bully, once prosecutor, now newly-promoted Prefect of Praetorians who'd replaced the evil *politico* Tigellinus. The list didn't end there. It went right to the top.

Taking all Quistus had – even his name – wasn't enough for Nero. He wanted it all. Omba knew the Emperor had been

bound to take from Quistus, one day, his one remaining posses-
sion: his life.

Assassins. Her heart thudded. Assassins sent by Nero. The
giant could crush a man's head in his hands.

She ran to the door. Jammed, it wouldn't budge. Her muscles
bulged. She spied an alley even smaller, twisting between Luca's
hovel and the next. She moved fast, her shoulders brushing
both sides. Pigs grunted beyond the wall. She reached up,
pushed with her feet, pulled herself over the top, and jumped
down into Luca's garden on the other side.

Pigs gathered around her, thinking she was food. A row of
holes low in the far wall funnelled light into a cellar. She heard
muffled voices.

'Quistus!' laughed the child dressed in golden robes, standing
in the brightly painted coffin on the table. Quistus knew neither
the strange wood nor the foreign style of painting. 'I know
your face; don't deny your name, Quistus. I know you're fearless for the truth, I saw it. Your debauched appearance doesn't
shock me. Sometimes disgrace is an asset. They say you're the
only man in Rome who isn't afraid, and it's true! I saw you
defy your ruler, the cruel Nero, and make him a fool in front
of everyone – I saw it with my own eyes in the Circus Maximus,
among the crowd of a hundred thousand! A crowd's one of the
few places I can hide, you see.'

Quistus studied the boy, perhaps twelve years old, though
the handsomely slanted eyes looked older. His voice was high-
pitched, the words tumbling too fast. He laughed too much,
close to hysteria.

'Do you like my game, Quistus? Isn't it exciting! A game
of life and death.' The boy's laughter rocked the table, which
was instantly steadied by the hands of the quickly-kneeling
Manas. 'Faithful Manas carried me through the streets of Rome
in this coffin, and I was quiet as a mouse! No one knew I
looked through the tiny holes, no one guessed I was inside,
alive! It's the first time I've escaped from the house for . . . oh,
weeks. Since that day I saw you save the lives of those slaves
at the Circus. It feels . . . for ever.'

The boy smoothed his golden smock, then without warning
threw himself horizontally from the table. Manas caught him
without a change of expression, setting him down carefully.

'Aren't I brave, Quistus? See, I'm brave. Why are you frowning? I don't allow frowns. It's rude.'

An and Chong looked nervous. Those two, An short and fat, Chong longer and sharp, both fawning like a lady's lapdogs on the boy, didn't matter. Neither did Manas, silent, watchful, obedient. Only the boy, this ridiculous boy, mattered.

Quistus turned his back. 'Ertola, kindly fetch me a jug of water.' He let her see his face: his head was bursting. 'I'm thirsty. Take Luca with you.'

'Quistus dares turn his back on me!' cried the boy. 'He's forbidden to turn his back! Wang Chong, teach him!'

'Highness,' Chong apologized. 'Barbarians . . . they're barbarians. To teach *yi* manners is like teaching dogs to dance. It can be done, but it takes more time than Heaven permits today. There's pressing business.'

'Chong, you promised Quistus was different,' the boy cried petulantly. 'You agreed, Yuan An. Where are his manners? He turns his back.'

'Highness, there's the matter of importance – you insisted—'

'She didn't kill him, An!' the boy cried. 'I don't care what you say.'

Quistus gulped straight from the jug. He didn't take his eyes from the boy.

An whispered to Chong, 'Do you smell the barbarian? He reeks of poison.'

'Poison?' hissed Chong.

'Wine. He poisons himself with wine. Slow death. Barbarians don't understand distilled spirits, fortunately for him.'

'An, quickly.' The boy overheard. 'Your gé gïn root will make him better.'

'Highness, I have none,' An said smoothly. 'We're so far from civilization. I've only my needles—'

'Far from civilization? It's Rome.' Quistus wiped his lips. He handed the empty jug back to Ertola and spoke to the boy. 'You have the advantage of me, lad. You know my name. What's yours?'

'Heaven has no name,' Chong said.

'It cannot be uttered.' An pushed between them.

'Let him speak for himself,' Quistus said.

The boy waved An away. He returned Quistus's stare. 'I am Prince Number Five. An is my major-domo, Chong my adviser.' He didn't mention Manas.

'Thank you.' Quistus sat calmly. He leaned forward, his eyes on a level with the boy's. 'I suppose, Prince Number Five, that Manas always succeeds in catching you when you show off? When it pleases you to throw yourself suddenly off a table like that, for example?'

'Of course he does.'

'And if, one time, he did not?'

The boy was confused. 'How could it happen?'

'If it did?'

'Duty is all he knows. The smallest injury to me, however accidental, would hurt him more than death.'

'What exactly would hurt him more than death?'

'Dishonour. Remorse. His spirit would wither and blow away on the wind. He would never join his ancestors.'

'Then you risk everything he loves very lightly.'

'You may call me Zhang,' the boy said thoughtfully.

'Highness! Protocol forbids – your name – the barbarian—' Too late. An, beads of sweat squeezing from his cheeks, bowing, made the best of a bad job. 'Senator Quistus,' he announced, 'you have the honour to be noticed by Liu Da, Prince Zhang, fifth and most beloved son of Emperor Liu Ming-Di of Loyang, ruler of all Earth under Heaven, direct descendant of God, Huang-Di, by whose mandate the Emperor rules the great family of China. Bow down!'

Quistus's head thudded. 'China? What?'

Chong said, 'Your little city, Rome, is at the edge of the earth. Great China is the centre of the world, and Loyang is the centre of China.' His fingertip drew the name in spilt wine across the table. *Qin.*

'Never heard of it.'

'*Qin,*' An said. 'Middle Earth, the source of all civilization, all silk, all spice, and everything good that comes along the Spice Road.'

'Which we pay a fortune in gold to buy, I believe.'

'You Romans don't know or care where your money goes, or realize how small you are,' Chong said. 'To you we're simply the East. You know nothing. You're ignorant of true reality.'

Quistus held his head. 'Young Zhang here's fifth in line to all this power, wealth, civilization and so on?'

'No, Quistus, not fifth. He is first. The Mandate of Heaven will fall to him.'

An nodded. 'His father the Emperor had a dream of five cranes flying over the palace, and the fifth flew faster and became first. The omen was unmistakable.'

'If you believe in omens,' Chong muttered.

'Zhang's four elder brothers were found unworthy. The Emperor decreed that his most beloved fifth son, Zhang, by Consort Jia, be adopted as his first and foremost son by his childless Empress. Zhang shall be Son of Heaven.'

Quistus said, 'Young for it, isn't he?'

'I'm not young,' Zhang said, sounding very young.

Omba knelt by a light-vent, straining to overhear. Pigs snuffled hungrily at her legs. She shoved them away, cursing, and pushed her head and shoulders deep into the vent. Voices echoed below.

'If you're telling the truth, Zhang, you're a long way from home.' Quistus yawned. 'What brings you to glorious Rome?'

'Why won't you believe us? *Qin* is the whole world.' The boy's eyes gleamed near tears with frustration. 'You have my word, Quistus, everything my *Ai* guardians tell you is the truth.'

'Quistus doesn't believe a word,' muttered Chong. 'I wouldn't.'

'The barbarian's too addled with wine to think.' An trundled obediently to Zhang's side, following some unspoken command. 'Highness?'

The boy whispered in a strange tongue. An bowed, retreating to the shadows. Zhang stepped so close to Quistus, face to face, that Manas took a sharp, protective stride. The boy waved him back. He said quietly, 'I see you don't believe me, Quistus. You think I'm playing some sort of childish trick?'

Distracted, Quistus tried to keep an eye on An, but couldn't see him. 'How would a twelve-year-old boy know what I think?'

'All my life I, too, have had enemies. I know.'

'Then you know, Zhang, that sometimes enemies play tricks.'

'An enemy,' the boy said, 'would make up a more believable story. And he wouldn't send a boy to tell it.'

'I don't—' Quistus gasped at a sliding sensation in his neck. He reached up but his hand was knocked away. An whispered close to his ear, 'Be still, barbarian.'

Ertola screamed, 'He's stabbed Quistus!'

Manas looked up as a shape moved in a light-vent.

* * *

Omba pushed at the filthy stones. The shadows below were deeper than ever. The man she'd first seen, An, stood behind Quistus. He'd thrust a blade into Quistus's neck. The blade gleamed silver, a thin, shining line. Quistus arched his back and tried to reach the hilt, but An knocked his hand away. Quistus sat without moving now. The assassin was killing him. Omba gripped the edges of the opening, pulling with all her strength, shouting, 'Master!'

The stones gave way and a pair of hands reached up from below, clamped on her wrists, and dragged her down.

'Be calm,' An said. 'It's no blade for killing, only healing. You're feeling needle number three.' Quistus sat peacefully. Nothing was important, only the faint burning sensation in his neck. Manas jumped, reached into a light-vent, and dragged Omba to the floor in a shower of stones and dust. 'Omba,' Quistus said. 'Faithful Omba.' He watched them struggle, their bodies rolling, the African princess kicking, biting, scratching for eyes and testicles. Manas lifted her and threw her down. A table broke. The coffin fell to the floor, smashed. Quistus stared curiously at the broken wood. 'Hollow tubes of wood,' he murmured. 'Never seen before . . .'

Quistus's headache leaked into the needle. His sight cleared. 'Omba.' He came to his senses. 'Stop. Stop it, both of you.' He pulled her back, smelling cardamom. 'That's enough. Zhang, tell your man. Make it an order.'

Zhang said, 'Manas.'

At once Manas turned to the boy. Zhang nodded. Omba and Manas slapped each other, hissing, then stepped back. Quistus gave them a few breaths to calm down. 'So, Omba,' he said, 'you've found me.'

She stared at him through her one good eye, the other swollen shut, making out the needle in his neck.

'Needle number three,' An said quickly. 'Only temporary. Not a cure. For that I would need needle number nine.' He plucked out number three, wiped it on his sleeve, and replaced it with eight others of various sizes in an oblong leather case. 'Not so much pain now, I think?'

Quistus rubbed his head. 'It's a miracle.'

'No miracle,' An said. 'Just *zhong yi xue*. Chinese therapy medicine.'

Omba whispered, '*Chinese*, Master? What?'

'You know as much as I do. From where these civilized folk come, we're barbarians.'

'I'm no barbarian,' Omba growled. She spat at Manas, who growled back. An held out his hands, palm-up for peace. 'Enough! A spirit of enmity between us brings bad fortune on us all.'

Omba whispered, 'His fingernails, Master. Like daggers.'

An folded his long fingers back into his sleeves. Quistus said, 'It's good to see you, Omba. And I thank you from the bottom of my heart for your concern. But I'm no longer your master.' He sniffed. 'Cardamom?'

'Vulpus the spice-seller bought me. Knock-down price.' Omba unclenched her fist, revealing the spices crushed during the fight, and smiled. 'He'll wonder where I am.'

'Get back before he posts you missing with a bounty on your head.'

She sneered at Manas. 'You really think you can trust this lot? You need me more than Vulpus does, Master.'

Zhang stared at a spot of blood on the back of his hand. He didn't seem to know what to do with it. Manas knelt. He wiped away the speck as reverently as though he touched the hand of a god.

'More blood is spilt.' The child turned to Quistus. 'This is the second unfortunate incident today. The blood of ordinary humans must not touch me. It's desecration.'

'I think you'd better tell me about the first incident, the one that brought you here.' Quistus sat, resting his elbows on a table. 'Since it's obviously so important. Isn't it?'

'Murder,' An said. 'Horrible murder.'

'It could have been worse,' said Chong. 'Much worse.'

The child stared at his hand, defiled by the barely-visible stain.

Quistus said, 'That's why you seek me, Zhang? To find a murderer?'

'We know who the murderer is,' Chong said. 'We can't believe it.'

'It's Zhao,' An said. 'In Ruyang I served as magistrate, where I discovered the invariable rule that the one who discovers the murder is the murderer.'

'Such a belief just makes crimes easy to solve, An,' Chong complained.

'The safety of Heaven is paramount,' An hissed. 'A preventive execution ensures—'

'Yet we can't believe it's true,' Chong sighed. 'Logic fails us. An, we talk of dear Zhao. If *she* is the murderer—'

'She?' Quistus interrupted.

'If *she* is the murderer nothing makes sense. It's illogical. It makes us very afraid.'

'Who is Zhao?' Quistus asked patiently.

Zhang's unbroken voice replied. 'Zhao is mother, sister, daughter to me. Her love and loyalty and kindness towards me are perfection. She cannot be the murderer. Yet her hands were bloody. You must prove Zhao's innocence, Quistus. Don't make me order her to die.'

II

The Villa Paria

Quistus settled into the hired sedan chair, its interior dark and airless, furnace-hot from the sun. He lifted the curtain flap, watching Chong and An hurry the boy past Luca in the alley's shadows. The door slammed. Zhang faced him, excited. The sedan chair swayed, throwing them forward at each other as it was lifted, the slave at each corner settling a heavy pole on his horny shoulder. All were Vitellius's men, captured Germans prevented from escape not by chains but by infirmities, carefully matched. The blinded pair at the back had no choice but to follow those in front, who between them had the use of only two arms, an ear and a single tongue. The one with the tongue barked gruff Latin. 'Where to, Lord?'

Zhang didn't know where he lived. He lifted the curtain and whispered to Chong. 'Chong says, the Villa Paria.'

'To the Paria on the Viminalis Hill,' Quistus ordered. He was surprised. The Paria was, or had been, one of the best houses in Rome, really more than a villa though not quite a *domus*, but palatial enough, and for rent since Nero ordered the suicide of the ancient and politically troublesome Paria family. The slave with hearing made signs to the one with speech, who barked, 'We obey, Lord!'

The sedan turned past Triton's trickling fountain. The slaves took up their rhythmic, swaying tramp through the heat-shimmering streets of Rome. When Zhang tried to peer out, An, who jogged heavily alongside pouring sweat, hissed and snapped the curtain closed. Zhang peered through a gap on the other side, trying to see around Omba, who padded silently on bare feet, on stones that must be burning hot under the fierce sun. Manas prowled in front, elbowing people who got in the way.

Quistus nodded at the view. Only the boy mattered, and a boy's trust must be earned. 'Impressive sight, eh, Zhang? Rome was founded over eight hundred years ago, by gods.'

The boy shrugged. 'That's nothing. Three thousand years ago one god joined all Chinese families together in brotherhood. I am God's son by direct descent. One day I'll worship Heaven, *Tien*, for my people. My prayers to my – *our* – ancestors will be for all Chinese families, bringing health and good fortune. The Son of Heaven brings together all peoples and makes us all one family, one earth, one China.'

'Our Roman buildings are like white cliffs.' Quistus pulled the curtain. 'That gold statue of Jupiter stands hundreds of feet high. A million people live here. Rome's greater than any other city, greater than any empire the world has known.'

'Our Chinese cities are vast,' Zhang scoffed. 'Our empire is the world itself. Chong says only twenty-five legions defend your borders, yet Ban Chao commands hundreds of legions in my father's name.'

'Yet here you are in Rome, not in China.'

'I chose to travel, Quistus.'

'Hmm,' Quistus said, again thinking how old and tired those dark, upward-slanted eyes looked in one so young. 'Travel. A wise choice, I'm sure.'

An, bobbing anxiously around the vehicle, flapped the curtain down. Quistus spoke in the shadows. 'You travelled all this way here, Zhang, yet you haven't introduced yourself to Rome. Where are your emissaries, royal cavalcades, showy gifts? They say the royal visit to Rome of King Tiridates is costing Nero a fortune in shows and games. But no Roman's even heard of *Qin*. Nero hasn't welcomed Prince Zhang or held games in your honour, or, perhaps, even heard of you. You live in hiding, in fear. Why?'

Zhang tried to sound haughty. 'The imperial affairs of *Qin* are none of your business.'

'In fear of your four elder brothers who now find themselves junior to you, who don't even share the same mother?'

The sedan jerked, tilting uncomfortably as it was carried up the Viminalis. Zhang looked for An or Chong, but there was no one to advise him how to respond. He looked Quistus in the eye. 'You don't know us. My brothers love me, Quistus. Liu Xian, Liu Gong, Liu Dang, Liu Yan, all my elder Liu brothers back home –' he entwined his fingers – 'like that.'

'Then why have you run away to Rome?'

'I never run away!'

'Who wants you dead?'

'Zhao is innocent, that's all I know.' The boy's face was younger than ever, yet plainly exhausted. 'Please, Quistus. Help me.'

'Why me?'

'Because you have nothing to lose. Because you're not An or Chong.'

'What of your father, this all-powerful Emperor?'

'The Emperor believes—' Zhang swallowed. 'No messengers return. My father believes I'm dead, surely.'

'Yet here you are, alive.'

'Yes.' A single tear trickled down the boy's cheek. 'Here I am.'

They were nearly at the Paria. 'The coffin that hid you from the people of Rome,' Quistus said. 'What wood was it?'

'Not wood, grass.' Zhang wiped his cheek. He shrugged. 'Bamboo. Very common. I haven't seen any growing here. Why?'

'I haven't seen it either. You really have come far.' Quistus sat back, satisfied. 'Do all Chinese speak Greek?'

The boy shook his head. 'None know of Greece.'

'But you do. You do. A long journey for you indeed, Zhang, with time enough to learn a language.'

'Quistus!' Chong stuck his head through the curtain, puffing, as the sedan was carried up a final set of steps. 'You ask too many questions.'

'I thought that was what you wanted.'

The sedan was set down under a marble portico and the boy got out. Chong whispered, 'No, Quistus. We want answers.'

An whispered through the curtain on the other side, 'The right answers. Zhao found the murdered body, Quistus, therefore she is the murderer. You will find her guilty. His Highness will believe you. Peace will return to our household.'

Quistus watched An and Chong hustle the boy into the house, hiding him between their bodies. Was he really in such danger? Each side of the Paria's imposing entrance was let out to shops, as was usual with fine houses. No sign of a doorman. Omba went in, then returned. She nodded to Quistus. Safe. Manas stared down the street. The scene seemed normal enough to Quistus: snack-sellers touting from trays, scurrying slaves, important patrons strolling in togas, clients swirling around them like suckerfish. It was much too hot, people kept to the shadows. An came out and paid off the German with a handful of silver coins, not bronze. 'Glory to you, Lord!' cried the German, and the sedan chair was gone at a run before An realized his costly mistake. Maybe he didn't care.

Quistus turned. 'Show me what you want me to see, An.'

An shrugged. 'It was not I who wanted you here.' A Prince's word was law, even if he was only a boy.

After the brutal sunlight outside, the house's interior struck cool and dark. An closed and locked the heavy iron-studded door quietly, replacing the long bronze key on a hook. Quistus took his time looking around the narrow vestibule. He stepped on to the raised platform beside the door. Where was the doorman who should be sitting on the three-legged stool? *Ostiarii* were an unfree but proud race, often going back generations, and none ever turned down a visitor's penny, but the stool was empty today. The viewing hatch to the street was, as usual, set high so that the doorman eyed whoever was outside in safety. The platform had been washed but here the pale mortar between the tiles stayed brown as blood. An said, 'Chong believes the doorman was killed here, and dragged—'

'The doorman was killed?' Quistus was surprised. A doorman, however proud of his greeting skills and memory for faces, was nobody. 'A man of no importance was the victim?'

'Indeed.'

'He was Chinese?'

'He was Roman, Quistus. The only Roman in the house. We needed someone who attracted no attention, able to turn away visitors in Latin. He spoke enough Greek for us to understand him.'

'Greek as well as Latin? An unusually good doorman.'

'The best,' An said. 'He was yours.'

Quistus shivered despite the heat. The Villa Marcia was buried deep in his soul, a bone from someone else's body, someone very different; he was no longer that man. Old memories surfaced, haunting him awake. 'Cerberus?' He cleared his throat before he could speak. 'Cerberus served me and my father before me at the Villa Marcia.'

'We know, Quistus,' Chong called from another room, echoing. 'We purchased him at the imperial auction deliberately. He never tired of telling stories about you.'

Quistus bent his head. 'I'm sad Cerberus's death brings me here. He was loyal and greedy, but he never took a bribe against me.' He touched his cheeks, taking a deep breath. 'Show me his body.'

'It hasn't been moved from where it was taken,' An said bleakly. 'That was impossible.'

Quistus followed An into the cavernous entrance hall where Chong waited. The far end was a broad marble stairway crowded with people, all facing him, all Chinese, all silent, wearing all styles of clothing from ragged to exquisite, all with eyes downcast.

He murmured, 'The royal household, I presume.'

'Our household-family. Each one loved and trusted. All have proven their loyalty a hundred times.'

By the first step a man was pushed forward between two guards. Plainly of great strength, he seemed paralysed by fear. His hands bound tightly behind him, he was thrown to his knees. His eyes were black, wide, his skin waxy with sweat. A sword was held to his neck. 'We're just in time,' An said with satisfaction. 'Captain Lo. Dereliction of duty.' There was a splitting sound, a heavy spurt of blood, and the head rolled. The body was dragged away, someone fetched the head, and women with buckets cleaned up.

'Last night Lo guarded these steps,' An said grimly. 'He slept. When shaken he smelt of *yapian* – opium. Yunyazi—'

'Yunyazi?'

'Our court magician. Yunyazi examined Lo with a Truth Spell—'

'I'd have welcomed the chance to question Lo myself,' Quistus said mildly. 'With or without a Truth Spell.'

'Yunyazi's powers make a drop of sweat talk, believe me. Lo saw nothing. He'd taken enough opium to make a horse sleep.'

'Captain Lo was a hero of Falling Waters Bridge,' Chong said sharply.

'Enough!' An said. 'This time, he erred.'

'Don't execute anyone else before I've questioned him, An.' After a moment's hesitation, Quistus added, 'Or her.' A thought struck him. 'Does anyone else here take opium?'

'Wild Swan, our second best dancer. So sad. Opium is given to her.'

'Why?'

'She's dying. There's little hope. A most distressing disease.'

'I'm sorry.' Quistus lowered his voice. This was the part he dreaded. 'Where was Cerberus's body found?'

An and Chong went to one side of the stairs, revealing a corridor where Zhang waited with obvious impatience. 'At last!' The boy grabbed Quistus's hand without etiquette, drawing a reproving hiss from An, and pulled him to a doorway.

Sunlight poured through high, barred windows. A kitchen, obviously. Zhang dragged Quistus excitedly to the water cistern. 'See!'

The stone cistern was brimming with blood. The space seemed too small to fit a whole man inside. The face floated on the red scum like a mask, blank, downward-staring eyes already baked brown by the heat. Gently Quistus wiped the old man's skin clean with his hands.

'Cerberus,' he nodded.

'Chong said to leave him there,' Zhang said. 'He said don't touch him. I ordered it.'

'You did right.'

'Remember Heaven can do no wrong, Quistus,' An said in a low voice.

Quistus turned, angry. 'Wait outside, An. You too, Chong. Where's Zhao?'

'Under guard. She says nothing new, just the same story over and over.'

'Send her in.' An and Chong shuffled in reverse, never showing their backs to the child. Quistus held Zhang's shoulder until they were alone, then lifted him casually on to the table among the pots and pans. The boy sat swinging his legs like any boy. Manas, a sharp curved *sica* through his belt, blocked the corridor with his broad shoulders. His fierce blue gaze never left the boy. Quistus heard the entourage murmuring on the stairs but couldn't see them. He'd need to talk to each one, perhaps twenty or thirty in all. It wasn't going to be quick.

He asked gently, 'Are you well, Zhang?'

'You think my father's son is afraid to see a man's blood?'

'That's not what I asked.'

The boy's lower lip trembled, then was stilled. 'These people are all my family. We're *family*, Quistus.'

'I understand. What's the first you knew of this terrible tragedy?'

'Everyone shouted when Zhao screamed in the middle of the night. I didn't hear her but the shouting woke me. I sleep behind thick walls, hidden at the back of the palace –' he corrected his Greek – '*house*. At once Manas, who lies at my door, rushed in to protect me. I wasn't frightened.'

'I know, I know.'

'Chong ran to tell us Zhao had discovered something terrible. So terrible that no one except An believed, at first, that she could have done it.'

'An dislikes Zhao?'

'An, my major-domo, is a brilliant man. Zhao, my teacher, is a brilliant woman.'

'Your teacher?'

A woman's voice came softly from the doorway. 'Yes, I am Zhao.'

The girl stood calmly between two guards. She was much younger than Quistus had expected. Her hands were tightly knotted by leather thongs, her ankles hobbled together. No one was taking any chances. Manas drew his *sica* and stood between her and the boy as Zhao was dragged into a beam of sunlight.

Quistus blinked, surprised. She was beautiful. Everything about her was wrong – she was too tall, within an *uncia* of his own height, and her tight-pinned topknot of deeply black hair made her even taller. Her forehead rose high over dark slanted eyes, the eyelids creased to give her an air of cynical, world-weary intelligence. Her gowns were silk and satin, embroidered with fiery mythical beasts. She'd been permitted to wash her hands but her left sleeve was crusted with dried blood. For a moment her gaze into Quistus's eyes was direct and piercing, then she bowed her head in submission to the boy.

'I see you're left-handed, Zhao,' Quistus said, with a nod at her sleeve. A mocking smile lifted the corners of her lips. He'd made a mistake already. She said nothing to help him out.

He said, 'Aren't you?'

'This is Quistus the barbarian,' Zhang said. 'Look at him, Zhao! On this matter he speaks with my voice. Answer his questions!'

She raised her eyes, looking firmly at Quistus, not Zhang. However close her relationship with the boy in private, in public he was too wonderful to be observed by mortals without permission. She waited while Quistus studied her, frowning, perplexed by her. She threw him by saying, *'Dominus?'*

Lord. She spoke Latin. Quistus hid his surprise, unsuccessfully – her dark, deep eyes missed nothing important – then in Latin replied sternly, 'Tell me exactly who you are in this household and what you saw.'

'I am Zhao of the family Ban, unworthy and unenlightened younger sister of the virtuous twins Ban Gu, the imperial historian, and Ban Chao, eternally victorious general of the Outlands North-of-the-Wall—'

'Not Latin gibberish!' the boy commanded. Zhao was instantly head-bowed, silent. 'Speak properly. An always says you're too clever for your own good, Zhao.' He looked to Quistus for approval. Quistus realized the boy's emotional turmoil, his deep terror that Zhao was guilty. He'd called her mother, sister, daughter. His teacher too. She looked no more than eighteen or so, closest to the boy in age of anyone he'd seen. If Zhang had a friend, someone who really knew him, she was Zhao the accused.

She whispered in Greek, 'I was born in Fufeng. At the age of fourteen I took up the dustpan and brush in the house of my husband, Cao Shou.'

Quistus said, 'He's here?'

'He died two years ago, when the kidnappers—'

'Only last night's events concern us, Zhao!' An called from the corridor. 'Quistus doesn't want to hear the life story of a guilty woman.'

Quistus stuck to Latin. 'Zhao, are you the only one who speaks our tongue?'

She replied in Greek, obedient to the child's command. 'I am, Quistus. Languages find lodging in my silly, unsophisticated head. I meant no harm by it.'

'Who taught you?' Quistus already knew the answer.

Zhao visibly forced herself not to look at the cistern. 'Cerberus spoke enough Greek for me to learn a little Latin.' She added, 'He often talked of you. He was ancient with wisdom. He claimed you taught him to have two faces.' She gave a small shudder, believing it. Quistus realized how *foreign* Rome was to these people.

'Not literally two faces, Zhao.' Such intelligence in her, yet such naivety. He explained, 'Our god Janus looks both ways. A good *ostiarius* is the spirit of Janus at the door of a house, witnessing the comings-in and the goings-out.'

'I was wrong to speak to him without permission. I understood little of barbarians, and learned much.' Polite defiance, but defiance. She knew her own mind.

Yes, and she must know more about us Romans than anyone else in this crowd, Quistus thought, little though that is. But I don't understand *her* at all. He adopted Zhang's commanding tone, which she seemed to expect. 'Tell me what you saw in the kitchen last night. Leave nothing out!'

'At which moment shall I start?'

'When you came into the kitchen!' Quistus pretended impatience. 'Why were you here? Speak!'

'I was thirsty for a cup of water. The moon was high.' She took a deep breath. '*Ban ye*, deepest night. I left my room. I came down. I backed against the door, almost closing it.' She leant back, almost closing the door, muffling the sounds of the house, reliving the moment. 'Dark in here, full of shadows.'

'How did you see?'

'The moon's glow.' She pointed at the high barred windows where the sun now shone. 'And I carried my lamp.'

He nodded at shiny, pale pieces by the cistern, scattered among brown fragments of pottery.

'Yes,' she said, 'that was my white porcelain lamp. I carried it from my room in my right hand, being right-handed.'

'Ah, yes, right-handed,' Quistus said uncomfortably. He gave up his commanding tone. 'Describe everything just as you saw it, Zhao.'

'I looked around me . . . I thought, These pots and pans shouldn't be on the table. I sound foolish, trivial. Must I tell you everything?' She shot a glance at Zhang.

'Yes, tell him everything!' Zhang said. 'Prove your innocence!'

'I should not have been in here,' she confessed. 'It was wrong.'

'You needed permission to be away from your room?' Quistus asked.

'It's virtuous for the household-family to sleep at night, especially women. We're last to bed, first to rise.'

'But thirst awoke you early.'

'I dreamt I heard a sound.'

'What sound?'

'An echo. Like a door closing, a wooden mallet on stone, odd footsteps. It's difficult to describe.'

'Go on.'

'My mouth was dry. Dutifully I investigated as far as the kitchen but found nothing.' A rehearsed excuse. Her gaze met Quistus's for a moment. He noticed something about her and stepped closer. Zhao's eyes narrowed, squinting.

He stepped back. 'Go on. The pots had been moved to the table.'

'Yes, from the cistern lid. A bad spirit had moved them.'

'How do you know it was a bad spirit?'

'My lamp-flame sensed a ghost pass through. The flame bent to one side, then burned straight again.'

Zhang's eyes shone. 'The world's full of ghosts and spirits.'

Quistus looked behind the chimney breast. Nothing unusual: latrines, storerooms, steps. He turned back to Zhao. 'Then?'

'I took a jug—'

'This brown jug?' Quistus nudged the fragments with the toe of his sandal.

'Yes, in my left hand, I still held the lamp in my right. I knelt at the spout on the side of the cistern but only a drip came out, hardly enough to taste.'

'She drank blood!' Zhang said with boyish delight.

'Quiet,' Quistus ordered. An, who'd pushed the door ajar to eavesdrop, drew an appalled breath. Quistus had insulted Heaven again.

'I'd already decided to be quiet,' the boy said with dignity. 'She may continue.'

Quistus said, 'So, Zhao, you decided to lift the lid and fill a jug with drinking water – as you believed it to be – straight from the cistern?'

'Yes.' She paused, frowning. 'No. No, I remember, at that moment there was a flash of lightning, green, then red, and one of your barbarian gods gave a great clap of thunder.'

'We know the exact instant of your discovery,' Quistus said, pleased.

'Half Rome heard it,' Omba called over An's head.

'Ertola called it a noisy star,' Quistus remembered. 'Probably a shooting star, a thunderbolt of burning iron falling from the sky.'

'Fallen from Heaven,' Zhang said eagerly, looking at Quistus. He couldn't keep his mouth shut when Quistus was around. 'A message from the spirit world, a sign, yes?'

'We'll ask Yunyazi the precise meaning, Highness.' An bowed. 'Your magician always knows such things. He will tell us, no doubt, that the shooting star foretold Zhao's guilt.'

'Or her innocence,' Quistus said.

'There's no such thing as omens from the spirit world,' Chong insisted. 'The noise of thunder, like that of shooting stars, is made by heat and light, not Heaven. Even if omens and gods existed, why announce the death of a mere doorman?'

Omba pushed into the kitchen. 'Master, listen. I know shooting stars. On autumn nights they scratch Kefa's sky from side to side. This was no shooting star, I swear. Each person spoke of it differently. Those far off saw a silent flash. People in the Subura said it was brilliant and noisy. One girl claimed she saw a flower grow from the Viminalis among these fine houses here, burst into bloom above the rooftops, and die. It was close by, Master.'

Zhao said softly, 'Yet a shooting star falls, not rises.'

'Zhao knows everything about astronomy,' Zhang told Quistus proudly. 'Writes books.'

'But no flower grows in the dark.' Quistus shook his head. 'The girl you heard was mistaken, Omba.'

Zhao murmured, 'Green and red. A green stalk growing, blooming into red petals. The flower was a rose.'

'Stick to what you actually saw,' Quistus prompted.

Zhao turned back to the cistern. Now she trembled. 'I dipped the jug, I touched his – his hand, fingers – I lost my mind, dropped everything, the light went out, I screamed.'

'Master, look at her,' Omba said reproachfully, bringing a stool.

'She may sit,' Zhang said.

Zhao sat. 'By moonlight I saw my hands were black with blood, my left sleeve too, where the jug broke. I tried to lift his body, I couldn't, he was stuck, only his face came up, I was screaming for help.'

'You poor girl!' Omba exclaimed. 'Master, you can see she can't tell a lie. This is awful for her. And she screamed for help, which means—'

'She wanted to be discovered.' Quistus drew a deep breath. 'Lift his body out.'

'Manas!' Zhang ordered. Manas called one of the guards to the cistern to help him. The second guard held his blade to Zhao's throat, just in case.

'Go on, Zhao,' Quistus said.

'There's no more to tell. Everyone came.'

'Who arrived first?'

'An. I heard Chong shouting for Lo, then when he didn't come Chong came anyway, then Yunyazi the magician and his little yapping dog – I can't think clearly. I'm so ashamed of losing my self-control.'

Manas thrust his muscular arms elbow-deep into the cistern, lifting under the body. Blood and water splashed across the floor, spreading. The body, tightly wedged, wouldn't come. Manas and the guard bent double, lifting together, grunting.

Quistus knelt beside Zhao. 'Did you do more than scream? Did you kill him?'

'No.' She turned, close to him, her gaze unfocussed. 'No! My loyalty to the Prince is complete. I'll die before I harm him. Why should I kill a doorman, a friend, a loyal servant?'

'This isn't about Cerberus's death,' Quistus said. 'The lock was unbroken, unforced. But Cerberus wouldn't unlock the door at night. Why kill a doorman? To let someone in, obviously.'

Chong called, 'But no one came in. No one was seen. There was no attempt on Prince Zhang's life. The house was searched, it was my first order. Cellars, attic, every possible hiding place. No one.'

'Perhaps the intruder's motive was not assassination,' Quistus said, 'just simple theft. He got in somehow, Cerberus discovered him, was killed, and the thief ran off when Zhao screamed.'

'The house contains treasures priceless to us, but nothing was stolen.' Chong added, 'Why would a simple thief bother to hide Cerberus's body?'

An called, 'The only reason an intruder could have for being here is the assassination of Prince Zhang. The child is Heaven and Earth to us, our life, our hope for the future. He is *Qin*. Can't you understand that simple fact, Quistus?'

Quistus turned to Zhao. 'You were the accomplice, the person inside. You killed Cerberus—'

She wailed, 'No, Cerberus was my good friend! Why should I kill my friend?'

'You had to unlock the door, Zhao. Someone came in. Else why unlock the door?'

'No.' She dropped to her knees, her forehead to the stone floor. 'I spent all afternoon alone with the Prince, teaching. I could have killed him any time.'

'That's true,' Zhang said. 'We were sewing. And poetry.'

'Poetry? Sewing? Why didn't you tell me before?'

'I assumed you knew. Everyone knows my routine.'

Quistus lifted Zhao's face. 'Someone wants the boy dead.' He held her chin, forcing her to look at him. 'Obviously you're too close to Zhang to do the deed yourself. In Rome a murderer costs a few *sestercii*, so you only had to let someone in to do your dirty work for you. You'd drugged Lo earlier, he knew and trusted you, you'd hidden the drug in a sweetmeat, a gift. That got Lo out of the way. You couldn't face killing Cerberus, but he trusted you. You chatted, not for the first time, in Latin maybe, distracting him as you unlocked the door and let in the murderer. Cerberus was unarmed but he shouted for help. Your accomplice killed him to silence him and hid his body in the cistern, an impossible task for a woman.'

Zhao gazed at him steadily, dark brown eyes in a white face. 'Your accusations are lies and you know it.' She jerked her chin from his grip. 'If what you say was true, why is my beloved Prince still alive? Why did I scream?'

Quistus rubbed his face wearily. He was too tired to think.

'Why did the would-be killer hide the body, wasting time, instead of getting on with the job? If Zhao is innocent, why not kill her too, as she arrived so conveniently illuminated by lamplight, instead of allowing her to raise the alarm?'

'Tell us the answer, Quistus!' Zhang commanded, but Quistus was silent. He only had questions. He turned, realizing he'd almost forgotten the men at the cistern. They'd changed their grip. Manas grunted, muscles gleaming along his arms. He and the guard hauled with all their strength. '*Huuhhh!*'

The body came up with a sucking noise. The two men lifted it overhead, dragging the limbs free of the cistern. The arms and legs were twisted beneath the torso, the neck broken. Bloody liquid flooded from the unblocked spigot until someone turned it off. The two men laid the body on the soaked floor and stepped back, unmoved.

Zhao covered her mouth.

'His joints were torn to make his body small enough.' Quistus's voice was almost too low to hear. 'Cerberus was crushed to make him fit.' He crouched. 'His throat's cut.' The doorman's tunic was torn to tatters across his chest and stomach. 'Stabbed in his heart. His belly too.'

'It's butchery,' Zhao whispered.

Quistus touched the final cut. 'His genitals. Almost severed.'

'This was no murder,' Chong said. 'It was a ritual killing.'

'A barbaric ritual,' An said nastily, and Quistus saw himself as they saw him: a barbarian to make sense of a barbaric act. His stomach rose in his throat. He tasted wine. Cerberus's mouth hung open, dribbling blood.

He heard Zhao say, 'Do you still believe I did it, Quistus? Do you believe I *could?*'

Zhang cried out, 'Quistus has proven Zhao innocent!'

Quistus bent in half. He vomited red wine that mingled with the red blood.

He awoke in a high, darkened room, naked but for the sweat-wrinkled towel under his buttocks. A strap around his forehead stopped his head dropping on to the needles through his nipples when he passed out. Yellow ribbons tied his wrists lightly to the arms of the chair so that he couldn't pull the needle out of his penis.

He remembered An saying, 'Needle number nine.'

Needle number nine, longer and slightly thicker than the others, had been thrust carefully into his neck. The hilt burned with a tall, incense-scented flame. The burning, itching, healing sensation from the silver needle was pleasant if he didn't move. The long flame was just visible in the corner of his right eye. It bent, scalding his ear, if he tilted his head. Each time the door opened the draught bent the flame and his hair crackled. The day was stiflingly hot, the thick walls of the Villa Paria holding the heat in, not keeping it out. Sweat trickled down his face and spine. He felt peaceful. They weren't trying to hurt him, only heal him. *Zhong yi xue.*

The room's lone window, high up, was barred to keep out thieves, heavily draped to keep out light. It made him smile.

The door opened. Omba wiped the sweat from his body with long sweeps of her hands. She left. He called, 'Omba?' But the door closed. He nodded peacefully. His mind went round and round.

What monster would murder a man so horribly? Why?

Later the door swung and Omba wiped him again. 'You stink of metal, Master. It's wrong for a Roman to stink among Chinese. I'll send the girl with towels.' She flicked his sweat from her long, strong fingers. 'An says it's the wine coming out of you. You hear me, Master? He says you'll never need to drink again. Ever. You'll be a fit servant of the Prince, part of his family.' She added, 'Everyone is family to these people.'

Quistus found his voice, obsessed. 'If no one came into the house, why was Cerberus killed? Gentle, loyal Cerberus never hurt anyone. *Why?*'

'Rest, Master. You collapsed. A seizure.'

'The Prince told me, *A crowd is one of the few places I can hide.* It made me think, Omba,' he said dizzily. 'The killer's still here. He's in the house. An assassin hiding in plain sight. A trusted face waiting to strike again.'

'Zhang's heavily guarded.' Her voice came and went. 'He's locked in his room. Only Manas sees him. They've heeded your advice. They're frightened. Who else can they trust but you? You're indispensable.'

'Indispensable,' Quistus muttered thickly. His tongue felt twice its size. 'Omba, go back to Vulpus. Tell him you were attacked, waylaid in the street, any excuse. Serve him today. Tomorrow I'll buy your freedom.'

She looked at him with deep contempt. 'You're poor as I am, Master. You're as much a barbarian to these Chinese as I'm a barbarian to Romans. I don't want your freedom.'

'Listen, Omba. I'll charge them a fee. An's got so much silver he doesn't know what it's worth.'

'You've lost your wits, Master. Does a gentleman work for money?' He'd offended her. 'If you grub for a fee, you're no better than a common lawyer.'

'You're a snob.'

'You've insulted me. You can't treat me like this after what we've been through.'

'Look at me, Omba.' In her good eye – her right eye was still swollen shut – he saw his naked reflection, the flaming needle in his neck. He looked ludicrous. He'd put on twenty pounds in the last two months. His skin was soft and flabby, white as dough except for his ridiculously sun-darkened face and hands. 'Omba, I don't know what will happen to me. If I work for these people, you'll be free. You must want to be free.'

'You need me,' she grumbled. 'Someone's got to look after you.'

'My life isn't in danger. Only Zhang's.' He smiled to make her go. The smell of burning incense made him terribly sleepy. 'I'm safe.'

'Promise?' she called from the door.

'Omba, I'm safe.' His eyes closed. 'I promise.'

Quistus was wrong. He was in more danger than any of them. Just by waking up that morning he'd survived the first murder attempt against him. In a few minutes his second journey to the door of death would begin, and this time there would be no turning back; the investigator was also the victim. He wouldn't fully realize that until it was much too late.

Omba, leaving, crossed the atrium of the Villa Paria. Sunlight streamed through the open roof on to the colonnade of white pillars, one disfigured by a curved line drawn in soot. Obviously Chinese had the same trouble with graffiti artists as Romans.

She'd first met the gnarled servant Shu when Quistus was carried out after his collapse. Now the old man, a battered, too-small helmet jammed on his head, strapped into an ominously-holed leather breastplate too large for him, carried a spear. Shaking, spear wobbling, eyes round with fear, Shu guarded the entrance of the Villa Paria in place of Cerberus. Without a word he slammed the heavy iron-studded door open, shoved Omba outside, slammed it closed. She stood looking around her, glad to be out of the house. In there they were jumping at shadows.

Rome shimmered like an open furnace. Not a breath of wind, even here on the hilltop. The brilliant sunlight hurt her eye.

Quistus didn't want her. She *must* be free. No choice. Omba was upset. She rubbed her wet eye and told herself it was the sun.

Time to face Vulpus. She loped down the empty, sunlit side of the street towards the Subura. Crowds kept to the shadowed side and she made good time.

A curse came from behind her, then voices shouted. Someone knocked over an apple-seller's basket. Apples rolled down the street, spreading from a man standing in the shadows. Everyone grabbed what apples they could and ran, but he didn't look, or steal, or move. He stood deaf to the apple-seller's accusations. His sea-green cloak was hooded, his face shadowed. Omba felt him watching her, examining her. Chinese hid their faces in Rome. Maybe he was a messenger sent by Quistus or the Prince recalling her to the Villa Paria. But this man stood as deeply motionless – as *poised* – as an athlete at the starter's whistle.

A gust of wind lifted the silken hood. A flash of gold skin, tattooed cheekbones.

At once he turned on his heel – barefoot, no sandals – and vanished from sight into an alley. 'Stop, thief!' The apple-seller ran after him calling for the gods to help, for justice. You heard it a thousand times a day.

Omba knew sick people often wore a hooded *burrus* to hide a mutilation or disease. She tried to forget about it. A toddler trotted past clutching a big red apple in both hands, and she smiled.

The apple-seller in the alley stopped in mid-shout. He'd run out of breath.

A single apple rolled from the alley towards Omba. The apple-seller would run to claim it. He didn't. She snatched up the apple and ate it in three starving bites as she crossed by Triton's fountain into Pepper Street. It was the first food she'd eaten today.

Vulpus wouldn't be pleased to see her. She knew she'd need her strength.

*   *   *

Quistus dozed. The door opened on the tall, milky figure of Zhao. Three hours ago he'd accused her of murder. She closed the door behind her. They were alone. There was no one to help him. He struggled to move but the needle-flame bent towards his eye. The strap held his head. Zhao looked down at him in the way even Romans did these days: with contempt. Her black hair gleamed, piled high, held by long bone pins intricately carved.

'Quistus the barbarian,' she said in Latin. The colour of the ribbons at his wrists, golden yellow, meant he had Zhang's trust.

She knelt, opened his eyelids wide with her fingertips, and stared into his eyes. Her fingernails were short, her hands used to work. Her gaze seemed deep and searching, but he already knew she was short-sighted. No, her deep, dark eyes were looking beyond him, into his soul. He couldn't stop her. She'd changed her clothes, jasmine-scented. Silk monsters embroidered on her satin smock breathed fire, but exhaustion bruised her cheekbones.

'I must trust you,' she whispered.

She rocked back on her heels, blinking. He saw something glint on her wrist, a blade less than two inches long. He opened his mouth to shout.

'If I wanted your life,' she murmured, 'I wouldn't need an eating knife.'

She leant back against the wall, rested her slim hands wearily on her knees, and closed her eyes.

'Where have you been, you bitch, you monkey!' Vulpus was beside himself with rage, as she'd known he would be. 'Omba, monkey-bitch! Kneel to your master!'

She turned her head away so that his insults didn't hurt. He didn't call her *Princess* once. There was no point; Vulpus had no customers to impress. The morning shadows had swung and the stall stood full in the afternoon sun, unbearably hot, not a single client waiting, the trays and pouches empty but for dust and mould. Vulpus grabbed her neck-chain. 'Where have you been? Where's my cardamoms, my nutmegs?'

A woman passing said, 'Cardamoms? You have cardamoms? My sister will pay double.'

Vulpus hit Omba's shoulders with the chain. 'You see what you've done? I've nothing. Today I could have made my fortune.

I'll have you whipped. No, I'll whip you myself.' The chain hit her chest, he didn't mind if the sackcloth on her breasts fell off. She held on tight. 'Well?' he demanded, knocking her to her knees.

'I was attacked in the street. They stole everything. Look.'

Vulpus fell silent. He noticed her swollen eye and scratches. Obviously she'd put up a fight. She opened her hand and he sniffed her palm. 'Cardamom.' He nodded, convinced. 'Yes, even a cardamom is worth stealing at these prices.'

The worst thing happened. Vulpus helped her to her feet and hugged her, his hawk nose stuck in her cleavage and his soft white fists feeling the small of her back. 'If only you knew what I've been through today. It's not over yet. I need you, Omba.'

Quistus slept, drugged by incense smoke. The strap held his head up. The noise of wooden hammers softly striking on tiles awoke him. Not until the door opened did he recognize the sound as footsteps. A girl's footsteps.

He stared. She stood on tiptoe, yet was no taller than a child. The pile of towels she carried teetered higher than her head. Her eyes peeped around the side to find her way to him. He'd never seen a girl so exquisite, so perfect. She had the round face of a doll, almost a mask. Her skin was flawless, white as chalk, her eyelashes black, her lips exotic buds of vermilion red. She was enchanting.

'Excuse, Quistus!' she laughed in Greek. 'Omba said, bring towels—'

Zhao woke, rolling smoothly to her feet, crouching, fists extended. She saw who it was and relaxed at once, asking something casual-sounding in Chinese. The girl laughed, something about so many towels, and Zhao settled back with a yawn.

'It's all right, Quistus. Meet Little Pelican.' She closed her eyes. 'You're complimented indeed. Or maybe she's just curious to see a barbarian close up.'

Quistus watched Little Pelican place the towels carefully in the corner. 'Is she a servant?'

'No! A dancer. A very fine *Wu* dancer, trained in Chu, better even than poor Wild Swan. She's no child, Quistus. It takes many years of bravery and dedication to achieve Little Pelican's skill at *Nuo* and *Tiaoshen*. A *Wu* dancer is like a sorcerer. The self-discipline of her years of training, her self-denial, is intense.

She's a wonder. Little Pelican dances the line between the worlds of gods and men.'

'She's lovely. I'd love to see her dance.'

'That sacred privilege is for the very few, Quistus,' Zhao said without opening her eyes. 'When Little Pelican really was a child, long ago, all her small toes were carefully broken and folded under. Her feet were tightly bandaged to force each heel bone into the instep. The bandages were tied tighter each time. As she grew up her bones were broken again and again, as necessary, to make her feet perfectly small and pointed, a lover's joy.' Little Pelican's feet were less than four inches long. 'For that reason, though not high-born – I don't even know who her father or mother was – she was treated as a lady even before she showed her genius as a dancer. Those special wooden clogs are called lotus shoes, so that she walks on her toe with as little pain as possible.'

'Surely she can't dance in those?'

'You'll never know, Quistus.' Zhao's voice faded. She was asleep.

Little Pelican bowed gracefully to Quistus. She picked up a towel in another towel with beautiful good manners. Carefully she wiped the sweat from his face, avoiding the needles. She towelled his chest, his belly, his thighs, and his feet just as carefully. Then she bowed respectfully to the sleeping figure of Zhao.

'Thank you, Quistus,' Little Pelican said so softly as she departed that he thought he dreamed her voice. 'Thank you for finding our dear Zhao innocent.'

'I need you to look tough, Omba,' Vulpus commanded. 'Tougher. No talking. Frown. You get shoved, shove back twice as hard. That's good. You frighten even me, eh?'

Omba padded beside him towards the reeking warehouses, bored. Vulpus insisted on holding her chain, showing everyone what a big little man he was. They came under the city wall to the riverside, palaces standing cheek by jowl with shacks, wharves, docks, more shacks and warehouses, beached barges. The Tiber stank, its thick waters olive-green with drought, bridges striding tall on mudbanks. People woke from the heat of the day and pissed on the mud. Human shadows silently watched from doorways as they passed, Jews who offended the gods, Moloch's child-killers, even blood-drinking Christians. Each sewer outlet trailed a dark fin of slime crawling with fishermen setting nets for lamprey.

'Remember. Tough.' Vulpus climbed steep wooden steps set in the end wall of the Spice Guild warehouse. 'I'm meeting an important man, one of the Spice Guild masters. You won't have heard of him. His name's Vitellius.'

'Vitellius!' Owner of Luca's tavern, and much else.

'Prices have gone crazy, Omba. If I don't buy new spice, what can I sell? If I don't sell, I starve. To buy stock at the new prices, I've got to borrow a fortune.'

'From *Vitellius*?'

'It's a business investment,' Vulpus said nervously.

A Phrygian at the door checked them for weapons and pushed them in.

At the far end of an airy loft three men reclined at a balcony table over the river, drinking steaming white wine from thick glasses. Omba noticed a fourth full glass, still steaming, by an empty place. Who'd been sitting there a moment ago? Nothing was said.

Vitellius hasn't changed, she thought. More than ever he looked like a frog crossed with a spider – round belly, thin arms, an ugly face with wide, unsmiling lips. He'd called Quistus *patronus* for years, just one of a great man's *clientela* begging and fawning for favours. How times changed. Now Vitellius, his fingers stuck to the elbow in every pie, after a long career of lying, cheating, stealing and the occasional murder, had grown great while Quistus fell.

She didn't know the two men with him. 'Roco and Dorca,' Vulpus whispered. 'Sons.' He coughed, waiting to be noticed. Someone – probably another of Vitellius's many illegitimate offspring – brought a cooked chicken to the table. A chicken did not divide happily into three instead of four. Roco reached for a leg then, seeing his father's greedy eyes, hesitated.

'Vulpus, my old friend.' Vitellius permitted his greasy knuckle to be kissed.

'This small gift is for you, *patronus*,' Vulpus fawned, offering a whole nutmeg. Omba hid a smile, knowing he'd found it stuck between his floorboards.

Vitellius clicked his fingers for a grater. 'Omba. What are you doing here with this fool?'

'She's mine. I bought her. Very pricey.' Vulpus made his heightened status clear. 'My African princess.'

Roco said, 'My father knows exactly who Omba is, Vulpus.'

'You *are* a fool, Vulpus,' Dorca rumbled. He was as ugly as his father.

'He wasted all his money buying her,' Roco said. 'Everyone knows he wants her. Not a wise business decision.'

Vitellius pulled off a chicken leg. 'Tell me, Omba, how is my dear *patronus*, Septimus Quistus?'

'As well as you'd expect in his situation.'

'I'm so sad to hear that. Is there any more I can do?'

'I know you helped him as best you could, risking Nero's anger to shelter him. Luca's was a better bolt-hole than nothing. Thank you.'

Dorca whispered in his father's ear, 'Quistus is missing from Luca's.'

Vitellius gave no sign he'd heard. 'I'd have done more for my old friend Quistus. I tried to warn him but he wouldn't listen. I'd have purchased you myself, Omba, but times are—' Omba thought Vitellius would say *hard*, like any businessman, but instead he said, 'Dangerous.'

'I understand.'

'I'm sure you don't.' Vitellius waved his chicken leg imperiously. Metellus, one of his younger adult sons, fetched a nutmeg grater. He smiled at Omba, made even more handsome by the white streak across his hair, some childhood fight injury. Last winter he'd smuggled Quistus and Omba from Rome under the noses of praetorians led by the ambitious bureaucrat Stigmus. She noticed Metellus carried a very large knife in his belt. Not here to cook. His brother Stichus waved to Omba from the shadows, also armed. Something was up.

Metellus whispered to Omba, 'You know where Quistus is?'

'Excuse me,' Vulpus raised his voice, 'but I have come here to discuss an urgent business opportunity involving considerable sums of money—'

'More.' Vitellius turned the leg under the grater, ignoring Vulpus. 'More. Not too much. Enough.' He sniffed the grated nutmeg luxuriously, dipped the spiced chicken in fish sauce, and ate quietly. 'So, Omba, where is he?'

'Why all this interest in Quistus?'

'I dropped by Luca's this morning with Roco. Routine,' Dorca said.

'Making sure our dear stiff-legged brother runs his business profitably,' Roco said. 'To our dismay we found somebody had already kicked his door in. We had to kick it in again. Luca's had a breakdown. He won't talk to us.'

'He hasn't talked to us since Roco broke his knee,' Dorca said.

'We asked him anyway,' Roco said.

'Luca's best whore's run off and Quistus is gone too.'

'That's bad news.' Vitellius tore off the other leg. 'With the whore? Was she pretty?'

Dorca shrugged.

'I can help you, gentlemen,' Omba said. 'Quistus is with the Chinese.'

Vitellius frowned at the unfamiliar word. 'Chinese?'

Dorca said in a tight voice, 'She means the Gold Heads.'

There was a silence. Vitellius stopped chewing. He jerked his eyes. Roco looked over the balcony, checking out the wharf below. The sun had dropped below the rooftops. 'You were followed, Vulpus? Anyone see you?'

'No, Roco.' Vulpus wrung his hands. 'I swear.'

'Sure?'

Metellus, drawing his knife, stood by the door. Stichus slid to the window.

'Maybe,' Omba remembered. 'Maybe I was followed part of the way to Vulpus's. Someone knocked over apples. A man, I think.'

'A man?' Vitellius chuckled without humour. 'That was no man. No man, indeed. Hooded? A cloak of silk, not wool? Smaller than you'd think?'

'If you say so.'

'A golden face, tattooed each side?'

'Yes, I saw that.'

'Gold Head!' Vitellius swore. 'Yet you're alive.' He went on thoughtfully, 'Why should it follow you? You're no one to them.'

'They follow everyone, they search all the time,' Roco said. 'You never know where they are. They're like the wind.'

Metellus called, 'If Quistus is with the Gold Heads, he's dead.'

Omba shook her head. 'The Chinese took him. They're looking after him.'

Vitellius watched her carefully. 'Where?'

Something in Vitellius's eye made her say, 'How should I know?' She added honestly, 'He's ill. Too much wine.'

'If he's been drinking Luca's wine, it's worse than a hangover.' Vitellius had years of experience at not looking guilty. He shrugged, spreading his hands, the picture of innocence. 'I make no apologies, Omba. I did what I had to. No one says no to Nero. The Emperor is the *patronus* of every Roman. That honour has been with us since the days of Augustus. I haven't been disloyal to my *patronus* Quistus, only loyal to the greatest *patronus* of us all, Nero.'

Omba stood. 'Luca was feeding Quistus poison in his wine? You two promised him safety but you were really doing Nero's dirty work?'

'Sit down. It's in the past. I swear I'll do Quistus no more harm. The situation has changed, changed deeply.' Vitellius made a small gesture for peace. 'Metellus, check the Phrygian isn't asleep out there, or dead.'

'What?' Vulpus gulped. '*What?* What's going on?'

'Who are the Gold Heads?' Omba asked quietly.

'They're fucking deadly,' Dorca said. 'They moved in on us a few weeks ago. That's all you need to know. What's this about Chinese?'

'They're from the East. They call their country *Qin*.'

'Never heard of it.'

'I have,' Vulpus said. 'I've heard that name from silk traders. No one knows how silk thread is made. They say the *Qin* do it by magic, they're magicians.'

'They sound like Gold Heads,' Roco grunted. 'Metellus?'

Metellus slammed the door. 'All clear.'

'Doesn't mean they're not there,' Dorca said. 'We should get out of sight, Father.'

'I don't hide from anyone.' Vitellius tore off a chicken breast. 'No. No more nutmeg. I hate nutmeg now.' He turned to Omba. 'These are my streets. I don't give my streets up. The Gold Heads want war, I'll give them war.'

'Their heads are made of beaten gold,' Metellus told Omba. He shrugged. 'Roco saw one full face.'

'My knife made it bleed,' Roco said. 'Just gold leaf.'

'One single cut in its clothes,' Metellus said. 'You barely escaped with your life.'

'I thought you boys weren't afraid of any man?' Omba said.

'They're not men,' said Dorca. 'They aren't women either. They're sexless.'

'*Castrates?*' Omba shook her head. 'Eunuchs aren't fighters, they're too clever for bravery.'

'These creatures were never men, Omba. They were women. They're vicious and skilful. Metellus is right, I was lucky.' Pride made Roco add, 'A little bit lucky.'

'How can women be castrated?'

'They cut off their *mammae*. I saw through the torn clothes. Smooth-chested, no nipples. Not just one breast, like the Amazons, both.' Roco shuddered. 'No *papillae*, no *clitores*. That's what I think. Warrior virgins.'

'Such creatures would reproduce, if any man could bear to touch them, but without feeling or pleasure.' Dorca, a passionate man, had sired almost as many brats as his father. 'Without nipples the creature cannot nurture a child. What it cannot feed it cannot love. What purpose can it have in life?'

Omba thought, I know their purpose. They're assassins. The Gold Heads are in Rome to kill the boy.

'Obedience,' she said. 'Total obedience. That's their purpose.'

Did the Gold Heads kill Cerberus? It made no sense.

'Roco, Dorca,' Vitellius reproved his sons. 'Sexless women? Whatever next! You imagine far too much. I'm ashamed of you. Go, watch the street, all of you, and learn to be brave.' He clapped his hands. 'Go!'

He turned to Omba. 'Sit beside me. What I'll say is best said quietly.'

Vulpus took the opportunity to worm his way on to the bench. 'Worshipful *patronus*,' he said with a slimy grin, 'about the money . . .'

'What do you see?' Vitellius waved his greasy palm at the loft, filled only with shadows as the sun set. 'Where are precious spices piled to the roof-beams, as they should be? Pepper by the ton, a year's supply of cinnamon, an emperor's ransom of ginger, cloves, saffron, preservatives to keep food fresh, jasmine, bolts of silk, do you see them? No. Nothing. What can I do, Vulpus? Nothing. A forty-foot roll of ice-white silk is pricier than a house, and money costs a hundred per cent. Spices and silks – anything that comes along the Silk Road – is up in price ten times over, a hundred times, and that's if I can get them. I can't. You know why? The Spice Road is closed.'

Vulpus's lips moved. '*Patronus*, it cannot be . . .' he squeaked.

'I assure you of the situation. The Emperor himself is help-less. They say four thousand camels stand idle on the Parthian border, that the gates of Ecbatana are rusted shut. This year's payment of Roman gold, however, is already gone. Hundreds of millions, vanished into the East to pay for someone's army. So you see, Vulpus, you're not suffering alone.'

'Something must be done. Rome without spice?' Vulpus shuddered, more concerned with his own fate than Rome's. 'Who's to blame? There will be riots.'

'The Emperor,' Vitellius lowered his voice, 'is well aware of that. He blames these vile Christian cannibals to deflect blame from himself.'

'But it's not them?' Omba said.

'Of course not. How many legions did their Christus command?' Vitellius sipped his wine. He made a face because it was cold and the cumin had lost its taste. 'No. The Gold Heads have stopped the Spice Road, they and their allies. I know this for a fact.' He rubbed his face. 'The leader of the Gold Heads is a creature called Golden Turtle. He assures me that's his name in Latin. He's their god, their father. As children, the Gold Heads swear an oath of obedience until death to him, and in return he promises them life for ever. He's a magician, he calls himself a *Neidan*. He's made of solid gold.'

'A solid gold man cannot live.'

'I saw him with these eyes, Omba. There was a moment's truce between us. Golden Turtle is obese, as big as two men, he hardly walks. His voice squeaks like Vulpus's, only worse. He's a eunuch. His body is hairless and indeed he appears to be made of gold. He eats gold for food, they say, like Crassus did.'

Every Roman knew that story. A hundred years ago Licinius Crassus, the richest man in Rome, led forty thousand soldiers east against the Parthians to secure the Spice Road for Rome for ever. His army was cut off, trapped and massacred. Crassus's son Publius, in a vain attempt to rescue his father, was killed with every man in his legion, V *Scythia*. The Parthians captured Licinius Crassus alive.

'They murdered him by feeding him molten gold, but he couldn't die,' Vitellius said. 'Who knows the truth of it? Many legends were born that day. Perhaps a man may live turned into gold. Perhaps the man who survived was in fact Publius. Many believe that Publius led his men into the east behind the Parthian lines rather than return in disgrace to Rome. Who knows? People believe anything. Thirty years later Emperor Augustus negotiated the return of prisoners and captured eagle standards, but no trace was ever found of Publius Crassus, his men, or the eagle of V *Scythia*.'

'Could the Gold Heads close the Spice Road, Vitellius? Are they an army?'

'I doubt there's twenty of them in Rome. It's enough, if Golden Turtle has the Parthian empire on his side. It's said even the Parthians watch their backs, there's whispers of a huge barbarian army gathering in the east. An army led by warlords wearing silk.'

'*Qin*,' Omba said, thinking, Whose side are they on?

Vitellius rubbed his face wearily. 'I was face to face with Golden Turtle. He was dressed in silks so fine I saw his gold belly and backside. He taunted me, opening and closing his gold fingers like crab claws. "Spice Road open. Spice Road closed. Spice Road open. Spice Road closed." He can do it. It's closed, isn't it?'

Omba leant forward. 'What does he want?'

'He wants me to find some boy called Prince Zhang and hand him over to be killed. Which, of course, I have been sincerely trying to do. I want my streets.'

'Then find the boy quickly!' Vulpus said. 'Unless this Golden Turtle gets what he wants and the road is opened very soon, I'm a broken man. Find him, great *patronus* Vitellius, and save me.'

It was almost dark. Vitellius gazed at the spice-seller with frog eyes and wide, unsmiling mouth, venomous as a spider. 'It's not so simple, fool,' he said. 'Others are involved now. Others who are higher, greater.'

'Who?' Omba said.

'Higher. Greater,' Vitellius said, unblinking.

Vitellius sat alone for a dozen breaths after the spice-seller and Omba were gone. Then he called, 'You heard, Tigellinus?'

A door creaked. Vitellius shifted uneasily as the perfumed Sicilian sat beside him in the dark and drained the fourth glass of wine.

'Yes, Vitellius. I heard.'

Tigellinus the Sicilian (who preferred to be thought Greek) was what Crassus had once been: by far the richest man in Rome. Thanks to Quistus, he was no longer the second most powerful man after the Emperor, no longer Prefect of Praetorians. Tigellinus's all-too-public fall from the Emperor's favour, his humiliation cheered by the mob packing the Circus Maximus, had been drastic, alarming, and must be reversed. To be rich but powerless in Nero's Rome was unimaginably dangerous.

Gaius Sophonius Tigellinus had worshipped power for more than thirty years. For power's sake he'd slept with the wives, mothers, daughters, sons and, if necessary, horses and dogs of three successive emperors, and reputedly Caligula himself, as well as (of course) Nero; thus Tigellinus had kept himself, in politics if not always in bed, firmly on top. His mind was sharp as a gutting knife thrust deep in the political heart of Rome. For the past week he'd been sleeping in his Aemilian palace with Nero's empress, the gorgeous Poppaea, while Nero was away playing with her lookalike, the boy Sporus, by the sea. Tigellinus was the sort of man who'd do anything to get back the power and pride he'd lost. Anything at all. Less than thirty-six hours ago, his chance had come.

Vitellius shivered in the heat, just to sit beside a man of such admirable ruthlessness and single-minded brutality. Not Greek at all.

'Six hours in the saddle to Antium yesterday, at the Emperor's command,' Tigellinus growled. 'Rome in uproar, prices rising, Nero in a fine temper at his seaside palace, dressed like a whore, his tailor crying, advisers scurrying like ants, even Seneca called from retirement. War looks inevitable, we're sending whole legions east. They say this *Qin* empire is bigger than anything. The Emperor's shouting for Quistus like he did last time, panicking, thanks to Seneca's whispers. Nero calls me to his bridal bower – he's marrying his pretty boy – and he begs for my help, crying like a woman. Six hours back to Rome again, two horses died under me, my arse is on fire. A glass of wine with my old friend and informant Vitellius and what do I hear? There's a *Qin* prince actually here somewhere – *somewhere* – in Rome. And guess what, Quistus is with him.' His voice rose, his fists clenched. '*Quistus!*'

Vitellius refilled his glass. Tigellinus drained it to the dregs.

His voice was low, savage. 'I know how to hurt him. I know his daughter Lyra is alive and well – for now – and I *know*—'

Tigellinus smiled. Revenge was best served cold. His time was coming.

'Quistus must live, Vitellius. You'd better pray he doesn't die. The Emperor commands his presence in Antium, *statim*. No excuses.'

Vitellius was shaken. 'To find Quistus, you must find the Chinese and the boy Prince Zhang. Before the Gold Heads do.'

Tigellinus's smile broadened. 'Me? No thanks. I'll be back in Antium before dawn. I don't like bringing the Emperor bad news, it's fatal. I hardly imagine the abducted Quistus confided his destination to our stupid friend Luca, so I think the thankless task of finding him is someone else's job, don't you? I have just the man in mind.'

They watched the full moon rise while Tigellinus's fresh horse was fetched.

'Awake!'

Quistus woke with a start. Moonlight, flickering flames, long candles. Someone was in the room with him – someone more than the sleeping figure of Zhao. The newcomer was tall, made taller by a conical hat, and white-bearded, with long, bony hands. At his feet sat a small white dog with alert eyes and a wagging stump of a tail. The dog yapped once.

The man murmured, 'Be silent, Fu.' The dog was silent; even its tail stilled.

The man bent over Quistus, strongly unwashed, his beard smelling of boiled vegetables. A bright red flame sprang from the needle in Quistus's neck.

'Be still, man, for your own sake!'

Zhao yawned, turning in her sleep. The smell of incense was overwhelming. Quistus tugged the ribbons on his wrists but they were stronger than they looked, or he weaker. The red flame rose, sparkling fiercely.

'She won't wake until I say,' murmured the man. 'Be aware that I am Yunyazi. Yes, you've heard of me. Some call me the *Wei Boyang*. I am he himself, the Prince's imperial magician, skilled beyond measure in the transcendent arts.'

Quistus tried to spit. He couldn't. Sticky clay filled his mouth, caustic, bitter. He moved his head to follow Yunyazi's swaying movements but the flame turned his sight red. His hair crackled.

'Chong sent for me, Quistus. You're lucky he has bright eyes. Lucky he sent for me. Lucky I agreed to come. I like luck.'

Quistus croaked, 'Are you the murderer?' He choked, swallowing the foul clay before he could stop.

Yunyazi's voice came from Quistus's shoulder, breathing into his ear. 'If I were the murderer our Prince would be in Heaven. So would you. I never kill. Except to bring back to life.'

'What?' Quistus asked dully. The taste of clay rose in his throat.

'Clay and herb and fire will flush your body of poison, Quistus. Your mind will clear just as sunlight burns away fog, and you will know yourself.' Yunyazi walked around the chair three times. 'An was so sure you'd poisoned yourself with wine as a way to self-murder that he failed to observe the obvious truth. But Chong is a rational man who noted, the moment he first saw you, the blue colour of your gums. A symptom that does not accompany wine. Of course I was interested. A magician sees through appearances to Truth.'

Yunyazi walked backwards, round and round, touching his fingertips to the needles in Quistus's body. Coloured flames sprang from the hilts, green, blue, yellow, showering vermilion sparks. 'Be still!'

Quistus shut his eyes, wincing. He couldn't breathe. The flames rising from his nipples burnt his nose. He stuck his chest out but his flaming penis burnt his ribs.

'Indeed you are a Stoic, able to endure pain and suffering without discomfort or fear.' Yunyazi stretched out his hands and the flames subsided. 'Impressive.'

Quistus recovered his breath. His body trembled. The magician picked up the little dog, Fu, and stroked its perky ears.

'There, Fu. That was easy for us, wasn't it?' He nodded. 'Yes, An is a loyal servant and a faithful politician, but a foolish doctor. Fortunately Chong told us of your seizure, nausea, headache, delirium. Added to the darkness in your gums – fascinating. We knew at once, didn't we, Fu? Someone slowly but surely poisoned you with lead. Probably in your wine.'

Quistus felt his sweat dry. His mind was clearing. 'Luca?' he said. Then he said, 'Vitellius?' He thought some more. '*Nero.*'

'You're safe here,' the magician said. 'It's our murder you're

investigating, not your own.' He plucked out An's needles one
by one. 'I am *Zhenren*, a true man.' As he threw down the
needles he chanted, 'I am *Waidan* and *Neidan*. Heaven reveals
its secrets to me.' The little dog barked.

Yunyazi flicked away the ribbons holding Quistus's wrists.
'You'll find my advice essential to your enquiry, I'm sure. I
will solve everything. When we find our traitor, we've found
our murderer.'

Quistus stood. 'Not necessarily.'

'What? How so?'

Quistus turned to the sleeping figure of Zhao and spoke in
the sharp tone Yunyazi had used earlier. 'Awake!'

And Zhao awoke, smiling to see that he was better.

'I must warn him,' Omba whispered. Best to speak soft in the
Subura after dark. 'Please, Vulpus, let me go to him. My master
needs me. He doesn't know what danger he's in. His own *cliens*
betrayed him, tried to kill him. I must tell him of the Gold
Heads. *Please.*'

Vulpus tugged her chain, looking around fearfully. 'These
streets are too dangerous for a woman. There's robbers about.
See me to my room first. Then we'll talk.'

Omba looked over her shoulder, sure they were followed.
She saw nothing. They were there. Gold Heads, or Vitellius's
sons? Could be either. It seemed half the world wanted Zhang
dead and the other half wanted him alive. But which half was
which? Was Vitellius's fear of Nero greater than his hatred of
Golden Turtle?

She thought, Maybe *everyone* wants Zhang dead.

They reached the *insula* safely but the dark stairwell frightened Vulpus. He wouldn't go up alone. Omba, sighing angrily,
strode with him to the sixth floor, taking the steps two at a time
to Vulpus's one, watching impatiently as he unlocked his door.
He pushed her inside to check for intruders then unexpectedly
jumped behind her, looping her chain around a roof-beam. A
padlock clicked closed through the links. 'Vulpus!' She twisted,
grabbing him, catching his cloak in her fist, but he leapt back.
There was a tearing noise. The chain sprang taut at her throat.

'There. You're safe.' He was careful to stay out of reach.
'Breathe, Omba. That's better, don't hurt yourself, don't struggle,
don't look at me like that. What else can I do? It's been the

worst day of my life. I'm a broken man, you heard Vitellius. You're all I have left, where's your heart? Still you call *him* your master. No, if I let you go to Quistus, you won't come back. What about poor Vulpus? I've got to think. I must think . . .'

Zhao insisted on making tea for Quistus and Yunyazi in spite of – or because of – the late hour. Both magician and patient, drained by the cure, would appreciate care and refreshment. Prim and immaculate in her ankle-length *cheongsam*, she half-filled a small shiny pot with green leaves, topped it up with almost-boiling water until it overflowed, let the mixture steep for six long breaths, and poured the greenish brew of *Erh ya* into tiny cups. Yunyazi sniffed, savoured, swirled, sipped quickly, and replaced his empty cup with a sigh of satisfaction.

Quistus watched. Romans drank only medicinal herbal teas, but years of Omba's Oromo coffee infusions had taken away his fear of novelty. Zhao, bowing her head, placed a teacup in front of him.

His big fingers fumbled clumsily with the fine porcelain. She hid her smile. 'No. Like this. Gently, Quistus. Not war.' He copied her delicate motions as best he could. 'Two swallows.' Her lower lip caught between her teeth in fascination as he drank like a horse. The big Adam's apple in his throat bobbed when he swallowed. His lack of refinement repelled her and made her curious. A Chinese man could not be changed, for he was already perfect; a barbarian could be improved. Who'd want to, though – he almost broke the cup putting it down.

'More tea!' Yunyazi ordered, tea-minded. One cup was never enough. Her hands performed the ritual without thought while the men talked. She listened to them with only the surface of her mind while her heart was busy.

Quistus said, 'Yunyazi, you questioned Captain Lo?'

'Indeed, with a Truth Spell.'

'Henbane, perhaps?'

Yunyazi raised one hairy grey eyebrow. 'Even a barbarian is not totally ignorant. Yes, tincture of henbane. Scopolamine. He confessed anything true.'

Had Quistus even noticed the tea or her skills? Zhao asked, 'Does this tea please you?'

'Good,' he muttered. That was all. A barbarian, she decided, didn't use two words where one would do. She refilled his cup, staring. She'd teach him to drink Chinese, eat Chinese, dress Chinese, be Chinese. She could change him, educate him. Heaven knows he needed it.

Quistus said, 'Lo was innocent.'

'Yes. He'd been fed the opium in a fortune cracker. In his case the fortune foretold for him was, I suppose, disgrace and death.'

'Who gave it to him?' Quistus asked.

'His memory was broken.' Yunyazi drank a cup, two quick swallows. 'I deduced the cracker from the crumbs on his chest. A gift from someone he trusted, probably a woman.'

'Are you sure?'

'A woman would have easy access to the kitchen. Lo liked women.'

Already she'd improved Quistus, Zhao decided. She'd burnt his filthy tunic and found proper clothes for him, the silk under-smock and long satin gown that he now wore, blue-green to match his eyes. He'd grumbled, flapping his arms in the wide, shiny sleeves. He had no idea of style. She'd hidden a giggle behind her fingertips, imagining. If only he'd known she'd dressed him in her own clothes, let out to fit his broad shoulders! None of the men had been tall enough – except for Manas, who mostly wore iron plates, leather straps, buckles – for Quistus not to look silly. At least he appeared a little bit civilized now. She'd teach him manners, how to move, perhaps even speak a few words of the civilized tongue – she blinked. She'd been daydreaming. 'What?' she said, flustered. 'What did you say?'

Quistus repeated, 'I'll start with Zhang. Zhang's the key to everything that happens.'

'No. You can't. He's only a boy. It's night.'

'I'll need to talk to everyone. Who knows when the killer will strike again? I haven't much time.'

'He's asleep.' She burst out, 'For you even to say his name aloud is profanity! Quistus, why can't you behave *properly*?'

'I answer to Zhang and no one else,' Quistus said sharply. 'I speak with his voice. You heard him. You have to do as I say as though it came from him. Call An and Chong if you want.'

Yunyazi sipped a final cup. 'Perhaps that would be wise.' He snapped his fingers, whispering to a servant, who scurried away. He closed his eyes and laid his hands lightly on his knees, waiting, then realized Quistus was no longer sitting among the teacups. Yunyazi cursed all *yi* and hurried out, closely followed by Zhao.

Quistus stood in the roofless, moonlit atrium. He tried several doors that opened and one, slightly smaller, that did not. He turned. 'You walked through the atrium last night, Zhao?'

She sighed. 'Yes, at about this time. The moon was higher, of course.'

'And you, Yunyazi? Where were you?'

The magician drew himself up. 'I do not answer such questions. I am everywhere.'

'Then you know everything that happened. Perhaps you're the guilty one.'

'I was in my rooms,' Yunyazi said, 'flying between life and death.'

'You mean asleep?'

'You ask questions very rudely. I shall not answer.'

'Asleep?'

'I never sleep.'

'Then you were awake. You heard Zhao scream?'

'No.'

'His rooms are near the back of the house,' Zhao explained.

'I only heard the one noise,' Yunyazi said, 'the—' He stopped, finding no word in Greek. 'The *baozhasheng.*'

'The what?'

Zhao struggled to translate the word into Latin. '*Fragor.* Explosion.'

'What's that? What is *explosion*? Explosion of what?'

Yunyazi pointed at a pillar. 'Have you not seen the soot? The sound was definitely a *baozhasheng* in the sky. It grew from here.'

Quistus stared at the white walls and pillars. *Atrii* were used for family cooking in the open air so they usually had soot-blackened walls; the word meant black. But this house fed so many mouths that the kitchen had been put downstairs and the atrium was pristine white, except for the ascending trail of black soot up one pillar.

He brushed his finger across the mark, licked his fingertip. Not charcoal from a cooking fire; a bitter taste, metallic. 'A celestial painting,' Yunyazi said. 'The thunderclap attracts the spirits to gather round such dazzling, but brief, beauty rising as an offering from Earth to Heaven.'

Zhao touched her forehead. 'I'm such a fool. The flower so many saw and heard . . .'

Quistus took a deep breath. 'You're saying someone planted a flower here that grew like lightning into the sky? Can you do that?'

Yunyazi looked down his long, dirty nose. 'Heaven seeded the earth with secrets to be discovered, Quistus. Magicians such as I and Fu devote our lives to such mysteries.' He picked up his little dog, stroking it fondly. 'Isn't that right, Fu? We uncover the secrets of Heaven. Light and dark. Man and woman. With the elixirs of the *Cantong qi* and the *Jinbi jin* and the Alchemical Scriptures we reveal the unity of yin and yang. You yourself saw us conjure the fires of many colours upon your body to cure your spirit of its dark, leaden yin, did you not?'

'I saw.'

'Then you must believe. The Celestial Flower spell is simply contained in a different way.'

'Did you plant the Celestial Flower?'

'No.'

'A Roman could not have done it?'

Yunyazi chuckled, scratching the dog's ears. 'Such a glory has never been seen in the sky of Rome.'

Quistus said, 'But a Chinese could have made it grow and blossom with such a loud noise?'

'I could have, if I wanted.'

'But no one else?'

A shadow crossed Yunyazi's face. 'A wicked spirit could have watched me practise my spells, and learned.'

'Who?'

'I don't know. Wicked.'

Zhao interrupted impatiently, 'How do these words save the Prince's life? How do they explain the death of Cerberus? We're wasting time.'

'Disrespectful woman, be silent!' Yunyazi was offended. 'Get about your housework. A woman learns nothing spying on the talk of men; it's beyond your comprehension. Go!'

'Stay,' Quistus said.

Zhao lifted her not-so-meek head. 'The entertainments in the sky have no purpose, Quistus. They're just light and noise, *yanhuo*, art of fire. *Yanhuo* are –' she shrugged – 'they're beautiful, that's all.'

'So having murdered Cerberus, instead of killing Zhang the murderer decided to stop and entertain Rome with some *yanhuo*,' Quistus said mockingly.

Zhao's cheeks reddened. 'We know *what* happened; we've only to understand *why*. Perhaps it was coincidence, two entirely separate events occurring together by chance.'

'I don't believe it.' Quistus turned back to Yunyazi. 'Could you show me *yanhuo*?'

The magician bowed. 'Conjuring the spell takes a short while.'

Quistus said, 'I'll be with Zhang. Follow me, Zhao.'

'The Forbidden Quarters are at the very back of the house.' Zhao hurried to catch up. 'Manas is guarding his door. It's impossible to approach in secret. I assure you the Prince is in no danger.'

'Suppose Manas is the killer, biding his time? Have you thought of that?'

She looked genuinely startled. 'A brave man, a soldier who killed many of the Prince's enemies face-to-face in battle – would he knife an old, unarmed doorman in a frenzied ritual of cuts from throat to genitals?'

'Would he?'

'No. No man is more honourable than Manas, more total in loyalty to the Emperor and thus to the Prince. Anyway, he uses a curved *sica*, not a short straight blade.'

'A short straight blade such as you now wear on your wrist.'

'A kitchen knife, to protect you while you were helpless. To any traitor among us, Quistus the interrogator, you need to be next to die. You know that.'

'Don't be angry, Zhao. I wasn't accusing you. As I'm still alive, I trust you completely. I'd wager that's not the only knife missing from the kitchen, though. One killed Cerberus.'

'Then why slur Manas?'

'It took strength to dislocate the body's joints and force it into the cistern.'

'As if the other guards were not capable.'

'I'll talk to them too.' Quistus crossed the audience room to the peristyle, the private garden beneath the moon. Doors led off the colonnades to each side. 'Your room's behind one of these doors?'

A room as small as a cell. A thin, hard bed, neatly made. A

few possessions, nothing that couldn't be packed in a minute. She watched his eyes. 'We've been running for nearly two years, Quistus.'

'Since the Prince escaped his captors at the battle of Falling Waters Bridge?'

She was startled. 'Who told you?'

'Chong said too much. An shut him up. Who's the Prince running from, Zhao? What danger could be so *big* that even his money and royalty and father the mighty *Qin* Emperor can't save him? Why have you been coming west all this time?'

She bowed her head meekly. 'It's not for a woman to tell secrets.'

'Isn't it? Meek doesn't suit you, Zhao. I think you're clever and arrogant under your pretty skin. I think you're pretending to be less of a person than you really are because An demands it. All of them do, except maybe Chong. Even Yunyazi puts you down.'

She pressed her lips together and hid her face, as usual, but he overheard her angry murmur. 'The important one trusts me.'

'The Prince? Lucky for you.' Quistus lifted a couple of small but weighty leather pouches from the bed, sand-filled, held by a silken cord. 'What's this?'

All he saw was her piled-up hair. Head lowered, she wasn't talking. He put his fingers under her chin and made her look at him. 'Your eyes arc wet,' he said, surprised. She twisted away.

'It's nothing. I'm short-sighted, Quistus, as you'd know if you weren't so annoying. I can hardly see to read. What worse fate could there be for a writer who lives by books?'

He hefted the pouches. 'So?'

'A well-known cure. I tie them over my eyelids at night. The weight straightens my eyesight. The next day, perhaps two days, I can at least see to read.'

'Why are you upset? I've said little to upset you.'

'You've never been married, have you, Quistus? I can tell. No wife, no children.' She stared intensely. 'You've never been stranded fifteen thousand *li* from the ones you love, love desperately. I envy you.'

Yet she'd said she was a widow. He put down the pouches carefully. 'What exactly woke you last night, Zhao?'

'You're changing the subject. Why do you accuse me of being upset?'

'Answer me.'

'A sound like *clop-clop-clop*. Satisfied?'

'Knocking? Footsteps?'

She folded her arms. 'I was asleep.'

He turned to leave the room, irritated by her attitude. Manas, arriving, filled the doorway. Quistus stopped, eyeing the *sica* in the giant's hand. Manas rumbled in a deep, accented voice, 'The Prince will see you now, Roman.'

'So you have a tongue,' Quistus said.

The giant, expressionless, stepped aside. Prince Zhang came forward with a shy smile. 'Have you found the murderer yet, Quistus? Are you better? Who have you talked to? I want to know everything!'

Quistus glanced at Zhao. He was learning to read her subtle changes of face; this look, almost invisible, was a frown. 'I'd say we're making progress,' he smiled. Her left eyebrow straightened a fraction. A definite frown. She thought he'd made no progress whatsoever. He'd succeeded in irritating her almost as much as she irritated him.

'I couldn't sleep,' the boy said eagerly. 'I thought you'd find this helpful, Quistus. I'm so glad you're feeling strong. There's no time to waste.' His teeth shone like pearls as he held out a silk scroll wrapped in vermilion ribbon.

Vulpus snored on a pile of old spice sacks in the corner. Omba sat on the hard, splintery floorboards, furious, sleepless. The chain securing her iron collar to the roof-beam was too short to allow her to lie down. Good, no danger of comfort, of drooping eyelids. A crack of moonlight swung, gleaming on the padlock. Slowly she stretched her legs, rolling into a crouch. Vulpus cried out, 'Silvanus!'

She froze, unmoving. He turned over, muttering in his sleep in much the same vein as when he'd been awake. *Silvanus would lend him gold for spice. Good old Silvanus . . .*

She waited until he snored again, then stood carefully. The u-shaped hasp he'd pushed through the chain links into the padlock was held by two springs of bent metal inside. Her gold belt of tricks had been taken by Vulpus, probably sold; she bit a fingernail and worked it into the keyhole. It broke.

Vulpus flopped over. The blanket hung down, showing his foot still in its sandal. *Good old Silvanus, argued in the past, but always best friends, eh?*

Omba stared at the blanket. The night was hot. The chain clinked taut as she reached out, cutting off her breath. She strained downward, fingertips outstretched, barely touching the blanket's corner. On the second try she pinched the seam between her middle and forefinger, inching it gently towards her, and breathed again.

The blanket slipped from Vulpus's shoulder, revealing his clothes to the waist. His fear of fire was so great that he lay fully clothed on his cloak, ready to run instantly if the alarm was raised. His eyelids twitched. The smell of mouldy spice mingled with his odour of sweat.

She pushed forward, fingers straining. The chain tightened until she couldn't breathe.

The keys glinted on his belt, completely out of her reach.

'I'm glad you're getting on so well with our Lady Zhao,' the Prince said cheerily as they walked past the fountain splashing in the moonlit peristyle. 'Not everybody does, you know.'

'Really? They don't? Amazing!'

Zhao, her expression reposed, glided behind the Prince and Quistus as smoothly as if she moved on wheels instead of feet. An and Chong, who'd elbowed in front of her still shaking the sleep from their faces, ignored her. Pecking order. The boy led but kept Quistus beside him, outside the *Qin* pecking order. Quistus held the vermilion scroll the Prince had given him.

'They don't like her,' the boy nodded. 'They say she's fierce, self-willed, and worse, she can be . . . unladylike. Have you experienced her temper? No wonder they're afraid of her, secretly.' They climbed the steps to his quarters, a small suite of rooms behind one heavy, easily-guarded door. At once their footsteps squeaked loudly. 'Nightingale floors!' the boy laughed at Quistus's confusion. 'No one may approach me without being announced by nightingales. Squeaky nails. Her idea.'

Behind them Manas blocked the doorway with his broad shoulders, facing back along the peristyle with his arms crossed. Quistus had noticed at least two more guards behind pillars.

He looked around the room. Simple furniture, lightly built, easily packed away. Lacquered tables shone like mirrors with exquisite workmanship. He'd never seen anything like them. A landscape of embroidered silk hung down one wall.

'Actually, the singing floors were my idea,' An said.

'Mine,' said Chong.

'My father says Zhao is the most intelligent and virtuous woman in China. He has a most high opinion of her.' The boy sat cross-legged on a mat, watching Quistus expectantly.

Quistus remembered the scroll. He pulled off the vermilion ribbon with clumsy fingers. The silk banner unrolled from its wooden header, almost weightless, and he frowned at the columns of black brush marks that appeared. The silk continued to unroll until it almost touched the floor.

'My Family Book,' Zhang said. 'Every *Qin* household keeps a Family Book. Each person under my *Mianzi* – you might say patronage – is grouped by gender, rank and appointed task, with a short record of their deeds, personal relationships, moral character and ancestors. Yunyazi says this book is merely a tiny part of the great Book of Mankind written in Heaven.'

'These are all names?'

'All people, yes.' The boy nodded. 'Not all survive. The names here, marked with a dot beneath, gave their lives for me on our journey.'

'This many?'

So many names marked with the dot for death. His argument with Zhao, his goading of her, was trivial and unnecessary and Quistus was ashamed of himself. The boy selected from the much shorter list of the living. 'Yuan An, Wang Chong, Ban Zhao, Yunyazi . . .'

'I know them all by heart,' Zhao murmured. 'Little Pelican, Wild Swan, Shang, Shu . . .'

'We're the survivors, Quistus,' the boy said. 'One of us is the traitor. The traitor must not reach Heaven. His name must be erased from our Book. Find him.'

Quistus asked thoughtfully, 'Why are these rooms called Forbidden?'

'My people are forbidden to enter here without permission, on pain of death. Even to allow such a thought into their minds is forbidden.'

'It's law,' An said. 'The Prince who will be Son of Heaven is already sacred, sacrosanct.'

'Good,' Quistus said. 'They'll be nervous. I'll talk to them here.'

Omba's fingertips strained to reach the key. Her chest heaved for air. She couldn't hold her breath one moment more. She backed a step, letting the chain go limp, breathing through her wide-open mouth to silence her gasps.

She gulped, holding her breath as Vulpus muttered, 'No, no, she's mine . . .'

He sighed, then snored.

She breathed again, looking up at the roof-beam. The chain was strong but the beam was thin and cheap, bent by the weight of the roof tiles directly above, themselves rejects, cracked and brittle. She stood among spears of moonlight, slanting now: time passed.

She bent her shoulder under the beam, braced her hands on her thighs, and pushed. The wood bent upwards with a loud crack but wouldn't break. A roof tile slithered, rattling as it gained speed, and after a few moments of silence she heard it shatter on the cobbles sixty feet below.

Vulpus stirred. He opened one eye, seeing Omba sitting just as he'd left her.

Quistus looked up sternly from the table at which he sat. 'Your name is Yuan An?'

'You know it is.'

'What does your Prince expect of you?'

'I am the Prince's chief *Ai* guardian and major-domo, appointed by the Emperor himself.' A smile creased An's fat lips at seeing the barbarian so obviously impressed.

'You must be a very important man,' Quistus said.

'Indeed.' An smiled. 'My revered father and grandfather both served the Son of Heaven of their day and were pious and incorrupt. I myself have—'

'Where were you when Zhao screamed?'

'In bed, asleep.'

'Alone?'

An swallowed. 'Yes. I was first to hear her scream. At once—'

'At once you ran to the kitchen.' Quistus ticked off the name in the Family Book. 'You may go.'

Omba held out her arms for balance. She stood on her left foot and slowly stretched her right leg out straight. Carefully she drew in her arms, muscles twitching as she wobbled, clasping her hands under her right knee to take the strain. She pointed her foot. Her heel brushed Vulpus's thigh and she grunted, quivering, lifting higher, stretching her toes towards the keys.

Nowhere near close enough.

She arched her back like a bow, bending her left leg, thrusting her right leg forward. The chain tightened, almost hanging her. Her big toe touched the key.

She felt her leg cramp.

'I am Wang Chong.'

'Yunyazi tells me I have to thank your sharp eyes for saving my life.'

Chong bowed, seated though he was. 'The honour is mine. I know you for a Stoic and a fellow logician.'

'So, fellow logician, who killed Cerberus?'

Chong looked flustered. The Prince watched eagerly from one side, obviously bursting with questions, but each time the boy opened his mouth to interrupt Zhao very softly cleared her throat.

Chong admitted, 'Logic has failed me.'

'I'm sure it doesn't fail you often.'

'Never.'

'Perhaps the murderer was a ghost.'

'Yes, a ghost!' the Prince burst out. Zhao cleared her throat. He made a face and watched silently.

'That's impossible. Ghosts do not exist,' Chong said confidently. 'I know everyone believes the dead have souls. I, however, do not. I can prove it.'

'Blasphemy!' The boy sounded thrilled, then covered his mouth with both hands before Zhao could clear her throat.

Chong said, 'If spirits exist they are naked, unless you believe clothes have souls as well as men. But,' he concluded triumphantly, 'has anyone ever seen the spirits of their revered ancestors in the nude?'

'Nevertheless,' Quistus said, 'there was a ghost in the kitchen last night.'

'No. That cannot be.'

'Zhao saw it. The ghost had piled pots from the cistern lid on to the table. It passed through her lamp-flame as it departed. The flame bent in consequence.'

'The murderer had moved the pots, obviously. As for the flame, it was bent by a draught of air.'

'Where could the draught have come from? The front door was closed.'

'Perhaps it was opened. The key was on the hook.'

'If the door was opened, who came in?'

'Perhaps someone went out.'

'How did that person lock the door from the outside and return the key to the hook?'

An idea struck Chong. 'Speaking of the front door is misleading us. Behind the chimney in the kitchen are toilets, storerooms, steps to the atrium—'

'Exactly. The backstairs for the kitchen slaves to bring up food.' Quistus nodded. 'So we know the murderer was still in the kitchen when Zhao arrived. We know he had the key to the backstairs. We know he used it to escape into the atrium. From there, who knows where? Thank you, Chong. That's all.'

Zhao looked shaken.

'You were in there with him, Zhao!' the Prince said, elated.

'We know one thing more,' Chong said, rising. 'We know he killed Cerberus, and yet he did not kill Zhao.'

The iron collar pulled tight under Omba's chin. Her skull was being ripped from her spine. Her left leg was a contorted slab of cramped muscle, veins and tendons standing out like ropes. She narrowed her eyes, ignoring her body's distress.

At last her toe curled under the key on Vulpus's belt. She shoved her whole foot under the belt. Vulpus moved aimlessly, waking.

She stiffened her foot. Now or never. 'What?' he muttered.

She jerked back, hard. Vulpus flew out of bed, dragged by his belt. She wrapped her thighs around him.

'Move and I'll kill you,' she whispered.

She grabbed the key from his belt and unlocked the iron collar. After a moment's thought she clicked it shut on Vulpus's neck and threw the key out of the window. From the door she looked down at him kneeling helpless on the end of the padlocked chain. 'One shout, Vulpus, and I'll come back.'

'I would have let you go in the morning,' he called. 'I was afraid,' he added.

She frowned. 'Afraid? Of what, Vulpus?'

'That I'd never see you again.'

She rubbed her neck and ran silently downstairs.

*   *   *

'What's your name?'

'Manas.' The bodyguard towered over Quistus.

'You're a man of few words, Manas.'

Manas crossed his arms.

'Everyone else has brown eyes. Yours are blue. Where are you from?'

'I am Kyrgyz.'

Quistus glanced at the Prince. 'One of the family of *Qin*,' the boy recited. Zhao nodded approval; he'd learnt his history and geography lessons well. '*Qin* is a great family of peoples, Quistus. The Kyrgyz are from the mountains.'

'You're very strong, aren't you, Manas?' Quistus waited for a reply, but the giant only shrugged his leather-strapped shoulders. 'I suppose you have the key to the kitchen backstairs?'

'No, Roman. My responsibility is the Prince.'

'Who does have it?'

'Captain Lo did.' Manas turned as a shadow fell across the doorway. He moved with amazing speed and lightness on bare feet, silently covering the space between the Prince and the door. The *sica* flashed in his hand, but only Yunyazi's little dog ran in, barking. Yunyazi, trailing a little smoke from his robes, arrived a few moments later.

'Thank you, Manas, that's all,' Quistus said.

Yunyazi carried an armful of leather pouches, beakers and, in the crook of his elbow, a thick, short tube. He bowed deeply to Prince Zhang and dropped them on the table in front of Quistus.

Quistus prodded the pile. 'This is *yanhuo*?'

'No, Quistus, these are raw spells.' The magician patted his robes until he found the source of the smoke, pulling out a glowing wick, which he handed to the Roman. 'Heaven hides its mysteries like riddles to be unearthed. That is why we dig mines at Yuyao, Mount Laojun, Xireg by the Salt Lake of Hoh . . .' Yunyazi paused for effect. 'I shall turn iron into gold.' He opened a pouch with a flourish. 'Powdered iron.' He took a pinch and mixed it on the table with soot from the lamp. Nothing happened. Quistus watched, disappointed.

'In Rome spells and curses must be spoken or written,' he said, 'or the gods don't hear.'

'Wait, wait. A catalyst is required.' Yunyazi pointed at the wick. 'Please.' He took it and touched the end to the small black mound, blowing, chanting under his breath. Fu barked. A glow started. Gold sparks appeared, then small golden flames.

'The table!' Zhao squeaked.

Yunyazi extinguished the sparkling flames with his hand. 'When I succeed in uncovering the spell that cools and preserves the gold flame, I shall make limitless gold for the glory of *Qin* and the Son of Heaven.' He bowed to Zhang, who looked pleased.

'That's all it does?' Quistus said.

'Where's red and green?' Zhao asked.

Yunyazi waved away the smoke. He took the bamboo tube and covered one end lightly with silk, upended it, and poured in a yellow powder. 'Celestite, the celestial sky-spell for red,' he explained. Next came an oily-smelling silver spell. 'This is for green.' Finally he took a spell which he called *Huoyao*, a black powder made of salt rock, charcoal and brimstone. 'Sulphur,' he told Quistus cheerfully, wadding the end with silk to hold everything inside.

'Where's the rose?' Quistus asked.

Yunyazi lit the end. There was a deafening bang and a burst of smoke. The embroidery on the end wall was burning, the table covered with green and rose-red flames. Quistus kicked the table over to put it out. Manas protected the Prince with his body, pushing him into a corner for safety. The two guards rushed in. Manas growled at them. They pulled down the embroidery and stamped on it.

Quistus picked up a piece of smouldering bamboo. 'This is what woke Rome,' he said. 'But why? Why go to all that trouble?' Before he could make a proper examination there was a wooden clopping sound. A grown-up woman ran into the doorway. She was as small as a child and Quistus remembered Little Pelican, the dancer who'd been kind to him. She gasped, dropping to her knees at the Prince's feet, her hair tumbling unpinned in grief. Even so she had the presence of mind to speak to the floor rather than look on Zhang without permission.

'Lady Zhao, you should come. Wild Swan is . . . I think her journey is done.'

At once Zhao hurried from the room.

Omba waited, watching from the darkness of the *Fortuna*'s courtyard. The winding street, shafted with moonlight and shadow, seemed silent and empty. No shouts from Vulpus yet. Had she terrified him enough? Maybe he wouldn't shout at all. No, too proud. Too in love with her, he'd say.

Someone would worry about him, surely. Someone would find him.

Still nothing moved, only cats and rats. Distant shouts, gangs fighting it out. The moon slipped behind the rooftops. A rat ran over her foot, which meant good luck. She'd waited long enough.

She moved quickly past Triton's fountain and turned uphill, then ran hard, drawing out a gap between her and anyone behind. Impossible for pursuers to hide going so fast, they'd be breathing hard and loud on the hill. After a few hundred paces she dodged into an alley and leant against a flaking wall, catching her breath.

She blinked, rubbing her eye. The swelling was going down. She took a peep round the corner.

Nothing, no one. No heavy breathing. She leant back. Didn't mean for sure they weren't there, though. Vitellius's boys knew these streets like their foreskins.

Rather than risk the main street she backed deeper into the alley, covering her nose: stinking rubbish. The mess slipped round her ankles. From rotten cabbages and pears and chicken bones, a man's head slid into the moonlight.

The apple-seller who'd followed the Gold Head into the alley still looked very angry indeed, but his windpipe was an 'O' of surprise. His throat had been sliced open with steely skill, cutting his Adam's apple in half. He'd died in perfect silence.

Zhao hurried from the Prince's rooms followed by An and Chong. Quistus stopped Yunyazi. 'You. I want to talk to you.'

'Not now. I must go to Wild Swan.'

'You've been giving her opium, haven't you?'

'I've been giving her merciful oblivion,' the magician said snootily. 'The infection is severe, there was never any hope. Wild Swan was hysterical. Only Little Pelican was brave enough to nurse her. Come, Fu!' He brushed past.

'Wait.' Yunyazi ignored him. Quistus turned to the Prince.

Zhang murmured, 'Yunyazi.'

Yunyazi stopped instantly. The dog sat. Quistus said, 'From the same stock of opium that drugged Captain Lo? Your personal stock?' The magician was silent. 'Tell him to answer, Zhang.'

Yunyazi admitted, 'I suppose some could have gone missing.'
'Who else has opium?'
'I understand it's widely available on the streets of Rome.'
'Indeed it is, but you're all afraid to go out, aren't you? So the drug came from you. How much is missing?'
Yunyazi licked his lips. 'A little. Enough.'
'So both the *yanhuo* and the opium came from your rooms. What a coincidence. Did you drug Lo?'
'A soldier's far too superstitious to accept anything from a magician.'
'Did you light the *yanhuo*?'
'No! Remember, Quistus, I healed you. If I were guilty, you'd be dead by now.'
'Well, Quistus? Is he guilty?' Zhang asked excitedly.
Quistus shook his head. 'He's careless. I want to know who has the key to his rooms.'
'My rooms,' Yunyazi said in a new, menacing tone, 'do not have locks. No one enters the room of a magician such as I without permission. Not unless they wish to be turned into a centipede and crushed underfoot.'
Quistus turned to Zhang. 'Can he do that?'
'Yes.'
Quistus said, 'Someone doesn't believe it.'
The magician appealed to Zhang. 'He knows I'm innocent. We're wasting time. Allow me to go to Wild Swan. There may still be something I can do. You know my powers.'
Little Pelican pressed her head to the marble floor. 'No, no, it's too late. Wild Swan, gone. She taught me all I know.'
'You have my permission, Yunyazi.' The Prince stood. 'We must go with Zhao, she'll be upset. The women were all close. They make better friends with each other than with men, I think.'

Omba pushed the apple-seller's body under the rubbish. She crouched, listening, wiping her hands on her thighs. The streets fell deeper into darkness as the moon dropped. She inched backward, finding a niche of total blackness, folded her legs under her, and waited. Not moving, hardly breathing, her eyes almost closed, only her heart beating . . . slowly.

The Prince, his floor-length tunic shining golden in the lamp-light, hurried from the Forbidden Quarters with Manas and the guards. Quistus watched Little Pelican raise her head from the floor. Her round, chalk-white face, thickly powdered, was streaked with flesh-pink lines of dried tears. He reached down without a word. Her hand was tiny and he lifted her easily to her feet – or rather, he reminded himself, the tiptoes that passed for feet, folded and twisted into points, yet called by Zhao 'a lover's joy'.

'I wanted to thank you, Little Pelican,' he said, 'for your kindness to me when I was sick. Thank you again.'

She backed. 'I must return to Wild Swan's room. Grief and sadness, mourning. There's much to do.'

'I'll walk with you.' They crossed the peristyle. She pinned her hair with shaking fingers, plainly nervous alone with a westerner. He couldn't see her face but spoke anyway. 'Obviously you and Wild Swan were very close.'

'Like a mother to me, she taught me all I know.'

'I know you gave her opium to ease her distress.'

'No, Yunyazi did. I'd call him when her suffering was too much to bear. When she woke she was delirious, screaming, out of her mind. Yunyazi understood. He's a good man.'

'You must be very upset.'

She stopped and turned up her face, smiling with tear-stained cheeks. It was an expression of pure pain. They walked on. He said nothing for a moment, distracted by the quick, clopping sound of her lotus clogs.

'That's what Zhao heard,' he said. 'Zhao heard you—'

'Yes?' Little Pelican was curious. 'Why, is it important? I kept vigil for Wild Swan day and night, it's no secret. I couldn't sleep.'

'So it was you in the *ban ye*. What woke you?'

'Look at my feet, Quistus. Are they not so very beautiful?' He lied. 'Yes.'

'Men desire me because of them. Do you desire me?'

'No. Not in that way. But yes, you're lovely.'

'You'd want me if I wanted you to.' Again she turned her face up like the actress she was, smiling through tear-stains, not afraid to show herself as she was. 'Do you think I chose these so-beautiful lotus feet? I was four years old when these mutilations were forced on me. Yes, mutilations. Imagine the pain. Imagine sleeping. Could *you* sleep so mutilated, so deformed, Quistus? That's why I walk in the night. Because I live in agony.'

She shook her head. 'Beg pardon. I can only mourn Wild Swan. I'm so tired.'

'Was anyone else awake? Did you see anyone?'

'I didn't even see Zhao. No doubt I'd returned to Wild Swan's bedside.'

Bowing their heads, they arrived at the little room where Wild Swan lay, where everyone gathered outside the door.

Omba smiled in the dark. When Quistus had stumbled on her staked naked over the anthill near the winter palace at Kefa, a thorn through her tongue to stop her swallowing the honey bait (its sweetness summoning a multitude of painful poisonous insects, scavengers and carrion-eaters to breakfast on her mucous membranes for the duration of her excruciatingly slow and agonizing death), he'd at once understood her lesson in palace politics. Power, whether exercised through men or women, was always the same. Only the details changed.

He'd asked, 'Do you want to live?'

Oromo society was female dominated, a melting pot of sisterly love and extravagant displays of affection, spite, intrigue, betrayal, reconciliation, treason, torture, incest and murder by every imaginable trick, scheme, ruse and deceit, all of it kept strictly in the family, or rather between the half-dozen or so families who mattered. The winner was the princess who survived long enough to prove her loins worthy of birthing a queen, a woman strong enough to rule women. No queen had lived past adolescence for nearly thirty winters; competition was fierce.

The hunt was one, just one, of the tests of femininity.

Not a sound now. The alley was black as the Styx.

By the plain of Kefa there were caves as black as this where you waited with only a sharpened stick – tonight Omba didn't have even that – and you waited, and waited, for the creature whose cave it was to find you. A poisonous snake seeking warmth as the night cooled, or lion, leopard, or wild dogs. It might already be in there with you, a deadly spider weaving her web only inches from your face. To hunt was to be hunted. You never forgot that lesson.

She looked from the blackness to the jagged map of moonlit gables and roofs drawn against the night sky. The moon set in the west. Darkness would be total for a while. Then dawn would show her up, and warning Quistus would be impossible without revealing the Villa Paria to their enemies.

Vitellius didn't know about the Villa Paria. Neither, she was sure, did the group he called the Gold Heads – the cloaked figure who'd murdered the apple-seller wouldn't have followed if it had seen her leaving the Paria, seen Shu the Chinese doorman. 'They're like the wind,' Dorca had said. 'They follow everyone, they search all the time.'

No, if the Gold Heads knew about the Paria, Golden Turtle would be there by now.

She reached out as though touching a spider's web. She'd been followed to Vitellius's. She didn't know it for sure but she felt it. Back with Vulpus, then her escape from the *Fortuna* . . . she sensed observation like a web being woven around her, even though her hands touched nothing but the innocent air.

One by one the high moonlit roofs faded into blackness. No one, Gold Head or not, could see her now. She found her way along the alley by blind touch, hardly breathing, stopping for minutes at a time, listening. A glow began in the east.

No one followed her. She reached the main street and sprinted uphill towards the Villa Paria.

'There's nothing I can do for Wild Swan,' Yunyazi sighed. 'She slips away from us. Don't blame yourself, Little Pelican. It's hard for even an expert such as I to foretell death's exact moment.'

The bedroom was smaller than Quistus expected, the woman drawing her last breaths more exotic. Younger, too, more like an elder sister to Little Pelican than a mother. Her face, once strong-boned and arresting, was bare of make-up, freckled, spotted, blistered as though by hot irons pressed to her cheeks and neck. Her eyelids fluttered, her chest heaving weakly with frantic half-breaths that rattled her throat. No one but Yunyazi actually went into the room, and even he stayed by the door. The smell caught at Quistus's throat. He stared at Little Pelican, amazed. For all her slightness and delicacy, the little dancer had been brave enough to nurse the poor woman through this terrible, disfiguring illness. He whispered, 'Plague?'

Yunyazi shook his head. '*Tianhua*. Small spot disease.'

'Varius.' Quistus nodded. 'I've heard of it in Egypt and Greece. Hardly here.'

'We brought it with us from Greece. Several servants died. We thought it was over, but a week ago –' he shrugged – 'Wild Swan.'

Zhao knelt. 'Wild Swan saved the Prince's life at Falling Waters Bridge. She danced with swords as his enemies crossed, she blocked the narrowest point, she cut the ropes. She would have died in the torrent, but Lo climbed down the knots and carried her up.'

The dying woman heard her voice. 'Zhao?'

Zhao cried out tearfully in Chinese.

Wild Swan lifted her head. 'Zhao!' Her pocked, suppurating hand reached from under the blanket, grasping. '*Zhao!*'

Yunyazi pulled Zhao back just in time. Wild Swan stared, her hand moving weakly, then she didn't move again. The life left her eyes.

Little Pelican fell to her knees beside Zhao. The two women hugged each other, weeping. Prince Zhang shivered. 'I hate death,' he said.

Quistus asked, 'Why did she call Zhao's name?'

'Who knows?' Yunyazi drew a coverlet over the dead woman's face. 'Who knows what fantasies of Heaven the dying see? Perhaps she believed she saw one of her ancestors through Zhao's shape. If so, she died happily.' He stopped, listening. 'Did you hear?'

Quistus frowned. 'Someone's at the door.'

'Shu has strict orders not to let anyone in,' Zhang said.

Omba beat on the heavy, iron-studded door of the Villa Paria. 'Shu, it's me.' She turned, panting, leaning against the studs. She was all right, no one had followed. Faint streaks of grey separated the Viminalis hilltop from the darkness of the Subura valley. Nothing moved. 'Shu, it's me! Open up!'

'Stay here.' Quistus left the room. The knocking was louder from the atrium. He heard the viewing hatch bang open and paused on the broad marble stairs, realizing Zhang followed. They heard shouting. The two guards ran downstairs to the entrance hall, leaving Manas beside the Prince on the top step, Quistus one step below.

'It's Omba's voice,' he called down. 'Let her in.'

'No.' Manas drew his *sica*. 'Why now? Why night?' An and Chong came running. An said, 'Manas is right.'

'No one comes in,' Chong said. He drew a sword from his robes but held it wrong, like an intellectual.

'*Meiyou! Meiyou! Jinqu!*' old Shu shouted through the peep-hole. The stool where Cerberus once sat fell over and he stood on the step, spear clutched nervously, helmet sideways. '*Jinqu, Omba. Liqai!*'

'It's her,' Quistus said, relieved. 'Let her in.'

'It's too dangerous,' An said.

Quistus turned on him. 'Why, An? Why is it too dangerous?'

'There are things you need not know, barbarian. Only matters within these walls concern you.'

Zhang looked from An to Quistus. He said quietly, 'Let her in.'

An's fat face set. 'Highness listens to the advice of a *yi*?'

'Shu,' Quistus called, 'let Omba through.' The old servant mumbled to himself, banged the hatch closed, straightened his helmet, pushed the long bronze key into the lock, and turned it twice. He opened the door enough for Omba to slip through. 'Quistus,' she called, 'I've found out something you should—' The door slammed wide, knocking Shu off his feet, his spear skidding over the mosaic. A blade flashed from the darkness. Omba shouted in pain. A dark figure swept past her, hooded, sea-green cloak rising like a wing as it ran into the entrance hall.

For a moment the figure paused, hood turning as it searched, then the hood fell back to reveal a shiny gold face. The gold skull was shaved except for a braided topknot. The eyes slitted at once, finding Prince Zhang.

'Guards!' Quistus said. He reached for his sword, but of course it wasn't there, only the silky-smooth hip of the gown Zhao had given him.

Omba rolled on her blood-red shoulder. 'Gold Head,' she called.

The Gold Head sprang for the stairs with astonishing speed. A guard swung his sword and screamed, dropping the sword with his severed hands on the handle. The Gold Head leapt on the marble balustrade, running uphill on splayed feet. 'Omba,' Quistus called, pointing at the spear, telling Zhang, 'She never misses.' The second guard swung, falling back with a knife in his fore-head. Omba threw the spear. It passed through the Gold Head's cloak like air, breaking on a pillar. Manas pushed the Prince behind him, jumped, skidded in the brains of the dying guard, yet recovered as nimbly as a cat. Too late; the Gold Head sprang along the step, whipping a long blade from its cloak, whirling the shining arc overhead to strike, eyes fixed on the Prince. Quistus turned to Chong. The Gold Head stopped in mid-stride. Surprise came into its eyes. It looked down, then as Quistus held tight on to the hilt, slipped slowly off the Chinese blade through its heart, tumbled downstairs, and lay face-down and still.

Shu gave it a kick to make sure it was dead. His wizened face cracked into a toothless, crazy smile, as though he'd done all the dangerous work.

Quistus returned the dripping sword to Chong. 'Thank you.'

'Thank you,' Chong said politely.

'You nearly killed us all, Quistus!' An shouted. 'You must take the blame!'

Zhang stared at the body, trembling. Manas hurried him to Zhao but the boy said, 'Let me see.'

Zhao forgot etiquette, wrapping him in her arms. 'Don't look, don't look.' She called angrily over his head, 'He's only a boy, Quistus. He should be in bed asleep, not witnessing an atrocity. You almost got him killed.'

'Let him see,' Quistus said. Zhang came forward. They walked downstairs together and Quistus prodded the body with his foot. 'I suppose this is the same one trying to get into the house last night?'

'No, Master. It wasn't.' Omba nursed the deep gash in her shoulder. 'The Gold Heads didn't know about the Villa Paria.' She swore under her breath. 'Until I led this one here.'

'He doesn't matter,' Zhang said. 'He's dead.'

Quistus said thoughtfully, 'More than one, perhaps?'

'No, Master, I swear I'd have known. Our secret's safe, for now at least.'

'But there *are* more?'

'At least twenty. Fanatics led by Golden Turtle.'

Quistus turned to Zhang. 'Who came through the door last night, if not one of them?'

'Highness,' An said smoothly, 'the barbarian has already failed you. All he does is ask questions. Dismiss him.'

'You saw him save my life,' Zhang said. 'Bow down to him.'

An gritted his teeth and bowed.

Chong whispered, 'Did you hear what the slave said? She

knows about Golden Turtle.' He, too, bowed, hissing to An, 'You were right. We can't stay in Rome. There are places even farther away to hide . . .'

'The Gold Head's body must be burned,' Yunyazi interrupted. 'Golden Turtle, a *Neidan*, may bring it back to life. That's what he promises, but I think we have nothing to fear from ashes.'

Quistus said, 'Get your shoulder looked at, Omba, then we'll talk. You know more about what's going on than I do.' He turned to Zhang. 'You've got some explaining to do, boy.'

An was furious. 'Highness, your divine self must not allow the barbarian to speak to your Highness so rudely.'

There was a silence like a held breath.

'*Must?*' Zhang turned slowly. 'You said *must* to me, An?'

An prostrated himself.

'Quistus,' Zhang called firmly, though in a high, nervous voice. 'I want you to see. I shouldn't have listened to my foolish advisers.' He clicked his fingers for the dead body to be rolled over. The gold face turned up, gleaming, staring. 'You see, Quistus, gold is for the Son of Heaven. It's the divine metal given to the first Emperor by God, Huang-di. It is the mandate of Heaven. For anyone below the rank of marquis to own gold is treason. This gold face is itself treason, open rebellion, a declaration of war. Worse, it's blasphemy, an attack on everything sacred we believe in.' Zhang dropped on one knee, pointing. 'See, tattoos. Here, the left cheek, means Xu. The right cheek is Ying.'

'At last we know for certain,' Chong breathed. 'Prince Ying of the Xu Consort Clan. It's him. Curse him, curse his mother. Finally we know our real enemy, the cause of all troubles.'

'I never liked my uncle,' Zhang said. 'Funny. I was right.'

An whispered, 'Ying may be Emperor by now. Everything is chaos.'

'No,' Zhao said. 'Not while my brother commands the army.'

'An army fifteen thousand *li* to the east.'

Omba took her hand from her shoulder. 'There's trouble closer to home than that, Master. Do you trust your old friend Vitellius?'

Quistus shook his head. 'On Nero's instructions, Vitellius ordered Luca to poison me. He had no choice, but—'

'I had an interesting talk with Vitellius.' Omba took the Gold Head's sword and, with the point, scratched the hard, dead face. 'Gold leaf, just as he said. He reckoned – rather, Dorca and Roco did – that the creature isn't even a man.' She sliced the black silk open across the chest. 'No nipples. No breasts. Right again.' She lifted the skirts with the point. 'It was female. See what's missing?'

Manas looked disgusted, Chong interested, and Zhao covered the boy's eyes. 'Quistus, that's enough. The Prince has had no rest.'

'I've got more questions than answers, Zhao.'

'One day he'll be Son of Heaven and he'll rule the whole world. But tonight, he's just a child. He needs his sleep,' she said fiercely.

Quistus sighed, agreeing. 'We're all very tired, Zhang. A lot's happened. Maybe Zhao's right, we should get some sleep.' He added, 'I'm going to.'

Zhang yawned. Quistus watched Zhao take him upstairs, then called, 'When you wake, Zhang, you'll tell me everything, won't you?'

Manas ordered the guards to be doubled. Omba gazed thoughtfully along the sword. 'I don't mind,' she growled. 'I'm not afraid of warrior virgins.'

He was always gone in the morning.

The lad who limped beside the road from Gaul was obviously penniless, exhausted, near starving. Travellers saw what he'd been through by his stick-thin legs caked with filth and dust, tattered holes for boots, rags for clothes (except for the once-classy broad-brimmed hat, now battered shapeless, given him by a lady), a smelly strip of leather bandaging his left hand. His skin was burnt nut-brown by the sun, his hair scorched blond; his eyes were large and sad, liquidly dark, irresistibly innocent. He was obviously too poor to steal from, too thin to be worth stealing; no work in those scrawny arms. Women (he was too shy to let them bind his wounded hand) wanted to wash him clean and feed him up, brush those unruly blond streaks, make that needful face laugh. Men, moved either to take pity or advantage, failed to notice the boy's determined chin or the fact that he rarely blinked, except when he was lying, which he did only for his own good. More than one innkeeper, farmer, farmer's wife, or her daughter – even *all* her daughters – attempted to seduce him in return for giving him a night's shelter, and if any succeeded he didn't care, for he was a skilled thief. They were all water off a duck's back to him, all fish in the stream, for he was always gone tomorrow.

'I got something to tell you, Senator,' he rehearsed a thousand times a day as he walked in the burning heat of the sun. 'It's the truth. I *did.*'

It was a hard road but not as hard as the place he came from, the town between two rivers called Ravens' Hill by locals, that Romans called Lugdunum.

'I swear it's the truth,' he'd say, imagining his reward. The reward kept you going and made everything you did all right, even proper. You got a chance like this once in a lifetime. You couldn't not take it.

Six weeks had passed on the road.

Each mile was thousands of paces for the boy, ending in a stone marked with the miles to Rome, one less than before, then another mile began. Mile followed mile and days and weeks until he almost forgot where he came from. The great river was part of someone else's life, the Via Julia Augusta no different from the Via Aemilia Scauri, and even when the Aurelian Way traced the Italian coast and the miles fell to single figures – whatever that meant: he couldn't count – Rome seemed no nearer.

But he never forgot the name of the man who'd spoken to him on the bridge, never forgot the message, or the promise. In Rome he'd be rich, rewarded with gold coins, good food, new clothes, and a room in a great house for as long as he wanted.

'I swear to you it's true,' he whispered, clenching his fist around the bandage. 'I *did.*' And one day when he was walking half-asleep the Seven Hills shimmered in the distance, suddenly clear, enclosed by white walls, covered with white buildings.

He'd reached Rome at last, centre of the world, the end of his journey and, as it happened, the beginning. Rome was when the boy's troubles really began.

People swept him through the gates, elbowing him, knocking him aside, too busy to see him. He kept asking, 'Bright Armour Street?' No one understood his simple pagan speech. He wandered the broad boulevards gazing in awe, sent first to a street of metalworkers, then coppersmiths, who shrugged and sent him to the ring-makers' street. The light had been failing by then and they were packing up, but one old man cocked his head. 'You mean *Armilustri*,' he'd said, and pointed.

It was a street of fine houses, well cared-for behind high walls, and the boy's spirits rose. Halfway along one house stood out from its smart neighbours, ivy across the door and shutters hanging off, and he hoped this wasn't his long-sought destination. Something – perhaps the ache in his left hand – told him it was. His feet crunched over dry leaves on the step. He brushed away the cobwebs to reveal a small blue-glass plaque set in the wall, but he couldn't read.

'You won't find anyone there,' a passing slave called. 'No one but ghosts, that is. That's the Villa Marcia.'

The boy whispered, 'The Villa Marcia.' He stared up at the deserted house.

'Want to know what happened there?' the slave called.

The boy shook his head.

His name was unusual in Rome: it was Viridorix.

III

Rome Burning

Three men rode like the wind from Antium, purple cloaks and plumes flying, steel armour flashing. Their horses, fresh at Bovillae, were already lathered, whipped ragged. A command from Nero was a matter of life and death – yours, if you didn't look sharp.

The two praetorian troopers, both Scorpions, dismounted at the Appian Gate. They held the third man's horse while he slid down.

'Get on with it,' Stigmus ordered. 'You know where.' They marched ahead, shoulders barging, kicking people out of the way with their spiked boots. Yet as he followed their broad backs, Stigmus mused that Tigellinus, obviously weary from his hasty return from Rome last night to the Emperor's side, had been so helpful that it was almost suspicious: *Why not try the place called Luca's tavern, eh?* Stigmus had learnt never to trust Tigellinus's helpful suggestions, but to his surprise the Scorpions knew the place. Top men, both. The heat, the weight of armour, his tight leather under garbs and thick cloak, made Stigmus's squat, compressed body ooze with sweat, yet at this moment he was the most powerful man in Rome.

He savoured that.

Only two months ago he was a mere *specialis* of Nero's dreaded *Cognitionibus et Fides*, the Office of Understanding and Faith. Born a slave, he'd won success in his chosen career by arranging the suicide of his father's wife, the murder of his high-born father and the crucifixion of his brother – inventiveness which first brought him to the Emperor's attention – leading to well-rewarded prosecutions nailing up Christian abominations who wouldn't call Nero God. But still, a mere *specialis*.

His mission to Britain with Quistus, bungled though it was, was Stigmus's great stroke of luck. He'd escaped the horrendous Brits with his life – just – and the fabulous carcanet of fire diamonds called the Phoenix too, which he'd stolen from the only girl he ever loved, but in the Circus Maximus Quistus had tricked him into giving it to Nero as a gift. Stigmus, despair at his loss transformed into elation at his reward, was thrust into disgraced Tigellinus's place as Prefect of Praetorians by the grateful, fickle Emperor.

Early this morning, as Prefect, he'd been summoned to Nero's bridal bower in an echoing, crowded, gossiping bedroom of the Antium Palace, the silk drapes enclosing the squeaking bed showered with rose petals and Sporus giggling inside. Stigmus waited by the nuptial candles to be noticed, helmet under arm, sweating even then: fear, pure and simple. Nero the God, Supreme Pontiff, had that effect on everyone.

'My dear Prefect, you will find a certain man with no name and bring him to Me. At once.'

The giggling began again. Stigmus swallowed hard. He knew exactly who Nero meant, yet everyone knew that Quistus had disappeared.

Then Tigellinus smirked, 'I may be able to help you, Stig, my friend.'

Yes, good old Tigellinus *Sicilianus* (not that most people dared call him that, as Stigmus did, to his face), maybe he wasn't so bad after all.

The troopers left-turned by Triton's fountain, tramping down a narrow alley in single file. They stopped at a locked door, kicked it in, and followed tumbling chairs and tables downstairs. Stigmus waited a moment, wondered if he should draw his sword, then went down. The cellar stank like a pigsty. The troopers bent the innkeeper over one of the filthy tables not broken or used in the barricade.

Stigmus scowled. 'Where is he, Luca?'

Luca, sensibly, babbled none of the usual lies and excuses. 'I know,' he said. 'Him. Yes, he was here. I wouldn't tell my brothers, but I'll tell you. What's in it for me?'

'Cut his other knee off,' Stigmus commanded.

'Listen!' Luca squealed. 'Foreign gentlemen came, and *they* smashed up the place. Then my bastard brothers. Now you're the third lot, and my best girl's run off. What's in it for me today?'

Stigmus drew his sword.

'The foreigners took him,' Luca cried. 'I'm no fool, right? I followed them upstairs, didn't I? I kept my ears open. I heard him order the idiots carrying the sedan chair. The Villa Paria.'

'He'll live,' Stigmus said. The troopers looked disappointed. It was afternoon already, the heat was unbearable, and as usual the smell of smoke hung over the summer-struck city.

'I want to help you.' Quistus sat cross-legged like Zhang, who was bright-eyed after his morning's sleep. 'So, Zhang, you have to help me.'

Zhao, kneeling between them in the way that made her almost invisible, made tea. She tasted, nodded that it was safe, and Zhang took the tiny cup. Two swallows. 'You slept well, Quistus?'

Quistus also took two swallows. 'Always.' He hadn't. Sleeping awoke the dream that was a memory, the memory too terrible to face. He had a powerful desire to drink himself to nothing. He needed something stronger than tea. His hands shook.

'You and I have good *ganqing*.' Zhang watched Quistus's hands. 'I knew it the moment I saw you. I've not regretted my decision. We understand each other.'

'We both know you came to me for the same reason you employed Cerberus. I'm a Roman and you can trust me.'

'Do you have children?'

Where did that come from? Quistus was shaken. 'We aren't talking about me.' Zhao, pouring more tea, shot him an interested look. Quistus the Stoic, openly emotional. Why? He hadn't denied it when she accused him of having no wife, no children – of being, by implication, a man empty of feeling. Of course, a man (at least, a Chinese man) never changed; perhaps it was she who had changed, she who had feeling after all.

The boy said, 'Are your children like me, Quistus?' He waited for a reply, but there was none. 'I wish I could play with someone my own age. I'm ashamed.'

'Ashamed?'

'I'm frightened of dying.'

'I won't talk about children or death.' Quistus knocked over his cup. He set it right. Zhao refilled it to the brim. He said, 'Tell me about the tattoos. Xu and Ying.'

Zhang looked hurt. 'Are we friends?'

'Yes, we're friends.' Quistus took two swallows. 'We have good *ganqing*.'

'Zhao, you may tell him.' Zhang turned to her.

'To understand Xu and Ying,' she said, folding her hands neatly, 'first, necessarily, you must understand Golden Turtle and the Gold Heads.'

'Go on,' Quistus said.

'The Son of Heaven gives lands – sometimes whole countries – to his princes, dukes and kings to rule in his name.'

'Family, of course.'

'Sons, brothers, cousins, uncles, related at least by marriage.'

Quistus said, '*Qin*'s one big happy family.'

'It's true,' Zhang said. 'So my eunuchs always told me.' He explained, 'A prince is brought up by eunuchs so that he's safe from politics.'

'What happened to yours?'

'They were . . . involved in politics. I no longer trust eunuchs.'

Zhao said, 'Each year the Prince is commanded by his father the Emperor in Loyang to visit the Autumn House in Chen. We all look forward to it; the palace is very beautiful with gardens among mountains and streams. The way west skirts Mount Laojun and winds steeply to the Wei river, heavily forested. An ideal place for a surprise attack led by the Duke of Chen.'

'Fire arrows,' Zhang said. 'Men fighting on fire. Confusion.'

'Many were killed, carts burnt. Our guards died defending

the Prince's palanquin, the travelling-house carried on the shoulders of many men.'

'They were killed under us,' the boy said. 'The house fell. I was taken prisoner with Zhao and the women. Cao Shou, Zhao's husband, was executed to encourage our good behaviour.'

'I'm sorry,' Quistus told Zhao. She lowered her eyes.

The boy continued, 'Fortunately, An and Chong had dropped behind with the heaviest carts, delayed by mud, or they would have been discovered and killed with my eunuchs, who, having outlived their usefulness to Chen, had . . . had not sought sufficient assurances for their safety.'

'Who was Yunyazi with?' Quistus interrupted.

'A magician always travels at his Prince's side. The Chens were too frightened to kill him, weren't they, Zhao? They took us to the tower in the mountain pass but released him when he said he'd change them into worms. They thought the snow would do their work.'

'What of Captain Lo?'

'When we were taken as hostages he fell back in the trees with about fifty men, many injured. We thought he was dead. We had no hope. It was icy cold in the stone tower when the snows came. Instead of killing us – as he should have done; he'd already been paid – the Duke, a weak and greedy man, decided to obtain a ransom to double his money. No doubt the thought of murdering a "divine" child preyed on his mind, as Zhao's whispers intended. She's so clever! Finally the Duke agreed to send her to the Emperor with cunningly-phrased demands.' The boy smiled, nodding for Zhao to continue. He liked this bit.

'As soon as the tower was hidden behind cliffs, arrows rained down, killing the Duke's escort around me,' Zhao said. 'Yunyazi had found Lo and his men. They'd seen the tower was too strong to attack, reached only by a single rope bridge over the waterfall. However, the Duke had made one serious mistake. An and Chong had been with the carts carrying the silver *sycee*, about twenty thousand Kuping taels' worth, uncaptured.'

'And gifts,' Zhang said. 'Lots!'

'And gifts,' Zhao agreed. 'So we decided on a trick—'

'Her idea,' Zhang said. 'An tells everyone it was his idea, but it was hers.'

'After long days and nights we hauled the wagons along the precipice to the bridge, pretending I returned from the Emperor.

When I displayed the ingots of silver "ransom" to the soldiers on the tower, the gate was thrown open – and Captain Lo, whose men had hidden on the cliffs during the night, swinging from lines, attacked instantly. They succeeded in bringing the Prince out, but it was close. The Duke's men poured after us across the bridge.'

'But Wild Swan danced, and cut the ropes?'

'She saved us. We thought we were safe. The Duke and his soldiers had fallen to their deaths and we had only the weather to fight.'

'But it didn't work out like that?'

'We sheltered at an inn from the storm. In the morning the Prince was gone. He'd been kidnapped. That same night, the inn was attacked by two Gold Heads. They were killed by Lo's men, but it was a dreadful shock. Who'd sent such creatures? We even feared it was the dead Duke of Chen, reaching from beyond the grave. Their cheeks were not tattooed at that time, their rebellion against the Emperor not openly expressed.'

'What of the Prince?'

'He was lucky,' Zhao said. 'If he'd been at the inn, he'd've been killed.'

'It was awful!' Zhang said. 'I'd been kidnapped by spice traders. Awful men, brutes. They stuffed a bag over my head and tied me over a disgusting animal. After a day I wanted to die. A week later I wished I *was* dead. They brought me through the Celestial Mountains and tried to sell me in the market at Xireg. All they got was a few *wazhu* and a bag of salt.' He brightened. 'Imagine my pleasure when the person who bought me took the disguise from her face – it was Zhao!'

'That luck was only the start of our troubles,' Zhao said. 'An decided it best we hide in the hills above the village and send for help to the Emperor. Instead, we saw our messenger dragged back to the market square by Gold Heads. Golden Turtle tortured him to death with fire and water, knowing we must be watching, taunting us with our friend's dying shrieks.' She shook, haunted. 'The eunuch clicking his gold fingers, "Save him, yes! Save him, no!" Of course, we couldn't.'

'I offered to give myself up,' the boy said. 'Golden Turtle had called out he wanted only me, the others could go. But after the terrible things we'd seen and heard, no one believed him. We held a council of war.'

'Obviously the road to the east was closed off to us,' Zhao said. 'Our only hope was to head through the mountains to the stone desert. At Kashgar the Gold Heads nearly caught us. We heard they came running into Bukhara only a week after we left. They're tireless. They pull Golden Turtle in an immense covered wagon, the roof turned up at each corner. It's full of Searching Spells. The people of Kangju – you call it Sogdia – begged us to leave their territory, nowhere was safe. Bands of fierce, bearded warriors roamed the length of the Zeravshan valley searching for us, as unwelcome to the Kangju as to us. From descriptions of the warriors' brutality and clothing – raw fleece – and the terrifying reputation of their *shanyu*, Punu, we realized the Gold Heads were in alliance with *Qin*'s most ancient enemy, whose army now dared to ride far west of the Great Wall.'

'Ancient enemy?'

'The Huns. Why else build a wall of five thousand *li*?'

'Never heard of them,' Quistus said.

'From Ecbatana we reached Antioch. At the coast we took ship to Athens, breaking our trail. Again we thought we were safe. Eight months later, on the eastern horizon, we saw a black ship with golden sails, and knew we were not.'

'So here you are in Rome,' Quistus said. 'Still hiding.'

'Undiscovered,' Zhang said. 'Rome is a big city. Golden Turtle's Searching Spells haven't found us.'

Quistus wondered how much longer that would last. 'You told me the Gold Heads weren't tattooed at first. But now they are. What's worse than Golden Turtle? Who are Xu and Ying?'

Zhao began, 'We now know that Chen was only a finger-puppet—' She stopped, wide-eyed, listening.

Quistus crossed the squeaking floor. He pushed past Manas. 'Knocking at the door. I already told Shu not to answer. I don't want anyone seeing Chinese.' He crossed the peristyle. An and Chong came running. 'Out of sight, you two. No living Gold Head knows you're here.' He glanced at the atrium corner where the dead warrior's body had burnt safely to ash. 'Omba!'

She came running, her shoulder stitched by Manas. Quistus said, 'Probably just some kid selling vegetables.' He knew it wasn't; from the staircase the knocking sounded like thunder. 'Shu.' He jerked his thumb to the kitchen, then pointed for the two guards to hide behind pillars. He looked round, checking nothing Chinese showed, then opened the peephole a crack.

'Got you,' Stigmus said. 'Open up, you bastard.'

Quistus blocked the doorway. 'My old friend Stigmus,' he greeted his lifelong enemy. 'What brings you here?'

Stigmus shoved past. He looked appreciatively around the grandiose hall, empty except for Omba. She growled. In the past they'd tried to kill each other in various nasty ways.

'What an imposing house,' Stigmus drawled. 'One might almost call it a palace.' He sheathed his sword, unable to hide his envy a moment longer. 'How do you do it, Quistus?' He hissed with frustration. 'How do you always fall on your feet like this?'

'You remember my name.'

'So does Nero.'

Quistus watched the two Scorpions. The one on the left stood by a pillar with a Chinese guard hiding behind its bulk. Omba breathed in noisily, drawing the Scorpion's eyes to her breasts through the red silk dress found for her by Zhao, almost long enough but extravagantly tight.

'Nero took my name,' Quistus said. 'You heard, you were there. It's his now.'

'Maybe you could have it back.'

'Maybe I wouldn't want it.'

'Why not?' Stigmus's face screwed up. Quistus drove him crazy. 'Why does Nero want to see you? Why *you*?'

Quistus laughed. 'You mean you don't even know why you're here?'

Stigmus's cheeks flushed as red as Omba's dress. 'Bring him!' he told the Scorpions. 'Stop staring. The woman stays.'

Quistus showed no sign of the inner turmoil he felt; at least the Prince was safe, and Stigmus had been distracted from searching the house.

Almost at once, as they walked from the Viminalis, smoke swept along the street. Nobody knew where it came from, then under the aquaduct by the Circus Maximus a surge of people pushed them back. Someone shouted that a fire on the Caelian Hill, caught by the hot easterly wind, had leapt along the wooden shops on Cyclops Street into the alleys, setting ablaze the narrow streets around the Appian Gate.

'Nothing to worry about,' Stigmus grinned. 'They say Tigellinus lights these things, you know? They always start when he's out of town with clean hands. When you're the richest landlord in Rome, you always want more. They even say Nero wants Rome burnt, just to make space for a bigger palace.' He chuckled, shaking his head, and turned right. 'We'll requisition horses from the imperial post at the Ostian Gate. The coast road's not much longer, and it's flat.' The change of plan took them along the Vicus Armilustri, past the derelict Villa Marcia. Quistus tripped. 'Your old house,' Stigmus grinned. 'That must hurt.'

Quistus said nothing. At an upstairs window, he was sure he'd seen the face of a boy looking out. He shook his head and walked on.

'What?' Stigmus goaded him. 'Too many happy memories?'

'What can we do?' the Prince asked.

Omba sat. She looked at Zhao.

'We wait,' Omba said. Zhao poured fresh tea.

The road by the sea was heavily wooded, the coast dark, un-inhabited. Only the full moon flickering through the trees, and the gleam of waves breaking on their right, made travel possible. Even so it was well past midnight when Quistus saw the little lights of Antium scattered around the bay, dwarfed by the fierce dynamic glow of Nero's steep, vaulted palace on the cliff top. The wind whirled great draughts of sparks from bonfires blazing on the cliff edge, illuminating the paved squares and sprawling colonnades like day. Nero's builders, Severus and Celer, thought big.

Quistus dismounted, stretching his legs by the third portico. The night's feasting was over, revellers had retired inside with the *arbiter elegantiae* to refine their debauchery in private, and those too drunk or full to stand, or who stood but weaved or puked too near the edge, were carried away by their slaves. A few tired-looking unlucky whores let the wind cool their naked, fake-jewelled bodies while they polished off the wine dregs. Boys dressed as girls crawled under the tables to sleep, or lay snoring where their lovers let them go. Quistus watched thoughtfully, estimating how many had banqueted and fornicated under the moon tonight, and at what expense. He turned as Stigmus reappeared with a man he recognized, the subtle freedman Epaphrodites, now Nero's private secretary. 'What?' Stigmus said. 'You two know each other?'

'Indeed,' Epaphrodites said smoothly, not dropping his gaze from Quistus's eyes. 'I trust you still have that agreement on linen paper, sir, marked with the Emperor's seal?'

'Safe,' Quistus said.

'*What* agreement?' Realization dawned on Stigmus. 'Gods, that's why you're still alive!'

'Except for extremely recent developments,' Epaphrodites said, 'perhaps not alive.'

'You tricked the Emperor somehow.' Stigmus gave an unsteady laugh. 'He tricked Nero – and lived!'

'No one knows what was written,' Epaphrodites said. 'It was penned by the Emperor's own hand, sealed by him.'

He took Quistus's elbow, drawing him privately along a corridor, low-voiced. 'I should mention, sir, that the Emperor is not now quite so amused by the agreement as when he signed it. In fact the only reason he hasn't sold *his* property – the Villa Marcia – is because he believes his unwise promise may be hidden there, somewhere.'

'I'll bear that in mind, Epaphrodites.'

Epaphrodites opened a door. 'He's retired with his new wife for tonight, sir, and commands you to attend him in the morning. There's someone to see you first.' He bowed, closed the door behind Quistus, and was gone.

'Knew you'd come.' Seneca was an old man now, once Nero's tutor, the master who'd lost control of his pupil, the humane *consiliarius* of a tyrant. Dislodged from power, his life threatened by Tigellinus, Seneca the fox bumped between his fabulous villas in a poor cart and lived stoically on bread and water to hide his wealth until his turn in power, he dreamed, came again. He still believed that Nero, with his energy and artistry, could be made into one of Rome's greatest Emperors – if he'd only listen to Seneca. 'Congratulations on still being alive,' the old man said. 'Didn't expect it, frankly.'

'I'm sure congratulations are mutual.'

'Why are you wearing those extraordinary clothes?'

'It's a long story. Why are we both here?'

The room's walls were of pearly oyster shell. Seneca hobbled to the glass window, looking out on darkness. 'Because a wind blows from the East.'

'Really?'

'Why do I always feel you know more than you say, Quistus?'

'I can't imagine.'

'Nero hates you more thoroughly than he hates any man – left alive, that is – yet he knows your special talents. Above all else, he knows your heart is Roman; so in a strange way that he finds acutely unpleasant, Nero trusts you, even though he doesn't always get the result he planned for.'

The two men watched each other in the dark glass. Seneca gave way first. 'So, Quistus, two days ago, when I suggested your name to Nero in relation to the situation we face in the East, he overcame his scruples and his intense dislike of you and reluctantly agreed to send Tigellinus to bring you from Luca's tavern.'

'What situation in the East?'

'There you go again. Then Tigellinus returns from Rome empty-handed with new and alarming information, and suddenly Nero's screaming for Quistus, all is forgiven, and sending that blunt tool Stigmus to find you at any cost.'

'I'm flattered, except for his choice of Stigmus.'

'Here's something you don't know. Yesterday's rather bloody entertainments here, and the feasting to celebrate so much death – a thousand notables served with the twelve foods of the Zodiac, Falernian wine a hundred years old – cost Nero half a million *sestercii*. Tomorrow's entertainment will cost three times as much. All held in honour of King Tiridates of Armenia. Who? Where?'

'A country between Rome and the East.'

'Yes, yes, I know. Exactly. And the Parthian Empire – also to the east – is no longer our enemy but our friend. The murder of Crassus is forgotten, the lost eagle a trivial oversight, all's forgiven.'

'There's always wars, and rumours of wars, from the East.'

'This time the rumour has a name.'

'Oh?'

'*Qin*,' Seneca said, pronouncing it wrong.

'Ah.'

'You're making me work very hard. Tigellinus claims you know them. An empire as great as – perhaps even greater than – Rome.'

'Perhaps.'

'That you even know someone called Prince Zhang.'

'*Zhang*,' Quistus nodded, pronouncing it properly.

'King Tiridates, with his contacts to the East – part of the Spice Road passes through his kingdom – tells us Zhang will be Emperor of *Qin*. If he lives.'

'If he lives,' Quistus said carefully, 'I'm sure that Zhang, his father's favourite son, will be a good friend to Rome.'

'And his father, the Emperor of *Qin,* most grateful for the return of his favourite son?'

'Yes.'

'Exactly what I told Nero.' The old man rapped his stick, pleased.

'I understand there are difficulties in the way,' Quistus said. 'Golden Turtle. Gold Heads. Huns.'

'That's what I said!' Seneca grinned. 'Nero thought of you at once.'

Omba swirled her cup. She glowered at the tea leaves. 'I've had enough of this stuff,' she burped. 'An acquired taste, you say?'

'We call our tea ceremony *Erh ya*,' Zhao purred. 'Actually it's a Buddhist ritual. The religion is achieving some popularity in our country.'

'My father's a tolerant man,' Zhang said. 'Some say Buddhism, too, is an acquired taste. Many still believe that the Emperor should be revered before any foreign god.'

Zhao cleared her throat.

'Honoured teacher,' Zhang said earnestly, 'a government, like any creature, cannot survive with two heads. The Emperor's ministers are trained and examined by the rational wisdom of Confucius, and serve the Emperor, not any other god.'

Zhao rearranged the teacups, tight-lipped.

Omba yawned. 'Don't you even have coffee? In Kefa we pick the beans off bushes, crush them into honey or wax, and roll them into balls. One keeps you going all morning. I'd rather have coffee than tea any day.'

'We must try it.' Zhang stretched. 'I'm tired.'

'We have no coffee,' Zhao said firmly, 'only tea, and my Prince should be in bed.'

When she returned the two women sat quietly, worried. They

tried not to think what might be happening as the hours passed without word. Later Little Pelican came in wearing mourning rags, her eyes huge and sleepless. Omba patted the mat and the tiny dancer sat between them, her grotesque feet folded under her, sharing the companionable silence while the long night turned into day.

'Quistus, you will stand in the shadow of my magnificence,' Nero commanded. 'No one shall stand between me and my fellow god, Sol, the Sun.' As always he was nervous before a performance. Despite the coming battle he wore no armour, only a singer's flowery silk *synthesina* to his ankles, and seemed impressed that Quistus, unexpectedly, was silkily and similarly dressed; imitation, obviously, was flattery. The hydraulic platform crowded with the usual boring old toga'd hangers-on sank, with loud mechanical groans, beneath the palace towards the shimmering aquamarine grotto beneath.

'Indeed I shall,' Quistus said. Rock walls slid past. There was no railing.

'You mean *not*,' piped Sporus through his veil. The boy looked eerily like the empress whose place he took, even wearing Poppaea's perfume as well as her clothes. 'Your grammar was wrong. Indeed I shall *not*.'

Quistus frowned. 'I shall *not* stand in His shadow? Great Caesar, Sporus confuses me.'

'I admire your clothes,' Nero said. 'Excellent taste.'

'I don't like him,' Sporus hissed. Quistus smiled and turned to Tigellinus, who slept with Poppaea more than Nero did.

Tigellinus told Sporus, 'Everyone near the Emperor should keep a very tight grip on his tongue today, and think before speaking.'

For a sufficient moment, Sporus looked frightened.

Nero muttered, 'Suppose the crowd hate me? Suppose there's no applause? What shall I do?'

The platform shuddered to a halt on glowing blue waters lit by shafts of submarine light. A gleaming trireme, *Apollo*, decorated in silver and ivory, awaited the royal pleasure. The entourage jockeyed, scrambling for precedence on the high stern. Stigmus tripped on the gangway. 'Careful, Stylus,' Nero called. 'If you fall in the water your armour will drag you down, and we'll never see you again.' Everyone stepped away from Stigmus. Nero never did get his name right; two bad omens in one.

Nero waved his wrist, the *trierarch* clapped his chest in salute, and at once the vessel slid from the cave's narrow mouth into brilliant sunlight, the royal entourage shuffling nervously in Nero's suddenly-appearing shadow. Golden oars were unshipped by highly-trained Greek rowers, the purple sail set, and the trireme moved rapidly across the sparkling waters towards Antium's harbour walls, crowded with spectators on wooden grandstands in the natural amphitheatre of the bay, where the battle fleets faced each other, half with purple sails and the others, slightly less impressive, white. That was Tiridates' fleet. Nero called Quistus to the highest viewing platform over the stern. 'I love winning sea battles, don't you? I've a genius for it, you'll be impressed. I built this harbour especially. I love winning.' He lowered his voice. 'I always do win, Quistus.'

'Great Caesar honours me by returning my name.'

'Not yet! I am the world's greatest artist. My eyes see farther than you can possibly comprehend.' The vessel changed course. Tigellinus and Stigmus shuffled carefully lest their shadows touch the Emperor. Sporus looked beseechingly from the main deck, downwind of sixty sweaty oarsmen. Below them more oarsmen, called fart-catchers, kept time in the shadows, and farther down still more *thalamites* worked in stinking darkness. The drum thudded time. The adjudicator's flag flew from the lighthouse. Astrologers would choose the moment for battle to commence. Sea monsters and mermaids swam in the harbour, and from the rocks heavily wigged and powdered sirens sang bewitchingly to the sailors.

'There he is!' Nero waved cheerily to King Tiridates on the flagship of the opposing fleet. Tiridates, an impressive-looking, bearded man wearing a turban, returned the wave glumly. Quistus reckoned the Armenian knew what was coming. Spectators towed on rafts bedecked with banners and food-laden tables cheered for Nero. On other rafts women waved, shaking their hair, taking off their clothes. 'Not yet,' Nero ordered angrily. 'They mustn't besmirch men's honourable battle with their filth. Oh, why not?' Nearby a raft of monkeys had been provided with masts and rigging to swing from, chattering excitedly. 'See!' Nero pointed, enchanted. 'The crowd love them. All my genius.'

'Look,' Quistus said, 'one's wearing a veil.' Nero shielded his eyes, peering.

'Looks like Sporus,' Stigmus joked heavily. Tigellinus drew breath, prepared to be outraged if Nero was, but Nero hadn't heard.

Tigellinus smiled instead. 'The Emperor appreciates wit, Stigmus. Speak louder next time.'

'I don't need your advice, *Sicilianus*,' Stigmus said. Still the flag on the lighthouse flew steadily. No doubt, Quistus thought, Nero had arranged everything to the finest detail; if Tiridates thought he was in for anything like a battle, he was about to find out that it was a play. As always in Nero's plays, the lead actors would enjoy a fine performance, the audience would applaud and the chorus would die. Only *Apollo* and Tiridates' ship, *Tigranocerta*, were manned by free men. The rest were chained to their benches.

'Watch.' Nero gripped Quistus's shoulder. 'I've a few surprises for the king.'

'I'm sure he'll love you even more for them.'

'Men do love me,' Nero said, 'for I am more than a man.'

A smaller, white-sailed vessel was passing ahead of *Apollo*, withdrawing to position before start of play. Nero ordered the drum speed to be doubled, driving the trireme forward. The oars flashed. Foam poured over the bronze beak projecting from the bow. Men waved from the other ship, then, too late, tried to change course. Nero's flag dipped and the flag on the lighthouse dipped in response, signalling the start of the show. Nero clapped with excitement. 'Break her in half!' *Apollo*'s bronze beak shattered the smaller vessel's oars and rammed her amidships. The impact didn't need to breach the hull, only roll it over. Triremes were narrow, their three decks making them top heavy. The white sail slammed into the sea and *Apollo* rose up as the vessel rolled under her. 'Too fast,' Nero sulked. 'No singing.' *Apollo* slid over the drowned hulk. A few men struggled up, splashing, and at last they heard screams. 'You hear that, Quistus? But their song gives me no joy. I can't help it, even perfection depresses me. It's my artistic nature. I'm never satisfied. What am I to do about the East? Hmm?'

'Can even great Caesar stop the sun rising?'

'Yes. Yes, I can, Tiridates is teaching me the powers of the Magi. The sun may rise as often as it wishes, Quistus, but I can no longer tolerate the closure of the Spice Road. Rome's great families can't live without pepper on their fish, it seems. To Hades with them. But even the price of bread has shot up, and that *is* disturbing. In fact, it's a crisis. The common people blame me personally for every penny on a loaf.' He ordered a turn towards a gaggle of small white-sailed boats. Gladiators gathered on *Apollo*'s foredeck, bronze armour glinting, armed with tridents like sea gods. 'The East is the most serious threat Rome has faced. I've sent seven legions to the Parthian frontier under General Corbulo. Yes, seven.'

Seven legions. Tigellinus and Stigmus shuffled as the Emperor's shadow swung, trying to overhear.

'Top eagles,' Nero said. 'III *Gallica*, VI *Ferrata*. I've bled Syria of V *Parthica* and XII *Fulminata* despite the Jews. V *Macedonia*, so Moesia's stripped bare. My beautiful XV *Apollinaris*. And that's not the end of it.'

The ship lifted again, the stern grating on the wreck. Quistus gripped the rail, hard. Beneath him a couple of hundred thieves and rapists were drowning in chains, making it difficult to adjust to the change in scale. Seven legions was an immense force, more than a quarter of the entire imperial Roman army. Both he and Nero had forgotten about shadows. His own shadow fell across Nero's still-handsome, bloated face.

'Corbulo's orders are be ready, do nothing,' Nero said. 'Everything's rumour. Rumours of a rebel Hun army under rogue *Qin* command somewhere beyond Parthia. True? False? Nobody knows, but the Parthians are shitting with their pants up, Tiridates is so terrified he begs for friendship, and the more I slap him the more he kisses my hand. Gods, Quistus, an army of millions?'

'Prince Zhang told me the Emperor has hundreds of legions.'

'Hundreds! You believe him?'

'A woman I trust as good as confirmed it. She claims her brother's their general. I suspect the Emperor's troops don't know Zhang survives in the West. They believe him already murdered.'

'But this rogue *Qin* faction is in league with the Huns?'

'They know he's in Rome. I don't think we can keep the boy hidden much longer. The Gold Heads must be close to finding him. It's only a matter of time.'

'Corbulo tells me these Huns are frightful. Utterly barbaric. Eat meat raw,' Nero said thoughtfully.

'Apparently they've fought the *Qin* for a thousand years. Even a huge wall didn't keep them out. Now they're coming west.'

'The next Emperor of Rome will not be a *Qin*, Quistus. Or a Hun. I promise you that.'

'Nevertheless, the threat is significant.'

Nero decided. 'Does this boy trust you?'

'Except for the woman, I'm all he's got.'

'What about her?'

'If she were ever shown to be a traitor, he'd willingly die of grief.'

'That's straightforward, then. You'll adopt this boy Zhang as your son, and take him back home.'

Quistus stared, dry-mouthed. He couldn't speak. His belly had been slit and gutted. He looked down, and seemed whole. 'I can't adopt a son,' he croaked.

'You will adopt him as your son to show Rome's friendship and goodwill. You *will*, Quistus. You *will* return him to the *Qin* Emperor. With the boy gone – or at least not here – the Huns and the *Qin* rebels will have every reason to return home, and there they can all fight amongst themselves as much as they like.'

'I can't—'

'I know you had true sons of your own. Yes, very tragic. You don't have to take your loss so seriously, Quistus. This *Qin* brat has to believe in you, you must make him trust you like a father. Adopt him as your own. I myself was adopted. It doesn't mean anything, it's politics.' Gladiators leapt from *Apollo* on to the decks of smaller vessels and Nero applauded, his hands hollowed like roof tiles in the Greek fashion, the signal for general applause. While the butchery and drowning of prisoners was going on, and a few desperate hand-to-hand combats were played out, interrupted by humorous chases involving a naked sea goddess, Nero ordered oil poured on the waters. He raised a flaming torch like Jupiter Lucetius, God of thunderbolts, and threw it into the oily waves. They watched the ships float in flames, burning. Men jumped. 'Ah, they're singing at last. Time to get alongside Tiridates and take him prisoner.' The battle proceeded to its carefully choreographed climax. Quistus hardly noticed. He felt ill, overheated by all he'd seen and heard.

Tiridates, brought aboard at the dockside so the audience

witnessed what was said, threw himself theatrically at Nero's feet. The speeches were rehearsed; Quistus heard their words echo off the crowded stone walls. 'My God, I am your slave.' The Armenian had a deep voice, louder and more rolling than Nero's. 'I crawl on my knees to you, my God, worshipping you as Mithras.'

Nero played his lyre, then sang. 'You have acted wisely in giving yourself to me personally that you may experience my grace. I now make you King of Armenia, so that you and others know that I have power over kings, and the power to give and take away kingdoms.'

Tiridates looked up. He whispered, 'It's not fair to hit a man when he's down.' Nero laughed, replaced the turban with a crown, and raised the king to his feet.

'Ah, these people.' Nero wiped his hands and came back to Quistus. Stigmus was listening to the report of a travel-stained praetorian.

Tigellinus said, 'Quistus looks fevered. Your presence quite overawes him, great Caesar.'

'I'm all right,' Quistus said.

'He's been at the Falernian.' Tigellinus made drinking signs.

Nero gripped Quistus's arm, hard. 'I *am* Rome, Quistus. You won't fail Rome, will you?' He added, 'Succeed, you'll have your name. Fail me, don't bother coming back.'

'Success or exile, Quistus,' Tigellinus grinned. 'Success or exile.'

Quistus, swaying, shook his head. 'He's seasick,' Nero said contemptuously.

'This man says the fire in Rome's spreading out of control,' Stigmus called. 'As soon as it's stopped, it starts again in a dozen places.' He stared at Tigellinus. 'No doubt we have you to thank for that, eh, *Sicilianus*?'

Tigellinus said nothing. Nero coloured. Stigmus stood without moving. Then the blood drained from his face, leaving him as pale as a stone statue.

Nero turned to Tigellinus. 'Prefect of Praetorians,' he said deliberately, 'you will, of course, use all measures to contain the fire.'

Little Pelican brought a box and joined Omba at the window. She clambered up and together they watched the smoke move from east to west. The smell of burning timber made the air feel even hotter. The light rippled as blue billows of woodsmoke drifted across the sun, making the city wavery and colourless.

Towards evening they saw the first dull flames peep above the rooftops of the Caelian Hill. Almost at once points of orange fire sprang up in the eastern suburbs, brightening as night fell, and smoke began to blow over the Viminalis.

'It won't reach here,' Omba said.

'How was I to know?' Stigmus, hoarse from shouting, struggled with the enormity of his personal disaster, his fall from power as sudden and as stunning as his rise. 'How was I to know *he* ordered it?'

He clung despairingly to the pony that carried him to Rome. He'd been stripped of his *insigniae* of rank (Tigellinus had made sure *that* happened). He kept his cloak but the six praetorians, Scorpions all, riding stallions in close escort, no longer took, or even noticeably heard, a single command he shouted at them. Their orders were to make certain he followed *his* orders.

'You will make sure Quistus reaches Rome. You will ensure he takes Prince Zhang into his care, by force if necessary. You will escort them under close guard to Ostia with all possible speed, and see with your own eyes that they board the trireme *Pharsalia* for Antioch, where General Corbulo's legions will protect them. Then you will report back to me, at my pleasure.' Nero had smiled.

Report back to me. Stigmus didn't like that part. He didn't like that smile at all. He covered his head with his cloak. He'd accused the Emperor to his face of incendiarism. It wasn't the sort of accusation you survived, especially if it was true. He couldn't believe his own tongue had done it. It wasn't his fault. Quistus had tricked him into it somehow.

Stigmus threw off his cloak. Beside him Quistus rode in a drunken stupor. He ignored Stigmus when shouted at. Night was falling and in front of them the city was burning.

Omba watched wind-driven flames grasp the Caelian and Esquiline Hills, pushing bright fingers into the narrow streets below. The temples and stately buildings of the Palatine were dark but new fires – set either by men, or sparks – sprang up on the Oppian hill. These were much closer, blocked only by the darkness of the Subura from the classy slopes of the Viminalis.

She imagined the fire reaching into the cheek-by-jowl *insulae* of the Subura valley, blowing into the warren of flammable shops, storerooms, hovels. If, *when*, that happened the Viminalis would burn, too, from rising heat and wind-rushed sparks. 'Better wake Zhao,' she told Little Pelican. 'The Prince, too.'

'If it reached here,' Little Pelican whispered, 'where would we go?'

'Just wake them.' Omba turned back to the window. Oddly enough she found it difficult to worry about the Prince and what Quistus would expect of her. The strangest thought had come into her mind, a mental picture of a man padlocked by his neck to a roof-beam, listening as the fire came closer.

The Ostian Gate was packed solid with refugees fleeing Rome; no hope of men on foot pushing through that lot. The praetorians formed a wedge on horseback, spurring into the crowd, whipping the flats of their swords at anyone who didn't get back sharpish. Someone threw a stone. Stigmus's pony staggered. The tall Scorpion called Brumus pulled it up by the bridle. 'I can do it,' Stigmus shouted. Brumus held on for a while before letting go. He didn't care what Stigmus said.

The Scorpions broke through. They rode fast through deserted streets, avoiding big crowds, scattering groups of looters, desperate men pulling down buildings with hooks, busy lighting firebreaks, swaying under piles of furniture, women shepherding children, old folk wandering. The foul orange sky made everything look diseased and rotten, ready for burning. Stigmus noticed Quistus swaying in the saddle. Still got a bag of wine hidden away.

At the Villa Paria two Scorpions were already beating the door with their swords. Brumus gave orders; the praetorians tied ropes from their saddles and pulled the door off. They rode into the house. Quistus, blinking, rode after them.

Two Chinese guards stood on the stairs, swords level under their eyes. Another pointed a crossbow. The string creaked. Omba came round a pillar with a short, fat *pugio* dagger in each hand. Shu prodded Brumus with his spear. Nobody else moved.

'We've got orders,' Brumus barked in Latin. 'Nobody gets hurt, right?'

Quistus lifted his head. He spoke quietly in Greek. 'My

friends, these men are helping us. Put up your weapons. We've come to take the Prince home.'

'Hurry up!' Brumus shouted. 'I'm not staying here all night.' He knocked clothes from the women's hands. 'Not that stuff. Just what you stand up in. Get out.' He pulled Quistus's horse round, slapped its rump. 'Do something useful, you. Look after the women out there. Stop them taking stuff out.'

Omba touched Quistus's knee. 'Are you all right, Master?'

'Fetch the Prince.' Quistus was burning up. 'Quickly. Ostia. Tell them Ostia. Get Prince' – his mind couldn't grasp the boy's name – 'get him to the old port. *Pharsalia.*' He squinted at her, seeing a horrible look come into her eyes. It was pity.

Omba ran back into the house. People came along the street followed by smoke. They shouted something. Whatever it was, it was coming. Quistus grabbed Stigmus by the shoulder, pulling him off his pony. 'Help Omba. Get them out.'

'You filthy drunk,' Stigmus said. He went into the house. Quistus tried to tell the women, mostly servants and cooks, what was happening. They couldn't hear a word for the noise of fire and yelling. They bowed politely, distracting him, then a few bright souls rushed out with a pushcart piled high with whatever belongings they could salvage. Others stole a mule cart and ran between the shafts, skidding, tossing anything useful down the steps, pots, pans, cutlery, drapes, a long roll of carpet, a chair perched on top. Quistus realized that this situation – grabbing everything, running for their lives – was entirely familiar to them. They'd done it so many times before. One woman ran out clutching a copper cauldron, her face wreathed in smiles of relief.

Brumus stood in the doorway. He drew his sword and shouted orders. Zhao came out wrapping the Prince in a gold cloak. A praetorian gave up his horse. Manas swung Zhao and the boy together into the saddle. Yunyazi, Fu barking at his heels, strode from the house with a servant pushing his handcart behind him, Little Pelican on top clinging to a chest of drawers, sticks, scrolls. She cried because the body of Wild Swan was left behind. The praetorian who'd given up his horse stood with a gold arrow through his neck. The black feathers quivered, vibrating, then stilled. The praetorian turned to Brumus and fell flat.

'Gold Heads!' An shouted.

'Roofs,' Chong pointed, ducking. A praetorian chucked a spear into the smoke.

'Move out,' Brumus ordered. An arrow hit the woodwork by his face. He broke it with his sword. The lamps went out in the house.

Stigmus half fell outside, pushed by Omba. 'That's the lot.' She lifted him into the saddle. The pony twisted, bucking. Stigmus drew his sword. An arrow thudded and the praetorian without a spear came backwards off his horse, not moving as it rolled on him. Omba grabbed the reins and threw Yunyazi over the saddle without dignity as the horse came up. 'Move, magician.' She slapped its rump with the flat of her dagger. The little dog ran barking after the horse. No one noticed Omba slip back into the shadows.

Brumus jumped from the step on to horseback. He held the reins in his sword hand and snatched the bridle of the Prince's horse. 'Hold on.'

'I do know how to ride, thank you.' Zhang's voice was high but calm. Zhao wrapped her arms tight around him, protecting him with her body. Manas ran in front. The horses trotted forward, the servants jogging alongside, carts bumping behind. Quistus thought the carts would slow them but downhill they rolled faster, the men running for their lives between the shafts. Fu yapped excitedly, sounding like a squeaky wheel. An arrow clattered on the cobbles. The ground levelled and they pounded along the Vicus Armilustri. Quistus heard a clash of weapons behind them, a couple of praetorians fighting a rearguard action.

He peered. Smoke swirled from a side street, abruptly condensing into a solid shape covered in ash, and for a moment he thought the man they'd burnt to ash had come back to haunt them. The head lifted and he saw the gold face turn towards the Prince, too late. Manas cut the Gold Head in half without slackening pace.

The road widened. The way to the gate looked clear enough. Brumus called Manas and turned back to help his men. Manas ran holding the Prince's bridle. Quistus slackened pace, staring, then reined in. Stigmus almost rode into him. He followed Quistus's eyes to the Villa Marcia.

'Are you out of your mind?' Stigmus shouted. He looked back fearfully. The last of the servants jogged past, two old retainers with a barrow, one pushing and the other holding it up.

No sign of Brumus. 'Stay if you like, Quistus. To Hades with you!' Stigmus spurred away.

Quistus looked around. The city was as quiet as a burning city could be; the ground trembled slightly with the roar of distant flame. He groaned and slid from the saddle. His legs bent; he tottered against a wall, then pulled himself towards the door of the Villa Marcia.

The door opened before he reached it.

Omba slipped back into the shadows by the Villa Paria. She waited until the coast seemed clear, then ran – ran almost slap into them, half a dozen at least, black figures. And something else, that thumped as they set it down.

She side-stepped behind a column under the portico. No way forward, and she'd be discovered in another moment. She walked backwards, keeping the column between her and them, stepped over the broken door, then turned and ran between the pillars flanking the vestibule into the entrance hall. Footsteps behind her. No time for thought. She crossed the darkened hall and leant back against the kitchen door, then peeped round.

Black-cloaked figures raced round the hall, as light and quick on their feet as children, cloaks flying, faces glinting by the lamps they carried. The Gold Heads called rapidly to each other but she didn't know the words, Chinese. She looked overhead, hearing their footsteps race upstairs. Meanwhile more shadows moved into the vestibule.

Omba stared. Her heart froze.

On the pillar next to the entrance, perfectly obvious to anyone leaving, sooty fingers had smeared a five-letter word. The letters were so hasty and roughly formed that for an instant her mind couldn't make sense of them.

OZTIO

'*Oztio*,' she whispered. 'Ostia!'

Who'd been last out? Yunyazi? Stigmus? She had the horrid feeling she'd been the last one. The lamps had been out. She'd walked right past it . . .

A sedan chair was carried into the entrance hall. The eight Gold Heads carrying the chair set it down as though afraid of breaking glass. They removed the roof and sides. There, raised on a seat like a throne, sat the most obese man Omba had ever seen, a man as round as a turtle, his arms and legs pulled into the rolls of his flesh, a man of solid gold.

Vitellius had called him a *Neidan*. Yunyazi had used the same word. A man who could bring back the dead.

Golden Turtle put out his arms to be lifted. He grunted, wheezing, belly swinging. Omba expected the tiles to break under his feet. He was hairless and the filmy silks left no doubt that he was a eunuch. Behind his bald head Omba saw *Oztio* on the pillar. No one had looked round yet.

Golden Turtle squealed orders. His slitted, fat-enfolded eyes gleamed, peering from side to side. He was angry, very angry. Cringing figures brought a *Qin* gold cup. He drank, crushing it, then smiled like a gold necklace as Gold Heads rolled a body down the stairs. Omba recognized Wild Swan, wrapped for burial.

Golden Turtle kicked the body. He stamped on it with his solid gold heels, squealing with rage.

Omba knew there was nothing she could do. There was nothing but danger here. She moved quickly past the water cistern to the backstairs. At the top she broke the lock with her dagger, moved cautiously into the darkened atrium, then swung up on to the roof. Still she heard Golden Turtle squealing and thumping. He wasn't going anywhere; maybe he was so angry, so obsessed with his revenge on the body of Wild Swan, the hero of Falling Waters Bridge, that he'd never notice *Oztio*, or the Roman letters would mean nothing to him. Maybe he was a fool.

Omba dropped into the side street and ran to the Subura. There was still time.

'I got something to tell you, Senator.' The boy backed down the corridor as Quistus staggered forward from side to side, his shoulders pulling damp plaster from the walls. 'I swear to you it's true, sir. I *did*.'

Quistus squinted at him. 'Viridorix, the urchin, *puerulus*?'

'Yes, sir!' The boy sounded relieved. He pushed back his long, blond-streaked hair. 'It's me, sir. I prefer the term fisherman to urchin. You do remember me.'

'The bridge, boy fishing. You lied. Said you saw her. Lyra.'

'Yes, sir, I did. And—'

'Riding on a white horse.' Quistus staggered. 'Liar.'

'No lie, sir. Plain as I see you. How could I have known what she looked like if I hadn't seen her, or told you she was wearing a cream cloak, which she was, as only you yourself had seen?'

Quistus put his hands to his face. 'Dunno.'

'You aren't yourself, sir.' Viridorix put the Senator's arm round his shoulder. 'Steady now. Find you a place to lie down. Bit of a night on the town, have we, sir? Come on now.'

'No, this way.' Together they staggered down the corridor towards the door at the far end, the mahogany panels inlaid with mother-of-pearl dolphins.

'Gave me a bit of a shock, sir, finding your house empty like this,' Viridorix remarked conversationally. 'Not what I expected.'

'Rome's burning. Wrong time to come. Why are you here?'

Viridorix blurted the words he'd rehearsed so often. 'I saw her, sir.'

'You said.'

'No, sir, don't get me wrong.' The Senator stood stock-still, staring at the door like it was locked or something. Helpfully Viridorix pushed it open. He knew the house well by now. The door squealed loudly on its hinges. 'What I meant was, I saw her *again*.'

The *therma* was the family-sized hot pool at the centre of the Villa Marcia, once heated from below, the walls colourful murals of underwater scenes. Quistus stared, trying to make sense of it as it now was, dusty, lifeless, bloodless. The pool had cracked, the water drained, only cold debris remained, echoes, memories.

'Saw her again?' he muttered. 'Lying.'

'Let's find you somewhere more comfortable.' Viridorix tugged at the arm over his shoulder. He was getting desperate. 'Look, you said there'd be a reward, right?' The Senator wasn't listening. He was staring at the pool – rather, the hole where the pool had been. He pulled away from the boy, staggering by the side, almost falling in and killing himself. Viridorix scampered, alarmed, but the Senator kept going. Another door, less obvious, opened into a cold, dark anteroom, a steam room once decorated like a grotto, the shells now strewn broken across the floor.

Viridorix already knew the house had been searched by something worse than thieves. No furniture that wasn't broken, and in the old study the plaster had been hacked off the walls, the floor dug up. He'd lived off apples from the tree in the peristyle garden with whatever snacks he could filch from markets and sneak back, but this house had ghosts, and he didn't want to stay here another night. He watched the Senator gaze round the walls of the steam room as if remembering, then lightly touch a landscape of nymphs playing in seaweed – and it swung open.

'A secret door to a secret room.' Viridorix ducked after the Senator, impressed. 'Better than most.' Quistus turned briefly. 'I mean, sir, my sister works at the public baths in Lugdunum. They all have 'em, secret rooms, spyholes, so you can watch women without their clothes on. Wish you hadn't, sometimes.'

The Senator tried to step up on to the bench. He couldn't make it. Viridorix placed his shoulder helpfully. The Senator pushed down and reached into the top of a corner. His hand disappeared deep among cobwebs for a moment, then came out gripping a square of heavy folded linen paper, wrapped in a purple ribbon, sealed with thick red wax.

A complicated pattern had been pressed into the wax by a ring. Viridorix recognized the Emperor's face. He looked at the Senator with new respect.

The Senator slipped the sealed letter into his clothes. He was shaking, sweating. 'How long have you been hiding here, Viridorix of Lugdunum?'

'You *do* remember me, sir! You remember what you promised me on the bridge, when you were coming back from Britain?'

'Anything, for the truth.'

'You hooked me, sir. I wasn't going to forget a promise like that. I didn't think it would ever happen – good things don't. But two Mondays after that very day, sir, I was fishing, like usual, and there she was. She was. She came riding from the north – same road you took – white horse, same cream cloak, sir, but I mean, filthy dirty. Same girl, exact same. Your daughter, I swear.'

The Senator ignored distant shouts, the thud of a wall falling. 'You're wrong. She could have been anyone.'

'I shouted out her name, sir. Lyra. *Lyra!* I called to her. And she jerked round at me at once, big grey-green eyes, sir, like yours, then rode on. She knew her name.'

'You're making it up. Very convincing. You're a good liar.'

'Yes, sir, I am a good liar,' Viridorix said urgently, 'but I *did*.'

'Get out of here, Viridorix.' The Senator shook his head. 'This house will burn.' He sounded like he might burn with it.

Viridorix followed him past the pool, along the corridor to the entrance. Then he said, 'I can prove it, sir.'

The Senator waited. His face dripped sweat.

Viridorix unwound the smelly leather bandage from his left hand. The long strip came off at last and under it his palm was clean, uninjured, holding a coin. It had been there so long that its impression was stamped in his skin. He held it out.

Quistus took it. He looked at it. He moved to the doorway and studied it under the glowing red sky. He glanced at Viridorix, then back to the coin. Turned it over, God with a circled head holding a crown. He whispered the Greek inscription aloud: '"*Barbarikon*".' He read around the face on the front: '"*King Gondophares, the Saviour*".'

'See, I followed her to the inn, sir. Stole it from her room. Next day she rode off to the east.'

'The east?'

'As Rome's my witness.'

'You swear you stole this from Lyra?'

'It was the best I could do. I swear it. I wanted a bracelet or something with "Lyra" on it, but she was sleeping with a man. I had to be dead careful.'

'A man?'

'Big fellow. She called him Septimus.'

'Gods!' Quistus whispered. 'She wasn't sleeping with him, Septimus is her brother.' The Senator looked more shocked than any man Viridorix had ever seen. 'They're alive. Septimus and Lyra lived.'

Viridorix looked pleased. 'Just a matter of the reward, then.'

Weary men carried buckets but they were half empty. Omba ran by Triton and the dry mouths of the sea monsters, only green slime left in the fountain pool. The men came back with empty buckets, shouting. They threw them down and ran away. The fire leapt the street.

She ran up the *Fortuna*'s stairs, knocking aside women and children, the wooden stairways a jumble of furniture, rubbish, people, shouting. The building quivered, heat stroking the walls.

Smoke flickered up the light-well from stuff they'd thrown down earlier and now couldn't reach, burning. She pulled the women by their hair. 'Get out.' She pushed them, kicking, her eyes streaming. 'Get your children out, go.'

No one on the fourth floor except thieves. No one at all on the fifth.

She climbed the ladder to the sixth floor, Vulpus's hut on the roof. He knelt at the end of the chain just as she'd left him, except that he looked terrified. He gave an awful grin. 'I knew it. I was right. You had to come back.'

'You lump of shit, why didn't you shout?' She broke the roof-beam, pulled the chain off the splintered ends. Above them the tiles slid away leaving a hole of dark sky, red smoke.

He rubbed his knees. 'Bet my life on you, didn't I?' He grinned.

'Doesn't mean anything. Get out of here!' She bundled the chain into his hands. 'Go. See you in Hades.' The stairs were burning on one side. She jumped a flight, slammed into the wall with spread hands, looked back. No Vulpus. The stairs collapsed, pulling easily from the wall, cheap builders. She ran down before she fell down.

He'd turned back, frightened of the fire. She'd known about that. Should have dragged him down with her.

She looked up from the corner. The *Fortuna* burned, every door and window pouring flame into the night. A few people milled in the street. They held their hands over their heads as if the sky fell. Someone threw an empty bucket. Omba stood by an abandoned cart piled with someone's life. A man ran up to it and ran away with a cushion.

A voice remarked calmly at her shoulder, 'You're hard to keep up with, Omba.' She recognized one of Vitellius's sons, Metellus, with the white streak in his hair. Behind him stood various other brothers armed to the teeth. 'We've a common enemy tonight.'

'Are you serious?'

He showed her the blood dulling his knife.

A tile crashed. Vulpus waved from the roof. He held something, he'd gone back for it – spice, whatever, he'd given his life for it.

He let it drop through the air.

Omba picked up her gold belt of tricks from the cobbles.

She'd worn it when he bought her, part of the deal. She looked up.

Their eyes met. Flames were coming up all around him. 'Hades, no,' she whispered. 'No, Vulpus, don't!' He'd jump rather than burn.

Omba leapt on to the cart. She held her arms wide.

The Senator collapsed in the doorway. Viridorix stood beside the body wondering what to do. Quistus was his only hope of a reward; Viridorix had nothing else, no back-up plan, no second best. He looked round, seeing how fast the fire came forward. 'Come on, sir, no time for sleeping now. Let's get you in the saddle. Hup.'

He lifted the unconscious man's hand, let it flop.

The horse nibbled grass between the stones. Viridorix pulled the reins over its head, kept hold. He got his arm under the Senator's shoulders. 'Bit of help now, Senator. Sit up. That's it. Heavier than it looks, your arse.'

'Heard that,' Quistus muttered. His legs moved. 'Help me.'

Viridorix grunted. The Senator pulled himself up by the horse's girth. Viridorix got his arm round one leg and lifted. The Senator straightened, swung his foot, got aboard. He slumped forward over the saddle with his arms hanging down. Viridorix took the reins, then stopped. He went back to the house, jammed his battered straw hat over his head, and closed the door carefully. You didn't want those ghosts running after you.

He led the horse by the reins, joining the stream of people along the Armilustri. The Ostian Gate was nearest. He'd never felt so frightened and helpless. The Senator looked like death. Viridorix was afraid he was dying. The Senator's face bumped against the horse's neck, swollen, red as a burning coal. There was a rapid clop of hooves as a mule came past. He paid attention because the mule was ridden by a woman the colour of night, wearing a gold belt. Her sweat shone like fire. She was holding a man in front of her, a lot smaller than she, hanging limp. She glanced at Viridorix.

'Hoi!' he called. She reined in. 'I saw you before,' he said. He could see she remembered him. He added, 'With him.' Omba lifted the Senator's face, startled.

'Is he wounded? Were you attacked?'

Viridorix said, 'I think he's dying.'

She grabbed the reins. 'Hold him tight. If he falls, I'll cut your ears off.' She remembered Viridorix all right. She pointed her dagger at the scarred, dangerous-looking thugs moving along the walls behind her, one with a white streak in his hair. 'And if I don't, they will.'

Viridorix gulped. He held on tight.

Zhao's horse cantered into night like a black wall. The experience was absolutely terrifying. Only Rome like a burning map gave any sense of direction. As the city shrank beneath the horizon she began to see more clearly, glimpsing the road angling darkly among dark hills, the marshes slightly darker. Manas ran behind, holding the horse's tail. Further back still was Stigmus, sword drawn for show. Faintly the moon's glow glimmered in the smoke, gleaming off the sea ahead, and she made out the Prince's cloak shimmering gold between her arms. As the smoke cleared she worried how bright the moonlit cloak looked. She heard him laughing, finding joy in adversity as she'd taught him, though she hadn't meant it this way. 'We're free!' he cried. 'Faster!'

'Hush,' she said, overwhelmed by the disaster. What a fool she'd been to leave the Prince in gold, a perfect target. Yet to dress him in anything else would demean him, tarnish his glory. Better to die honestly.

Best not to die at all. She trusted the horse to see better in the night than she. She heard hoof beats and one of the praetorians rode beside her. His small shield was gone and he had an arrow in his armour. He cursed in Latin, which she understood. She covered the Prince's ears.

The trooper rode ahead, swearing. Behind her she heard the people running, the rumble of a cart. They were taking turns to pull for their lives. What a wonderful house-family they were. A gold face leapt into the moonlight; the trooper came off his horse. Zhao shut her eyes.

She ran them both down.

'Zhao,' the Prince said after a while, 'you know you did that?'

Zhao said something for which a girl could lose her head. 'Be quiet please.'

Prince Zhang sat in silence, shocked.

*　　*　　*

The mule cantered, the Senator's horse trotted on the leading-reins, and Viridorix ran beside its belly, hanging on. He was terrified the Senator would slip and fall and Omba or the thugs would tear his ears off. It might be sensible to give up any hope of reward, quietly fall back, and hide in the dark until they were gone.

There was a noise like a handclap. Viridorix stared at the arrow sticking from the saddle, its gold shaft gleaming in the moonlight, black feathers fluttering. He ran faster.

The *trierarch* of the trireme *Pharsalia*, Captain Myron, was Greek but his vessel was Roman, part-owned by Tigellinus, so instead of a crew of highly-trained, highly-paid professionals, Myron had to make do with Roman scum, brutes accustomed to brutality. All 170 slaves rowed in chains, slept in chains, shat and vomited in chains, and died in chains. At first, as a Greek, he thought all this was rather beneath him. But he had to admit it was economical. A *trierarch* could make a good living.

He stood by the steering-oar high on the stern, a small, iron-faced, frowning man with a plump belly and carefully tonged hair. Unless you were rowing aboard a trireme, there wasn't much to do except eat and drink well and keep the scum hauling in time. His frown deepened because he didn't like being woken in the middle of the night by some messenger, even from Tigellinus, telling him to look sharp. Myron's frown meant trouble for anyone in his power – which, for a captain, meant anyone aboard his ship. 'How many?' he demanded. 'Some Prince, and how many you say?'

The messenger shrugged. 'To Antioch,' he called, and set off back to Nero's Antium.

Myron's frown intensified. He didn't like the fire behind the hills; trouble in Rome. He didn't like mooring instead of anchoring; the brutes caught the smell of women ashore and tried to break out. He didn't like a night departure, the old harbour was filthy with sandbanks. He didn't like rowing across half a sea to Antioch, ten days' hard hauling even with a good wind, double that into the teeth of an easterly. Most of all, he didn't like surprises. A surprise brought out the worst in him.

He heard hoof beats between the warehouses. 'Wake 'em up,' he ordered. Canes whacked on sleeping backs. The men woke silently, grumblers and swearers with their lips sewn together, just a hole for water and porridge. A woman and a boy wrapped in a gold cloak rode along the dock. The biggest man he'd seen ran behind the horse.

'Poseidon's prick!' Myron said. 'A woman!' No one took a woman on a ship. His eyes widened as carts, pushcarts, handcarts appeared, pushed by more women as well as men. They swarmed aboard up the ropes as easily as gangways and started chucking stuff aboard too. The woman with the boy met him eye to eye on the quarterdeck. 'My name is Ban Zhao. The Prince requires a cabin to himself.'

'You're not having my cabin,' Myron spluttered. 'You're not coming on my ship.' Mean-looking foreigners with swords jumped aboard. He didn't like the look of them and neither did his free sailors, but the newcomers made nasty faces and there was a flurry of drawn weapons. The sailors shrugged and checked the rigging. A couple of bowmen deployed in the bow and stern. An old man with a spear walked around Myron, scowling. A girl the size of a child stood on tiptoe, her face a grinning mask, mourning rags whipping in the wind, as if death itself came aboard. On the dock a praetorian cantered on horseback, blade in hand, his cloak the colour of veins' blood by moonlight. 'Captain! Prepare to sail. No delay. Your life depends on it.'

'I'm not sailing with a woman,' Myron said. 'No women.'

'That's Brumus, a centurion,' said Zhao.

'He's Poseidon's chief ball-polisher for all I care,' Myron said. 'Get your women off my ship, and get yourself off.' He stared at the dock as a dark woman came riding a mule, someone hanging on her with an arrow through his leg. Behind them a boy ran beside a horse, steadying a man slumped over the saddle. The boy's strength was almost gone. The horse halted and the man slipped down against the boy, then fell all the way. 'I'm sorry,' the boy cried. He tried to pick the man up.

'That does it,' Myron said. 'Stop. Stop, all of you. I'm in charge. I'm Captain Myron and I'm in charge, do you hear me? Exactly what is going on here?'

Omba heard their bare feet rattling and jumping over the tiles of the warehouse roofs, closer. Gold Heads. She shoved Vulpus against the ship; willing hands lifted him. She tossed one of her daggers to Viridorix. 'Cut the bow rope.'

'What?'

'The rope at the front. Cut it.' He scampered. He was a fast boy, quick on the uptake. She shouted at the servants chucking embroideries aboard, pointing at Quistus lying in a heap. They grabbed him by his clothes and sandals, running crabwise. A bowman jumped down to cover their retreat. The crossbow mechanism clacked loudly, shooting a heavy bolt. A shout came from the dark, defiance, pain. 'Don't shoot!' Stigmus ran from the shadows where he'd been hiding. He scrambled aboard. Calmly the bowman fitted another bolt and wound the mechanism.

'Get aboard,' Omba said. Brumus charged past in a clatter of hooves, sword swinging. She cut the stern rope. The bowman fired coolly into the Gold Heads leaping on Brumus. The Roman went down. He came up fighting. There was a sound of men running between the warehouses then a roar of deep voices as Metellus and his brothers charged the throng.

Omba grabbed the servants dragging Quistus, heaving them aboard. The wind was moving the ship out already. The stern gangway fell with a splash. Viridorix swung against the ship's bow, dangling from the rope he'd cut. His hat dropped off. Someone pulled him up and tousled his hair. The bowman shouldered his weapon neatly. He ran along the forrard gang-plank, leaping aboard at the last moment as it fell into the black waters.

The wind blew. The men fighting on the dock dwindled to shadows. No one saw Brumus. The sounds of battle faded away, leaving only the splash of waves rocking the ship.

Stigmus turned to the captain. 'You'll put me ashore at the first opportunity. That's an order.' But he thought, When I go back to Nero, I'll be killed.

Omba glowered at the drummer who sat cross-legged above the rowers, a hollow log propped between his trembling knees. 'You.' She jabbed her dagger under his chin a couple of times. He grinned like a monkey and took up the rhythm. The oars creaked, driving the ship forward.

A hand grabbed her shoulder. 'Poseidon's balls, who do you think you are? I am Captain Myron, and—' She seized him by the armpits and threw him over the side.

Zhao leant over the rail. The water looked dirty.

'Omba,' the Prince called quietly. He knelt by Quistus.

Yunyazi stroked his little dog. 'Careful. Don't touch him.'

Quistus's eyes were open, the whites showing. Someone brought a lamp. His face was a spotty, suppurating rash. 'No,' Omba whispered.

'He's dying. *Tianhua*,' Yunyazi said. 'His life is held in the hands of the gods.'

'Gods?' Chong scoffed. 'What gods?'

Quistus's lips split softly as he gasped for air. 'Not Antioch. Pelusium. Arsinoe.' His back arched in agony. He gasped, 'Hippalos. *Hippalos*.'

IV

Lost Souls

They were alive. He heard their laughter from the *therma*. He knew what would happen. (He woke screaming.)

The corridor stretched as he ran. Their laughter turned to shrieks. The door decorated with dolphins slammed shut in his face. Locked from the inside. Barred with iron. (He woke screaming.)

He beat his fists on the heavy mahogany panels. Dark drops of blood spattered mother-of-pearl. One by one their shrieks stopped. He couldn't open the door. He never could. (He woke screaming.)

There was a brilliant flash of light from above, brighter than the sun. A voice cried, '*Quistus. Awake!*'

The door swung slowly open.

He felt King Gondophares' coin in his hand.

'*Where?*' He barely recognized the thinned, pained voice as his own. '*Where am I?*'

'Not the Middle Sea—'
'That's for certain.'

'Not Antioch—'

'Nowhere near there.'

'You'll never guess. Not the *Sinus Arabicus*—'

'The Red Sea—'

'Far behind us. You were delirious. Then you slept like a dead man.'

Uncomfortable silence.

'For more than a week. We followed orders—'

'It wasn't easy—'

'Well, none of us had heard of Pelusium—'

'Except Omba—'

'I'd heard of it, actually. I just wasn't quite sure where it was.'

'Shut up, Stigmus.'

'I'll have you know Stigmus is an important man.'

'Shut up, Vulpus.'

'Anyway, the port of Pelusium. At the mouth of the Nile—'

'One of the mouths—'

'The Gold Heads never heard of it. They're in Antioch by now. With the Roman army. Poor Gold Heads!'

'A thousand miles away!'

'More—'

'If they survived.'

'Golden Turtle would have brought his dead ones back to life.'

More uncomfortable silence.

'But even *she*'d never heard of Arsinoe—'

'And *everyone* had no idea at all where Hippalos was—'

'Except one old man on the Arsinoe waterfront.'

'Come to that later.'

'Omba was the captain of our trireme. She promised the men on the oars—'

'When we reach Pelusium, you shall all have your freedom!'

'But not until. So—'

'You've got to row faster than you've ever rowed in your lives—'

'And they did! Eight days, Ostia to Pelusium!'

'So I freed them at Pelusium, as she'd promised,' came Zhang's voice, 'and I gave them the ship too.'

'No use to us.' Viridorix. Bad Greek. They'd been teaching him Greek. Time *had* passed.

'Everyone at Pelusium knew where Arsinoe was,' Omba said.

'Across the desert—'

'By sailing boat.'

'Up the Nile—'

'The Pelusius, one of the mouths of the Nile.'

'You already told him that. Even if the Gold Heads *had* followed us by magic to Pelusium, we'd have given them the slip again.'

'Then half a day in a cart to the canal—'

'A flat-bottomed boat pulled by camels—'

'Real live camels!' Viridorix's voice shone. He'd never seen them before.

'And the royal canal comes past the lakes—'

'To the *Sinus Arabicus* at Arsinoe.'

'Where we asked the old man. And he said—'

'"Do you mean Hippalos? Or *Hippalos*?"'

'Either will do!'

'"The man or the ship?"'

'Both!'

'So here we are on Captain Hippalos's ship, *Hippalos*.'

'Good old Captain Hippalos.'

'Sailing for a week—'

'Bad winds this year, kept him ashore. Easterlies. For months—'

'He usually sails east in *Aprilis* or *Junius*—'

'His bad luck, our good fortune.'

'So here we are. The ocean—'

'*Indicum Mare*.' The two boys spoke reverently. 'The Indian Sea.'

They helped him sit up, turning him slowly, and Quistus saw a sight so rare and vast that no words described its emptiness and terror, a blue ocean stretching from horizon to horizon without sight or sign of land, featureless, unmoving, infinite.

Captain Hippalos of *Hippalos*, an ally of Quistus since their Judean spying days, once Greek but nowadays turbaned and with a gown of parti-coloured Indian wool that covered his feet, was a brave and greedy man. He was also, as Quistus had remembered, a genius.

Hippalos's genius was simply for seeing the obvious. He kept his eyes open. From watching flights of migrating birds he'd stumbled across the greatest (and best-kept) trading secret in the world: that in early summer steady winds will blow any Egyptian ship that raises a sail straight to India, and in November, after a sufficient calm for unloading and loading, blow her home again. The merchants of Sind and Peshawar had guarded this secret for centuries. It made his fortune.

Once in India, Hippalos saw from the sun and stars that the coast obviously runs not from west to east – as Romans believed from the deceiving tongues of Sind and Peshawar – but north to south. No need for the long, intricate and expensive journey hugging the shores of Arabia and Persia, dodging rocks and pirates. Hippalos simply sailed straight across the safe, deep ocean until he saw the sun rising over India, and turned left. He made his second fortune.

To anyone used to shallow Roman seas and their variable winds, *Hippalos* was an extraordinary-looking vessel, stumpy, wide and too tall, at least until fully laden. No oars or oarsmen – a lack to bring out any shore-hugging, lee-fearing Roman in a cold sweat – made even more room for cargo. Below decks, *Hippalos* was packed with two hundred tons – four hundred cart-loads, a thousand camel-backs – of Egyptian linen, topaz, coral, glass and more. She was a Silk Road in herself. At year's end she'd sail the trade winds home laden deep with sugar, frankincense, myrrh, cotton, silks, indigo dye wrapped in rhinoceros skin, even cinnamon. Not for nothing (Captain Hippalos knew better than anyone) was the Spice Road called the Subtle Road. With five hundred million a year in Roman gold to play for, the overland route blocked and prices touching the sky, new ways quickly and quietly sprang around any difficulty. Not all were roads. He meant to make his third fortune on this voyage.

A greedy man on his third fortune is even greedier for his fourth. The sudden arrival on the dockside of thirty exotic *Qin* looking anxiously over their shoulders, scared but somehow also scary, concerned him; the sight of his old friend at death's door worried him; Omba's talk reassured him; An's Kuping-stamped silver ingot convinced him. Welcome aboard.

'Close your eyes.' Omba held his shoulders, a water ladle to his lips. Quistus sipped. He sighed and she laid him back. The shadow of the sail moved across his eyelids.

'What happened, Omba?'

'Master, there's something you should know first.'

He mustered his strength. 'Spit it out.'

'You died.'

'Yes, you did!' Viridorix called.

Somebody hushed him.

'We saw you die,' Zhang said. 'You didn't move.'

After a while Quistus said, 'Am I dead?'

'You're alive, Master.'

'Then how can I have been dead? I don't remember it.'

'Yunyazi brought you back to life.'

After a long while Quistus said, 'How do I know?'

'Good point!' Chong exclaimed. 'Appearances must be questioned – life is made of shadows—'

'You died in the storm,' Viridorix said. Zhang nodded. 'Where the sea narrows and the great ocean begins. The deepest hour of the night, *ban ye*, when people die.'

'And you died.'

'Yunyazi lit candles in the bottom of the boat. The sea dripped everywhere. We could hardly hang on. Yunyazi chanted the *Cantong qi* and the *Jinbi jin* and the flames went up—'

Even Zhao chipped in. 'The spells he put you through before, Quistus, they were nothing.' (He heard An hiss, 'Silence, traitor.' Zhao flinched as if struck.) But nothing stopped the cheerful voices of the boys.

'Lightning flashed! Thunder rolled, a signal from the gods.'

'And you lived! It was awful. You sat up with a scream.'

'Mind you, you'd been doing a lot of screaming.'

'Opium.'

'Dreams.'

'Nightmares.'

'Depression,' came Yunyazi's voice, 'is a distressing feature of the disease.'

Quistus's mind was racing, but he was too tired to hang on to his thoughts. 'Signal,' he said. 'It was a signal.'

'Yunyazi.'

'You wished to speak, Roman?' The magician stroked the little dog's ears.

'Thank you for saving my life. Again.' Fu gave a yap, taking credit. Quistus murmured, 'You said I was dying of *tianhua*. I heard you say it.'

'Indeed.' Yunyazi sat cross-legged. 'And you did die.'

'So the boys keep telling me.' Zhang and Viridorix fished from the stern, An fussing between them, trying to keep them apart. No sign of Zhao on deck; in disgrace apparently. 'I'm lying here with nothing to do except think. Yunyazi, how does a person catch *tianhua*?'

'From someone who already has it, or who knew someone who has it.'

'Wild Swan died of *tianhua*.'

'Indeed.'

'Yet you brought me back from death, not her.'

'Her time had come. Yours has not.'

'How do you know?'

'You have work to do. Unfinished work.'

'Which is?'

'You told me once that there is a murderer *and* a traitor. I agree. Yet the murderer cannot murder and the traitor cannot betray. It is a very *Qin* insight, Roman. You are a little like us,' Yunyazi said modestly.

Quistus tried to think clearly. 'I saw Wild Swan for the first time in the moment of her death. Little Pelican nursed her, but she didn't catch *tianhua*. Others were there, but they didn't catch it. Why me?'

'You think you caught the disease by accident, Roman? Someone tried to murder you.'

'Why?'

'Obviously, to stop your investigation exposing them. It's long been known that pus weeping from an infected person's skin transfers the disease, especially to a small cut or abrasion. Easily done without the victim's knowledge. A traditional method of murder in *Qin*, regrettably. The disease remains invisible for some days, giving the murderer time to cover their tracks, even to shine with innocence.'

'And the murderer is not infected?'

'Perhaps clothing is secretly touched to the sufferer, then carefully given as a gift to the victim.' He gave an oblique look. 'Your clothing – burnt and thrown overboard, not this gown you now wear – was given you by Zhao, was it not?'

'Yes, but . . . Zhao's been kind to me. So has Little Pelican. Chong has helped me, even An has not opposed me, and Manas and the others—' Quistus's mind went round and round. He lay back exhausted. 'Why were Wild Swan's dying words *Zhao*? And she tried desperately to touch her, or reach her.'

'I don't know. They'd known each other for several years, trusted each other through adversity, but they were not close friends. Dancers stick to their own clique, and Zhao's prickly.'

'I need to speak to her.'

'Very well.'

Quistus called the magician back. 'Tell me, why does Omba ask me to close my eyes when she gives me water?'

'Ah,' Yunyazi said, and went.

Zhao lifted the hem of her long, shiny gown, showing her toes, moving gracefully across the waist of the *Hippalos*. Her shadow swung from side to side with the heaving, creaking, rolling of the ship. Her hair was pinned, her eyelashes perfectly blacked, quite at home. She waited patiently where Quistus lay on the straw mat by the rail. His eyes flickered, waking. She placed her fist in her hand and bowed.

'Sit, Zhao. You look well.'

It was wrong for her to sit beside him; she knelt. 'You're recovering your strength, Quistus.'

'Thanks to your care.'

'And Little Pelican's, too. And the other girls'.' She pointed to them busily at work in the bow, sewing, repairing, talking, never still. 'Fen, Genji, Lien, all cleaned you—'

'And you? Did you?'

'Are you embarrassed? I'm no different from them.'

He switched to Latin. 'I think you *are* different, Zhao. Thank you for the gift of clothing at the Villa Paria. I liked the colour.'

She said quickly, in Latin, 'They were my own clothes. I selected them with my own hands. No one else touched them.'

'So you alone are to blame for what happened to me?'

'They were clean. If they were infected, from Wild Swan presumably, I don't know how it was done. They were never out of my sight.'

'Why did Wild Swan cry *Zhao* as she died?'

'I don't know. We respected each other. Perhaps the opium had worn off. She was in despair. You know about despair, don't you, Quistus? I heard your nightmares. Wild Swan didn't know what she was doing or saying.'

'She tried to grab you. Perhaps she was trying to warn us.'

'She was *dying*, Quistus. Who knows what was going through her mind. I know Yunyazi's been speaking, spreading poison. An and Chong say the same thing. As usual,' she said bitterly, 'they all leap to find me guilty.'

'They're envious of you.'

'They're men! How may they be envious of a woman, pray?'

'Because you're more intelligent.' He added, 'And more beautiful.'

Her cheeks couldn't blush beneath the thick white powder. She looked away. 'I'm sure you're mistaken.'

'Well, more beautiful, anyway.'

She lowered her voice to a fierce whisper. 'You just say so because you're thinking those thoughts, because you haven't had a woman for weeks. You're like a Chinese man.'

'You're wrong, Zhao. I haven't been with a woman since my wife died more than four years ago.'

She stared away from him, showing the back of her head. She hadn't known he had a wife.

'I'm still married,' Quistus said. 'I can't help it. Zhao.' He reached up with an effort, touching her shoulder. 'Let me see your eyes. I have to ask you a question.'

She turned with hurt eyes.

He said, 'Prince Zhang is still protecting you, isn't he?'

'He still believes in my innocence. An still does not. Chong wavers. Perhaps those two are the guilty ones. They'd dropped back in the forest with the money before Chen attacked, their lives were in no danger, they didn't fight at Falling Waters Bridge—'

He interrupted her tirade. 'If Prince Zhang gave you an order, Zhao, would you obey?'

'How could I not obey?'

'If he told you to kill yourself, would you?'

She stared, then stated the obvious. 'Yes.'

'If he told you to thrust a knife into your heart, would you do it?'

'Yes.'

'If Prince Zhang told you to kill *him*, would you?'

'Why are you asking this?' She looked around, then remembered they were speaking Latin. The women laughed and chattered in the bow, carefree, men repaired ropes, trailed lines for fish, searched out the sail's cool shadow, repaired their weapons, and Captain Hippalos, his hands behind his back, swaying with his ship, yawned, belched, and sniffed the wind.

She whispered, 'I would kill him if he ordered me.'

'You'd kill Zhang.'

'Yes. To obey is my legal duty, to disobey unthinkable.' She trembled, cold in the tropical heat. 'Quistus, don't—'

'If the Emperor himself ordered his son to die?'

'Then Zhang would die obeying his father.'

'But if the Emperor ordered *you* to kill Zhang?'

Zhao wept. She shook her head, trying to hide emotion. 'You make me hate you. You can't ask me this.' Her face smudged, white and black. She couldn't think how to clean herself, her hands were worse. The women in the bow noticed her distress and fell silent.

'Zhao,' Quistus said. 'I need to understand.'

'No! I would *not* obey the Emperor. That command would be murder, it could not be given. The Son of Heaven *is* the law. If he breaks the law he breaks himself. Heaven would withdraw its mandate, its blessing, from his rule, and his house would fall.'

'Thank you, Zhao,' Quistus said gently. 'I'm sorry I hurt you. I had to know if you were lying.'

'Could I lie to you?' she said, so that he almost missed it.

Genji shuffled to Zhao and whispered, asking if she was all right. Zhao nodded. Genji, flashing Quistus the briefest look of accusation, shuffled obediently backwards.

'You shouldn't let her dare look at you like that.' Zhao dabbed her eyes with her wrists. 'She was rude. I'll punish her.'

'Until I understand you all,' Quistus murmured, 'I'll never find the murderer. Please don't punish Genji.'

Zhao stood. He'd put her through as much as he'd intended. Black streaks trickled from her eyes down her white face. The black had mingled with vermilion from her lips, then she'd succeeded in wiping the mess over her cheeks and nose. Nothing hidden. She looked naked. She was real. She bowed for permission to go.

'No,' Quistus said. 'I want you to give me a drink of water.'

Zhao looked round. Omba wasn't on deck, Yunyazi was deep in conversation with Hippalos. There was no one to tell her what to do.

She went to the barrel, dipped the ladle, and returned.

She held it to his lips. Quistus stared at his reflection in the water.

Days passed, just the same. The wind blew the sail and the sail pushed the ship, and the ship lifted and fell and trailed foam over the long, slow waves, yet never moved. Every day they were at the exact centre of the ocean, the horizon coming no closer, falling no farther behind. The sun rose on the bow and set on the stern, where the boys fished with long lines. Zhang, initiated into the mysteries of bait, was nearly as expert and loudly opinionated about hooks, maggots and mackerel guts as Viridorix.

Sunset gong. The women, laughing busily, ran from the bow as one and carried Quistus below. Dawn gong and they returned him to deck, laid him beneath the awning, fed him, made sure he was comfortable, and laughed among themselves. From their jokes he picked up a few words of Chinese. One day he asked Genji, 'Why Zhao not help?' Genji pretended not to hear. He asked the same question at sunset, and again at dawn. 'Why not?' Until she answered.

Polite, busy shrug, moving away. 'Men say not, that all.'

'She say so too? Because I look different now, Genji? She hate look?'

'No.' She glanced him in the eye for the briefest moment. 'Men no like Zhao. She no like men. All men, not just you.'

In Genji's world of the house-family An and Chong were men, the Prince too awesome to mention, and Stigmus and Vulpus beneath notice, not men at all, only foreigners. 'Me?' Quistus smiled. 'Me foreigner too?'

'You speak *Qin* a little. We try make you *Qin*. You man, will be. Rule number one, men not smile. Not look good. Lose face.'

He laughed. He was careful to learn more Chinese words, and all their names.

Where they laid him in the waist was the centre of the ship. From here Quistus could watch and see everything. His mind was busy. He squeezed rope in his hands, regaining strength.

An and Chong wore square sun hats. They stared from the stern, worried. Quistus asked Captain Hippalos to send a lookout up the mast. No black ships, gold sails; nothing at all. Quistus wondered if General Corbulo still waited with his army in Antioch. By now the consternation of Nero and

Corbulo must be a sight to see; he and the Prince had disappeared into thin air.

Quistus grinned to himself.

Again An shooed Viridorix away from the Prince when he thought no one was looking. He didn't like him with Zhang. Quistus called the boys over and they showed off their catch, fishes stranger than any seen before. He nodded, watching them side by side, similar in height and weight. 'Viridorix.' Thoughtfully he pulled Viridorix's hair into a topknot.

'What?'

'I was just thinking—' Quistus changed the subject. 'Fish for supper tonight.'

'I caught more than him,' Zhang said.

'Never did!'

'Look, this one's all scarred, like—' Zhang covered his mouth.

'Like him,' Viridorix said. 'What? I've seen worse.'

Quistus had been able to take a few steps, sponging himself in seawater, his weakened body pocked and scarred where the scabs had peeled. He'd hardly recognized his face. 'You mean it's an improvement on what I looked like before, right, Viridorix?'

'That's the spirit, Senator,' Viridorix said. 'Omba let me keep my ears although I dropped you. She said if she cut them off I'd be even uglier than you.'

Stars swayed above the ship. Quistus, unable to sleep, joined the three men by the lamp on the stern. Still no sign that they were followed. Yunyazi crouched, busy.

'Thanks to Yunyazi's Spell of Wayfinding, old friend, we've made very good time.' Captain Hippalos helped Quistus the last few paces. The captain and magician had obviously been adjusting something at the feet of the Egyptian at the steering-oar. 'I've followed a course directly for our destination.'

Fu's pink tongue licked leftovers from the magician's beard. 'Spell of Wayfinding?' Quistus queried.

'Heaven buries wonders to be found, as I told you.' Yunyazi revealed a basket protecting a wooden contraption from the wind. Inside, from a stick carefully marked with spells hung a stone shaped like an arrowhead, balanced by a fine thread around its middle. It swung with the motion of the ship, yet always pointed in the same direction. The Egyptian glanced and gave a tug on the steering-oar.

Yunyazi set it spinning. 'An iron stone of the north never forgets its way home.' He passed his hand over the spinning stone. Fu barked. The stone slowed, steadying, again pointing over the port bow.

Quistus said, 'North? How do you know?'

Yunyazi nodded at the North Star, Polaris. 'Even in cloud or fog, the spell-stone never forgets.' He turned as if absent-minded. 'Captain, what did you say our destination was, exactly?'

'I didn't,' Captain Hippalos said smoothly. 'Trade secret.'

'The same place Hippalos goes every year, of course,' Quistus said. 'Barbarikon.'

Sunset gong. Tonight was the ship's feast night, a small fire carefully lit in a brazier under the copper cauldron. To the delight of the Chinese, Hippalos offered a small quantity of a delicacy new to Rome, *oryza* – rice. Fish, chicken from the coop, spices and a little seawater for seasoning were quickly added. Fen, the beaming cook, threw in a paste of flour and water she'd dried in strips in the sun, *miantiao* – noodles. Stigmus made a face. 'That's paste, *pasta*, not honest Roman fare.' Quistus noticed he ate as hungrily as everyone else. Knives and plates were clumsy with this new sort of food; the *Qin* used their fingers and small sticks.

Stigmus, after a little wine, claimed the Emperor had ordered him to keep a close eye on Quistus. 'I'm the Emperor's eyes and ears here. You'd better hope I give you a good report, Quistus.' Stigmus, after more wine, wondered if he could get away with claiming to still be Prefect of Praetorians. Who would know? Quistus had looked ill during Nero's mock sea battle; maybe he hadn't heard, or taken in, its appalling sequel. Stigmus started to feel a lot more cheerful.

Vulpus used his elbows to clear a place beside Omba. The ship's carpenter had sawn the fetter from his neck and Vulpus was already the hero of the fire at the *Fortuna*. 'I ran back into the flames to get something precious my poor sweet had lost.' He pointed at the heavy belt she wore. 'There, my gift to her, along with her freedom.' Omba ignored him. 'I had to jump for my life. She's worth every penny.'

'I caught you, you shit,' Omba said. 'I had bruises for a week. If that cart hadn't collapsed you'd be dead.'

'I took an arrow through here for her.' Vulpus showed his thigh, a small round scar on each side. Omba got up and sat by Manas. No one else liked sitting with the giant bodyguard, he ate off the plates beside him as well as his own. He reached to help himself from Chong's rice and Omba took a piece of fish from Manas's plate and swallowed it. Manas scratched his head.

Quistus looked back to where Zhang ate alone in the stern cabin. He persuaded An to let Viridorix join the Prince. 'He's Roman, An. That means you can trust him, remember?'

'It's important the Prince is not contaminated, debased by human contact. Especially of his own age.'

'It's important that he stays alive,' Quistus said, adding, 'they're just children.'

'No,' An said smoothly, 'the Prince is not a child. He's the Prince.' But he'd relented. 'Your urchin may taste the Prince's food for poison.'

'Poison?' someone said. 'Here?'

Omba called, 'Is the traitor still among us?'

Somebody whispered, 'What of the murderer?'

There was a deep silence. The rigging creaked, foam hissed along the hull, but they were so used to these sounds that they no longer heard them. An breathed out through his nose, looking at Zhao.

'I'm sure of it,' Quistus said.

'So am I. There's something you don't know,' Omba said. 'It's been preying on my mind. See, I went back into the Villa Paria to escape Gold Heads. Somebody had left a big scrawled message telling them where we were going.' She added, 'You didn't mention the change of plan to Pelusium until we were aboard the trireme. But everyone knew we were going to Ostia, you shouted it from horseback in the entrance hall, remember?'

'If you say so.'

'Everyone heard. Well, someone going out wrote *OZTIO* on one of the door pillars. Easy. Fingers dipped in lamp-black.'

'Oztio, not Ostia?'

'Exactly. Someone who'd heard the name for the first time and got it a bit wrong. Or maybe they just couldn't spell.'

'The Chinese don't write Roman letters,' Quistus said.

Zhao cleared her throat. 'Actually, I do.'

'You, again!' said An.

'Yes. Cerberus taught me.'

Quistus asked, 'Were you last out of the house?'

Zhao shook her head. 'I came with the Prince. Many others followed.'

'It's not safe for her to live,' An said. 'How much longer must we ignore a guilt that parades itself so insolently in front of our eyes?'

'I'm sorry, Zhao.' Chong was distressed. 'Perhaps An's right. Just to be on the safe side.'

She burst out, 'Then ask the Prince to order me to die.'

'Wait a moment.' Quistus asked Captain Hippalos for some old bills of loading. He turned one over and handed the blank side to Zhao. 'You know what to do.' She touched a finger to the bottom of the cauldron and quickly wrote 'Ostia'.

'Doesn't prove anything,' An said. Zhang wasn't here to protect her. 'Trying to prove people guilty is useless; you just *know* they are.'

'Now you, An,' Quistus said.

'But I was one of the first out!' An complained. Quistus pushed a piece of paper into his lap and nodded at the cauldron. An blacked his fingertip. He drew a line.

'Not Chinese,' Quistus said. 'Roman.'

'I – I can't.'

'Then you don't know as much as Zhao,' Quistus said. 'Not for the first time, An.' He pushed the paper at Chong, who shook his head helplessly.

Quistus turned to Yunyazi.

'I refuse,' the magician said snootily.

'One of the last out,' Omba called.

'I can write *Ostia* perfectly,' Yunyazi sniffed. 'I know everything. I already knew we were going to Pelusium. Had I been the traitor I would have written *that* and betrayed Quistus's little trick from the start. Therefore I am innocent.'

Quistus looked interested. 'I didn't decide on Pelusium until I met Viridorix at my house. I'd intended to go to Antioch, let things happen Nero's way. You know everything, do you? Then you know what Viridorix gave me that changed my mind.'

Everyone looked at Yunyazi. Yunyazi shrugged. 'Yes.'

'Do tell.'

Yunyazi stroked Fu. 'I killed this little dog,' he said, 'and raised him from the dead.'

'I appreciate these tricks,' Quistus said, '*if* they really happen, but I need to know—'

'A silver coin with Greek writing. Let me think. "King Gondophares, Saviour".' Yunyazi pulled his beard thoughtfully. 'On the reverse, "Barbarikon".'

'Barbarikon?' Captain Hippalos gave Quistus a sharp look. 'What a coincidence.'

Quistus shivered at the magician's words. He said to Yunyazi, 'You saw the coin when I was unconscious.'

'I did not.'

'Viridorix told you.'

'He did not.'

'Thank you, Yunyazi. You're as helpful as usual.' Quistus asked Omba, 'Who came next?'

She tried to remember. 'It was Stigmus – no, there was a handcart. Little Pelican got aboard.'

Quistus handed the paper to Little Pelican. The dancer sooted her finger then started to cry. Zhao said, 'How could a dancing girl like her possibly know Roman letters?'

Quistus took the paper back. He gave it to Stigmus. 'Your turn. Just for the record.'

'You think *I*—' Stigmus sighed helplessly as Omba looked mean. 'This is ridiculous. Very well.' He scribbled *Oztia*, then looked embarrassed. 'Oh. It's a simple mistake to make.'

Quistus tapped the paper. 'Your name.'

Stigmus shook. He scribbled his name, *Stigmuz*. 'Look, it's your fault, Quistus. You made me nervous.'

Omba said, 'I wish it *was* Stigmus, but it could have been anyone. The lamps had gone out by that time. No one saw.'

Quistus sighed. He threw the papers overboard. 'Perhaps the dog wrote it.'

'So, my friend,' Captain Hippalos said, bracing himself on the stern rail against the sway of the ship. 'Still searching.'

Quistus sniffed the wind blowing from the sunset. 'Perhaps.'

'Have you told these people?'

'No.'

'Not even Zhao?'

'Why should I?'

'When are you going to tell them the truth? You decided against Antioch because of Lyra, chose Barbarikon because of her. All because of a coin stolen by an urchin, that may mean nothing.'

'Actually, I decided against Antioch the moment I heard Nero's plan.'

'The obvious route.'

'Too obvious. The Parthian desert, Corbulo's legions sweltering in heavy armour, a supply train trailing dust to the sky, five miles a day, Gold Heads behind us, Huns ahead. The same place Crassus came to grief. And then how much further to *Qin*? An army would never make it. I wanted nothing to do with Corbulo. He's my diversion.'

'Barbarikon. The back door. The secret way.'

Quistus shrugged.

Hippalos, too, sniffed the wind. He ordered the sail shortened. 'The coin means nothing. It tells you nothing of where Lyra *is*, my friend; only where she *was*.'

'She's been to Barbarikon once so she may return. The coin was important to her. In Lugdunum she still carried it in her clothes although Barbarikon was thousands of miles away. And she rode away east.'

Hippalos turned the coin over. 'All that hope, because of this.' He handed it back, hanging on against a sudden roll of the ship. 'What of the boy, Prince Zhang? Will you betray him for Lyra? Will you give *him* up, Quistus? Or will it be her?' He shook his head. 'A man who serves two masters is assured of an interesting life.'

'I can't help Zhang. I've done all I can for him.'

'He's thousands of miles from home. His eyes shine when he sees you. He wants to show you his latest catch, his new design of fish hook, he wants your approval. You think a boy like that knows his father? Probably meets him once a year.' The captain handed the coin back. 'Perhaps something in you died after all.'

The trireme was rolling heavily, drifting off the Nile, when the fishermen found her. Adrift for a week or more, they guessed. Weed clung to her like long green hair beneath the sea. The oars dangled, clattering, rowed by the waves. Her sail twisted in the wind, torn, throwing out ropes like tentacles, then again fell still. No one at the steering-oar, the drum silent. The father cupped his hands and shouted.

No answer.

He spat out a fish scale. 'You,' he ordered his sons. 'There's money in it.'

They shook their heads, afraid. 'Cowards,' he said. 'I'll tell your mother.'

He turned the little boat into the shadow under *Pharsalia*'s stern. The youngest boy looked sick. He said he smelt something rotten. The father grinned, showing he wasn't afraid. 'What can smell better than rotten fish?' He smacked the boy's head to show he was stupid. 'Maybe her anchor dragged. No one aboard. This is the best day of our lives.' He threw a rope up, but no one caught it. He heard a whirring sound like a song humming under someone's breath and shook his head, not recognizing the tune.

His eldest son called, 'If her anchor dragged, why's it stowed on the bow?'

He looked back, giving his useless boys once last chance, then scrambled up the side. He swung his leg over the rail. And stopped in mid-air. That was what it felt like.

They'd been freed from their chains, every one of them, strong men going as far as he could see into the darkness at the bottom of the ship, every one of them free. They'd stayed at their oars. He saw them with dislocated shoulders, torn, bruised muscles, the skin hanging off their hands. They'd rowed for their lives. Not fast enough.

Their faces, he would never forget.

The smell wasn't rotten, not yet. It was blood, blood everywhere. The song was flies.

He threw up the way he'd come, and jumped.

Sleepless, Quistus thought about Hippalos's hard words. If he met Lyra would he know the woman she'd become, changed as she'd be by her experiences, a new woman, no longer a child? He'd know her. He'd known her, instantly, from the one glimpse he'd had of her. He'd know his own flesh however changed Lyra was. He could no more turn his back on her than he could turn his back on himself, lose her any more than he could lose himself. He'd tried already, in Luca's tavern, and failed.

He stared at the dark. *Ban ye*, the hour people died. The ship heaved and rocked. He heard the wind wail, spattering noisy rain. He waited until dawn, then went aft to the stern cabin. Manas catnapped at the door, *sica* in hand. His eyes flashed instantly. He checked the Prince would receive Quistus, put his hand on Quistus's shoulder for a minute while the Prince made ready, then pushed him in.

Zhang sat by the opened shutter, watching grey seas pile up behind the ship. Just when it seemed she'd be overwhelmed, the stern rose and the sea passed harmlessly underneath. 'I know why you've come, Quistus.' Zhang wore his gold cloak. He didn't look round. His voice was solemn, deeper than when he played at fishing with Viridorix. The cloak by itself turned him from a boy into a young man, a Prince. 'I know it looks bad for Zhao. The gift of infected clothing. But still—'

Quistus sat at the table. Viridorix slept in the bunk, his head turned away.

'If she was guilty,' Quistus said, 'what would you do?'

'Nothing. Accept my fate. Everything would be worthless. I'd die.'

'I thought so.'

Zhang turned. A wave rose up behind him, almost filling the window, foaming, then slid beneath. The ship's timbers groaned and they both hung on to the table. 'Captain Hippalos told me your secret, Quistus. Your children. That's a very bad secret.'

'Yes, it is.'

'Viridorix said there was something worse, too. Every Roman knows it, but not I.'

'Some people believe I killed them.'

'A murderer to investigate a murder.' Zhang looked interested. 'Did you? *Could* you?'

'I don't know. I can't even imagine what happened.'

'Zhao, too, has a secret. She has two young children from her marriage. Did she tell you? I thought not. Twins. About three years old.'

Quistus asked immediately, 'Are they hostages? That explains—'

'No, you see, they're in the care of the Emperor. Safe in Loyang.' Zhang made a small, sad gesture. 'But, like your own children, almost limitlessly absent. They are her heart, Quistus. Yet here she is, with me. That's how I know she's innocent.'

'Does An know about—'

'No more than he knows your secret, and I won't tell him, or anyone else. Children are their parents' weakest point. That's why the Emperor was attacked through me. Zhao knows this.'

'Is that why she never mentioned them to me?'

Zhang scratched his chin, where the first fine hairs of manhood straggled. 'Zhao is a little like a mirror of you, isn't she?'

Quistus thought.

The Prince said, 'Zhao is loyal to me even though it takes her a world away from her own flesh and blood, from everyone she loves. I need the same loyalty from you. You may not desert me, Quistus.'

'Hippalos talks too much.'

'You do not have my permission to leave.'

Quistus sat, angrily, without asking permission. 'I'll tell you what I know. The rest—'

'*Know* isn't enough without loyalty. You've sworn no oath to me, it was enough that you were Roman, an outsider. I need more commitment, Quistus. Our journey is harder from now on.'

'Oaths aren't everything, Zhang. Like every Roman, I've sworn an oath to Nero.' Quistus gave a short laugh.

'Not the same thing.' Zhang, too, sat. 'Stigmus repeated the conversation between you and Nero to me.'

'Don't believe a word he says.' He wondered how much Stigmus had said.

'Nero ordered you to adopt me as your son.'

'Well, that happens to be true.'

'That would be acceptable to me,' Zhang said. 'A simple exchange of rings would suffice. Until we reach Loyang.'

'I can't,' Quistus said. He got to his feet and went out. Zhang called, 'Manas.'

Manas pushed Quistus back.

Zhang changed the subject with his usual arbitrary decisiveness, almost like a sleight of hand. 'Tell me what you've discovered so far.'

Quistus sat. Viridorix swung his legs off the bunk, wide awake all the time, and at once both the boys were not Prince and urchin, just any boys, enthusiastic and heartless.

Zhang said, 'You see, Quistus, when you were delirious you muttered "signal" and lots of strange things—'

'We all heard you,' Viridorix said. 'But you don't make any more sense than Yunyazi.'

'You've been awake how long, Viridorix?'

'Just this moment,' Viridorix said cheerfully. 'Didn't hear a thing.'

Quistus waited. Zhang jerked his head. Manas closed the door, and they were alone.

Quistus stared at his hands, still swollen and scarred. 'Cerberus was killed by an assassin let in to the Villa Paria by an accomplice already inside. Right? No. It never made sense. Wrong way round. Cerberus was killed because someone was breaking *out*.'

'Why not kill him cleanly?' Zhang asked excitedly. 'Why cut him and stab him from his throat to his you-know-what?'

'Gold Head-type ritual, maybe.'

'No. Yunyazi would know. He would have said.'

'It doesn't matter,' Quistus guessed.

'I think it does matter. Ritual's important. Confucius teaches—'

'What matters is, with Cerberus dead, the killer or his accomplice went off to find the Gold Heads and bring them back to assassinate Zhang.'

'But I'm still alive,' Zhang said.

'Not if he'd found 'em,' Viridorix said. 'Right, Senator?'

'Right,' Quistus said. 'Meanwhile, the other fellow took Cerberus's body to the kitchen in case a guard did his rounds or Lo woke. The odds of discovery were rising rapidly against them – but they were desperate, at their wits' end, they'd been in Rome for months and the Gold Heads had no idea where they were, and might move on from Rome any day. Where to conceal the body from casual inspection? The larders were locked. The cistern.'

'You said "he",' Zhang said.

'Only a man would be strong enough.'

'Could have been two women,' Viridorix said, 'head and feet. My sister—'

'Some of those cooks are very strong.' Zhang nodded. 'You should see their—'

Quistus said, 'Wild Swan knew, or suspected, who the traitor was weeks ago. Maybe she threatened to go to Zhang with her suspicions. That's why she was killed.'

'Wild Swan died of *tianhua*.'

'She was murdered. Murder by disease.'

Zhang whispered, 'In the moment of her death Wild Swan tried to warn Zhao.'

'Yes. Zhao was the only one Wild Swan knew for certain she could trust. The women talk among themselves. She knew about Zhao's babies.'

'I'm surrounded by lies, concealments, half-truths,' Zhang said.

'Welcome to politics. Whoever it was heard Zhao thirstily and unexpectedly coming to the kitchen and saw her lamp. No time to get out up the backstairs, not then. Hid behind the chimney. When Zhao's lamp-flame bent, it wasn't a ghost, it was the draught from the front door opening and closing. The one searching for the Gold Heads had returned empty-handed and put the key back on the hook, mission failed. The cooks would discover Cerberus's body in the morning; he might be missed much earlier. Whatever the failed traitor and the murderer who couldn't kill Zhang did, they had to do before then.'

Zhang nodded. 'They couldn't get to me because of Manas at my door.'

'More than Manas stopped them, Zhang. Everyone takes an oath of loyalty to the Son of Heaven, and to you personally as *Mian*, patron, house-father. The murderer can't kill you. Can't touch you. To *Qin*, loyalty and family are everything, yes? If a man breaks his oath he loses his soul, his name's erased from the Family Book. It's as though he, or she, never existed. Family loyalty. Wonderful thing.'

'They needed the Gold Heads,' Zhang murmured. 'Prince Ying of the Xu Consort Clan, my father's brother, believes he should be Emperor, that he's the rightful Son of Heaven, cheated of his birthright. Golden Turtle and the Gold Heads swore oaths to him. The Duke of Chen was one of his creatures.'

'So,' Viridorix said cheerfully, 'as long as you're with us, however many traitors and murderers there are among us, you're safe.'

Zhang didn't smile. 'Until a sail appears.'

'Or there's an unfortunate accident.' Quistus explained. 'Murder by omission. Failure to warn you someone's behind the door with a dagger, snake, poison, whatever.' Zhang looked depressed.

'Club,' Viridorix said. 'Spear. The edge of a cliff.'

'Be very aware of your safety at all times, Zhang. Fishing from the stern could be very dangerous for you. Don't go near the rail. Don't slip. Don't—'

'So,' Zhang looked firmly at Quistus, 'what did the traitor decide to do?'

'The same thing they'd done many times before. Left a clue, something that showed where to look. How else did the Gold Heads keep catching up with you, time after time, Kashgar, Bukhara, Ecbatana, Antioch, all the way to Athens?'

Zhang shook his head.

'A signal,' Quistus said. 'In this case *yanhuo*, not yet invented in Rome, something that could only be Chinese. *Yanhuo* over the Viminalis. Here we are.'

They heard an argument outside. Omba stuck her dripping head around the door. 'Captain says get on deck. Didn't you hear the rain?' She struggled against Manas. 'Get off me, you oaf.'

On deck, seamen spread a spare sail for fresh water. Warm rain swept over them in torrents. The wind blew the sail away. Someone fetched heavy, oily cloaks. Quistus shook his head, soaked already. The squall passed over and he saw land on both sides. Hippalos was shouting. Quistus couldn't hear and went to the stern.

'Yunyazi's wayfinder is too good,' Hippalos said grimly. 'We're in the estuary, I think. I don't know where the island is.'

'Island?' The sea, beaten flat by another squall, was brown and silty.

'I think we're in the river,' Hippalos said. 'Have we passed the island?' The lookout came shinning down the mast. Hippalos shouted, 'Where away?' There was a banging noise. The ship lifted, grinding. A rock shuddered along the rail, throwing up timbers. The sailors ran to the other side, shouting. An, pudgy white face wobbling with fear, pushed Zhang at Quistus. 'I cannot swim. He cannot.'

'I can swim,' Quistus said.

'Viridorix can't swim,' Zhang said.

'Stay with me, both of you.' He turned to Manas. 'You?'

Manas looked away so that he wouldn't lose face. He couldn't swim. The women and servants ran back from the bow. The ship struck again, hard. People fell, sliding across the deck as the vessel leaned. Vulpus grabbed Omba, then slipped, pulled her down, and they both fell. Stigmus, resplendent in his praetorian's purple cloak now black with rain, drew his sword. He hung on to a rope, feet sliding, and looked sternly in control.

Quistus told Hippalos, 'Rocks, both sides.'

'I'm aiming for the sand.' Hippalos clung to the steering-oar with the Egyptian. Quistus pushed Manas. 'Lend a shoulder.'

Manas said, 'I stay with the Prince.'

Quistus saw the thin pale strip of beach, trees behind. For a moment he thought they were safe but a reef darkened the surf. *Hippalos* rolled on her side, cargo breaking loose, grinding, wedged. People slid into the water or stood on the hull, crying and shaking in the jungle heat.

Quistus cut the ropes, letting the sail fly.

'My name is Thomas ben-Joseph. You're safe here. Don't be afraid.'

'I heard of you in Judea, Thomas. A Christian, aren't you?'

Zhang watched wide-eyed. Stigmus gave a shudder at the sight of the white-haired cannibal who ate the flesh and drank the blood of his three-in-one god. In Rome – and Jerusalem, come to that – they knew how to deal with these people.

'I'm a Christian and a Jew,' Thomas agreed. 'The brother of Yehoshua, called Jesus. His twin brother, in fact. He needed me to do his work here.'

'Pleased to meet you.'

'Welcome to my mansion.' Thomas was about seventy years old, with a strong, gentle face. He gestured at the ramshackle hut on the waterfront, his house. 'I'm a very important man now, you see,' he chuckled. 'An architect must have his own mansion and many servants. A builder his thousands of helpers. A carpenter his workshops and apprentices.'

Quistus looked around the dripping hovel. The monsoon had turned the earth floor to mud, the few pieces of furniture growing like weeds. 'You're an architect, builder, carpenter, all three?'

'And digger of foundations, plasterer, coppersmith, goldsmith—'

'Who pays you?'

'King Gondophares.'

'Ah,' Quistus said. 'King Gondophares. Saviour.'

'I baptized him and he bade me build a palace here, the

greatest palace ever seen on the Indus, a palace to stand for eternity.'

Quistus stepped outside to the beach, where Thomas's boat was pulled up. The crew was extraordinarily numerous, which had meant leaving most of them on the island while the Prince's entourage was ferried ashore in stages. Hippalos and his crew stayed with his ship, wedging her with sheer-legs as the tide retreated, checking the damage. It looked bad. Water still poured from the holed hull. Thomas's boat set off again, crowded with enthusiastic rowers.

'Palace?' Quistus gazed round the thatch rooftops of Barbarikon, jetties standing in the grimy water, swamps, tall trees, low hills. 'What palace?'

'You have to imagine such a miraculous creation.' Thomas pointed. 'That hill. Those trees felled. The whole hill levelled, then built up again. A magnificent palace, a truly great monument to King Gondophares.'

'When are you starting?'

'About thirty years ago.'

Quistus and Omba exchanged looks. 'We're very grateful for your hospitality,' Quistus said, 'but we need to move forward on our long journey.'

'Impossible,' Thomas said cheerfully. 'The river's in flood. You'll be here for a month at least. Then the barges can start moving cargoes upstream to Minnegara.'

'Have you seen any strangers? Strange faces?' An asked.

'There are no strangers here, brother. We're all brothers.'

'Gods,' Stigmus swore. 'They're all Christians.' He gazed round the smiling Indian faces, everyone talking Greek at once. 'Who does the work around here? Where are your poor, your slaves?'

'Gone,' Thomas smiled. 'All are Christian brothers in the community now. All paid for by King Gondophares' gold. The meek have inherited the earth. There are no more poor.'

Stigmus stared. 'That's all you're doing? Giving them money for no work?'

'The kingdom of Heaven will not be built on earth in a day, or out of stone. I promised Gondophares a monument to make him immortal. These people, their children, the meek, the sick, the saved, are Gondophares' true palace, and their gratitude is his immortality in Heaven.'

Stigmus barked with laughter. 'You mean he has to die before he can live?'

'Does the King know that?' Viridorix asked.

'We eagerly await the return of our brother the King from the war. My annual reports of our progress have filled him with joy and the desire for peace.'

Quistus muttered, 'These kings are half-Parthian, half-Indian. They're always fighting each other.'

'The Prince,' An hissed, 'cannot live in one of these hovels.'

'It would be better,' Quistus said in a low voice, 'if you'd didn't keep calling him *Prince*.'

The golden eunuch sat on the verandah of his great wagon overlooking the booming Laodicean surf, drinking gold. Around him his children – the nearest a eunuch could come to having children, and he loved and trained and spent his soul on them as dearly as children – feasted him on powders and potions of gold, tinctures of gold, elixirs of gold, golden eggs, peacocks wrapped in gold leaf, sands and slimes of different colours which when brought together, spellbound, made gold; and golden waters, slurped from gold cups.

'Pelusium,' he said thoughtfully. Despite his bulk, Golden Turtle's voice was high and metallic, an aspect of his great strength, for he was proud to be as strong as metal. 'Pelusium,' he repeated, then shook his head. An was a coward, the Prince was weak, and who was this man Quistus, a mere Roman, a barbarian, not even a chieftain?

Pelusium. That meant the Red Sea route, the Indian Ocean. Why go so far south? A ship must hug the hostile coasts of Arabia and Persia, harassed by pirates every mile of the way. To land and cross the desert on one of the Subtle Roads made even less sense. Once at sea they must keep going.

They had Yunyazi with them, he reminded himself. Barbarikon made sense. From there up the great river, across the mountains to join the Road at Kashgal, for example. That made some sense.

He clicked his fingers for the piece of paper found in one of the rooms of the Villa Paria, covered with fine black brushwork. He studied the dense symbols, squinting his golden eyes. The spy assured him Quistus was not expected to live.

Yet, Pelusium. That didn't sound like An's choice.

He called his favourite child to him, stroking his hard hands on the eager, delicate face, the teeth filed to points. 'Take ship to Barbarikon. Find the Prince wherever he hides. Kill him. I travel by land. Bring his head to me at the Imperial Palace in Loyang. Go.'

The Gold Head nodded sharply, veiled its face with black silk, and when he next looked, was gone like the wind.

'Pelusium,' he muttered. It still smelt like a diversion. He turned his gaze to the Laodicean hills. From here, and Antioch a few miles away, any number of roads led east. The obvious choice. The only one, really. Corbulo's legions, with all their commitment, organization and expense, could not possibly be a diversion. Rome, even at her peak, could not afford such a waste; and Rome, as it happened, had been burnt to the ground, and her mad Emperor scratched for every penny to build a palace bigger than Rome over the ruins.

Golden Turtle had promised Rome to Punu, King of the Huns.

He swept his arm across the table, scattering everything with a long crash.

'We travel east by road. Rome's finished. If Corbulo follows us, we lead him into the Huns, and finish him too.'

The children hurried to pack up, faces shining. They were happiest worked hard, and never happier than when promised a chance at death.

Golden Turtle thought about Prince Ying and Dowager Consort Xu. He thought about less than succeeding. He sweated gold.

Thomas's food was as simple as his dwelling. An, renting one of the better merchant houses in town, no longer allowed the Prince into the apostle's hovel, now buzzing with mosquitoes. 'The rains will stop soon.' Thomas broke bread in his soup. 'How go the ship repairs, Quistus?'

'Slowly.' Over the past month the cargo had been offloaded into barges and warehoused ashore. 'The planks are easy to replace but some of the ribs are stove in. That's difficult work. We've done the best we can.'

'I'll send more carpenters.'

'You're very kind already, taking so many off work at the palace.' Quistus frowned as Viridorix snorted in his soup. Zhao taught the Prince lessons during the day under An's watchful eye, while Viridorix ran wild. Quistus had brought him to keep him out of trouble. He heard voices on the beach, Vulpus talking learnedly of the price of cloves with Yavanas, a spice merchant. Yavanas's agent in Peshawar, a Kushan, was ill and the merchant cursed him and all the thieving short-changers of the *chowk* Yadgaar because the busy time of year was coming, cargoes upriver, cargoes down, money was to be made – or lost.

Quistus looked round, distracted. Through a hole in the wall he saw the timber lookout tower built under Chong's supervision on the island. Shu, just visible by his spear, watched for any sail from the west. So far nothing. Any day now – Thomas assured them – the trade winds turned from westerly to northeasterly, off the land. Then they'd be safe from Gold Heads. As the Indus subsided, flat-bottomed barges would slide downriver with precious goods from Peshawar, the mountains, China.

Quistus showed Thomas the Gondophares coin. 'This was stolen from a girl in Lugdunum,' he said, without looking at Viridorix.

'So? A long way from here. But coins travel.'

'Yet she must have obtained it here.' Quistus watched the apostle carefully. 'She must have been here.'

'Ships come and go.' Thomas wiped his mouth with bread. Viridorix watched round-eyed. He'd expected human flesh to be served up by the Christian. Goat soup was something of a disappointment, but he still hoped for a good tale to tell the Prince. If necessary, he'd make up something sufficiently gory.

'You'd remember her,' Quistus said. He couldn't go on.

Viridorix filled in. 'Green-grey eyes, big. Very pale skin, strong cheekbones. Reddish blonde hair, curls over her shoulders. A long cream cloak, maybe?'

'You mean Lyra.' Thomas stood with his arms outstretched, giving thanks for the meal.

'One moment,' Quistus said. 'You met her? Here?'

'She stood where you stand.' Thomas thought, remembering. 'Yes, Lyra. Brown skin, not pale. Her hair very dark brown, almost black, as you'd expect here. Hindu, not at all Roman in appearance. Rome's little more than a myth in these parts, even Alexander the Greek is a fading memory. On her forehead she wore a red mark like a flame, a kumkum bindi.'

'Kumkum bindi?'

'Perhaps she was to be married. She was very restless. Hardly ate. Up and down to the door.'

'When was this?'

'Not two years ago. Wouldn't mistake her eyes.'

'You're sure her name was Lyra?'

'As God's my witness. I showed her King Gondophares' palace.'

Quistus thought about it. 'I'd like to see this palace,' he said.

Thomas led them through the trees. The hill was a hive of activity, trees lying where they fell, men pushing barrows of earth in circles, slopes giving way to haphazard terraces and stumps of pillars, finally a flat, muddy summit covered by a low maze of unfinished walls. Viridorix jumped up, walking along them with his arms outstretched. Quistus said, 'This is what you showed her? This building site?'

'She was amazed.' Thomas put back his head, pointing at the empty sky. 'These huge porticoes, winding staircases, great pillars and courtyards and splashing fountains, roofs shining with gold.'

'Lyra saw them?'

'My dear Quistus, she pointed them out to me.'

'Oops.' Viridorix shook his feet. 'Stepped in a fountain by mistake.'

'How long did she stay?'

'Only a few days. She left in a great hurry.'

'By land or sea?'

'Riding north.' Thomas waved his hand at the causeway surfacing in the marshes as the floods eased, though dark clouds in the west promised showers. 'Some urgent news. Bad news. Yes, a terrible hurry.'

'You're sure she rode north.'

'As God's my witness.'

Quistus bit his lip. He stared north, beyond the first sails tacking down the great brown river. A glinting serpent inched on the causeway, probably a formation of men in armour. Over the flood plain, green hills shimmered with distance, and farther still, a hazy scrawl of mountains marked the top of Gondophares' kingdom. In the heavens above the mountain ranges, faint pale clouds hung motionless in the wind, the highest peaks of snow that cut the world in two.

Viridorix said quietly, 'Good news for Zhang.'

*   *   *

Thomas could not be hurried. It was dark before they reached the rented house. Viridorix raced ahead to tell the news to Zhang, who came running out. 'Is Viridorix right? Will you swear the oath?'

'Yes. We'll go north together.'

An met them at the door. 'Is it true that your Emperor commanded you to adopt the Prince as your son?'

'If the Prince wishes it, in token of the friendship between the Roman and *Qin* empires.'

'I already agreed,' Zhang said, pushing inside.

'Highness—' An bleated, following. 'A Prince does not take decisions, only advice.'

'Thank you for your advice, An. I will adopt Quistus as my Roman father.'

An turned to Quistus with narrowed eyes. 'This is a very sudden change.'

'His daughter,' Thomas explained, 'rode north.'

'Listen, An,' Quistus said, 'I saw Gondophares' army on the causeway. He won't be as pleased with his palace as Thomas is. He's going to ask what his money was spent on, and he's going to be very upset. This will be a very bad place to be.'

'Gondophares shall marvel at the miracle,' Thomas said. 'I've waited for this moment for so long.'

Quistus said grimly, 'When these Parthian kings aren't at war, killing other peoples and calling it freedom, they kill their own people and call it justice. We need to go. Now.'

An said, 'But the wind—'

'We'll take barges. When the wind changes we'll row.'

'I'll order the lookouts back from the island.' Chong clapped his hands and servants ran out.

Zhang turned to An. 'Well?'

An sighed. 'Naturally I advise the friendliest relations and an exchange of gifts between the Son of Heaven and his Roman vassal.'

'That'll do,' Zhang said. He followed Quistus into the garden between house and beach. *Hippalos* lay moored at the jetty, the patchwork of repairs along the hull showing fresh yellow wood. She was about half-heavy with cargo. Lamps from the garden reflected on the water, showing barges working along-side. Yavanas watched, notching a wooden tally as bales of skins were swung on ropes, silk in carefully-wrapped rolls, turquoise and lapis lazuli in boxes. 'Double time,' Quistus advised the captain.

'Can't sail before dawn.'

'Get the barges ready.'

Hippalos shouted orders. The tempo of work increased. Quistus called Thomas to the garden. 'You're neither Roman nor *Qin*. You're our witness.'

'But he's a Christian!' Stigmus said. Vulpus saw Omba come into the garden. He left Yavanas and followed her like a dog in heat, knowing that beneath her contrary moods she was hiding her feelings for him, and persistence would finally win her. Running the Peshawar end of Yavanas's spice business, a business Vulpus already knew thoroughly, could make him a richer man than he ever was in Rome. He was growing his hair longer to fit in.

'Simple ceremony.' Quistus looked at his left hand. There was only one ring on his finger, very plain and simple. He hesitated, then slipped it off with difficulty. He handed it to Thomas. Zhang, looking serious, did the same with one of his own. Zhao watched curiously, noting the one he'd chosen.

'This is done in the sight of God.' Thomas touched the rings together.

'And all the proper gods,' Stigmus said.

'And our ancestors,' An said.

'Really—' Chong sighed.

Quistus told Zhang, 'I adopt you as my own son, my own flesh and blood, for as long as you wish.'

Zhang whispered, 'You are a father to me.' He repeated the words twice more, three times in all.

'*Amun*,' Thomas said.

The room was dark. Quistus couldn't sleep. He stood at the window, the ring on his finger illuminated by the flares on the jetty below. The ring was large, of flickering green jade, inlaid with the golden head of some mythical beast. From its nostrils sparked tiny rubies, flame. Zhao called such a beast *long* – the dragon.

Quistus tried to pull it off. It wouldn't move.

*   *   *

Zhang and Viridorix, laughing, hid together under the stairs. 'He fell for it hook, line and sinker.' Viridorix's laughter died away. He looked frightened. 'It was too easy. He wanted to believe it and he *did*.'

'Never tell him,' Zhang said. 'Never tell Zhao, never. She doesn't know Quistus had children from his marriage. She doesn't know about the tragedy. She'd die if she knew. Not because of Lyra, who's probably dead anyway, or at least far away, but because Quistus didn't tell her. It means he doesn't really trust her, deep down.'

'He can't trust anyone.'

'Perhaps.'

'Thomas agreed with everything I said. I couldn't believe he was doing it. He even called her Lyra. It obviously wasn't her.'

'What a stroke of luck.'

'He's mad, that Thomas,' Viridorix said.

Quistus ordered the shutters closed. Nobody in the house slept that night, except Thomas, dreaming he'd show a delighted and appreciative King Gondophares around his palace in the morning – a people's palace of well-fed, well-clothed towns-folk living peacefully in prosperity, thanksgiving and devout worship. At first light he woke for prayer and tried to go home. Hoof beats rattled past the house. Everyone stopped their work, listening pale-faced. It was dark indoors, the shutters muffling noise as well as light.

'You aren't showing Gondophares anything,' Quistus said. 'He knows about the palace. That hovel's the first place he's looking for you.'

'I don't fear martyrdom.'

'You'll go on the ship, Thomas.' The rushing hoof beats faded and work began again. Fen ran to the barges with her cauldron. Zhang and Viridorix followed, shooed by An. Along the beach a glow of flames rose. Thomas closed his eyes, then nodded.

'Such a beautiful palace, was it not?'

Quistus snorted. 'Yes,' Zhao agreed, 'it was beautiful.' They led the old man along the jetty to the ship. Quistus called, 'Where away, Captain?'

'Trade—' Hippalos stopped, seeing Quistus's scarred face, the look in his eye. 'Kerala,' he said. 'I'll take him south to Kerala. He'll be safe there.'

Thomas called from the deck. 'Look, the fool's burning his own palace!' Fires were springing up all over the town, people running. 'Doesn't he know what he's doing?'

Hippalos shouted orders. Quistus jumped from the jetty into the third barge, piled high around the half-dozen rowers with thrown possessions, the entourage's usual well-practised, last-minute exit. Zhang and Viridorix leapt quickly across the swilling waters, not wanting to be cooped up with An. Quistus pushed off from the jetty. 'Give way.'

Thomas called down, 'If, with God's will, you should ever reach Peshawar, ask for my Sethian brothers Yaldabaoth and Barbelo. Tell them I wish you well.'

The oars creaked. When Quistus looked back, *Hippalos* was moving past the island, her sail pale in the dawn light. The next time he looked she'd shrunk from sight.

'Row steady,' he warned. Shu caught a crab with his oar, falling on his back. The others were almost as clumsy. 'Give way together. Steady now.' The three barges moved awkwardly into the mile-wide river mouth, keeping well clear of the shore. Omba steered the second boat, Vulpus beside her coiling ropes helpfully. An, in the first boat with Zhao, slowed to let Quistus's vessel catch up. Quistus and Manas stepped the mast, Viridorix hauled the rope. The dawn wind filled the sail, brown foam rippled at the bow.

The huge red sun rose and behind the three tiny specks Barbarikon had already dropped from sight.

'Anything?'

Quistus looked back from the hilltop. Over the past week the smell of the sea had long gone, he hardly remembered it. They'd come this far and barely started. The river wound back through the marshes to the horizon, a map of dead-ends, false channels, shallow lakes, backwaters. It looked so simple from up here.

No signs of pursuit that he could see; only whirling flocks of birds. 'Nothing, Zhang,' he said.

They'd moored in the reeds every night, careful to pass Minnegara in the dark, in midstream. Now they'd reached the hills the river narrowed, flowing hard against them, and the north-easterly blew in their faces more often than not. At the first sizeable village they'd hidden up and Quistus had ventured out in disguise, spending bits and pieces of An's silver on carts and supplies, not enough to draw attention, and making sure he haggled for hours, bartering the barges.

'My feet hurt.'

'You'll get used to it.'

'Viridorix is used to it. He's got feet like leather. I'm supposed to travel in my own house, you know.'

Viridorix said, 'Carried by people like me—'

'That's the way it should be!'

'That's why I'm stronger than you.'

'You're not stronger, you're uglier. And you smell.'

'At least I don't smell of perfume.'

Quistus smiled behind his hand. It seemed extraordinary that the boys, so different, could be such good friends – in spite, or because, of the occasional snit. 'Get used to walking, Zhang,' he advised. 'Only cart drivers get to ride aboard, and those bullocks are for hauling, not riding.'

'Little Pelican's allowed to ride and she's nothing but a dancer.'

'Have a heart, Zhang.'

'She doesn't even dance, just mopes for Wild Swan. I've had no entertainment.'

'What about Omba's stories?'

'Manas will carry me.'

'If he carries you he can't guard you.'

'We're out of danger.'

'No. You see, Zhang, you never will be out of danger. Ever.'

They walked in silence for a while beside the rumbling carts. Zhang said, 'Viridorix could carry me.'

'He's no bigger than you. It wouldn't be fair.'

'Who said anything about fair?'

'I wouldn't mind,' Viridorix said, 'if we took turns.'

Zhang glanced coolly. 'Don't forget who you're talking to.'

'By the way, Zhang,' Quistus said, 'your gold cloak . . .'

Zhang got that look on his face, what Viridorix called his *Prince* face. When Zhang wore his *Prince* face, complete with straggly chin, even Viridorix wasn't his friend. Neither Zhao nor An could control him. 'This is me, Quistus. This is who I am.'

'Exactly, son,' Quistus said deliberately. 'A target.'

'Excuse me.' Omba walked alongside. Zhang would often listen to her because she was of royal blood and understood him, and over the campfire she'd tell the wide-eyed boys stories of palace life – short-lived, basically – in Kefa. At times like that, with just the quivering flames in the night and the stars receding overhead, both boys forgot who they were. 'I have an idea,' Omba said, pointing to a rock pool where the river touched the road. 'I think Viridorix needs a bath, don't you?'

Viridorix ran away chased by Zhang, laughing. Omba tapped her nose. It was Quistus's plan for the boys.

That night she blackened Viridorix's hair with camp-fire soot and braided his curls in a topknot. She and Zhao looked at each other, grinning. 'Keep still, Vix.' They dressed him in a shiny yellow smock embroidered with fiery vermilion dragons, a satin cap and shoes to match, and – not the gold cloak, an unforgivable *lèse-majesté*; An would've burst – a purple cloak with yellow yin-yang designs, not truly royal by *Qin* standards but impressive enough. 'I feel stupid,' Viridorix said. The women clapped, hugging each other.

An turned to Zhang. 'Highness,' he begged, 'don't allow this, I beg you.'

Zhang sniffed Viridorix's tunic. He'd never worn anything without perfume before. He pulled the coarse, sweat-slimy weave over his shoulders with a shiver of revulsion. 'There, now you stink like a proper boy.' Quistus unpinned Zhang's topknot before An could stop him and made him practise walking. 'No, not like a Prince. Relax. Slouch.' He called the opposite advice to Viridorix. 'Walk slow, breathe in, look people in the eye, make them look down. You're the great Prince Viridorix.'

Vulpus watched Omba, smiling when she smiled.

'He's the great *Prick* Viridorix,' Stigmus said.

Viridorix paraded importantly. Genji giggled into her fingertips. Fen held her sides, groaning. Lien wiped tears from her skinny cheeks. Even Shu woke and allowed himself a small toothless grin.

'Excellent, Viridorix,' Quistus remarked pleasantly. 'Now you're the one they're trying to kill.'

She stopped to drink. The river, no longer mud-brown, roared in its rocky bed, swirling in deep, sudden pools between gravel banks thrown up by the floods. She knelt between two boulders and splashed cold water on her face, then looked round with her hands on her daggers, hearing stones slide. She breathed out. 'Oh. It's you. I thought you were Vulpus.'

Manas watched the last of the carts going round the corner. The dust drifted off. There were a few ragged-looking trees with birds in but they couldn't hear them for the rush of the waters. The giant turned his shaved head back to her, watching her with unblinking blue eyes.

'No, Omba. I am not Vulpus.'

'The mountain speaks.' She cupped her hands and drank, then stood watchfully. 'Still here? I thought you were guarding the Prince.'

'Quistus says, if I guard the Prince it reveals who he is.'

'You'd better guard Viridorix then.'

'That would not be guarding the Prince.'

Omba wiped her hands on her hips. 'You know best.' He stood in front of her. She pushed past but Manas dropped his hand on her shoulder. He looked into her eyes, blue on brown. He didn't move.

She pushed him. 'Don't you start. I've had enough of that trouble with Vulpus.' She knocked his hand off her and walked away. He walked three paces after her, then put his hands on her shoulders from behind. 'You love Vulpus?'

She sighed, halting. 'I do not love Vulpus.'

'He loves you.'

'I know.' She shrugged.

'I love you.'

She pushed his hands off and turned. 'No. Stop this.' She shoved him away, tapping her fingertip above her eye. 'I haven't forgotten what you did in the cellar. You're not forgiven.'

'You kicked me here.'

'I hope it hurt. Pardon me if I don't look.'

'It hurt very, very much.' He stood close. 'You hurt me. You give me pain. I think of you when I should not. When I am on duty.'

She dropped her hands to her daggers. 'Stay back.'

He took another step, closer. 'I sewed your shoulder when it was cut.' He caressed the scar. 'Good job.'

She drew the daggers. He kissed her. She dropped them.

Manas smiled a little. He touched the palm of his hand lightly across her fine short knots of hair. He picked up her daggers and kissed them.

Vulpus came for a drink. He watched them for a minute or two. He was standing in plain view but they never saw him. He turned and went back to the road.

The ship carried one passenger, the Jonah. Nothing had gone right. First, they should never have taken the faceless man's money – a head wrapped in black silk, that's all you could see. No telling what was underneath, just shadows. You could imagine it, though. Sailors had lots of imagination. Something from the deep sea, maybe. Strange things deep down. You could imagine it.

After twenty days at sea, you could think of nothing else.

The one cabin. Never should have let him have it in the first place. He never came on deck, just sat on the hard, bare cabin sole all the hours of daylight and darkness, cross-legged, wrists on his knees and hands turned up, hood pulled over that black silk face, shadowed. Didn't move. Not asleep or awake, from what you could tell through gaps in the planks. Not natural.

The crew stopped at the door, faces flushed with wine and fear, wooden battens clenched in their fists. Someone had to go first. The ones behind pushed.

Day and night they'd rowed into the teeth of the east wind. The galley was built for the *Sinus Arabicus*, not the deep ocean. But she could row into the wind. The traveller had known that, and paid well. They should have known better.

They pushed Abaqa to the door. Abaqa was tall for a Persian, a good speaker with a deep voice, a distinguished manner and steady eyes, a natural leader.

Abaqa listened at the door. Not a sound.

'Go on,' they said.

Abaqa rapped on the door, opened it, and the door closed behind him.

The door opened and Abaqa came out. He went on deck. He wouldn't come back.

At the junction of the two paths Quistus let the carts pull ahead, not for the first time. He leant against a rock to work a stone out of his shoe. His blistered feet had healed but the constant rain and puddles left them wrinkled and white. He put back the cowl of his robe, cold rain instantly beading his filthy hair and beard, clinging to his eyelashes.

Birds he didn't recognize swept over the bare, rocky slopes, hawks, and bigger birds too. He couldn't remember what a gull looked like, or a sandy beach, or Rome. Grey rocks streamed into the grey sky, the carts no bigger than insects beside the white river. He could just make out a dot of purple cloak, Viridorix. No sign of Zhang at all. Good.

He looked back down into the mists they'd come from. The track dwindled from sight, empty. An was still obsessed that they were followed by Gold Heads. 'You don't know them, Quistus.'

Quistus didn't believe it, but Chong agreed with An, and Yunyazi, who saw everything – or claimed he did – had sat in his cart with night rain drumming on the roof and his eyes turned up, and said, 'I see it.'

And Fu had barked once.

Quistus turned the stone between his fingers. He threw it away.

The path on the right turned across the plain towards the mountains of Srinagar. They could have gone that way. In fact he'd chosen to stay with the main path on the left, beside the Indus, taking them to Peshawar – so their guides assured them. Quistus didn't trust the guides much and he thought bandits were a bigger danger than Gold Heads, although there'd been no hold-ups that came to anything much. The mountain men saw the heavy *Qin* crossbows, Manas looming with a *sica* in each hand and Omba at his shoulder, the carts suddenly bristling with swords, and melted away.

That had been another good idea, the women dressed as men, given swords they didn't have the faintest idea how to use, and told to look fierce.

Quistus rubbed the rain from his eyes. He let them go out of focus, seeing patterns in the rocks and mud – and there it was, a simple straight line of thread laid carefully across a rock.

A thread of lemon-yellow satin from Zhao's gown. He screwed it up in his fist.

Someone hadn't given up hope, and in more ways than one: not only were they showing the way, they were still trying to incriminate Zhao.

'Whip them.' The bullocks slid on the hard shale then tugged forward. The carts turned left, crossing the shrunken Indus on a ramshackle causeway with a wooden toll-bridge, newly repaired, and inched across the plain on level ground at last. Viridorix and Zhang, followed by Manas at a discreet distance, ran ahead. Zhang stopped to scratch. He spent a lot of time scratching. Viridorix's clothes, not only filthy but ingrained with fleas, lice and ticks, drove him almost out of his mind. He'd never experienced vermin before.

Quistus gazed at the walled town standing in the mist.

The rain-streaming Peshawari plain, almost entirely encircled by mountains, was mother to the many rivers whose floods had torn the deep, jagged valleys between the peaks. Here at the town gates the valley roads met and spread out. The guides assured Quistus there were many ways to choose to go from here: west along the Kabul river to Alexandropolis, or along the valleys northward, or across the lake country to the north-east, all of them requiring skilled and honest guides such as themselves.

'We need to rest,' Quistus said. 'Four days. No more.' An, exhausted, but not noticeably thinner, demanded eight days at least. Zhao thought entering Peshawar at all was too dangerous, and suggested one of the small villages nearby.

'We'd stand out in a village,' Quistus disagreed. 'In town, especially a market town, a busy crossroads, we'll blend in. You'll see.'

The track led to one of the eight gates they saw on this side of town. Quistus, and Zhao with her face covered, went ahead to the square. He remembered Thomas's advice and spoke to a bearded man with glittering eyes. 'Where may one find the brothers of Seth?'

'This very place.' The man responded in Greek. 'This is Sethian Square. All these people you see are brothers of Seth.' He swept his arm around the busy bazaar. These travellers and descendants of westerners, remnants of Alexander's armies, still called the town by its long-ago Greek name, Kaspapyrus. The Kushans had their own name for it, but the man was pleased that Quistus did not look like a Kushan.

'I'm searching for Yaldabaoth. We need rooms, a whole house, stabling.'

'Ah.'

'We can pay.'

'In money?'

'In silver.' Quistus added, 'And Thomas sends his regards.'

'Thomas! Wonderful man! Is he in good health?'

'He wisely travels to Kerala for that very reason, in fact.'

The bearded man clasped wrists. 'I'm Barbelo. I'll speak to my father, Yaldabaoth.'

The house was very tall with a steeply pitched roof, its front on the busy square, its back balconies hanging sheer over a foaming half-stream, half-sewer. 'How convenient,' Quistus said. The rooms were high, hung with brass lamps and embroideries, the wooden walls and ornate doors as riotously ornamental and overdone as the balconies, each one projecting slightly farther than the one below. He called An, who offered a Kuping-stamped ingot. Barbelo bowed and the ingot disappeared into his sleeve. 'My house is your house.'

'We won't need your servants,' Zhao said. Barbelo clicked his fingers and, within half a minute, the house was quiet. An and Chong sat on overstuffed yak-hair couches embroidered with suns and stars, and closed their eyes.

'Baths,' called Zhao from upstairs. 'There are baths but no water.' *Qin* servants were sent scurrying. Quistus had the carts drawn round and hidden in the courtyard. Fen prepared food from the Yadgaar bazaar bought by Zhao, with Zhang helping to carry purchases as her itching, scratching servant, under Manas's watchful eye. Zhang had never known such freedom and had wandered after her among the stalls with his eyes wide. Shu and the guards kept watch from the upper windows and balconies. Menservants carried water for the baths while Genji and Lien washed clothes. Stigmus took a third-floor bedroom with a view of the mountains, claiming it was barely adequate for a Prefect of Praetorians, while Vulpus moved into the attic under the top peak of the roof, with a bed at the side and standing room in the middle, and a small balcony projecting farthest of all, so he didn't soil the balconies below when relieving himself.

He made way politely for Omba on the stairs, making no attempt to speak to her. She thought he looked very sad. 'What's up?' she asked casually.

'Nothing,' he said.

Viridorix, dressed in purple cloak and green pantaloons, sat sulking on a big double bed. 'Why can't I go out?' he glowered. 'I wouldn't be a Prince for anything.' He called to the busy group by the fire, 'And I won't have a bath.'

By the fire Zhang sat bolt upright in a tall, beaten-copper

tub, his steaming, grimy body sponged almost transparently white by the more elderly menial women while his long hair was carefully washed and combed out by Genji and Lien. His eyes closed in pleasure at the lifelong familiar ritual. Back from the market he'd stripped off Viridorix's disgusting old tunic in the yard and personally set fire to it.

Down in the main hall Quistus and Zhao drank tea from a samovar. He showed her the lemon-yellow thread. 'If we knew who hated you so much, we'd know who the traitor is.'

'I told you, all the men hate me, except perhaps Chong. They fear me.'

'You overturn the natural order, being cleverer than they. And knowing it. Showing it.'

Two more swallows of the strong, bitter tea, and she looked him in the eye. 'Are you afraid of me, Quistus?'

'Should I be?'

'I have a secret. I have two children.'

He refilled her cup. 'Why are you telling me?'

'Oh . . . you knew. Do you know everything, Quistus? Now I feel like a fool. Well, I left them with my sisters and my brother, Ban Gu. I've travelled across the world and halfway back for the sake of my Prince. I hardly remember what my own babies look like. Not a very good mother.'

'Who else knows about them?'

'Zhang. I suppose he told you.' She shrugged. 'Chong, he's bright, difficult to hide anything from him. Yunyazi knows everything I suppose. And now you. The stranger. The outsider. I should be embarrassed.' She stared at her hands. 'Even my husband, Cao Shou, was scared of me. I realize that now. Everyone, except you.'

He took her cup and emptied it in the pot. 'Too much tea makes you drunk.'

Vulpus lay awake in the dark. He heard voices echoing. Omba talked. Her room was opposite his, right under the roof-peak, but at the front of the house. She was talking to someone, and Vulpus knew who.

He'd heard those slow footsteps on the stairs, then her door had creaked before the footsteps reached the top. She'd known he was coming.

Her visitor, her midnight lover, could have been Vulpus – all he'd have to do was walk out of his own room and into hers. Could have been him in there with her now, talking in low voices, watching her smile, her white teeth, her animation, the hot animal scent of her. But it wouldn't have happened. That dancing look in her eyes wasn't for him. Never would be.

He loved her. He burned for her.

Her contempt broke Vulpus's heart.

He opened his balcony door and stood listening to the rain. The overhanging eaves kept him dry. Lamp-lit windows illuminated the stream below. Beyond the rain-streaked rooftops a horned moon curled like a blown candle-flame under the lid of cloud. The clouds reached down, the moon went out, the rain intensified.

Plenty of openings in the spice trade here. No trouble about that. Yavanas's man was dying of bright-blood coughing and, like Vulpus, had no sons. There had been that connection between him and the dying man, that natural understanding for each other, that sterility.

Vulpus lay listening to their voices. His *phallus* was so stiff he thought he might break. Manas laughed. Manas never laughed. Omba made Manas laugh those deep rolls of laughter. She, too, was laughing now. They fell silent.

Vulpus closed his eyes. The wall banged. He heard them roll along it, kissing.

Manas uttered a word in a foreign language. More dust from the wall.

Vulpus pulled the pillow over his head, trying to hear the rain.

'I'll be your guide,' Barbelo said smoothly, with a glance at An, the repository of Kuping-quality silver. 'But only to the top of the mountains. From there you make your own way down.' The rain had stopped. He nodded at the frosted, sunlit roofs of the town. 'Winter comes. You have little more time for rest, or you rest until spring.'

Quistus unrolled a goatskin map. 'Which way do you suggest?'

'The obvious path is the Khyber Pass, either west to Alexandropolis, or north up the side valley to Chitral.' Barbelo ignored the map, not knowing how to read it. 'Onward to Kashgal. There you meet the Road.'

'If we did not wish to be so obvious?'

'The lakes and rivers. By Mingaora, or Khalabat. Follow the Indus to its sourcc.'

Quistus studied the map. 'Lake Khalabat looks good. We could sail that and save forty miles.' Stigmus prodded with his blunt finger. 'Then the Indus out of the north end?'

'On foot, yes. The river shrinking smaller all the time, right to its source.'

'And follow the valleys down the far side?' Vulpus, watching, said nothing. Barbelo nodded, 'Yes.'

'It's a long way.'

'Keep to the valleys, Quistus, then turn to the sunrise when you reach the flat stone desert, along the line of mountains. Those are the outreaches of *Qin*, the end of the earth. I know no more.'

'What do you think, Vulpus?' Quistus asked.

'I don't know,' Vulpus said. He shrugged. 'Lake Khalabat. Why not?'

Later he knocked on Omba's door. She was busy packing. 'What do you want?' she asked coldly. Manas sat on the bed, polishing a *Qin* long-sword. 'You can talk in front of him,' she said.

Vulpus had wanted to talk to her alone, badly. He wanted to say, '*I love you and I always will. I need you and you've broken my heart.*' In fact he said, 'I've decided not to go.'

She might say, '*I've decided to stay here too. Manas has his duty to the Prince so he's going on. We don't really love each other. You're not so bad, Vulpus. Let's set up in business together.*'

She said coolly, 'What's that to do with me?'

'Nothing. Nothing really. I just thought you should know.'

'Now I know.'

He wanted to say, '*I was your master once. I could have had anything I wanted of you, but I gave you away of my own free will, because I love you. You see, I needed you to learn to love me of* your *own free will. Stay!*' He said, 'I hope we can still be friends.'

She tied some heavy cloaks in a bundle. 'Well, I hope we never meet again. Goodbye.'

'Goodbye,' Vulpus said. 'I expect to be very rich. I'm going to be a big man round here.'

'Goodbye,' she said firmly.

*　　*　　*

Everyone complained as they walked, softened by their days of rest. Almost at once a wheel fell off a cart, but Barbelo, walking with Quistus at the head of the column, told him carts wouldn't be needed much longer; they'd use boats, then carry most of what they needed on their backs. Barbelo was under the firm conviction that Viridorix in the purple robe was the Prince, and Zhang in goatskins the Prince's servant. 'He is a very bad servant. The Prince is foolish to keep such a lazy servant. He should hit him very hard to teach him.' Barbelo kept this up for hours, slapping at Zhang whenever he came close, giving him jobs to do.

The track to Mingaora curved off to the left, squiggling abruptly into the mountains ringing the plain. Quistus slowed his walk, letting the carts overtake him, not seeing anyone acting suspiciously. After a while he walked back to the junction.

Nothing; nothing to show which way they'd gone. He let his eyes lose their focus, and there it was, a few hundred paces along: four hand-sized stones exactly evenly spaced by the roadside to Lake Khalabat. When you knew what to look for you couldn't miss it. He kicked them away angrily and walked on.

A minute or two later a thought struck him and he came back, picked up the stones, returned to the junction, and spaced them carefully by the road to Mingaora.

You couldn't resist a single rider on a good black horse, a fool too proud to pay for an escort. First the fast-moving plume of dust, then the urgent hoof beats, finally the rider in black on the black horse coming into sight, a dream of horseflesh to keep you in milk and women for a year. Any half-awake farmer, goatherd, shepherd, yak-musterer, stone-breaker, beard-sucker, bored out of his mind with fighting brothers and chucking pebbles at chickens, was instantly a bandit. A man who could afford a horse like that would be carrying gold, wearing good clothes too, with boots. All it took was three or four of you together – four, actually, today – in the good place at the corner where the road from Barbarikon split, tough mountain men with a sword or two, rocks to hand, and Kanishka by good luck already on the high boulder sharpening his spear, and you had your ambush.

The man in black rode fast but leaning alertly from side to side, looking for something at the roadside. Kanishka threw the spear. It was a beautiful throw, no chance of ruining the horse. Kanishka could hit a hawk in flight at a hundred paces, even against the sun. The man in black moved his arm, steel flashed. The spear broke in pieces and Kanishka arched from the boulder holding his throat, not making a sound. He landed on his head and the horseman rode over him. The three mountain men stood their ground as he rode past, then two slumped wearily, cut to pieces, and he came back for the third. The third man ran, tripped, crawled on the stones. Finally he rolled over. The horseman, his face wrapped in black silk, touched his sword to the prone man's blinking eye.

'Which way Peshawar?'

The bandit pointed. The horseman pushed lightly until he felt stone, retrieved his dart from Kanishka's throat, and took the Peshawar road, cleaning his sword.

Barbelo said they felt tired because they reached so high above the earth. As they approached the realm of the heavens their bodies were being deprived of the life-giving ether that sustained them.

Quistus was floating in mid-air.

Yawning, he sat on the long, graceful bow of a yellow-painted boat, staring between his feet into crystal-clear waters that went down for ever. Long ago the Khalabat Valley, and the Indus flowing through it, had been blocked at the southern end by a mighty landslide, and the result was this long mirror-lake winding between the mountains. The white peaks plunged through the waters to a vanishing point in the sky beneath the boats. Half a dozen similar craft followed, apparently also floating in air, towing ripples across the mountains and sky below, carrying the entourage under elegantly curved canopies. The last boat was larger, loaded with a single two-wheeled chariot made of cane, a mule, and a small herd of black and brown goats. 'Indispensable,' Barbelo had promised. 'You'll see.'

'They're as smelly as Vix,' Zhang said.

'I smell like a Prince now,' Viridorix said smugly, 'and you're too clean for a peasant. Get dirty if you want to be safe.'

By late evening they stood at the north end of the lake.

Quistus reckoned they'd saved three or four days' walking on foot. They camped on the strand where the youthful Indus swirled into the still waters. He gazed at the valley rising into the clouds. 'We start at first light.'

In these deep valleys the sun rose long after daylight, and set long before dark. Shadows were colder than ice, the sunlight too hot.

'We're climbing closer to the sun,' Barbelo warned, 'yet it will grow colder. Nothing makes sense here.'

Zhao said, very Zhao-like, 'Then Icarus's wings didn't melt when he flew too close to the sun, they froze.'

'That story,' Barbelo said huffily, 'is a myth. You'll see.'

Quistus led. The path steepened and they were all tired, pushed down by their heavy packs. 'The air grows thinner as we approach God,' Barbelo called through blistered lips. 'The cold sun burns, yet gives no heat.' The cane cart bumped, pulled by the single mule, Little Pelican hanging on tight. Fen's goats foraged pasture at the roadside, grass and shrubs growing thinner and harsher each day. In return they gave milk, yoghurt, butter, grease against sun and wind, dung campfires for the bitter nights, a warm body to cuddle, wool, meat, bone soup, even stock and gelatin to flavour the thin vegetable stews that were soon their staple diet.

'This is a terrible place.' Fen shielded her eyes from the glaring peaks. 'Soup boils yet stays uncooked.'

That night it snowed, but wind swept the slopes clear. Sometime during the day the cart broke. Little Pelican rode the mule, her tiny feet pointing down the flanks, snow on her head and shoulders.

Quistus climbed with a stick. He couldn't talk with Barbelo and keep walking. They stopped. Both men were gasping. 'This, Barbelo, no. This can't be. Not the right way.'

'Many times,' Barbelo gasped. He nodded. 'Breathe through your nose, or your lungs dry.'

Quistus breathed through his nose, shaking his head.

At the start of each day he led with Barbelo, then dropped back past the people staggering forward. The guards were strongest but carried most. Quistus joked with them but they only understood strength. He slapped them, scowling, cursing, and they pulled ahead. The women kept going with a dogged wiriness, except Genji, who cried and leant on the mule. Fen winked and patted her belly. Quistus whispered, 'Who?'

Fen whisper-gasped, 'People say, father is Shu.'

'Shu's too old.'

'That's what Genji thought, silly girl.'

Each day the column stretched thinner. The rear trailed into camp after dark. Quistus and Omba walked at the back, pushing, persuading, encouraging, threatening.

He turned to her. Clouds rushed along the valley, snow whirling. 'I should never have brought them this way, Omba. I'm killing them.'

Vulpus was pleased with himself. He'd landed on his feet. Prices here were low by Roman standards, haggling was the same anywhere, and Yavanas's man, *requiescat in pace*, kept a big ledger of contacts. Vulpus's old skills hadn't deserted him, his lying tongue still transmuted a sack of dusty pepper into the treasure of King Midas himself, and he'd treated himself to a new cinnabar-red cloak. Each evening he came home to Barbelo's house – where he'd arranged to stay until the guide's return – eating minced lamb off a stick, carrying a bigger bag of gold than he had set out with in the morning, exhausted, elated by his labours, and congratulating himself on his deceitful skills. He made sure the heavy, ornate front door was shut, locked, and barred behind him – once or twice he'd had the feeling he'd been followed, the bazaar was full of thieves – lit the ornate hardwood lamp, and went up to his room humming cheerfully.

He closed the door and sat on the bed, dreaming of Omba by lamplight. He imagined the shadows were her. After a while he leant back and slept, and woke with a finger to his lips.

Vulpus moved his hands at his side. The finger stayed where it was.

'Shhh.'

A dark figure bent over him. He saw his old cinnabar-red cloak crumpled in the corner. Vulpus shook. The worst thing was not being able to talk. He could talk his way out of anything. He tried to talk with his eyes.

A knife. A soft ripping feeling on his leg. Vulpus voided helplessly. The dark figure touched his thigh, the small round scar on each side where the arrow had gone through. Certainty.

It reached up one-handed, threw back the hood from its head, unwound the black silk from its gold face. Vulpus's guts wrenched but he had no more to give.

The finger moved from his lips, clenched to a fist around his hair, and flung him through the balcony door without letting go. Vulpus dangled over the drop by his hair. He clung instinctively to the arm holding him up. The knife touched him with a numb feeling, his hand came off, he watched it go.

He had a choice. He let his right hand slip, hanging completely from his hair, swinging. He sobbed, cradling his arm. He shouted, 'Don't let me go.' Shouting was all that kept him up. He shouted at the calm gold face, 'I don't know where the Prince is.'

His hair skidded through the gloved hand, stopped with a jerk.

'Lie. Liar. Seen you. Heard you. Lies.'

'I love you, Omba,' Vulpus shouted.

'Lies.'

He shouted, 'Don't let me go and I'll tell you.'

A cold, unpleasant pause.

'For truth, I not let you go. You sleep on pillow tonight.'

He shouted, 'Alexandropolis.'

The Gold Head studied him. 'No.'

'Chitral,' Vulpus shouted. He wept. 'Turn off to Chitral.'

The gold face inclined slightly, then shook slowly from side to side.

His hair slipped another inch through the gloved hand. Vulpus looked up calmly. No one had ever doubted a word he said with this look in his eye. 'Mingaora, I swear. It's Mingaora.'

The knife whipped. Vulpus's body plunged headless into the stream.

The Gold Head carried Vulpus's head in front of it. It laid the head on the pillow, smoothed the hair and pulled the covers to the neck with an odd domesticity. 'I kept my word.'

The dark figure on the black horse reined in at the junction. Beside the track to Mingaora lay four hand-sized stones, evenly spaced.

The Gold Head smiled and kicked the horse to a gallop along the road. High above the rider a kite soared unseen on her outstretched wings, turning in the rising air, her keen gaze revealing the mountains and valleys laid out far below. Above Mingaora the snow began, the valleys narrowed, peak stood on peak, and the path – if it could have been seen beneath the snow, even by the most hawk-eyed – bent to the north-west.

The kite twisted in an updraught, swept higher by the storm swirling from the north-east, briefly glimpsing the line of figures in the high peaks, their divergent path leading them with every step farther from the determined figure racing on horseback, two valley systems – soon three – to the west. Then the storm blew over them all and they were gone.

The kite let the wind sweep her south, towards richer pickings.

'Gods,' Quistus whispered. He leant on his staff, the wood worn shiny by his hands, feeling smooth against his bearded cheek. The storm had blown over. His boots straddled the knife-sharp ridge of snow between two peaks. Around him a thousand lower peaks shone like diamonds. The ends of the world were laid out around him, immense, gently curving beneath the bowl of the sky, in every direction. He felt close enough to touch the sun.

'This is as far as I go,' Barbelo said quietly. 'From here, simple. Downhill.'

Downhill. Far harder than uphill, half-blind with snow, the goats long gone, the mule lame. Manas carried Little Pelican on his shoulders, but the mule had shown such spirit that no one would eat it. It hobbled after them, a faithful good luck charm, and gradually they started helping the mule as much as they helped each other. Drips of water slid down the snow in the gullies, trickles turned to streams. Thin grass poked around rocks and bordered the high, mossy tarns with living green. They followed a river cutting through the soft black earth into a deep, stony channel, gathering force. The valley steepened, white waters leapt from a cliff top into the air, and they could get no farther. Zhang and Viridorix ran forward excitedly. The women called them back with shrieks of alarm.

Quistus, with Omba holding his heels, crawled to the edge of the waterfall. He peered into the rainbows of spray, thinking he saw a patchwork of fields below, then shook his head. 'There's no way down,' he called back in Latin.

A man came from behind a rock. 'Well, well. What a surprise,' he said calmly, in the same language. 'How do you do. My name's Publius Crassus.'

V

The Lost Legion

'I was so amazed I nearly fell—'
  'I grabbed you, Zhang. I saved your life.'
'You never did, Vix.'
'Did! You looked so surprised—'
'Latin!'
'Anyway, Publius, you'd come out with that old-fashioned Roman drawl of yours—'
'Old-fashioned? Has Rome changed in only a hundred years?'
'"How d'you do, I'm Publius Crassus"—'
'Not quite like that but near enough—'
'Last thing we expected.'
'And Omba gave a shriek and let go of Quistus's ankle!'
'Didn't let go. I held on to his toes.' Omba chewed a mouthful of snails in garlic. One of the pretty Roman girls – or rather, part-Roman girls raised to be fully Roman – helped her to more wine.

Zhao looked into her cup. She murmured, 'I thought I would die, too.' No one heard.

'Actually just my big toe,' Quistus told Publius, reclining in the familiar comfort of a Roman couch. Even the bread tasted of home, prepared in the traditional oven. Publius had changed into a slightly musty toga and sandals, his grey ringlets carefully curled on his forehead, but most of the men at the long tables wore heavy woollen farming tunics. Everyone watched the strangers closely. Quistus was familiar enough with buildings like this from garrison towns in Britain and Germany, except that here the roof was low thatch, with pillars of polished wood instead of stone, and few windows. Smoke rose from the central fire through a hole in the roof. Shields hung along the rough, gloomy walls. An outpost town, definitely, but he'd seen worse.

'Anyway, we all thought Quistus was going over the waterfall—'

'So did he!'

'Didn't you, Quistus?'

'Yes, boys, I felt very undignified. My clothes fell over my head—'

'And you had spray up your arse!'

Deep laughter from the men. They had Roman manners and coarse Roman soldiers' humour, but eastern eyes – some of them blue, by Kyrgyz mothers.

Zhao the censor cleared her throat. Zhang muttered, 'Well, he did.'

'Then Publius ran forward and hauled Quistus up by the knees.'

'Not a moment too soon.'

'Or else,' Publius Crassus drawled, 'you would have arrived in Nirvana rather more precipitously than would have been good for you, Quistus.'

'I'm very grateful for your quick thinking, Publius. And that you climbed so far in search of a lost goat.'

Publius stood. He raised his voice. 'Soldiers, fellow Romans! We welcome our guests from home, even the ones who are *Qin*. Treat them well, though we are dishonoured men. Yet do not let your shame at being alive make you bitter or excessively subservient. Take even the *Qin* into your homes, as Romans, for they are under the protection of a Roman.' He indicated Quistus. 'We all have questions.' He waited. 'Servilius.'

'Just one question, sir.' A man stood up far along one of the tables. He swallowed, looking at Quistus, then hitched his belt with blunt fingers. 'Will Rome ever forgive us?'

'So this is Nirvana.' Quistus looked around the village in the bowl of the mountains as he walked with Publius. 'I've heard the myths. I never thought they were true.'

'The Huns who lived here – and died – called it Nie-Ban.' Publius nodded. 'Nirvana is a good place. We're sheltered from wind and the local warlords, the air's dry and we don't get much snow, but the soil's stony and the winters are long. It wouldn't be the first time the crops have failed.'

'What do you do when that happens?'

Publius shrugged at the neatly-ploughed fields, each furrow straight as an infantryman's sword. 'We starve, Quistus. Or we resort to . . . other measures.'

From here the valley looked almost perfectly circular, its grassy concave slopes sweeping down and out from the high southern cliff where the waterfall hissed. Dotted between the fields were small thatch villas and huts. Roughly in the middle of the valley, by the reedy lake and carefully-dug rectangles of fishponds, the ice broken morning and evening, the thatch village was laid out in the grid pattern beloved by soldiers. Smoke hung over the smithy. The mess hall where they'd eaten had by far the broadest roof, but not the highest: that honour, Publius pointed out, went to the tall trestle watchtowers guarding the stockaded entrance to the valley, where the stream meandered into the flatlands beside the Roman-straight line of stony approach road.

Quistus asked, 'Other measures?'

'Paid work.'

'You're mercenaries?'

'When needs be. The *Qin* claim this territory but the Emperor can't enforce his laws. Warlord fights warlord, dog eats dog. It's sport. To them death is life, they fight until their peasants are killed, crops destroyed, summer wasted, eke through the winter on what they've stolen, drink themselves blind, and plot next year's war. They have no idea of the real business of war, the business of *winning*, how to build mantlets to besiege a town, how to advance under fire without taking casualties. So, our services are for sale. We haven't forgotten who we are, Quistus. We have no honour but we remember how to fight like Romans.'

Publius turned away from the village along an uphill path. It ended in two giant boulders beneath the cliff, a mossy hut draped with skins in the vee between them. Two soldiers stood to attention at the entrance. Their Roman armour was old, old-fashioned, much repaired, but serviceable. The man on the left wore new greaves on his shins, strongly made. The second, a girl with dark eyes, was square-jawed yet lithe, with a scar down her cheek. Publius nodded. 'Yes, Quistus. We need everyone. No human spirit's wasted here.'

The guards crossed spears, blocking the entrance. Their eyes were steady.

'They're proud of Rome,' Quistus said.

'They are.'

'I wonder if you realize how time has moved on. Rome has forgiven you, Publius. You've done nothing wrong. A man does not bear responsibility for the sins of his ancestors.'

Publius turned angrily. 'You don't understand. Our great-grandfathers ran from battle. General Publius Crassus and V *Scythia* were cut off from the main army at Carrhae, surrounded. Their situation was hopeless, too many stupid mistakes had been made; it was time for them to die. Publius saw a way out – perhaps was *given* a way out by the enemy – and he ran and his men ran. Six thousand men cut and ran for their lives from Carrhae. Perhaps they meant to regroup, attack the Parthians from the rear, save the day, but once they'd started running they couldn't stop. They ran away behind the Parthian lines while the rest of the army was massacred, including Publius's own father Licinius, abandoned, tortured, murdered.'

'Those men weren't you, Publius. They were your ancestors. It was a hundred years ago. Their name lives on in you and your men, not their crime.'

Publius gave a jerk of his head. The guards raised their spears. He pushed through the skins and Quistus ducked after him into darkness. The hut wasn't a hut. It was a cave dug into the hill.

'Nothing changes, Quistus.'

Publius lit a flame and held it high. A mossy shrine threw back the light. The eagle of V *Scythia* gleamed on its standard among tattered banners, purple cloth woven with the always-familiar gold letters SPQR: the Senate and People of Rome.

'Do you know how hard Emperor Augustus tried to get that lost eagle home?' Quistus murmured.

Publius looked sharp. 'Emperor? What Emperor? What of the Republic?'

Quistus shut his mouth. Within a generation of Carrhae the fabled Republic had ceased to exist, except in the nostalgia of old men and the conceit of laws, and Emperors ruled. By now it was possible – probable – that Rome had entirely ceased to exist. Best to keep quiet.

'A slip of the tongue, Publius.'

'Well, the Parthians couldn't return the eagle even if they wanted to. They didn't have it.'

'A fact they understandably neglected to mention.'

'After his victory and his atrocious torment of Licinius Crassus, the victorious Parthian King, Orodes, rode east in pursuit of my great-grandfather. Publius Crassus surrendered rather than waste the lives of his men. They were allowed to live, but not as soldiers. Treated as cowards, contemptuously stripped of arms and armour – they hid the eagle – and even their names, they were forced to settle as farmers in the Zeravshan Valley. They were, in effect, hostages.'

Quistus murmured, 'Even their names were taken? That's a terrible thing to lose.'

'You think they forgot who to be? No, they were Romans. They didn't forget. When Orodes died some ten years later, over the next few months they quietly got together by night and voted, most of them, to make a break for it. They knew they could never go back to Rome, but they could strike east along the Silk Road. They planned their escape in total secrecy. Most had taken local women, many had children they'd brought up as Romans. On a festival night Publius and his men raided the Samarkand commandery, seized their weapons and dug up the eagle. They took back their Roman names. Some of the foreign wives stayed behind, but the children knew their duty. They were Romans. They marched across the mountains with their fathers. Girls as well as boys.'

Publius lifted the flame over his head, walking deeper into the cave. The circle of light set man-shaped ranks of brass, bronze and steel gleaming in the shadows, lorican breastplates and shoulder guards standing among rows of helmets, swords, javelins, shields, even hobnailed sandals, an army awaiting the breath of life. Publius's voice echoed between the rock walls. 'Six thousand men ran away from Carrhae, Quistus. A thousand died at the plough, another thousand stayed in the valley. Five hundred died crossing the mountains. The rest reached Nirvana and took it from the Huns.'

Quistus touched one of the helmets wonderingly, dented and brazed. 'And the Roman children had Roman children.'

'Each one proud of his or her name.' Publius Crassus turned, the light falling in deep shadows across his face. 'A thousand are left. We are the survivors.'

'Romans,' Stigmus said with satisfaction. 'Civilization at last. Wine. Bread. Pretty girls speaking Latin. What's your hurry?'

168   *Philip Boast*

'Why don't you stay here with them?' Omba said angrily. A month had passed. It felt longer.

'I might just do that.'

'Enough bickering,' Quistus said. 'Another month, maybe two, until the weather changes for sure.'

They were holding a council of war in Zhang's hut, or as An called it, the palace. Zhang had insisted only Viridorix be allowed to sleep here with him. Manas kept guard from a small hut by the gate in the high wall. An finally agreed because the 'palace' had only one door, one room, no windows, and the walls and thatch roof were two feet thick to keep out cold – except for the hole in the top to let out smoke – and to muffle the constant, roaring wind.

'Publius Crassus would make me welcome here,' Stigmus predicted comfortably. 'A Prefect of Praetorians doesn't ride by here every day, I'd wager—' He stopped, eyes wide. Quistus held Omba's *pugio* dagger to his throat.

'Stigmus,' Quistus said, 'you tell Publius you're the Prefect of Praetorians, and I'll kill you myself.'

Zhao looked interested by Quistus's sudden ferocity. To her he was like a mirror that, moved suddenly, revealed a completely unexpected profile.

'But it's true,' Stigmus lied. 'I'm the leader here. Everyone knows it. Nero ordered me to make sure you do what you're supposed to. Don't you like it?'

'Publius is a hundred years out of date.' Quistus sounded calm but he didn't withdraw the dagger. 'He likes it that way. A hundred years ago there was no Praetorian Guard because there was no Emperor to guard. A small praetorian cohort went with generals to war, that's all.'

'You don't frighten—'

Omba drew her other dagger. Stigmus snapped his mouth shut. They both had it in for him. When things went wrong they ganged up on him and Omba started reminiscing about unfortunate events in their past, such as the time he'd strangled her and left her for dead, a situation, bad in itself, that had grown rapidly worse for her. The bitch didn't like him to forget it. 'But I *do* frighten you, don't I, Stigmus?' she whispered.

Stigmus tried to ignore the knives at his throat.

'Publius thinks Rome is Jupiter and Mount Olympus rolled into one,' Quistus said. 'He dreams of a perfect republic he's never experienced, that actually never existed. To him – to all these sons and daughters of V *Scythia* – we're Roman republicans of perfect virtue. Let's not shatter their illusions. Talk of praetorians, emperors, anything like that—' he wagged his finger. 'Understand, Stigmus?'

'Yes,' Stigmus hissed.

'If he says a word I'll kill him,' Omba said. Quistus thanked her and handed back her dagger.

'I'm glad that's over,' Zhao said. 'However, if Stigmus represents any danger to the Prince, let's kill him now. I know he's Roman, but—'

'In Rome, women behave,' Stigmus muttered. He knew this lot weren't serious, not really serious. When he'd been a child people always tried to frighten him. It didn't work. He was careful not to meet Omba's eye.

'I agree with Zhao's logic,' Chong said approvingly. He liked Zhao, not only because he enjoyed her razor-sharp mind (if she agreed with him), but also because he felt she was less feminine (and so less threatening) for being much taller than An, yet, reassuringly, only a little taller than him. Neatly assured of his superiority over both Zhao and An, he gave a very rational *Qin* smile.

Quistus sighed. They were all tetchy. The constant dry, blasting wind with day after day of dry, gritty, wind-blasted snow wore tempers thin. They'd been cooped up like chickens, keeping secret Rome's moral decline from Publius, and (given Publius's distaste for *Qin*) pretending that Zhang was only a minor Prince of Wei province experiencing a local difficulty; there was always the tense nagging feeling, as winter dragged on, that time and great events were passing them by closer to Loyang. No one trusted anyone. Couldn't risk it. One of their number, perhaps present here, now, a friend sitting with them at the table, had killed Cerberus with a particular horror. Another used dark arts to light a grotesque flower in the skies of Rome, a beacon for assassins.

'I have this to say,' Zhang said suddenly. 'We must not fight amongst ourselves.'

'I agree,' Quistus said.

'There's trouble,' Yunyazi said, and Fu barked.

'You're all in trouble,' Stigmus glowered. 'I hate the lot of you. Shut that dog up.'

'We should send a messenger east,' Zhang said. 'I know it failed before, when Golden Turtle caught and tortured our friend to death in the market square at Xireg to dissuade us from further attempts, but failing once doesn't mean we'll fail twice.'

Quistus nodded. 'He's speaking sense.'

'We're not expected now,' Zhang said. 'A messenger may be able to reach my father for help.'

'I agree,' Quistus said. 'Publius has horses. They're hardy. A man alone could ride to Loyang.'

'You've no idea of distances in *Qin*,' Chong said. 'They're vast. Even now Loyang's half a world away.'

'A man needn't ride all the way,' Quistus said. 'Only to loyal territory.'

An looked at Chong. Chong said, 'Where's loyal territory? Chen Province is certainly up in arms against us, no doubt with a new duke burning to avenge his father. Prince Ying holds Chu Province in the palm of his hand, a huge and wealthy land, and for all we know all the other provinces—'

'Send more than one messenger,' Omba suggested. 'By different ways. That's what we princesses do in Kefa.'

'Does it work?' Zhang asked.

'Two out of three.'

'What does that mean? Two of three live, or two die?'

'Two die so that one gets through.'

Quistus turned slowly. Something was wrong. Yunyazi shook. His eyes turned up.

'We should send messengers,' Zhang was saying. 'An? Your view?'

Viridorix, wrapped in the purple cloak for warmth, woke. 'As long as it isn't me,' he yawned.

'I was going to suggest purchasing the mercenary services of these Romans,' An said. 'But there's a rather serious problem. I've spent the last of the silver.'

'*What?*' Quistus demanded.

'Renting Barbelo's house. That was the last of it.'

'That's very bad news,' Quistus said, watching Yunyazi.

Chong was saying, 'An's an idiot with money.'

'There's trouble,' Quistus said. 'Yunyazi—'

Yunyazi strode forward, lifting the door latch. The door banged open, letting in the wind. Outside Publius stood against the dark, his hand raised to knock, surprised. 'How did you know I— Has someone told you?'

'Trouble,' Yunyazi said. 'Danger.' The little dog jumped into his arms.

'We've found a man.' Publius braced himself against the wind. 'Is this what you've been hiding from us while you take our hospitality?'

Quistus said, 'What man?' They pulled on their heaviest clothes and followed Publius towards the meeting hall. Flames from braziers at the guardhouse threw up sparks. The Roman called back through the storm, 'This morning, before the weather broke, our flatland patrol spied a large wagon some distance off on the plain, a broken axle. Men could be seen repairing it unaware of our presence. The prisoner had climbed a hilltop with a couple of helpers, probably to scout the way. Taken by surprise, his helpers unexpectedly put up a very stiff fight. I've two men dead. Two men, Quistus. One of my girl soldiers badly injured.'

Quistus said, 'What does this have to do with us?'

'You'll see.' Publius gave him an angry look. 'You know more than you say.'

They went into the meeting hall, setting the rows of tall-flamed tapers fluttering in the wind. Publius's soldiers stood guard with drawn swords. Omba hissed, 'It's him.' Quistus turned at once, holding his cloak wide to conceal the boys behind him.

'Get back.' He spoke low and fast. 'Manas, get the boys back to the palace. Two more guards, front and back. Move.' Manas grabbed the boys and ran with them into the dark. Publius watched coldly. Zhao followed, slamming the door behind her.

A gold man stood by the fire, made golder by his long black cloak, warming his vast golden belly at the flames. He twisted without moving his feet, sweat and melting snow trickling down his shiny face, hairless chest. 'Ah.' He pointed gold fingers as fat as lobster claws. 'You are Quistus. With such a scarred face, you are lucky to be alive, I think.'

'Saw him at the Villa Paria,' Omba murmured. 'Kicking Wild Swan's corpse.'

'Golden Turtle,' Quistus said.

'Keep him from the fire,' Yunyazi said sharply. 'Allow him no tricks. Kill him now.'

Golden Turtle spread his hands and spoke *Qin*. Yunyazi replied. Chong whispered in Quistus's ear, 'Insults. They call each other a fraud.' Chong didn't know Quistus had learnt Chinese from Genji and Fen. The words were a lot worse than *fraud.*

Quistus poured wine into a cup. 'You must be cold, Golden Turtle,' he interrupted loudly, holding it out.

'I only drink gold.' Golden Turtle knocked the tin cup aside. 'Only from gold.'

'Kill him now,' Yunyazi said.

'We talk too much of killing each other,' Quistus said. 'Maybe there's no need for it.'

'You'll die,' Golden Turtle said. He pointed at An. 'And you. And you, die. All of you. I'll see your heads in Loyang.' He grinned. 'The Prince spiked beside his father.'

'Yet,' Quistus warmed his hands at the fire, 'you're our prisoner, not the other way round.'

'Kill him,' Yunyazi said.

'I am gold, a man transmuted,' Golden Turtle said. 'Gold is not destroyed.'

Quistus asked, 'Is Loyang where you were going?'

Golden Turtle shrugged. 'I shall go to Loyang if I wish.'

'Perhaps you'd like to come along with us.'

'You won't get that far.'

'We were doing so well.'

'Prince Ying and the Divine Dowager Xu, living consort of the God Guangwu, will see you wriggling on the point of a sword first.'

'So Prince Ying is not in Loyang after all?'

Golden Turtle hesitated. 'He will be.'

'Not if we get there before him.'

'He'll know you're coming.'

'Will he? Here you are, not looking like you're going anywhere. You can't tell him we're on our way. He'll get a nasty surprise when he sees the Prince alive and well, won't he? Is the Emperor already dead?'

'He is not to live for much longer.'

'If he dies, the new Son of Heaven rides with us into Loyang to claim his birthright.'

'The brat will die first. I can do things you can't imagine.'

'Kill him,' Yunyazi said.

'We aren't afraid of you,' An said, 'you – you liar!'

'Liar?' Golden Turtle raised his high, screeching voice. 'For example, it is true your man in Peshawar died screaming.'

'Vulpus is dead?' Omba said quietly. 'You killed Vulpus?'

'You must be Omba.' Golden Turtle flapped one hand in parody of a man dying helplessly. He screeched, '"I love you, Omba!"'

She flicked out her knives. 'Omba,' Quistus said sharply.

'He's telling the truth,' she sighed. 'Vulpus said that, I know. He's dead.'

'At the cost of my own child,' Golden Turtle said sadly. 'Vulpus saved you with his dying breath. I've paid a high price for all I've achieved. Look at me, how great and grand I am. Yet I have no life. No testicles, I am a smooth man. No balls.'

An murmured in Quistus's ear, 'Prince Ying keeps them safe in a jar, no doubt, to guarantee Golden Turtle's loyalty. Eunuchs are reunited with their manhood only at burial. That's why they're trusted so utterly. No soul wants to go through eternity without his most important bits.'

'I think Golden Turtle always tells the truth,' Quistus said. 'He's a proud man. He knows he might as well tell us everything. He knows Yunyazi won't let him live through the night. He might be difficult to kill, but he also knows Yunyazi will keep trying until he finds a way.'

Publius said firmly, 'Whatever you think this man's done, I won't allow any killing of prisoners. Our justice is Roman law.'

Quistus shouted, 'Who is the traitor?'

Golden Turtle held up his hands. 'I thought you might ask. I'd already decided to tell you. You want to know who your traitor is? His name is – Yunyazi!'

Yellow smoke billowed from the fire.

Quistus crawled, coughing. The smoke grew brighter as flames ran up the wall. A javelin thudded where he'd been a moment before. He found a sword. No Golden Turtle, only overturned chairs and tables. Omba crouched. 'He's gone. Gold Heads. Ropes, I think.'

'At least they don't know where Zhang is.' Their eyes widened, hearing screams outside. 'They were on the roof. Saw us coming. Manas and Zhao took the boys back—'

They ran into the dark. Quistus stumbled off the track, losing his sense of direction. He sprinted across a dark field. The wind pushed his face. He found the track and ran beside Omba. They dashed through the gate together. Manas lay face-down by the braziers, his skull blood-red. Omba screamed. She dropped beside him, cradling his head. A guard lay dead with arrows in him. Quistus ran through the open door. The wood had been split by weapons; the boys had tried to hold it closed. Quistus slipped, skidded on the greasy straw floor. His head hit the wall.

The single room of the palace was strangely thick with smoke. Zhao lay dead or unconscious behind the door. He'd slipped on the satin hem of her gown, her cerise gown that had made her look taller than ever.

Viridorix knelt by the open fire in the middle of the room, huddling the purple cloak around his shoulders. He shuddered. The Golden Heads had thought he was Zhang. But close to, he didn't look anything like the Prince. He looked like any Roman boy. 'They didn't touch me. They didn't touch me.'

'Zhang?'

Viridorix looked up. Zhang fell from the smoke-hole. He landed in the fire and jumped, scattering embers, patting sparks from his ragged clothes, his face stiff with fright.

'Zhao!'

Zhao's eyes opened, deep as night. Quistus held her.

'Quistus,' she murmured. 'You are . . . mildly concerned about me.'

She gazed at him, smiling, but he knew she could hardly see him. 'You need to wear your sand pouches,' he said.

'They hit me from behind. Perfect vision would not have helped me.'

'Your clever hiding place saved Zhang's life. He's all right. Shaking, but all right. So's Viridorix.'

She nodded sleepily, the bruise spreading over her temple. 'But how are you, Quistus?'

'Golden Turtle escaped.'

'I hear your heart beating.'

'Golden Turtle said Yunyazi is the traitor. Of course, that means the traitor is anyone but Yunyazi.'

She dozed, then said, 'Unless Golden Turtle is playing a double blind, telling us the truth to mislead us. I always doubted Yunyazi. He has *yanhuo*. He has opium. He's strong enough. His brain is brilliant and strange. And flawed.' Quistus suspected her mind was wandering. 'You're strong, Quistus. Your arms are warm, your heart is steady.'

'Sleep now,' he said.

Her voice changed, very soft and dreamy, un-Zhao-like.

'I wrote a poem for you, Quistus. When we were at sea, just before you died.

'"She waits at the window of her high tower

For her husband to come home from the war

But while she dreams of his loving embrace

His bones whiten in a foreign field

And four years pass never to be reclaimed."'

'Your embrace is so warm,' she murmured. 'Your heart is as steady as a rock. We're so very, very far from home.'

'This is going to hurt.'

Manas sat cross-legged. Omba stood behind him in the dawn, the curved needle between her teeth dangling catgut. She pulled the flaps of skin together over his skull and sewed. At no time did he move or make a sound.

When she'd finished she whispered close to his ear, 'I've got something to tell you.'

A moment later Manas yelped, whipped round and stared.

Golden Turtle slid awkwardly from the plough horse on to the black backs crouching below. He stamped to the great wagon, stopped at the stairs and held out his arms, and they lifted him aboard.

'Stay back!' he ordered.

The wagon leant on its broken axle, useless. A single gold lamp lit the central area, hung with veils of silk, tapestries, embroideries, beautiful lacquered furniture, gorgeous pillows, a thousand drawers and secret compartments, spell-books, curse-scrolls, treatises, alchemical works. Golden Turtle ignored them. His face softened. 'My beautiful child,' he whispered.

The emaciated figure on the bed tried to sit up. Its fingers and toes were gone, replaced by stinking bandages. It turned its golden face eagerly to his voice, ragged holes in place of nose, lips, ears. Even its eyelids had rotted. No hard-earned torturers' skill had achieved such a perfectly hideous result, only the bitter mountain tops. Golden Turtle stroked the cheeks in sympathy, kissed the rider's forehead, and broke its neck.

'You were too ugly to come back to life,' he shivered.

He pulled open the drawers, scattered their contents, piled

the scrolls and books over the corpse, took the lamp, and retreated. He held out his arms.

'We must make haste now,' he called as he was lifted by his arms and thighs on to the sturdy plough horse. 'Run, my children, run. To the East with you.'

He swung the lamp through the open door. After a few moments the wagon lit up with a roar, shooting flames of green, vermilion, yellow, gold, blue, high into the night sky. Golden Turtle didn't look back.

'Romans, soldiers of V *Scythia*, hear me out. I didn't tell you of our danger because I wanted to protect you. I was wrong. Prince Zhang, as you must know by now, is no minor prince of Wei. One day, perhaps sooner than he hopes, he will be the Son of Heaven.'

Quistus, standing on a table, lifted up Zhang beside him in his gold cloak. Zhang was calm, perfectly self-controlled, wearing his *Prince* face. It was the day after the storm. The roof above the blackened walls showed patches of blue sky. The tables and beams half-burnt in Golden Turtle's fire lay piled in the corners of the meeting hall. Publius, tight-lipped with anger, had summoned all the people of the lost legion to a forum. At dawn folk started arriving from the outlying farms, men and women carrying weapons, looking after children between them.

Quistus studied the faces watching him, judging their mood. Everything had changed. Golden Turtle was no longer chasing them. He was in front, blocking their way. They'd lost a good man, though Manas's wound looked worse than it was, and Zhao had made a full recovery. Publius's support couldn't be counted on, he knew he'd been lied to, or at least not informed. The meeting might swing either way. Two soldiers of V *Scythia* had been killed, a third injured, others hurt fighting the fire. The balance of blame might shift towards or against Quistus and the *Qin*. Some faces were grim.

'Prince whoever,' someone shouted. 'What's he got to do with us? What about that gold monster? How did he make fire so fast?'

'Why didn't you warn us?'

A girl soldier shouted, 'Two men dead.' He recognized her from the scar down her cheek.

Publius said, 'Let Quistus speak, Aurelia.'

Quistus gathered his thoughts. Zhao stood like a pillar of calm, yet delicate, slim as a flame, her fingertips lightly pressed together. Her face was chalk-white, the bruise masked as though it did not exist. Her eyelashes perfectly black, lips perfectly vermilion, revealing nothing of her feelings. But he'd learnt to read her through and through in the flutter of an eyelash, the smallest twitch in the corner of her lips. Every detail of her posture, her movement, her stillness, sent him a message.

'The blame is mine.' Quistus raised his voice decisively. 'Romans, I was wrong, and wronged you, in more ways than one. Wrong not to tell you I hid the Son of Heaven among you. Wrong not to tell you of Golden Turtle. Wrong not to tell you about Rome.'

The hostile muttering faded to silence. The girl in the bronze helmet called uncertainly, 'Tell us about Rome?'

A broad farmer carrying a spear called out, 'What's this about Rome?'

'The Republic is dead.' Quistus waited, letting them absorb the shock. 'There's no Republic. The Senate's a sham, the army a shadow of its glorious past. The great families have been wiped out one by one, murdered or ordered to commit suicide by an Emperor who killed his mother, married a boy, dresses as an actor, and can imagine no greater glory for himself than burning Rome to the ground.'

Publius broke the shocked silence. 'But, Quistus—'

Quistus spoke forcefully. 'Rome is destroyed.' He pointed at his eyes. 'With my own eyes I saw Rome burn.' Zhao moved her head a fraction. He gave them no time to think. 'Prince Zhang and these brave people—'

'People.' The farmer spat. '*Qin*.'

'Yes, they're *Qin*,' Quistus shouted. '*Qin* who have built a greater culture and empire than Rome is now.' Zhao bent her middle finger a fraction of an inch. He'd hooked them, now draw them in. He lowered his voice. 'Prince Zhang fled from China to Rome, seeking help. Rome – decadent Rome, not the proud Rome your fathers and grandfathers knew – turned her back on Zhang.'

'Except one Roman did not.' Zhang's voice broke, honking. 'Quistus stood by me. He adopted me as his son.' He told them of the dangers they'd been through together.

'A son,' the farmer muttered. 'That age, too. Quistus took a heavy responsibility.'

The girl, Aurelia, nodded. 'Quistus's actions speak louder than words.'

'Spoken like a true Roman,' Publius said. 'Deeds, not their shadows.'

Quistus let them finish. He continued. 'Zhang took shelter among you. Among Romans. Soldiers of V *Scythia*, you are the true Romans now. *You*. This boy, this Son of Heaven, seeks your help.' He lowered his voice to a murmur. They strained to hear. 'I have no silver to offer you, only glory. Will you turn your back on Prince Zhang, and on me, a Roman like you? Will you tell your children "I did nothing", and cling to the past in even greater shame, running from glory like your ancestors did?'

A moment for them to think. Zhao's little finger twitched.

The farmer called, 'What sort of people do you think we are?'

'I think you're the sort of people who don't run away from a fight!'

They roared for him. He shouted, 'You'll earn the gratitude of a grateful Emperor!'

Quistus raised his arms for silence. 'No. No, I don't ask you to do this. I ask only for – I will only *accept* – volunteers, men and women who hold an honourable death higher than a shameful life. You saw Golden Turtle. You saw the Gold Heads. You saw what you're up against. Well, they're ahead of us now. Golden Turtle let slip that Prince Ying and the Xu Consort Clan aren't in Loyang. The Emperor's still alive, besieged maybe, but alive. They'll do everything they can to stop us reaching him. We'll take casualties, people will die. There will be ambushes. Poisoned water. Arrows flying from the dark. If anyone here's afraid, let him or her—'

Publius touched his hand. 'You don't need to go on,' he said. 'You've got them already.'

'You'll make better time on horseback,' Omba said. 'Genji won't be going. She can't ride in her condition. Neither can Fen.'

'What, Fen—?'

'Apparently. More than two months.'

'Who's the father?'

'She says Shu.'

'Shu? Fen as well as Genji? What does Shu say?'

'He says it's An. An claims Yunyazi's the father. He says Yunyazi is a very dirty old man, very often.'

'Not as often or old as Shu.'

'Shu says Yunyazi and Lien . . .' Omba left a suggestive pause.

'Not Lien too?'

'She went sufficiently pale when I asked her.'

Quistus stroked his cheeks, now clean-shaven, pocked with scars. He sighed. 'I never realized it was going on.'

'Oh! You're the only one who didn't. The nights have been very long, very boring, very cold. You really didn't notice?'

'*All* of them expecting babies?'

'Well, not Zhao.' Omba let the silence draw out. 'You and Zhao are not.'

'Zhao?'

'It's obvious what she feels.'

Quistus stared at her.

'No, perhaps it's not obvious at all,' Omba said. 'To some people, anyway.'

'Well, I'm pleased you had more sense than to get involved in all these shenanigans.'

Omba said, 'Actually I'm going to stay with them.'

'We need you with us.' He stopped. 'Not you too . . .'

'Travel on horseback's no good for a baby.' She smiled. 'Me too!' She patted her belly. 'Don't tell me you haven't noticed?'

'I hadn't.' He hugged her. 'Who's the lucky father?'

'You really haven't noticed! Don't you open your eyes at all? You're so obsessed with finding traitors and murderers' – she slapped him playfully – 'you don't see what's happening in front of your face. It's Manas, of course.' She ran to the guardhouse and dragged Manas over, squeezed him tight around the waist, put her head on his shoulder. 'Tell him, Manas.'

'Quistus.' Manas bent his head to Quistus's height, showing the frightful scar. 'Omba must stay. Road no good for baby son.'

'Oh!' she said. 'He's already decided it's a boy!'

'You'll be parted from her, Manas.'

'No choice. The way.'

'I know. I wish you both all the best. You'll come back next year, Manas, and hold your son.'

'Semetei.'

'I don't even get to choose his name!' Omba said fondly.

The giant looked at the women working, loading carts and packhorses. 'Back to all our sons,' he said.

Omba went with him, then looked over her shoulder. 'Remember what I said about Zhao.'

Quistus shook his head. 'You're wrong about her. Zhao's cool, impressive, intellectual, and in perfect control of herself. She's much too intelligent to feel anything for a married man.'

'Oh, that,' Omba said. 'I forgot about that.'

Publius came over. 'The riders we sent have returned. The wagon was burnt out. Hoof and footprints led east. They gave chase for half a day, going hard. Nothing. They followed orders, turned back.'

'Thank you, Publius. We leave at dawn tomorrow.'

'Men and women over forty, and children under sixteen, will stay here. They're capable of defence, of course. Plus a garrison of a few hundred. That gives us about seven hundred volunteers in the saddle and on foot. Enough to deter bandits and local warlords.'

'Maybe some will join us.'

'Maybe we'll fly.'

'Our speed's that of the slowest cart anyway. We know Golden Turtle's more than half a day ahead, but he can't keep up that pace. He'll drop Gold Heads behind in ones and twos, maybe small groups, to harass us.'

'That's what I'd do.'

'So would I. Barbelo advised me to go down in the plain and follow the line of mountains east.'

'Very sensible.'

'Very predictable. I'll strike north-east, deep into the plain, then turn east. Zhang and the *Qin* know that way from their journey out.'

'The Taklamakan? Cold stone desert.'

'We'll carry our water with us.' Quistus nodded. 'It's worth the risk to wrong-foot Golden Turtle.'

'Very well. I'll give orders.' Publius saluted and hurried away.

Quistus turned to Zhang, who'd been listening quietly. 'I hope you're right, Zhang, that there is a way across the desert.'

It was the boys' last night in the one-room palace. Tomorrow, Viridorix knew, they'd set off for who-knew-where. His life felt like a constant journey and sometimes, like tonight, he saw no end to it except death. Manas dozed in the little gatehouse, or prowled the garden, or watched you blue-eyed from the dark, you never knew. Even Zhang was asleep now and there was no fun, no one to talk to.

Zhao sat between the candle and the embers of the fire, cross-legged on the earth floor, her wrists on her knees and hands turned up. Viridorix didn't know what it meant. Her lips moved silently.

He whispered, 'Zhao?' Her eyes opened. 'Who are you talking to?'

Her voice was soft, sleepy-deep. 'To my ancestors. To my dead husband, Cao Shou.'

'Why?'

'They're wiser than I, Viridorix. I ask their forgiveness for my stupidity, for my humanity, for my life.'

'Zhao, can I ask you something?' Viridorix crawled closer. 'Ask.'

'When I was wearing the purple cloak, the Gold Heads thought I was Zhang. They were all around me and they raised their swords and I knew they were going to kill me.'

'But they didn't.'

'They realized I wasn't Zhang. I was nobody. But I was sure I was going to die. I realized all I'd done was bad things, there was nothing else. No good side. All I could remember was lying to that holy man, Thomas.'

'Lying?'

'Zhang needed Quistus to come upriver with us so badly.'

'Yes, Viridorix.' Zhao nodded. 'We wouldn't have got this far without Quistus.'

'So I said to Thomas about seeing Quistus's daughter in Gaul.'

Zhao said nothing. Then she asked, 'Quistus's daughter?'

'Lyra. And how the Gondophares coin I stole from her meant she'd been in India. That's why Quistus came to India, part of the why, anyway. And the weird thing was, Thomas said yes, he'd seen her too—'

'Quistus has a daughter.'

'Her name's Lyra, and there's a son. I think he's Septimus.'

'A son.'

'And Quistus had about six more children, but he killed them. So they say. And his wife, their mother, Marcia.'

'He killed them.'

'Her too. That's what they say. He showed me the place, the Villa Marcia. I didn't like it. You could imagine it.'

'They say he killed them?'

'What I felt really bad about was Thomas saying yes, he'd seen Lyra, and I couldn't stop him going on and on about her to Quistus, although I wanted him to carry on in a way, because I could see Quistus would go with us because of her. And he did.'

'To Peshawar, because of her?'

'That's right. He searched for her in Peshawar, asked for her in all the bazaars—'

'He searched for her in Peshawar?'

'Of course he did. Just because of what Thomas said, and it was sort of my fault.'

'I never knew.'

'But I *did*. That's what I mean. Well, when there were all those Gold Heads around me aiming down their swords, and I knew I'd had it, I just felt . . . *guilty*.'

'Go to sleep, Viridorix.'

'It's been on my mind.'

'Go to sleep.'

Zhao sat without moving until the fire was cold and the candle was out.

Omba waited by the stony stretch of road between the watch-towers. Dawn was always a disappointment in Nirvana; the sun rose in the mid-morning, chipped from the peaks like a blazing, ice-cold diamond. The women with child lined the road beside her, Genji holding back the faithful mule, determined not to weep. As the soldiers came riding past the mothers with children held them up to be kissed, and some fathers held up older children to be kissed by their soldier-mothers riding out. Publius's wife held up their daughters. An odd wailing sound went up, the sound of certain departure rubbing against uncertain return. The old stood quietly. They'd seen it many times before.

Prince Zhang led the entourage, dressed in thick fleeces proof against arrows and assassins' knives. He nodded to Omba. Quistus held out his hand to her. Viridorix was trying not to cry. Manas ignored Omba lest he bring her bad luck. 'Manas!' she called. 'Your son will be waiting.'

An ignored Fen's calls, riding bumpily. He would have preferred to be carried in a sedan chair like a proper gentleman. Genji waved at Chong and he frowned, like a man thinking up a better design of saddle. He couldn't get the sword comfortable behind his shoulders. Fen waved at Shu, who did his wrinkly best to look like a fierce fighting man. Little Pelican rode in the cart holding a tasselled parasol overhead, the only girl – except Zhao – not to have taken a lover during the winter. Omba supposed that men (although it was unlike men to be fastidious) were repelled by Little Pelican's mutilated feet. Zhao came by sitting tall in the saddle, almost weightless, wearing no make-up yet pale as a ghost, the reins swinging lightly in her long fingers.

'You!' Omba called. 'Look after him.'

Zhao spared her a small, curious glance.

Omba climbed the watchtower. The plain spread out below her, the line of riders thinning into the dust, the heavier snake of infantry following with a steady rhythm. The sun shone glamorously off spears as it always did. She couldn't make out Manas but she knew where he was, near Quistus and the Prince. Yunyazi, wearing his beard inside his clothes against the cold, came last, swaying on top of the heaviest cart. He acquired treasures – pointless objects, stones, scrolls he said were treasures – wherever he went. Lien, standing alone, cried her heart out. Yunyazi ignored her. Fu stood on the seat beside him, barking.

The gates slowly closed, thudding heavily.

Omba stared across the plain until they were all out of sight, and even the dust had drifted away.

'Well.' She slapped her hands. 'That's that. Time to get some real work done around here.'

Sixty miles to the south, ten miles farther than the Silk Road (which obviously they'd not taken) that hugged the foothills, great peaks stretched across the horizon like a toothy lower jaw seen from the inside. The Taklamakan was the palate of a huge open mouth, a vast, sterile depression of dry rivers and dust. The road came from nowhere and went nowhere, one of the many Subtle Roads, a way around difficulties, blown over with sand and stones, perhaps not used for ten or fifty years, yet ready to be rediscovered in times of trouble.

And there had been trouble here. They rode past mummi-
fied men perfectly preserved in the dust, dried leather corpses
lying in ones and twos, sometimes whole battlefields preserved
from ancient, forgotten wars, exposed limbs and faces eroded
by the wind, tableaux of the unburied long-dead. The lost legion
marched in silence through these petrified cemeteries.

The fortress stood on a hillock overlooking a dry river, abandoned, roofless, its whitewashed walls wind-blasted to brown
rock. Yunyazi dug up a half-buried stone engraved with *Qin*
symbols. 'The Palace of Andirlangar.' Nearby lay other stones
inscribed in unknown tongues, *Nyatri Tsenpo*, kings, chief-
tains, warlords, robbers: all who'd claimed this forsaken place
and blown away.

They made camp in the echoing courtyard. The inner walls,
still white, glowed faintly in the starlight. 'You have your wish,
Quistus,' Zhao said. 'Do you remember, long ago, you asked
to see Little Pelican dance?'

'I remember. You said such sacred privileges were not for
the likes of me.'

'I'm only a woman, ready to be overruled by others greater
than I.'

Modesty from Zhao always struck him as false. He wondered
what she was really thinking.

She said, 'Now that we've entered the borders of Middle
Earth – though strictly speaking, of course, the whole world
is Middle Earth – Prince Zhang has commanded Little Pelican
to perform the Dragon Dance in celebration. It's a great honour.
This dance has never been seen by western eyes before.'

'I shall watch carefully.'

'It truly is a sacred privilege.'

'I shall watch it very carefully, Zhao.'

'You'll see her dance the line between gods and men. Aren't
you interested, Quistus?' Zhao's lips tightened. 'It's agonizing
for her. From agony beauty is born. You might at least appreciate what she's going through.' She led him to a high window
overlooking the courtyard. 'You'll get the best view from
here.'

Soldiers lined the rectangular courtyard below, their faces
and armour illuminated by the central bonfire on the sand. Zhang,
gold-cloaked, sat on the steps at one end on a chair someone
had found or quickly made. Stigmus stood behind him,

whispering in his ear. Quistus leant out, seeing Yunyazi directly below, busy with pots and powders. The magician had managed to salvage a few extra items from Golden Turtle's burnt-out wagon. That had been only a few hours after leaving Nirvana, when Quistus had ridden back to find him poking through the wreckage.

'Find anything, Yunyazi?' he'd asked.

'There are always things to be found. Finding is one of the principal ways Heaven communicates its wonders to the earth-bound.' Yunyazi had blown soot off a brass canister, shaken it to hear what it contained, and slipped it into his clothes.

Quistus had lifted a charred scroll. Yunyazi had snatched it, peering, muttering. Where the scroll had been Quistus saw a black silk sleeve poking from the ash. He pulled it out still attached to the rest of the clothes, and the cloak too. Yunyazi had nodded, murmuring, 'Yes, Golden Turtle attempted to burn a body here.'

'Not very successfully. Where is it?'

'Such things happen. Heat is drawn to Heaven. Often the earth remains cool beneath the fire.'

'What happened to the body?'

'It turned to ash and blew away to Heaven.'

Quistus had held the clothes. 'Maybe Chong was right,' he'd said. 'The dead do leave their clothes behind. Their spirits are nude.'

Yunyazi had pored over the scroll, muttering, and Quistus had ridden away.

He blinked, standing beside Zhao at the window. Drums were beating in the courtyard, softly at first. Yunyazi bowed to the bonfire. He raised his arms, and the flames rose. The Roman soldiers fell silent, then gave an uneasy shout of wonder.

Yunyazi lowered his arms, and the flames burned lower. He bent until his hands almost touched the ground. The flames had almost gone out. The courtyard filled with darkness.

Yunyazi stepped back with a cry, flinging up his arms. The bonfire hissed, flaring, and for a moment it seemed that the flames curled into a strange, fiery head that rose up – but it was just a bonfire again, just flames.

Quistus touched the ring Zhang had given him. A dragon's head. Zhao was watching him, the firelight shining down one side of her face.

He noticed Little Pelican by the bonfire. He hadn't seen how she got there. Her tiny figure trailed a long gown behind her in the dust, like a tail. Her shadow was longer than she, spreading up the wall. He couldn't see her face; she hid her head between her upraised arms, holding a pose.

She hadn't moved. Only the flames moved, the firelight dancing over her, her shadow dancing behind her.

The soldiers muttered impatiently.

Little Pelican stood on tiptoe. Her hair fell unbound in a long twist down her back, almost to the ground, where the end was tied with fluttering ribbons. She must be moving really, because now Quistus saw her face. Her face was a dragon's head, ferocious, full of vitality, its stylized mouth gaping wide. Vermilion ribbons hung from its nostrils.

Little Pelican turned on tiptoe, impossibly, smoothly rotating.

Zhao whispered, 'Can you feel her agony?'

'I can admire her skill.'

'I haven't forgiven you, Quistus.' Zhao moved to his other side, shadowed, ignoring the dancer. 'I never will forgive you. For making me suffer on the boat, hurting me to discover if I told you the truth.'

'You did tell the truth.' Quistus turned away from her a fraction, irritated by her interruption. Little Pelican, spinning very slowly, raised one leg until her foot touched her face, the dragon's mouth.

'Watch Little Pelican. Don't care about me, Quistus. Look away.' Zhao held the little kitchen knife from the Villa Paria.

He tensed, watching her. Zhao said, 'Don't worry, Quistus, it's not for you. It's for me. Why should you care?'

He turned fully to face her. 'Zhao—'

'Watch her dance, Quistus. Enjoy your great privilege.'

Little Pelican swirled in a slow circle, rotating from one foot to the other. The tail of her gown wrapped itself round her legs then flew out. The bonfire was brighter. The soldiers started a steady clap, increasing the rhythm.

Zhao held her knife at arm's length, almost touching him, both hands clenched, the blade pointed at her heart. He knew it would take real strength to stop her.

'Give me that knife,' he ordered. None of them ever disobeyed a direct command.

Zhao did. She pushed her fists against him. She pushed him

back against the window ledge. He could hear the dance behind him. She hissed, 'Is this how you killed them?' She pushed, hard, her arms collapsing until her fists almost touched her breasts, the knife pricking her dress between them, the point disappearing by an inch as though it already stabbed her.

'I won't live with your contempt,' she said. 'You won't lie to me now, Quistus. *How could you not tell me about them?*'

The knife had gone deep between her breasts, sliding almost to the hilt in the taut line of her dress. The point must be touching her skin. He said very carefully, 'I haven't lied to you.'

'*Everyone else knew you had a family!* Not I, not I. Cerberus never told me, he always kept your secrets. Viridorix said—' The knife trembled in her hands. 'You killed them. Somebody killed them. Perhaps you.' She pushed harder, squeezing her fists between their bodies. 'How could you never tell me?' She was weeping. The tears flowed. 'I had no secrets from you. Except one.'

Little Pelican whirled in a circle. She held long ribbons of flame in her hands. The ends touched the bonfire and burst into brilliant sparks flying around her as she whirled.

Quistus closed his hands over Zhao's fists but she pushed him with her body. He felt the blade touch her breastbone. 'What secret?'

'You know it, Quistus. It's the one you know. The one you won't admit.' She breathed into his eyes.

He said, 'I don't love you, Zhao.'

She pushed her face against his. 'No,' he said. Little Pelican whirled in the courtyard, red, green, yellow, sparks flying. 'Have her,' Zhao cried. 'Everyone else does. What's wrong with me, Quistus? From the very first moment I saw you, the very first, I loved you.' There was a loud explosion from the courtyard, like a thunderclap. The fire rose high, throwing deep shadows.

He tugged the knife from her, then held his hand. She'd cut him. He sucked the blood. She kissed his mouth. 'Zhao,' he said. She kissed him. He tore her dress. The knife had torn it already, he tore it wide. She bit him, her long fingers splayed against his face, they pulled each other down.

'Four years,' she whispered.

The cavalry of the Lost Legion rode ahead, scouting, but mostly the entourage stayed with the infantry at a slower pace. Quistus no longer bothered to check behind for clues left by the enemy – if, indeed, there was an enemy among them any longer. With Golden Turtle free and in front it was entirely possible that the traitor, job done, had stayed behind with the *Qin* oldsters and girls in Nirvana, and might never be found. The real enemy was in the East now. No news of the messengers they'd sent ahead in different directions; Publius felt that was a very good sign, as it was too soon for them to have returned with help, so they still had plenty of reason for hope. 'Do you agree, Quistus?' Quistus rode forward without answering. He'd obviously had a riding accident. His hand was bandaged and his face was red down one side. He'd stuffed one nostril with cloth. Quite possibly his nose was fractured.

Quistus rode without looking at Zhao. Zhao rode without looking at him, ignoring him, as cold and distant from him as he was from her. It was she who'd struck him across the face. *Ban ye*, they'd been lying on the cool stones, watching the stars, drawing deep breaths. The courtyard below had been quiet and empty, only embers remaining of the fire. Zhao had spoken first.

'You aren't married any more, Quistus. She's gone.'

He'd sat up but he was still naked. Zhao had held on to him, tight. She'd spoken with her lips almost touching his eyes. 'She's gone, Quistus.'

'I'm ashamed.'

'Don't be ashamed. She's dead. She's gone. Let her go.'

'I can't.'

'You *have*,' she'd whispered. 'You just have, Quistus.'

'I don't know.'

She'd leant back. 'Did you kill them?'

'I don't know—'

She'd struck him across the face. 'Of course you didn't!'

She'd held her hand. It felt like a finger was broken.

'Of course you didn't,' she'd sighed. 'And if Lyra's alive, Quistus, she's not here. She's not here.'

From Andirlangar the Lost Legion crossed the dusty oasis at Qiemo. The glinting line of Roman spears, helmets and shields followed the dry defile of the Qargan valley, swung south to Ruoquiang, and there rejoined the Silk Road. At first everyone was alert for danger when meeting travellers or passing through villages, but no one had seen a golden man or fighters wearing black. An advised Zhang to wear his gold cloak and sent people ahead to warn of the royal party's arrival. Villagers would come out to watch them pass and seemed friendly enough.

Stigmus rode beside Quistus. 'I've advised Publius that our messengers will expect to find us on this road, so we may receive news of friendly forces any day.'

Quistus didn't reply. Stigmus had noticed he didn't say much lately. Probably he'd tried to get friendly with Zhao, who was top-class after all, even without make-up, and received the same icy rebuff Stigmus had. Yes, the incredible was true; the ice-cold, snooty *Qin* intellectual had given up her white pancake and black eyes. She still looked extraordinary because of her height and spooky creased eyelids, but different, softer. A bit more human, maybe, more vulnerable. Still not Stigmus's sort, though, not needy enough, not much passion to be squeezed from that long thin frame. He fell back to the cart and struck up some chat with Little Pelican. The sweet little thing was just getting over her shyness. He was teaching her rude words in Latin and she picked them up in no time at all.

At Baxkorgan An was pleased when the village elders turned out to welcome them, making gifts of meat, honey and yoghurt that didn't have to be paid for. From there the Silk Road climbed, winding along the valleys of the Altun mountains before reaching the broad spread of the Qaidam Pendi, high, flat and hot. Midges swarmed from the salt marshes. That was when they saw the dot in the distance, shimmering in the heat.

'It's not a Gold Head,' Viridorix said. The boys had the best eyesight.

'He's one of ours.' Zhang peered. 'A messenger returning from my father.'

When the messenger rode by without stopping, they sent cavalry to bring him back.

The messenger had been tied to his saddle. His severed head was sewn to his hands.

That evening the second messenger rode into camp. 'Steady,' Quistus said. Only the first arrow, between the eyes, was golden, black-tuftcd. The others, all of them, were knife-chipped out of thin green wood, with rough-plucked vanes of goose feather.

Stigmus grabbed the bridle. He called, 'Look, Prince. He's been used for target practice.'

'Obviously,' Zhang said.

'Obviously,' Viridorix said.

'Not by Gold Heads,' Quistus said. 'An?'

An said quietly, 'These are Hun arrows.' Chong concurred.

Publius ordered the watch to the east to be doubled. The Romans, well-practised, dug a trench around the camp and threw up a stony earth bank, but found no trees for a stockade. The stars touched the horizon without dimming. No one slept that night.

Two out of three, Omba had said. Quistus wished powerfully she were here now. With any luck the third man had made it through.

At dawn the third rider appeared. He rode looking behind him into the rising sun, silhouetted, his horse stumbling and exhausted. Quistus caught him as he fell.

The man stared up. His lips were crusted with salt, his eyes wild.

'Give him water.' The man drank then convulsed, puking. He'd been drinking salt water, eating salt. His wild gaze found Quistus.

'Thousands,' he croaked. 'They're coming. There's a huge army of Huns coming.'

VI

The Sea Battle

Several days' travel to the east of the Blue Sea, a little farther than that from the Celestial Mountains, Prince Ying of Chu sat naked, except for his round black cap, in his bath. Only his head showed. His immobility in the steaming mineral waters required considerable presence of mind and intense personal discipline. So high had they come, so close to Heaven, that the normal rules of Earth broke down and it was possible to sit in water that was almost boiling. He was waiting for his breakfast fish to arrive.

The head of the valley was known for the medicinal quality of its steam pools. The tent in which he sat had been erected over one of the largest salt vents, boiling at its far end, merely almost unbearably hot at this end. Ying showed not one sign of discomfort, even though he was alone. Alone, that is, apart from the buzzing attendants who hung on his every word, the swarming lower orders who were not on the level of humans. One didn't notice them.

The tent was only a small part of the larger marquee that had been erected entirely over it, held up by poles as large as trees, topped by banners that flew in the wind. Beside it stood another white canvas palace almost as large, where the Dowager Consort Xu, his mother, was being painstakingly prepared for yet another day in her long, long life.

The valley below the steam pools, its rocks crusted with salt and minerals, teemed with barbarians of the worst, yet most indispensable, breed. Breed was the word for them. They bred like animals, in public, given the briefest opportunity. They cooked meat between their buttocks and the horse they rode. Their women were hideous lumps, their children screamed and grunted, and their fathers killed any who were weak or stupid. Ying breathed out through his thin nostrils, satisfied. He had to admit that it was an effective social policy; their brutality had made them into a strong people, a disciplined, formidable people in their way, although worse than animals.

Huns raped, killed, stole. That was it. No art, no buildings, no writing. What you saw was what you got. They were perfect.

From the water Ying raised the long, aristocratic nail of his little finger in a gesture of absolute command. The crystal tank containing the *huangyu* was carried in for his inspection. It was an old fish as long as his leg, like a carp but specially adapted to these bitter waters. He nodded and it was tossed in.

Huns had been his enemy for most of his life. Huns were his father's enemy, his grandfather's enemy; in fact the enemy of all his ancestors going back to God. Even now, somewhere in the north, the fool Ban Chao was fighting to hold back yet more Hun tribes. Nothing held back Huns. Building the greatest wall in history hadn't held them back. Ordering *Qin* farms and fields laid waste for hundreds of *li* to make a sterile border zone didn't stop them. Carrying the war into their own territory, burning Hun villages, crops, animals, children, women, slaughtering them by the thousand, ten thousand, hundred thousand, even much more – fifty million *Qin* roused to a fury of revenge achieved a great deal of death – merely encouraged the Hun to melt into the outer steppes, which were endless, to return as soon as one's back was turned, with even greater savagery.

It took Prince Ying to see one very simple fact: the Huns could never be beaten.

They could, however, be used.

Prince Ying was great friends with their unwashed *shanyu* King Punu. Punu had no table manners, none. Just to see him was agony, he crawled with grim vermin. He stood for every foulness that *Qin* stood against. Ying itched to drown him in a bath, to skin him clean. But somewhere beneath Punu's yak-greased hair lurked a sharp political mind. Such a mind leading such a people was easily subverted by such a man as Prince Ying, a man who had spent his life in the shadow of Emperors. A man who should have been Emperor. An Emperor who would bring the true religion of the Buddha to *Qin*. Around the tents a thousand priests, in saffron robes, chanted.

The Hun attacks on the East could not be stopped.

Ying had seen that the Huns had simply to be promised the fabled lands of the West. They could be turned.

Soon the boy-Prince would be dead. There was the small matter of Loyang still to be dealt with, but Ying's half-brother, the Emperor, would fall like a ripe plum to a horde of barbarian Huns under civilized *Qin* command. Ying's command. Mother's too, of course. Prince Ying would be the rightful Son of Heaven, and Mother would no longer suffer the term *Consort*. She would be Dowager Empress. He'd promised her.

The *huangyu* floated among the bubbles, dying, poaching nicely. Ying raised his fingernail for Golden Turtle.

The eunuch, entering, prostrated himself. He'd had the sense to wash himself of travel-stains, and his hard flesh had been buffed until he shone, but he'd forgotten the mouthful of *juelma* herb for which these Blue grasslands were famous. *Juelma* guaranteed eternal life. Ying had noted, however, that the peasants around here lived very short lives.

He said, 'You have been too long in the West!'

Golden Turtle swallowed the bitter herb. At a nod from Ying, attendants hauled him to his knees. Golden Turtle didn't dare look his master in the eye.

'Where is the Prince?'

'Four days west of the Blue Sea, Highness.'

Ying studied his fingernail. 'And my favoured one?'

'Alive. Not dishonoured.' Golden Turtle tried not to look at the large, fragile-looking glass pot placed behind Prince Ying. In it, a constant reminder of the consequences of less than perfect success, floated Golden Turtle's most precious and vulnerable bits, immaculately preserved. He added reluctantly, 'With the Romans.'

'Romans.'

'Perhaps staying back in Nirvana. Perhaps with them in the Qaidam Pendi. Impossible to tell.'

'Romans. Here. In *Qin*?'

'One hundred, no more,' Golden Turtle lied, gazing at the glass pot. 'Desperadoes. Battered armour, rusty swords, no crossbows. Barbarians.'

'Yet tales have reached these ears of fish-scale shield tactics proof against spears, towers that knock down walls, and swinging beams that throw stones.'

'My children will deal with them. The Prince's last pathetic messenger was allowed to escape and followed. His position is known.'

Ying held out his arms. Attendants raised him from his bath, revealing for a short but powerful moment his ample penis unshrunk by the hot water, having been carefully rubbed with snow lotus before his bath. The comparison with the shrivelled, pickled knobs in the pot could not have been more telling in his favour.

'Bring me his head,' Prince Ying smiled, 'or else.'

The *huangyu* was brought to him on an oval plate, gently steaming. Later he would have a word with King Punu. The map was almost ready. Then there was Mother.

'They know where we are.' Quistus looked around the circle of their faces. 'The messenger, poor fellow, would have been followed at a discreet distance.'

'Are we sure of that?' Stigmus asked.

'We dare not risk any other conclusion. We must change our plan. Where does this road lead?'

Zhao drew in the dust. 'This valley is flat grassland. Twenty days long, two days wide at this point. Hills and mountains to the north and south. There's a lake ahead.'

Yunyazi nodded. 'Shortly. We pass north of it.'

'We'll pass south,' Quistus said.

Zhang asked, 'You're sure the Gold Heads followed the messenger?'

'Yes,' Quistus said. 'I would've.'

Stigmus said weightily, 'I disagree—' but Publius shouted orders.

'South it is, Senator.'

'I don't use that title here,' Quistus said, but he knew it was a large part of the reason Publius the republican accepted his authority, even though under Nero *Senator* meant something very different from the old days.

'I know you don't use it, Senator,' Publius said, 'but I do.'

Zhao drew a circle farther east. 'This is the Blue Sea.'

'Farther,' Yunyazi said. 'Bigger. Much bigger. Yes, that's it. We have to get around the sea. There's a valley along the south side, flanked by the Celestial Mountains.'

'Towns? Villages?'

Zhang said, 'In Xireg, remember, I was sold for a handful of *wazhu* and a bag of salt. Golden Turtle tortured our friend to death in the market square. We know it. There's a road, and any number of tracks around the smaller salt lakes.'

'That's good.' Quistus nodded, thinking. 'What if we do the unexpected, go round the north shore of the sea?'

Yunyazi said, 'Marshes, grassland, hills.'

'So that's possible?'

'Yes, it's possible.'

'What lies beyond the Blue Sea?'

'The river valleys run down to Loyang, eventually.'

There was a moment of *Qin* silence. Quistus could see them thinking of the long green valleys of home.

'Then, ladies and gentlemen,' he said decisively, 'we should get moving.'

They kept the lake shore on their left all afternoon, guided by the thin finger of smoke that rose from its southern extremity. Quistus had thought the smoke marked a village or settlement of charcoal-burners, and meant to slip by in the dark, but as the sun lowered the single thin finger remained. No more fires were lit for cooking. Publius reined in. 'Doesn't smell right.'

They lay up for an hour in a shallow dent in the grassland, listening to the bells of yaks and cattle grazing. Wolves kept clear of the mass of men, but Roman armour was no defence against the mosquitoes, midges, gnats and bots that swarmed in whining clouds from the marshes. The soldiers rubbed each others' faces with mud, the girls laughing. 'Look what I found, sir, hiding with his herd.' A tough-looking Roman sergeant, every inch of her exposed skin black with mud, had collared a smokey-looking, nervously-smiling shepherd. No one could understand a word he said. He was blue-eyed, so Quistus called Manas over.

Manas listened. 'Man says it's a fort. Lookout post, *Qin*.'

'*Qin?*' Stigmus said. 'At last.'

'Bad men came last night. Fighting, screaming. Rode away into the sun.'

'The rising sun,' Stigmus said. 'He means the east.'

'Thank you, Stigmus,' Quistus said. 'Manas?'

'He says silence all day. Dead silence. He won't go near.'

'He's sure they rode away?'

'Short ponies. Men wearing fleeces. He calls them *Xiongnu*.'

'Meaning?'

Zhang said, 'Huns.'

'Huns!' Stigmus said.

Manas pointed. 'From the east. Many.'

'How many?' Quistus asked.

Manas barked something and the man gave a very short answer. 'He says, a herd.'

Zhao held up her fingers. The shepherd nodded. 'At least ten,' she said.

'Scouts.' Publius spat in his hand, crushed an insect. 'Raiders. He's sure they're all gone?'

'All gone.'

'I need to see before dark.' Quistus was curious. 'Who keeps a lookout post against the Huns out here? This is the middle of nowhere.'

'I think I know,' Zhao said. 'I'll come with you.' Quistus shook his head, but she swung into the saddle anyway. Zhao without make-up was not to be stopped, apparently.

'You're not going alone.' Stigmus drew his sword and ordered a phalanx of cavalry to fall in behind him. The soldiers looked at Publius. Publius nodded.

The horses cantered along the southern shore. One or two stunted trees grew in the marsh. The fort was a ditch-and-bank thrown around a small peaty hillock. Scrawny shrubs had been stripped and woven to make a lathe defensive wall at the top. A few Hun arrows stuck in the strips of wood, and the rest was holes where most arrows had passed straight through. Hooves had churned the neat turf slope to bare black peat. A couple of Hun bodies had rolled down and lay entangled with the *Qin* dead.

Quistus dismounted and clambered to the top. Stigmus was slowed by his drawn sword. 'Stay back, Zhao,' he called importantly from the rim, striking a pose against the sunset. 'Nothing to see here.'

Beyond, Quistus found a small, shallow declivity sheltered from the wind. The last stand had been here. The corpses buzzed with flies, blackened by a day in the sun. A Hun lay over the cooking fire, the source of the smoke. Quistus pointed at the small turf hut, its doorway low and dark. Stigmus covered the side. Quistus ducked through. After a moment his voice called out, muffled by the thick walls. 'Water.'

'Send water,' Stigmus called down to Zhao. He crawled into the hut, hand over nose. His eyes adjusted to the dark. 'Gods. He's not dead, is he?'

Quistus glanced round. 'He thinks we're Huns. He's terrified.' He said in Chinese, 'You're safe, man. We're friends.'

The soldier's imposing military moustaches stretched back to his earlobes. He held his arm at the shoulder, stripped of his *Qin* armour, left for dead. His legs kicked weakly. 'Don't come in,' Stigmus called, but Zhao ducked inside with the water. She held the skin to the dying man's lips. He couldn't drink. She asked him quietly, 'Who sent you?'

'I'm Ban Chao man.'

She glanced at Quistus. 'That's impossible.'

'He said Ban Chao.'

Zhao murmured, 'If he's with Ban Chao, one of Ban Chao's men, that's not possible.'

Quistus said, 'Ask him—'

She murmured gently, 'Soldier, where is Ban Chao?'

The man let go of his arm, pointing.

'Gods,' Stigmus croaked, 'he was holding it on.'

'North.' Zhao held the man while he died. He breathed, '*Zamashi.*'

She closed his eyes. 'He pointed north.'

'Don't treat me like an idiot,' Quistus said. Death always upset him. 'I know the word for north.'

Zhao snapped, 'I treat you like an idiot when you behave like one. This man is dead.' She shook.

'Shut up, you two,' Stigmus said. 'It stinks in here.' He stood in the doorway taking deep breaths.

'Zamashi, if you're interested,' Zhao hissed furiously at Quistus, 'is a border town in Gansu Province.'

Quistus nodded. 'To the north.'

'Exactly!' Zhao's lips compressed into a thin line. She made an obvious effort to relax. She knelt, covering the body with a ragged cannabis blanket.

Quistus said, 'Ban Chao, he's the same Ban Chao who's your brother, is he?'

'Congratulations.'

'Her brother?' Stigmus said.

Zhao nodded. 'The General commanding the Outlands North-of-the-Wall.' She shrugged. 'My elder brother, twin of the writer Ban Gu.' She shot a defiant look at Quistus. 'Twins run in our family.'

Quistus asked, 'North-of-the-Wall?'

'Anywhere Huns are to be found in the northern steppes, the Outlands.' Zhao sat. She put her hands to her head. 'I'm worried. I'm very worried. The Wall is three days' ride to the north. Zamashi is south of the Wall.'

'So?'

'If my brother is in Zamashi, he's crossed the Wall. This lookout post is highly illegal, Quistus. My brother's outside the borders of his command, disobeying explicit standing orders. He's committing treason against the Emperor.'

'He's gone over to Prince Ying and Golden Turtle,' Stigmus said.

She shook her head. 'I know Ban Chao.'

'Gods, it stinks in here,' Stigmus said.

They stood outside in the last red glow of sunset, breathing deeply, listening to the yelping of a wolf pack over the plain. Sergeant Aurelia, her scar an extra muddy line down her cheek, organized a defensive perimeter and burial detail.

Quistus said, 'Ban Chao could be in Zamashi because he's looking for Huns. They've gone from the north, so he's following them, following rumours, but he doesn't yet realize Ying's brought them this far south. A rider could warn him. Zhang boasted Ban Chao has a hundred legions in total. That probably includes sweepers, cleaners, pot-polishers, but—'

'It's still treason,' Zhao said. 'It doesn't make sense. My brother is the most loyal man I know. If he's come south, every man with him is marked for death. He'd never risk the lives of his men in such a way.'

'Yet that soldier told us with his dying breath, Ban Chao is in Zamashi.'

'A hundred legions, a tenth of that, would smash Ying to pieces,' Stigmus said. 'Him and all his Huns. The man who brought Ban Chao in on this would be quite a hero. The Emperor's rich, isn't he? Why should you and Publius get it all?'

'You still want to be a hero, Stigmus,' Quistus said.

'A rich hero,' Stigmus said. 'I'll show you. You think I'm a coward?'

'Even if Ban Chao is loyal, you really think he'd believe a word a barbarian told him?'

'He'd believe me,' Zhao said quietly.

'You'll just slow me down,' Stigmus said.

'My brother is no traitor, Quistus, and he'll believe any message I give him.'

Quistus drew a deep breath to say no.

He breathed out. 'She has a point,' he said.

'I don't want to let you go,' Quistus murmured. 'Now I've got you I want to keep you.'

'You don't say kind words to me. You don't say you love me.'

'I can't say that.'

'How can you say *that*?'

They were each a shadow in starlight. The stars came down to the lake, the waters were full of them. He sat facing Zhao on the grass, both cross-legged, their knees almost touching. Zhao rarely made an unnecessary movement. He thought, She's as calm as the water is.

'I miss my children too, Quistus.'

'I know. Do you know where they are?'

'If not in Ban Gu's care, then with my Cao in-laws in Fufeng. We would have sent for them to join us at the Autumn Palace. I don't think Shou's parents even know he's dead. The children are too young to understand, fortunately.'

'Life is tough.'

'No, it isn't,' Zhao said calmly. 'It's just life. *I* am tough.'

'You'll see them again. Two girls, or two boys?'

'One of each.' The air rustled as wings swept overhead. 'Like yours.'

'Viridorix saw them, Zhao. He saw them both, Lyra and Septimus.'

'Yes, I know what Viridorix said.' They heard the birds splash into the water. Ripples spread across the stars. In a little while the reeds tapped gently together. They heard a deeper splashing in the mud as though some heavier creature moved.

'Thomas saw her too, Zhao.'

'I shouldn't get your hopes up about Thomas. He was just an old man living on dreams.'

'He saw her.'

'Thomas also told me he saw his brother crucified and live again after three days. He built a palace out of air, of lies. How reliable a witness is he?'

'So when Thomas says something, makes some statement, it's always a lie? Maybe it's always the truth, you just have to see it in the right way. Maybe he did see his brother. He saw Lyra.'

'How long will you keep searching, Quistus? How long will it go on? Until your life is wasted, along with the life of anyone who cares for you?'

'I can't say it, Zhao. I can't say I love you.'

She touched his knee with her fingertip. 'You just did.'

They sat looking at the stars.

'Well, I don't want you to go.'

'Compared to a *Qin* man, you're so romantic and expressive, Quistus. I mean it. You are. You're different.'

He touched her finger. 'I'm going to send Stigmus with you, and fifty cavalry. He has the purple cloak. The Romans will accept his command.'

'Fifty's too many. I need to travel fast.'

'You've got to get through, Zhao. I've got to be sure. Tell

your brother I think Prince Ying is camped beyond the Blue
Sea with a Hun army, probably under rogue *Qin* commanders.
Maybe Ying can make mixed cultures work together under
strong military command; we Romans do, very successfully.
Being Huns they'll be spread out, foraging, living off the land.
They'll have livestock with them, mothers, children, old folk,
they can't move fast. Because they're so widely spread, they'll
be difficult for us to sneak past. Maybe we can't, maybe we
can. So I'm giving you fifty of the fastest, meanest men and
women on the fastest, meanest horses, and don't argue.'

'Now you do sound like a *Qin*.' Her teeth smiled in the dark.
'Finding my brother may not be easy. Just because he was in
Zamashi a week ago doesn't mean he's there now. He may
have returned to the Outlands.'

'Leaving his lookout post unsupported? Not if he's the man
you say he is. You're my wild card, Zhao. Don't let me down.'

'And when everything goes perfectly, and I do find him, and
he's still loyal, and he's close enough to make a difference,
and he agrees to risk his head, how will we find you?'

'Just follow the Huns. That's what I told Stigmus. It doesn't
matter what Stigmus knows, he doesn't speak Chinese, so I
kept it simple. The Huns will be on us like flies on honey.
We'll fight our way through. We don't have a choice.'

'I understand. And what do you tell me, who spoke *Qin*
from the age of eleven months, taught by my powerful brother?'

'We don't stand a chance,' Quistus began. 'If it goes badly,
or I think we have no chance at all, to save lives I may try to
steal a boat and sail Zhang to safety across the sea under cover
of darkness. I think I know who murdered Cerberus and hid
his body—' He spoke for another four minutes, telling her his
plans. Another muddy splashing sound came from the lake,
going away. He wondered if there were bears. He hadn't seen
any yet.

Zhao's smile came closer from the darkness. She'd leant
forward over her crossed ankles. 'That's enough talk.'

At first light the main body of Roman infantry, with a depleted
force of cavalry scouting ahead, marched south from the lake.
Yunyazi's cart rocked and thumped in the middle of the column,
Little Pelican hanging on to the seat beside him. It wasn't as
comfortable for her as horseback but he liked to talk, and she

liked listening. Viridorix and Zhang, identically dressed in padded armour, rode behind Quistus and Publius, with An and Chong following behind. An was miffed that Quistus had sent Zhao away without consulting him.

'But An, you kept telling me she was the traitor.' Quistus turned in the saddle. 'Well, if you're right, she can't betray us now.' The cavalry led by Stigmus and Zhao, riding hard to the northward by the lake shore, retracing their track of the day before, was already far from sight. An said nothing.

Quistus reined back to Yunyazi. 'Good morning, magician.'

'And to you, Senator, soldier, investigator.'

Quistus bowed in the saddle. 'And to you, Little Pelican. Dancer.'

'Promise me that one day you will see me dance,' she said reproachfully, and he realized she knew about him and Zhao. Little Pelican was observant; everyone else believed Zhao was a woman of ice, an intellectual incapable of feeling, whereas he knew she was capable of nothing else. Perhaps Little Pelican sensed it too.

'Promise me that one day you will dance for Zhao and me,' he said.

She turned her tiny body towards him, swinging her feet. She gave a sudden shiver although it was already hot, then a small sad smile. 'I surely will.'

'Yunyazi.' Quistus pointed at the line of mountain peaks closing from right and left, a few still pallid with snow, as the plain narrowed. 'The Celestial Mountains?'

Yunyazi nodded. He rocked between Fu and Little Pelican, the reins swinging in his dirty hands, and looked rather content.

'Why are they called Celestial? Because they're as high as the sky? Is there a way through?'

'You'll see, Roman.' Yunyazi didn't bother opening his eyes from his pleasurable doze. 'You'll see.'

Stigmus insisted on leading, which meant he sometimes looked round to see Zhao's horse cantering a mile off to one side or the other, taking advantage of some subtle lie of the land apparent only to her. Infuriating, showing off. He could tell his cavalry wanted to follow her, too, rather than him. The lake was soon behind them and the ground rose. After he'd led his sweating riders over one rocky spur too many, and had to turn them back out of a blind gorge, he reluctantly trusted her judgment. There was also the point Quistus had made – Zhao spoke Chinese. Without her, he couldn't tell Ban Chao anything. With an advantage that big on her side, he'd have to keep her firmly under his thumb. He'd wait his chance, she was bound to slip up, and then he'd be back in control.

Towards evening she followed birds to find a marshy lake. They made camp on the soft sedges, hobbling the horses to graze. The lake was salt but a small meltwater stream flowed from the mountains ahead. Some of the soldiers netted a cormorant as it surfaced with a fish in its beak, two catches in one. The cormorant tasted more fishy than the fish, and stringy too. Zhao showed them how to net small carp, scale, gut and roast them on sticks. Stigmus ate apart because he was an officer, chewing dried meat. The soldiers gathered around Zhao, picking up tips. One of the sergeants gave up her spare *sagum* cloak to Zhao as the day's heat fled into the enormous night sky, frost already forming on the rocks. Stigmus hadn't really noticed the girl before, dark eyes, square jaw, the scar up her face rather arousing. They settled to sleep. At last Zhao brought him a carp on a stick and sat beside Stigmus's fire, letting the smoke blow over her to keep off midges. 'We'll ride at moonrise.'

'I'll be the judge of that.' He chewed the fish. 'How much farther?'

She nodded uphill. 'There's a valley on the other side. We follow the Blue river upstream, it leads us between the peaks. There's a pass and we turn downhill near the source of the great Yellow river. From there it's not far across to Zamashi.'

'Now I don't need you at all,' he grinned.

'Quistus doesn't like you. I don't like you either.'

'Well, at least he thinks he has a reason.'

'I don't need a reason.' Fast, sharp tongue on her. She made him feel hot.

'You be a polite, obedient *Qin* woman. You don't fool me, I saw you arguing with him. You and me, we could work together. You hate him as much as I do.'

For a moment she looked curious. 'You think I hate Quistus?'

He said heavily, 'Do I look blind, Zhao?'

'I know you made love to Little Pelican.' She rolled away from him and pulled the *sagum* over her head. 'We leave at moonrise.'

*   *   *

The column of Roman infantry wound along the foothills in two sections, the royal entourage protected in the middle. Every two thousand paces a cavalry scout rode back, reporting no sign of Huns. The shepherds they passed swore they'd seen nothing, and their flocks were intact, so Quistus believed them. They passed a village or two and An hung the gold cloak from Zhang's shoulders. The villagers knelt at the sight of him, foreheads in the dust, overwhelmed by the presence of the divine child.

'Loyal,' An murmured. 'There's no Hun army here, Quistus. One small party of raiders, and you panicked.'

Quistus nodded at the Celestial Mountains closing to a line ahead of them as the great plain narrowed. 'Anyone can watch us coming from up there, and we can't see them.' They'd marched by moonlight last night, pushing forward under the cloak of mist clinging to the lakes and flooded salt pans.

Publius rested his soldiers in the shimmering heat of the day. Carts of brown salt heaped in clay jars passed them, rutting the road, trailing dust. 'Taking salt to the market at Xireg,' Chong said. 'Not worth much here, but in the lowlands each cart merits an armed guard.'

Quistus watched half a dozen carts rumble by, hauled by slaves and criminals gasping in the thin air. A line of miners caked with yellow dust, their ankles chained, came downhill from the mouths of the mines peppering the hillside to the low buildings Chong said were dormitories. 'They build them in the valley because the air's a little thicker here.' A wheel cracked and a cart went over, throwing out a load of ice-white snow on to the hot stones. It didn't melt. Yunyazi ran across, scooping up what he could in a brass pot before he was stopped.

'It's not really snow,' he told Quistus. '"*Qin* Snow" is one of the spells hidden in these hills by Heaven. In civilization the lords call it Hot Snow.' He let Quistus see in the pot. 'Saltstone, saltpetre. In Latin you call it *nitrum*.'

'That's why these are called the Celestial Mountains?' Quistus asked. 'Because of all the spells Heaven hid in them?'

Yunyazi nodded. 'The yellow dust is celestite. You remember—'

'The red rose?'

'Yes, Quistus. The red rose which blossomed over Rome was born here. Watch.' Yunyazi added a handful of charcoal to the pot, some pinches of other powders, then left the pot on the ground at the head of a short trail of powder. '*Huoyao!*' The trail burned busily, throwing out pretty coloured sparks. There was a bang that made them cover their ears, too late. 'Oh.' Yunyazi's mouth moved, but they couldn't hear him. The brass pot was gone. Only a small hole in the ground remained. Quistus rubbed his ears. 'An invisibility spell,' he whispered.

He turned. The base of the brass pot, jagged, much distorted, was embedded in the boards of the cart beside him, less than a foot from his neck. 'The spell must not be too tightly contained, or it grows angry.' Yunyazi wouldn't admit to being embarrassed. 'Injury results to the magician, and the enter-tainment value is lost.'

Stigmus groaned. He'd been in the saddle since moonrise, and it had turned into a hard day's climb under the hot sun, the bare rock too steep and crumbly to ride up, so they'd led the horses. Zhao called back from the ridge in a low voice, beckoning. Stigmus handed his reins to the dark-eyed sergeant and scrambled up. Zhao held him below the skyline. 'I thought I saw something.'

Stigmus took off his helmet and looked. The valley beyond was a remarkable and refreshing sight, bare slopes giving way to rich dark green woodland in each direction. 'Rhododendron,' Zhao whispered. From time to time between the rustling bushes and conifers he made out a line of white foam, the stream bounding down the centre of the valley. To his right the valley broadened and flattened into a blue haze.

Stigmus whispered, 'The Blue Sea?'

She jerked her head once, yes, then pointed left, where the valley steepened and turned north. 'Zamashi's that way, up the Blue river. I thought I saw movement.'

'Maybe we're in luck. Could be your brother.'

'Could be Gold Heads.'

'No. They don't know about us.'

She glanced at him. 'Golden Turtle doesn't have lookouts on the hilltops?'

'They'd have to move fast.'

'They do move fast.'

Stigmus thought about it. He was mortally tired of climbing. 'Any other way round?'

'No.'

'Then let's get on with it. You're imagining them anyway.'

Zhao turned. 'Sergeant Aurelia.' So that's the scarface's name, Stigmus noted for later. 'Short break. Share out the rest of the water, for the horses too. The stream down there is fresh, we'll pick up more later. I thought I saw movement ten minutes ago, nothing since. When we go, go quickly.' Aurelia clenched her fist in salute.

Stigmus said, 'You take orders from me, Sergeant, not the *Qin* woman.'

'Yes, sir.'

'Make sure everyone gets plenty of water. We'll be moving fast.'

Aurelia clenched her fist.

Zhao watered her horse, then drank. 'Gold Heads wouldn't expect so many of us,' she muttered. 'Quistus was right. We'll punch through.'

Stigmus waited until Aurelia was watching then put on his plumed helmet. Whatever their rank they liked a show. He was wearing his polished steel breastplate, the big musculature shining, whereas they only had cured leather. Effective but dull. Zhao said something to her, and Aurelia chuckled as she swung into the saddle. Stigmus decided he disliked Zhao even more.

They mounted up and Zhao went first without asking. That suited Stigmus fine, her horse skidded on the bare rock and he thought she'd go over, but she recovered and cantered into the trees, gone from sight almost at once. He raised his arm to the troop and his horse slid after her, recovering on the soft mat of fir needles beneath the conifers. He could hear the soldiers coming after him. They didn't like Zhao to get too far ahead. Rhododendrons grew more thickly closer to the stream, the waxy leaves slapping his face and armour. He heard the muffled thud of Zhao's horse's hooves now. He pulled even. 'Steady on. Don't want to run into a tree now, do we.'

She tightened her grip, urging her horse uphill along the side of the stream. A gold line whirred between them, thudding into a tree. Stigmus looked round, trying to see it. He heard shouts from behind. Zhao pulled away. 'Wait,' he said. 'Bitch, she took the fastest horse.' Zhao was shouting over her shoulder.

Aurclia came by fast, riding her piebald like a lunatic. She shouted his name.

Stigmus let go his reins long enough to draw his sword, then hung on again. The air was full of whirring. He heard the first quick clash of steel, then more. In front or behind? He couldn't tell. He wasn't a soldier. He was an investigator, a *specialis*. This wasn't what he was good at. Sounds to the right – no, now to the left. Faster.

Shouts. Clashes. Bangs, steel on steel. A yell, a scream, the first. Must shout orders. Trees everywhere. He put his head beside his horse's neck. 'Charge!' he called.

His horse put its head down. He felt it go over. 'Zhao,' he called. The horse somersaulted, slamming down on its back, on its saddle, beside him, he saw it. Fir needles flew out, a cloud, and he flew up and rolled over and over on the ground. A tree. Bang. Good advice. Don't hit the trees.

He lay on his back.

Head to one side.

Screams and clashing.

He saw his sword.

Am I hurt? Think about hiding.

They'll find you.

Crawled to his sword. Get up, get up. Grip sword, get up. Up. Beautiful Jesus, no. All the crucified with his name on them. They called Nero Satan. Just doing my job.

He blinked. Staggered back against a tree. Something soft. Someone.

'Take as many with us as we can,' Sergeant Aurelia said, her back to the tree, sword gripped in both hands, feet apart. Her face set.

Zhao? Where's Zhao?

Stigmus's head rotated. Bodies everywhere. Blood like dropped soup.

Three Gold Heads, closer. He raised his sword. Tried to concentrate.

Concentrate.

Three. They'd killed each other, Romans, Gold Heads, lying together. Only three. Bows, though, arrows. These three. Swords. Hands pointed like weapons.

He stood back to the tree with Sergeant Aurelia. He reversed his sword and jerked it through her heart. Armour. Everything, into the solid tree. Held up his hands, left her hanging there.

After that, there wasn't much need for words.

The three Gold Heads looked at each other.

'You need me,' Stigmus said in Greek. 'You need me too much to kill me.'

Quistus watched the sun sliding lower over the southern Celestial Mountains. Still no sign of Huns. All afternoon the Roman column had followed the long, pointing finger of Hoh Lake but now the land was rising. The mining road turned left across the salt marshes to the market town of Xireg, about five miles away, he estimated, on the far side of the valley. Ahead of them the valley narrowed towards a skyline pass some miles off, probably only a few hundred paces wide, difficult to tell yet. Might be an ambush. No way of telling what lay beyond. The scouts would report later.

He looked back. Yunyazi's cart had stopped in some bushes. Yunyazi was always doing this, stopping to talk to miners, or questioning someone who looked like a merchant. Quistus rode over. He heard voices, Yunyazi talking to Little Pelican in the back of the cart, teaching her something or boring her with spells. A round white bottom rose up and went down, small pointed feet clasped on each side. The magician was making love to Little Pelican. She turned her face, watching Quistus entirely without expression, tears trickling black lines from her eyes.

He'd seen that look in her before, that look of pure pain.

She held tight to Yunyazi with lustful, repetitive cries, urging him on, looking sadly at Quistus. He'd heard Little Pelican was the only girl, except Zhao, not to take a lover last winter – so Omba, always up on such matters, had told him. He knew from his own experience Little Pelican was brave and kind – look how she'd cared for Wild Swan – but he'd supposed her mutilated feet put lovers off. Omba had called them grotesque, but he remembered Zhao saying they were 'a lover's joy'. Obviously Yunyazi thought so too.

A dancer is like a sorcerer, Zhao had said, *the self-discipline of her years of training, her self-denial, is intense.*

Little Pelican had even said, sadly, that she could make Quistus desire her.

They were all human. Everyone wanted to live. He rode away.

Not dead yet. Lie on your face, keep still. Warm soil pressing into your mouth and eyes, but that's good. You're alive, breathing, trying to. The sun hot on your back, good, that's worth living for. They thought you were on their side. As long as they stayed curious, you lived.

The three Gold Heads were killing their wounded. He risked a blink of his eye then kept it tight shut. Gold Heads suffered silently and died in silence. Soon after that the Roman screams stopped.

Good. Stigmus felt a rush of relief. No witnesses.

The three came back to him. If he looked up they hit him. He woke with the sun lower.

They worked fast now, binding his wrists into his back with leather straps. Not too bad. 'Good,' he said.

If he spoke, they hit him. He woke in agony from his wrists. They'd poured water over the leather, shrinking the bonds tight. No blood in his hands, no feeling. He tried to move his fingers. Maybe they moved, maybe not.

They lifted him on to a piebald horse and tied his ankles together beneath. More water. 'No,' he whined.

He tried to see Zhao's body. Bodies everywhere. Sergeant Aurelia standing against the tree as though still alive. They'd pulled his sword out, good. No one would know. She stood there, nevertheless, on her stiff, dead muscles. He knew he'd remember the look on her face.

He'd remember her eyes.

Good. You had to be alive to remember.

The Gold Heads moved fast, leading the horse downhill. Aurelia's piebald jolted him from side to side. He knew if he ever felt his hands again, they'd hurt as much as his wrists. From time to time they poured more water over the leather to keep it small.

They came down the valley towards the blue haze. He wished he'd paid more attention, remembered its name. The haze turned into blueness stretching as far as he could see.

They wet the leather with salt water from the sea and kept going. He was thirsty so they gave him salt water to drink. He could hear the waves breaking on his right, they headed east along the northern shore. The breaking sound went on all night under the stars. At dawn they rested on a beach, the three Gold Heads chattering among themselves like playful children, giving him more salt water until he thought he'd die of thirst.

He croaked, 'I can tell you where Prince Zhang is. I'll do it. For water.'

Grinning, they gave him salt water. They poured it over his wrists too, and tied a leather gag in his mouth. Then they took up the lead-reins and ran on. Aurelia's horse jolted after them along the seashore, and Stigmus vomited salt water down his nose.

Quistus rode beside An and Chong. The track to the skyline pass was steepening sharply now. Yunyazi's cart rattled a few paces in front of them, the magician sitting as usual between Fu and Little Pelican, much taller than either. Something must have showed in Quistus's face. 'Ah,' An said, 'you know about Yunyazi.'

'I suppose I do.'

'You saw him yesterday? He was busy?'

'Yes, very busy.'

Quistus remembered Omba saying that Shu, of all people, had called Yunyazi a very dirty old man. He expected An to go on about the magician. But An obviously reckoned Yunyazi was just doing what a man must. 'Little Pelican, it's all her fault,' he said wisely. 'Born very poor, no parents, knows no better.'

'That's why Yunyazi takes advantage of her?'

'What else can he do? She has no advantages. And she dances beautifully.'

'And lotus feet,' Chong said appreciatively.

'Lotus feet,' An nodded.

Quistus stared at the two men. 'Has Little Pelican been . . . busy . . . with other men?' Zhao had claimed something of the sort, he'd thought she'd spoken out of frustration.

'Such beautiful feet, Quistus, any man desires her.'

'You don't, do you, An?'

'Of course not. I have a wife back home in Ruyang.'

'Not you too, Chong?'

'Never, I'm a single man, a rationalist. I don't believe in love.'

'I wasn't talking about love,' Quistus said. Yunyazi's cart had almost stopped. Extra horses were collar-harnessed *Qin* fashion, and progress resumed. Little Pelican glanced back.

'As you say,' An said delicately, 'it's not as though it's love, as it lasts only a moment.'

'Those feet,' Chong admitted. 'Irrational, I know, but impossible not to desire her because of them. Have you really not noticed?'

'It seems beauty,' Quistus murmured, 'is in the eye of the beholder.'

'And she the only one not to fall pregnant last winter,' An said, 'thank Heaven.'

'She knows the spells to preserve herself from conception,' Chong said. 'Imagine, we would have been all this time without a woman.'

'Except Zhao,' An said. Both men shuddered.

The piebald hated Stigmus. It kept turning its head to bite his foot as if hungry for his leather sandal, but he knew it wasn't hunger. It was hatred. The horse knew what he'd done. He tried to kick it.

It jolted him deliberately. He kicked the beast as well as he could with his bound heels. When he dozed slumped over its neck, it threw back its head.

The Gold Heads stopped for a few minutes every hour. The eastern shore of the Blue Sea – after much fevered rumination Stigmus had recalled the name – curved away on his right. They kept going east, running over low hills. No more salt torment. Good. Looking up. The leather straps dried, loosening a little, letting blood into his hands, and the agony was as bad as he'd imagined. But that was good too. At least he'd keep his hands. Excellent. Everything would be fine. He'd think of something.

The horse nipped his sandal.

The sandal came off, he felt it drop.

The dry leather ties joining his heels slipped over his bare foot. Nothing held him in the saddle, he felt himself going. He tried to shout through the gag but could only dribble, jolting. He slid over and thumped on to his back on the ground.

He lay there.

The three Gold Heads surrounded him. They stared down their swords. Not curious, not angry. Dispassionate. They'd already decided about him. They'd continue until they'd completed what they'd decided.

The piebald threw up its head, breaking the lead-rein, and cantered back the way they'd come. A Gold Head ran after it but the horse galloped. The Gold Head returned.

'Walk or die,' it told him.

Stigmus made begging noises. They tied the lead-rein to his wrists. Two pulled him, one ran behind with the whip. He stumbled, weeping because he had only one sandal. It was the little things that mattered.

Stigmus fell to his knees on the long grassy hilltop. The evening sun threw his shadow into the valley beyond.

His eyes widened, staring.

Publius rode back. 'Quistus, you'll want to see this.'

They rode almost to the top of the narrow pass. At Publius's signal they dismounted and moved forward between the boulders, crouching.

Quistus stared into the long, wide valley below. Dust drifted between the hills. Beneath it darker patterns moved, too many to make out individual people unless they were away from the main groups. 'How many, you reckon?'

Publius shrugged economically. 'Enough.'

'Huns on the move.'

'Only a mile or two a day. They camp early. Tents, fires, children running around, fighting. When the wind eddies you can hear the babies crying. They corral the flocks and herds – look, they're starting now. My scout reckons there's more animals than men.' He pointed to riders moving fast from one side to the other, settling some dispute. 'They're the problem. We won't make it through.'

They watched cooking fires spring up across the valley in the fading light.

'This isn't the main force,' Quistus said definitely. 'We'll fall back to Xireg and secure the town.'

Publius said, 'My soldiers aren't in this for a last stand, Quistus. You promised them glory and a big reward, not certain death in the dust.'

'Leave a rearguard here. A hundred Romans will hold a thousand Huns if they're funnelled in the pass. Once the Huns get into the open ground behind us, Xireg falls.'

'The town will fall anyway.' Publius pointed into the blue distance, beyond the hills along the left side of the valley. 'The Blue Sea. They'll just come round the seashore.'

An pushed between them. He peeped over the boulder, blinked, then said, 'The fighting men will be with Prince Ying.

He must know from Golden Turtle roughly where we are. What he doesn't know is which side of the Blue Sea you will pass.'

'I know he doesn't know,' Quistus said. 'That's our only advantage. Zhao guessed the sea is about fifty, sixty miles across, much more than that to ride around in the marshes. Take a week maybe. Ying can't cover both sides of the circle.'

'Therefore he will wait until he does know.'

'You're a budding military man, An.'

'*Qin* strategy is simple,' An said. 'Overwhelming force, overwhelmingly applied.' He shivered, the pass had filled with shadow. 'I must inform the Prince. Let us pray for good news from Zhao.'

They saw her coming.

Zhao never did know exactly how many men were hiding in the snow. They came up all around her horse, snow showering from their padded white smocks, and by her legs and shoulders pulled her down among them.

'Ban Chao!' she shouted, but there was no reply. A sack was thrown over her head, her thumbs tied together and she was lifted back on her horse, all without a word. She saw nothing, but knew they were going downhill by the awkward hip-rolling motion of the horse. 'Ban Chao's men?' she asked, her voice muffled by the sack. 'Are you Ban Chao's men?'

Whoever they were, they weren't Gold Heads. It could have been worse.

The ambush in the rhododendrons had been over in a flash. The arrows had come from nowhere through the bushes and, as luck would have it, the first struck the thick leather cheek-piece protecting her horse's mouth. With the bit jerked between its teeth, the jammed arrow whipping about with every stride, there was no stopping the terrified animal bolting through the trees, no holding back. She'd seen Stigmus once but then he was gone, glimpsed Aurelia but she was gone too. Zhao's horse galloped through the bushes, somehow didn't hit the trees, jumped the stream, fell back, jumped again, and exhausted its panic on the uphill slope.

When it had slowed to a walk Zhao waited on the treeline, looking back.

Silence. Whatever had happened, had happened. No sign of movement but the Gold Heads could be climbing unseen through the trees right now. She'd tried to pull the arrow from the cheekpiece but it wouldn't come free. She waited for another hundred breaths, studying the valley for any sign of life, then turned the horse and kicked her heels.

The night had been bitterly cold, and the ridge was high. The weather on the far side was completely different, with mist and whirling snow, and then she rode into the snowfield with the men hiding in it pretending to be snow.

Her breaths sounded loud in the sack.

Trees, she felt the horse stepping over roots. She held her breath and heard wind in the branches.

She breathed again, then held her breath, listening.

A stream hissing steadily. Hands steadied her knees, a jump. 'Thank you,' she said, but couldn't tell if they heard.

Men spoke in low voices. She was lifted from the saddle. A door creaked, she felt sudden warmth. She stood with her thumbs together, feeling a rough plank table with her fingertips. Footsteps. The sack was lifted from her head.

Night, candles, log walls. A man stared at her, the golden arrow he'd been examining forgotten. He was wide and muscular, wearing white enamelled armour. His face was round, made fierce by a pointed black beard and sideburns that hung from his ears to his chest. His eyes, too, were fierce and penetrating, with a crease across each eyelid. His mouth opened. His expression slowly turned to such surprise that Zhao looked down not to laugh.

'Zhao?' he said. 'Not you.'

Zhao knelt. 'Ban Chao,' she said politely.

'That bandit Duke Chen killed you years ago!' He laughed, lifting her up, releasing her thumbs, embracing her. 'I hardly recognized you with your face bare, little sister.' He frowned, examining her critically at arm's length. 'Surely these parts are not so wild that you ride without attention to decorum and the dictates of fashion?'

The Jade Horse inn at Xireg was a large, ramshackle, organically-grown building with stone pillars around a central area and many doorways of varying age added behind them as necessary. The arrival of a Roman cohort, heavily armed and impatient, quickly had the effect of encouraging the previous occupants of the rooms to seek shelter in one of the lesser inns.

The market square had only four entrances, easily closed off, with a central shrine to the Son of Heaven, whose roof made a good lookout post. On one side of the inn stood the grey Hall of Imperial Monopoly, on the other the Hall of Exchange, with the rear of the inn as a sort of warehouse between the two where, so to speak, West met East. In Xireg, Roman gold – and a few things more precious than gold, such as onion seeds – that had started their eastward journey two or more years ago, were exchanged for *Qin* spices and rolls of silk, ice-white, gold, vermilion, beginning their long journey west.

Zhang's room, its rich merchant summarily evicted, was on the first floor. The balcony windows overlooking the square had been shuttered and barred as though it were winter, muffling the calls of the Roman lookouts changing guard on the shrine roof. Silver lamp stands put out sinuous tongues of flame, illuminating thick carpets, flock-papered walls and low, solid furniture. Zhang, gold-cloaked, sat on a raised seat draped with gold brocade. Quistus thought how alone he looked without Zhao's quiet presence kneeling at his elbow. An had sent Viridorix into a corner. Manas stood behind the Prince with his arms crossed, the flames flickering along the raised, scarred line of Omba's stitches.

Quistus gestured, introducing Publius and the centurions accompanying him. 'Our plan of campaign—'

Zhang interrupted, 'An tells me our situation is desperate.'

'Indeed,' An said. 'I saw the Hun fiends with my own eyes.'

'Serious, not desperate,' Quistus said. 'We must avoid giving battle. We'd lose. To win, we must keep Prince Zhang alive.'

'I agree,' An said. 'It doesn't matter if we all die, as long as the Prince lives.'

'Speak for yourself,' Publius said.

'I want to live too,' Viridorix said.

'We must draw Ying forward,' Quistus said. 'The Blue Sea lies between us. We must make him commit his forces to either the north shore or the south. We'll send a detachment along the south shore as a decoy, with Viridorix wearing gold, and make sure he's seen.'

'Ying will be aware of the thirty-six tactics used by the *Qin* military,' Chong said. 'Blowing a horn in the south to pass silently in the north is tactic number six.'

Publius nodded. 'Still, Ying risks the Prince getting through unless he responds. He must divide his army.'

'His command will be weakened and split,' Quistus said. 'He can't attack us by north and south *and* also guard hundreds of miles of shoreline, defend the east shore—'

'I see Quistus's plan,' Zhang said. 'There's plenty of ships and fishing boats. With Ying's army divided, Quistus and I will simply steal a boat and sail directly across to the undefended eastern shore.'

An looked amazed. 'Highness, you are a military genius.'

'The Romans fall back to safety in the mountains. In a week, I'll be in Loyang.' Zhang's eyebrows drew together and they glimpsed the ruler who would be Son of Heaven. 'And then Ying had better watch his back.'

'That is indeed my plan,' Quistus said smoothly. 'Do what the enemy least expects.'

Zhang whispered behind his hand, 'Zhao told me.'

'I know, son,' Quistus whispered. 'I'm using Roman military tactic number thirty-seven.' The Prince nodded wisely, then looked thoughtful.

An said, 'What if your scheme fails, and the Prince is captured alive?' He didn't need to say more. The consequences for Zhang didn't bear thinking about.

Quistus opened the shutters. He gave a signal. Yunyazi, waiting down in the square by an old water barrel, its lid firmly weighted with stones, waved back, lit a spill of paper, and ran into the dark as fast as he could. 'Oh,' Zhang said, pleased. '*Yanhuo.*'

'Not exactly,' Quistus said. 'Yunyazi and I have discovered how to make spells angry. In fact so angry that their entertainment value is entirely lost.'

The shutters blew in. Dust fell from the ceiling. They heard stones falling on roof tiles. 'The Prince,' Quistus said, 'will not be captured alive. If it looks likely, I'll blow up his boat.'

Zhang slept. The first finger of moonlight touched him through the broken shutter. Quistus put his hand to the door, coming in, and immediately Manas was on his feet, *sica* drawn, moonlight shining on muscle. He saw Quistus and nodded. 'I wake him now?'

'I'll do it.' Quistus paused. 'Do you ever sleep, Manas?'

'No.'

'Never?'

'Not for thirteen years.'

'When the Emperor appointed you his son's bodyguard.'

'Yes. A baby. Fresh-born.'

'And you've never been away from Zhang since.'

'I never will. You know me. Omba knows me. I will die for him. You know this.'

'Let's hope it doesn't come to that.'

'One day.' Manas shrugged. 'One day it will. It does.'

Quistus touched the giant's shoulder. 'Do you remember your people?'

'Kyrgyz? Little.'

'But you remember something?'

'All I know is my Prince,' Manas rumbled.

'You know I have to wake the Prince now, and where we're going? Moving fast, taking about half the Romans with us. They've already left, we'll catch them up by dawn. The Prince will be on horseback, but you're too big to ride.'

'I'll run beside him.'

'You'll keep up?'

'I can do anything for my Prince.'

'Very well.' Quistus woke Zhang. 'Wear warm, padded clothing. Your cloak stays here with Viridorix. We're leaving Xireg.'

'The spells are harmless until they're uttered,' Yunyazi assured Quistus. They were standing by the row of loaded carts in the market square. Torches flamed in angled brackets on the building fronts, illuminating the loading work as more carts were brought in. 'Without a catalyst they lie sleeping, harmless.'

'I thought you said flame was a catalyst?' Quistus said nervously by the light of the flames.

'The true catalyst is the incantations of the magician. The flame is merely the physical representation of the incantation. We are perfectly safe. I shall not say a word.'

Quistus swung into the saddle. 'Three days,' he ordered. Yunyazi gave an airy wave. Fu woke, scratched, and went back to sleep.

Quistus nodded to Zhang and they rode out of town on the moonlit north road, the escort of *Qin* bowmen riding behind, Manas running with a steady stride beside the Prince's horse, his head higher than the rider. It was mid-morning before they caught the Roman infantry marching uphill at double-time.

Packs swaying, they wanted to reach the hilltops before the heat of the day. They took a siesta on the summit, then in the afternoon dropped down into the broad valley of the Blue river and turned east.

Ahead of them the Blue Sea stretched to a far horizon dotted with a few islands, and nothing else as far as they could see from north to south.

'No,' cried Golden Turtle. He pressed his hands to his bare head. 'Not my children. Only three. Only three.'

'They will live.' The three Gold Heads gathered around him for reassurance. 'They will live again.'

Stigmus shouted in Greek, 'I demand to see Prince Ying.'

That was the last thing he remembered.

Stigmus pressed his sun-blistered face to the bamboo bars of the cage, thanking the gods for his luck. The cage was horrid, too low to stand up in, too narrow to lie down in. It stank from the last occupant, his or her body removed only when Stigmus, his helmet shoved on backwards for mockery, was locked in. He was alive, that was what mattered. The *Qin* were a civilized people, after all. As for the cage, he would have done the same thing himself. Prisoners talked. That was all there was to it.

Stigmus was more than willing to talk. Thanks to luck and foresight, he had plenty to say. Best of all, he was now on the winning side. 'Ha,' he croaked at the filthy Hun faces staring up from below. 'Roman helmet. Very funny.' He polished it with his elbow and put it on the right way round.

The cage was suspended by a long cannabis rope from three poles as tall as trees, joined at the top. Lucky again. Had they left him dangling down there at the level of the Huns, his fate might have been short-lived and nasty. Huns reeked of fat and smoke, boys threw shit, girls taunted him with bones and rotten meat, and both sexes made cups of their filthy hands for water which they let trickle to nothing in front of his eyes. Hilarious. Stigmus had wiped the salt from his lips, begging for pity. Big stumping Hun women had spat at him, teaching the youngest children, and he'd licked it. He had no more tears to give.

He'd whispered, 'I demand to see Prince Ying. I am His Excellency Stigmus, Prefect of the Praetorian Guard.' The idiots didn't speak Latin. They didn't speak Greek. The mothers stumped away, their brats clapping and running in circles.

Then everything took a turn for the better. Some *Qin* from the big marquee winched the cage high. No shade up here, but it was a big improvement on Hun women and children. Stigmus had peace and quiet to think, and from up here he got a good view of the place, two big marquees with flags flying at the top, the cage dangling from the tripod about halfway between them. A third, much smaller tent downhill was where the Hun king waited when the *Qin* brass summoned him to an audience. Beyond the *Qin* camp the broad once-green valley ran north to south, alive with Huns, movement, animals, smoke, dust. Through a gap in the valley wall he saw the Blue Sea to the west, maybe ten miles off.

He noticed a Gold Head slipping through the crowd. 'I'm on your side!' he shouted. 'You saw what I did. You saw. I proved it. Tell your master.' The Gold Head went without a glance.

Stigmus scratched his stubble. Lots of people in the valley. Maybe other valleys too: that looked like more smoke to the south-west. Ten thousand fighting men in this one. Maybe fifteen thousand. Sixty thousand people in all, including the women and children. Not many old'uns.

Sixty thousand people, a hundred thousand animals. They'd even planted a few crops on the sheltered hillsides. A whole slow, gigantic people on the move. One cohort of Romans, a handful of archers and a boy-Prince, against this lot. You could see which was the winning side.

Golden Turtle came from the big marquee. He looked up, shielding his eyes against the sun, then gestured for the cage to be let down. 'Yes,' Stigmus whispered. 'Yes, yes!' He wiped his breastplate, brushed his cloak with the palms of his hands. The cage bumped on the ground. Horns blew. A huge opening at the end of the marquee was flapped wide, drapes pulled aside, veils lifted, soldiers marched out and formed up. An older man, his face thin, skull-white, with pinched nostrils, came after a while. He stopped, examining Stigmus. He ordered Stigmus's head to be turned from side to side. His dark plates of *mingguang jia* armour were so highly polished that Stigmus saw the colour of his eyes in them. Had to be Prince Ying. As best he could in the cage Stigmus prostrated himself, like everyone else nearby.

Ying said, '*Da Qin?*'

Golden Turtle nodded. 'Yes, Highness, he's Roman.' *Da Qin* was their word for Rome, Stigmus knew that much. They assumed Rome was part of the Chinese empire. 'Lixian,' Golden Turtle added, the *Qin* word for Alexander. Stigmus wondered if he was being compared to Alexander the Great. He grinned hopefully.

Ying laughed. Stigmus understood that laugh. He'd laughed it many times himself, before giving the nod of the head that nailed a Christian. 'Wait!' he cried. 'Listen. I know where the Prince is. I know their plans.'

Golden Turtle stared, then turned to Ying. He spoke fast Chinese. Stigmus nodded eagerly, smiling, then cursed as the horns blew again. A huge ornate palanquin decorated with silver moons was carried from the second marquee on the shoulders of tall young men. Everyone fell to the ground. Stigmus prostrated his forehead against the bars, peeping. Ying bowed deeply as the palanquin was set down. '*Mother*,' he said in Chinese.

'Prince Ying greets his mother with filial piety,' Golden Turtle said.

She was the oldest woman Stigmus had ever seen. Her wrinkled face was almost destroyed by make-up, her nose hooked, nostrils flaring, the corners of her mouth pulled down to her chin. Her eyelids had been slanted back and lifted almost into her hair, which was vast and improbably black. 'Dowager Consort Xu is now the Dowager Empress Xu,' Golden Turtle said. 'Prince Zhang is almost ours. Victory is a formality.'

'I know Quistus's plan,' Stigmus said rapidly. 'Listen to me.'

'Ah, Quistus. The one who is not a coward.' Golden Turtle explained what he had said to Ying, who replied. 'Prince Ying demands, "What is this contemptible plan, coward?"'

Stigmus said, 'Water first.'

Ying smiled. Golden Turtle repeated, '"Water afterwards."'

Stigmus said, 'Quistus is going to fight his way through.'

Golden Turtle murmured. Ying turned away, snorting. '"No water!"'

'Six hundred Romans will kill six thousand Huns,' Stigmus said. 'I guarantee it. Can you afford that?'

Ying snapped one word. Golden Turtle said, '"Yes."'

Stigmus said, 'But that's not what'll happen. If you don't listen to me, you'll lose for sure. Tell him, Golden Turtle. Tell the Prince I know Quistus's *secret* plan.' He held up his one remaining sandal. 'Look, still muddy. I hid in the reeds. I heard him tell Zhao everything.'

Ying turned impatiently. One more chance. Stigmus said, 'Zhao was riding to her brother Ban Chao for help when we were attacked.'

'This we know,' Golden Turtle said. 'Zhao got away.'

Stigmus didn't like that news. 'But I didn't run away, did I? I killed a Roman soldier for you, to show I'm on your side. I let you bring me here. I'm an important man. You need me.' He raised his voice. 'Ban Chao's closer than you think. He's come south from Gansu Province.'

'That would make him a traitor.'

'Perhaps he is.'

Ying looked interested, but the Dowager Empress Xu spoke suddenly. Everyone bowed in reverence. Golden Turtle said, 'The Dowager Empress says, "This man is a coward."'

Stigmus said quickly, 'Your Highness, Quistus will sneak the Prince across the sea in a boat under cover of darkness. Probably more than one boat, so you don't know which one he's on.'

'Ah,' Ying said.

'Diversions north and south. While you're kept busy the Prince lands on the east shore, rides safely to the Emperor in Loyang, and you're finished.'

Ying turned to Xu. She uttered harsh words. Golden Turtle said, '"How do we know what you say is the truth? Torture is most effective in deciding such difficult matters."'

'Wait.' Stigmus grabbed the bars. 'Wait, I can prove it. Quistus knows who the murderer is, your traitor in Zhang's household. Quistus said, his exact words, "I know who murdered Cerberus and hid his body."'

Golden Turtle spread his hands in invitation.

'It's Manas,' Stigmus said.

Golden Turtle turned to Ying. 'Manas.'

'Ah.' Ying spoke quickly, nodding. Stigmus picked out the words *Manas* and *Kyrgyz*. Golden Turtle translated, '"Yes. Yes, indeed it is Manas. Manas the nationalist, the Kyrgyz freedom-fighter who dreams of leading his people to a new land, a better home. As he will, if he pleases me."'

Stigmus took a deep breath. He knew this was the most

delicate, important moment, on which his salvation rested. 'Then you know I speak the truth.'

Ying moved one long-nailed finger in a gesture of command. Golden Turtle said, 'It seems you've earned one sip of water, traitor.'

Stigmus drank the spoon dry. They didn't let him out of the cage.

Golden Turtle scraped a circle in the dust with his gold foot. He stabbed the east side with his toe. 'The port of Haihu. We'll get boats there.'

Quistus watched Manas running tirelessly beside the plainly-dressed Prince's horse. They came over the gently downward-sloping grassland to the western shore where the Blue river met the Blue Sea. The port of Buh was on the river arm of a sheltered headland where junk-sailed fishing boats, some with little houses on top for living quarters, were pulled up along the muddy shore. Others were fitted with long poles and aerial nets for catching the gulls, sandpipers and cormorants that flocked and swirled over the islands, with sticky, tar-covered arrows on long strings for bringing down geese. The islands were pale with guano, mined and carried ashore in white-streaked barges, and farmers spread the fertilizer over the narrow fields. A row of peasants dug peat for the charcoal-burners whose smouldering turf-covered bunkers, with huts for drying and smoking *huangyu* fish, made the evening air fragrant with woodsmoke. Trees, raw material for new boats, had been planted by the freshwater marshes, and where the road came to the river's edge stood landing stages of strong tree trunks. Here carts from the Celestial Mountains unloaded iron, copper, sulphur, celestite and saltpetre into heavy barges. A foreman assured Quistus that the two-day, sixty-mile journey by sea saved more than a week on the road time to Haihu. No getting around that; travel by water was much faster than travel on land.

Geese cackled in alarm as the Roman infantry secured the village, seized some small empty warehouses as billets, and put up leather tents on the smooth, grassy headland. Publius took some men, confiscated the boats and workshops, and left a guard. 'We aren't stealing anything from anybody, except Zhang,' he told Quistus with amusement. 'It's all part of the Emperor's monopoly system. He'll thank us.'

He and Quistus went round the camp asking for volunteers to sail a boat. Obviously no one from Nirvana had the skill but half a dozen girls who'd handled boats on the Nirvana lake said they could row. Quistus put them aboard one of the fishing boats and pointed at the sea's misty south shore to their right, brown mountains standing behind, which they'd seen from the other side a couple of days ago. 'There's a village about fifteen miles that way, at the foot of the mountains. Anchor offshore. Wait. You'll know what to do.' They watched the girls lay their armour in the bottom of the boat, bare their forearms, and row quite well on the calm sea before struggling to raise the sail. After a while the boat moved away as the wind puffed, gathering speed. Quistus and Publius looked at each other with raised eyebrows, impressed.

Late next morning heavy carts started arriving from Xireg, Yunyazi riding first with Little Pelican and Fu. The magician took over the largest warehouse and there, supervising a detail of head-scratching peasants, began the work of mixing spells and muttering incantations. From time to time there would be a loud hiss and a pop, a flare of sparkling flames quickly put out, or an exclamation of pain. Once Yunyazi came outside, his grey hair smudged with smoke, his beard singed, and put carpenters to work on the sterns of the clumsy barges as well as adding oars.

Ninety-four head of Roman cavalry rode in from the pass, sweating and dusty. Xireg was now undefended. Quistus called to the cavalry centurion, 'Viridorix?' The man nodded. 'Well done. Get food and rest,' Quistus said.

An and Chong arrived with the second convoy during the evening, the tail end trailing in at dawn. The guards reported no sight of Huns. Quistus had simply pointed to the east.

It was the third day. The sunrise glowed with brilliant, unnatural colours through the mighty haze of smoke rising far-distant beyond the sea.

King Punu glanced up at the Roman swinging in the cage with the air of a man considering chucking a spear, but the *Qin* was still doing what *Qin* always did: talking. They never did anything but talk. Listening to Prince Ying was like listening to the Wind God, Garud, trying to pick sense from the blare of the wind across the steppes.

'This is a map, your Majesty,' Ying said. Punu eyed Ying's women. *Qin* women were sexless ornaments, clean, pale, plucked, waxed, flavourless, meek, stinking of perfume. They didn't smell like real women. Anything was better than listening to Ying. He waved. A dozen beauties waved back. Ying turned impatiently and someone dropped the veil.

Ying began again. 'Imagine you are a bird, your Majesty. This is what you see when you look down. The sea.'

Punu looked down at his clothes.

Ying sighed. 'When you see the enemy, you will attack. Is that clear?'

At last, something that made sense.

'Let's kill the Roman,' Punu said.

The Huns were moving forward, stretching for a dark, busy mile along the eastern shore. Four men carried each leg of the tripod, the cage swinging high in the air. The Roman had stopped shouting.

'Let's save him for later,' Ying said.

Quistus walked along the seashore, the two Roman spearmen following twenty paces behind. The heat was already leaving the wind as the sun dropped. As always before a battle his belly and fingers ached and he wished it would come quickly, just so that it was over, but part of him wished it wouldn't come at all. Anything could go wrong. The sea looked wide, empty, tempting, dangerous.

A few people pointed across the river into the trees. He didn't see anything.

Plenty of last-minute work was still going on, but the boats and barges should be ready to start loading troops, horses and equipment in the morning. Yunyazi came from one of the workshops patting yellow dust from his robes. 'Don't keep frowning at me like that, Quistus. I won't let you down. These people have wives, you know. You should see their nimble fingers! They sew like gods.'

Quistus nodded at the headland. Zhang's tent was in the Roman encampment, no different from the others, except for its doubled guard. As the moment of decision approached, Quistus's great fear was the unexpected, the sudden something he hadn't thought of, an assassin seeing his last chance slipping away, motivated by desperation. He'd made sure that the

Prince wore padded armour, even under a gold cloak. 'Zhang will be inspecting the Roman troops, Yunyazi, a morale booster. Will you be there?'

'Busy.' Yunyazi turned away busily.

'You know,' Quistus remarked, 'a lot of the time, I thought the traitor was you.'

Yunyazi returned. 'Why?' he asked cautiously.

'Because you're such a prick.'

Yunyazi spoke carefully. 'A magician such as I cannot help being wise. If I appear to know everything, it's because I *do* know everything.' He added, 'Everything that Heaven allows us to know.'

'But you don't know who the traitor is. Do you?'

'That information remains obscure.' The magician hesitated. 'There is one thing you should know, that you haven't really believed until now. Something that you do know is true in your heart, Quistus, but not your head.'

'What's that?'

'You did die. There on the boat, in the ocean. You did truly die, and I did bring you back to life.' The magician turned on his heel and walked away, busily shouting orders again, humming spells under his breath.

Quistus opened his hands and looked at them. He covered his face and breathed deep. It was almost time. He beckoned the two Roman spearmen to stay close, but they stared over the river. A horse whinnied, prancing on the far bank, then plunged into the water. 'Seen our armour,' one of the spearmen said. 'That's one of ours.' The horse scrambled over the mud trailing a leading rein, broken. The man grabbed it. 'Sergeant Aurelia's piebald, sir. Pretty hungry, too.'

'Make sure it's fed and watered.'

'Yes, sir. Sarge was a pretty good rider, sir. I mean, this didn't happen by accident.'

'I know.' Quistus knew what it meant. *What if Zhao is dead? What will I do?* 'Make sure those weapon cuts are seen to,' he said. But his heart was thinking, *What if she's dead?*

The spearman called a soldier to take the horse. Quistus forced himself to think with his head, to put the chaos inside him out of his mind. 'Follow me.' He went uphill on to the headland, among the tents, calm and confident, joking with the soldiers by their cooking fires. It was their last night ashore. 'Soldiers, tomorrow we're going to make sailors of you.' Rueful laughs; few could swim. 'If you feel like swimming,' he joked, 'there's one golden rule. Take your armour off first.' That got a genuine laugh. 'This water's so salty, you won't fall in it, you'll just bounce!' He looked round, their grinning faces brightening in the firelight as the light faded, and part of him wondered what he'd do if Zhao was dead. He shut her out of his mind.

Zhang was waiting in his tent. Quistus left the spearmen outside. Manas stood watchfully. 'You're late, Quistus,' An said accusingly. 'It's too dark. The Prince will have to review the troops in the morning.'

Quistus stood between the Prince and Manas. 'It's never too late.' He pushed the Prince out of the tent and turned to face Manas, hand on sword, backing through the tent flap. 'Not you, Manas.'

Manas came through the tent flap like a bull. Quistus pushed the Prince to safety on the grass. The Roman spearmen stood on each side of Manas, the tips of their spears against his neck. There was a series of clicks as *Qin* crossbowmen prepared to fire.

Manas gazed at Quistus. 'You know I would never harm him.'

'No, Manas, but you'd allow him to come to harm, wouldn't you?'

'Manas?' the Prince whispered. 'But that's Manas.' He raised his voice. 'Quistus, that's Manas.'

'Stay back,' Quistus said quietly. He stood between Manas and the Prince. He nodded at the giant's belt. 'If you please.'

'You know I am an honourable man.' Manas lifted the two *sica* between finger and thumb. He reversed them, bowed, gave the hilts to Quistus. 'You know the Prince would not have lived for a moment if I was not.'

'Let me guess what Prince Ying promised you, years ago in the imperial crèche in Loyang, when the fifth Prince became first. Something not for yourself when the Prince was killed, because you were never expected to live, because living would be dishonour. It was something for your people.'

Manas shrugged. 'Kyrgyz.'

'You were to die trying to defend the Prince. But not trying too hard. No one could get past you if you didn't want them to. This way, when the time came, Ying's assassin would get through, and you'd die before the Prince.'

'That is not dishonour. That is death for me, life for Kyrgyz.'

'No one at the Villa Paria actually *saw* you guarding the Prince's door before the attack on Cerberus, they just assumed it; they knew your irreproachable reputation. No one saw you come forward through the house that night, since Lo was asleep. You carried Cerberus's body into the kitchen, easily strong enough, strong enough even to snap his joints to fit him in the cistern, quick enough to hide behind the chimney when Zhao unexpectedly came in, then let yourself quietly out up the back-stairs. You were back at the Prince's door ready to rush in after Zhao's scream. Am I telling the truth?'

Manas said, 'Yes. This is all true.'

'Later, when the Gold Head tricked its way into the Villa Paria to within an inch of the Prince's life, you slipped on the stairs at the critical moment. If I hadn't been there he'd have been killed for sure. In Nirvana, your head was cut. No doubt you were meant to die but even a Gold Head isn't perfect. My point is, you let it happen. You weren't to know Zhao and Viridorix would hold the Gold Heads back long enough for Zhang to hide in the smoke hole, or about the extra seconds of confusion because Viridorix was dressed as the Prince. I saved the Prince's life the first time, not you. Zhao and Viridorix saved his life the second time, not you. Am I right so far?'

'Yes. It was supposed to be as you say. Almost.'

'What have I got wrong?'

'I was certain to die honourably by the gatehouse, but at the last moment I defended myself and the wound was superficial.'

'Why would you suddenly do that, Manas?'

'Because I love Omba.'

Quistus's eyes narrowed. 'You risked everything you'd worked so long for, your dreams of a free nation for your people, because you loved Omba?'

'Yes. I love her.'

An laughed. He doubled over with mirth.

'I love her,' Manas said. An wiped his streaming eyes.

Quistus imagined Zhao lying dead. He heard wolves in the hills.

Manas said, 'You know the power of love, Quistus.' His gaze was sky-blue, steady. 'I needed to live.'

Quistus had to look away.

He sighed. 'Now we come to the bit I really don't like, Manas. You murdered Cerberus. No dishonour for you in that, he wasn't the Prince.' Manas didn't answer. Quistus pressed, 'Well? You murdered Cerberus, didn't you, Manas?'

Manas shut his lips tight.

Quistus said, 'What makes me not respect you is the terrible way you killed him, Manas. Those terrible ritual cuts. Why did you do it like that?'

Manas opened his mouth. He stuck out his tongue between bared teeth and bit, hard. Blood poured down his front. He spat out his tongue.

Everyone stepped back.

Manas broke the spears. He threw the spearmen against the crossbowmen. An arrow went off in the air. He was already gone, running through the fire, running downhill. An called out, 'Stop him!' but Quistus said, 'No.'

He watched the giant plunge into the dark river. In a minute or two Manas's shadow climbed up the far side, running to the left through the trees, a shadow fading amongst shadows. 'You let him get away,' An shouted.

'Manas was the murderer,' Zhang said, shocked. 'I can hardly—' He shook his head.

'I knew it wasn't Zhao,' Chong said. 'I always had faith.'

'Now we'll never know, thanks to Quistus,' An said viciously.

Zhang went into the tent, opened a trunk, and came back with a scroll wrapped in a vermilion ribbon, the Family Book. 'When I brush out his name, Manas will lose his soul. He broke his oath. He will never have existed.'

'He's heading west, not east.' Quistus, still staring into the trees, held the scroll closed. 'And he didn't break his oath, Prince. You're still alive.'

From the saddle, Viridorix looked down on the dark lands spread below him on each side of the ridge. Dawn would strike the mountaintops first. His horse found a single wild flower and ate it. The six cavalry troopers behind him on the blade of rock were as nervous as he was, but they weren't going to show it. 'Don't he look pretty,' one said. The other said, 'Suits him. Lovely in gold.'

'I'm not much good at riding,' Viridorix said nervously.

'You'll like it, lad. Easy as falling off a horse.'

'Fishing, now, I'm quite an expert. I could teach you something about fishing.'

'You're too small to teach me anything,' the trooper said.

'If you were a fish we'd throw you back.'

'Shut it, you lot.' The officer stood up in her saddle. 'Sun's rising.' Sunlight struck across the peaks around them, brilliant in their eyes, rippling down the slopes below. On their left the Blue Sea caught colour from the sky. From the shadows of the broad valley on their right, calls went up. 'We're seen. Couldn't miss us, could they? On the skyline.' Horns blared distantly, their sound spreading. 'Looks like we've kicked an ants' nest,' the officer said, pleased. She was blue-eyed; Kyrgyz blood. 'Hold it. Wait. Make your horse rear up, Prince, will you? Give the cloak a few flashes. Got to make sure.'

'Whoa,' Viridorix said, hanging on.

'Makes a lovely Prince, don't he?'

Far below them, the camps and straggly lines of tents and turf huts had come to life. People were running, lines of horsemen drawing brief patterns away from the corrals, spreading out, riding uphill. Viridorix said nervously, 'Now?'

'Hold it. Wait for it.' The officer held Viridorix's bridle. 'Steady.'

'Fast, aren't they?' Viridorix said.

'Steady.' She waited her moment, then slapped his horse's rump with the flat of her sword, and the troop set off galloping down the long hillside towards the sea. Viridorix looked back, grinning madly, the gold cloak flying behind him like a flashing gold wing. His eyes widened as the Huns came over the ridge like a breaking wave. Viridorix bent over the horse's neck, riding for all he was worth. Being lighter, he gradually pulled ahead of the cavalry.

The sun burnt through patches of sea mist. Grass gave way to a sandy beach where the boat was pulled up near a two-hut village. The sailors had thrown up a sand ramp during the night. They grabbed the horse and Viridorix rode from the ramp on to the boat, hanging on as they pushed off from the beach with oars. The troopers raced onward, splashing across the marshes, through islets of low trees, disappearing along the curve of the western shore. A few Huns split after them, following.

The girl sailors from Nirvana rowed Viridorix's boat a few hundred paces to sea then turned sideways just barely out of arrow range, giving the Huns along the shore the best possible view of the boy-Prince on horseback, his cloak shining in the sun. They put on their Roman armour so the *Qin* high command would know exactly who they were dealing with. Then they waved their swords one last time and, well-drilled, set sail to the north-west, a course to lay them along the headlands to Buh.

'Well,' Viridorix said, 'they know where to find me now.'

At Buh they'd been loading troops, horses and equipment on to the barges since first light. The barges slid downstream, some of the heaviest full-laden yet with only enough men aboard to man them, and they were good swimmers too. Others had thirty soldiers hidden behind lathe screens. Quistus watched them reach the sea and hoist sail, picking up speed slowly, following the wind east. Next came fishing boats, big enough to carry only one horse, eyes blinkered and nose invariably buried in a sack of grass, with someone to stroke its head soothingly. The two-man fishing skiffs came last, skipping light and quick across the waves.

Quistus knew he was taking a dreadful risk. He wrung one of the gold cloaks in his hands.

Maybe it would have been better, after all, to slip the Prince away through the mountains somehow, or ride north of the Wall in hope of chancing across troops loyal to Ban Chao. But was even Ban Chao loyal? No telling who'd put Aurelia's horse on a leading rein. Impossible to tell what was right or wrong. You could only gamble.

Gamble and lose. Gamble and win. It was only an empire.

The six cavalry who'd accompanied Viridorix rode in. The ruse had been successful; the Huns knew the Prince was crossing the sea on a boat. 'Well done,' Quistus told the grinning officer. 'Get yourselves aboard.'

He watched Yunyazi's cart being loaded on one of the ore-barges. Yunyazi climbed on the seat between Little Pelican and Fu, looking for all the world as though his cart drove the boat. The magician looked at Quistus, then looked away. No one knew what would happen. Little Pelican waved to him. Quistus spread his fingers and waved. She smiled and Fu barked, wagging his tail.

'We're ready, aren't we?' Quistus called out to Yunyazi. The barge turned easily in the river, pushed round in its own length by one of Heaven's discoveries that Yunyazi called a *duo* – a rudder, which he steered from the cart with a pole called a *duobing* – a tiller. Quistus shook his head. It was the weirdest contraption he'd seen. Yunyazi even had the Romans eating noodles.

'If not, my friend,' Yunyazi called back, almost beyond shouting distance, 'we shall entertain the enemy to death.'

Quistus watched from the bare headland. He thought it was the most ramshackle fleet that ever set sail. Nero would have been appalled. Publius said quietly at his elbow, 'People will remember us Romans for this for a thousand years, Quistus.'

'If they remember us tomorrow,' Quistus said, 'I'll be happy.'

They turned, hearing hoof beats. Horsemen in strange garb rode into the village below, tearing along, splinters flying from hooves on the quays, calling after the boats. They milled furiously, accoutrements jangling, horses pawing ferociously, then saw the two Romans on the headland and galloped up like thunder. A pony trotted neatly after the warhorses, the tall, slim rider with her dress spread as precisely as a lady's fan to hide her legs, holding the reins lightly between finger and thumb. Quistus swallowed. 'Zhao,' he said.

Somehow she curtseyed on horseback. Quistus laughed. He couldn't stop himself. 'Zhao!' he said.

The leader of the *Qin* wore snow-white enamelled armour and long, fierce sideburns, his head confined by a white dragon helmet which he swept off, shouting.

Zhao translated politely, '"Good morning. My name is Ban Chao. I apologize for being inappropriately dressed. The land round here is not covered in snow."'

'Welcome, Ban Chao.' Quistus bowed, speaking Chinese. 'I am Quistus.'

Ban Chao laughed. 'You speak too slowly for him,' Zhao said. 'He thinks you're funny. He doesn't like it.'

'Are you well, Zhao?'

'You must ask questions through my brother. But yes.'

'He laughs at me.'

'He knows about you and me. Or suspects.'

'Suspects *what*?'

Ban Chao shouted at some length. Zhao said, '"Where is the enemy?"'

'He said more than that.'

'I repeat only polite words. The enemy is all he's interested in, Quistus, not us.'

Quistus pointed beyond the sea and swept his arm across, showing the scale of the enemy. He asked, 'Where are your troops?' Ban Chao pointed at the men riding with him. Zhao coughed modestly.

Quistus said, 'You are the great Ban Chao, you command a hundred legions, and you've brought *thirty men* with you?'

Ban Chao threw his dragon helmet on the ground, shouting furiously.

'He says—' Zhao blushed. '"My arse is as sore as pulverized steak."' She listened patiently. 'He says he has fists of teak. Guts of a python. He has balls – testicles . . .' She stopped. 'Of solid iron.' She cut through the stream of words. '"Where is that bastard Buddha-lover Prince Ying?"'

Quistus grinned.

Zhao said, 'My brother is being very rude, because the great but rebellious Prince is the son of the God-Emperor Guangwu. My brother should apologize.'

'And his filthy consort mother and her slimy eunuch,' Ban Chao said without translation.

'We understand each other perfectly.' Quistus picked up the dragon helmet and handed it to the general. 'By being here you are in serious trouble, Ban Chao.'

'This is only a head.'

'How long before your main force arrives?'

Ban Chao folded his arms. He looked at Zhao. She translated fluently, '"It may be a short while."'

Quistus said, 'There *is* a main force?'

'"One swallow does not make a spring."' Zhao added, 'All these men are traitors for what they've done so far, Quistus.'

'There is *no* main force?'

'My brother says, "It is more important to arrive than to travel."'

Publius looked at Quistus. 'I like this man, I think.'

'Great General,' Quistus said, 'illustrious brother of a fearless sister—'

Zhao interrupted. 'My brother says he knows this.'

'This is your country, General. I can't tell you what to do.' Quistus held out the gold cloak. 'If you want to save the Son of Heaven, wear it. Ride around the north shore like the wind.'

'That's not strong enough,' Zhao said quickly. 'Tell him to ride like the strongest, fastest, most powerful, most smelly fart in the world. He mustn't stop. He must conquer everything in his path, roar like a dragon—'

Quistus stared at her. 'Zhao,' he said.

She turned impatiently, uttering a stream of Chinese. Ban Chao exclaimed and clasped Quistus's wrist. 'She tells me your plan. If it succeeds, women will sew embroideries of our likeness. I pray you live until tomorrow.' Ban Chao shouted to his men, swept the cloak around his shoulders, jammed his helmet over his head, and galloped away.

'I must attend to some business,' Publius said.

Zhao sat quietly on her pony. Quistus stared over the sea, watching the boats fanning out. She said, 'Are you a very little bit pleased to see me?'

'I am delighted in a small way,' he said, and touched her knee.

Prince Ying stood on the seashore. Wavelets broke against his armoured toes. On his left stood Golden Turtle, massive, shiny, his bare gold feet sunk deep in the sand. On his right King Punu, fleecy and sour-smelling, listened to a messenger. Punu nodded. 'Prince Zhang has been seen on a boat.' He pointed south.

'Told you,' Stigmus croaked from the cage. The sight of all this water was driving him crazy, even though he knew it was salt. 'See, told you the truth. You can trust me.'

'Send forces in case he tries to land,' Ying ordered Punu. 'Deny him the shore.' Punu shouted orders and men rode southward, jostling for the glory of being first.

'Launch the boats,' Prince Ying ordered. 'Golden Turtle, you will take command of the sea and kill everyone on it who does not submit to me.'

Golden Turtle bowed. 'And Prince Zhang?'

'Capture him alive,' Ying said, pleased with the eunuch's thoughtfulness. 'He's a boy, after all. Boys like to play. I'd like to play with him a while.'

Golden Turtle smiled.

Ying recalled him with a click of the fingernail. 'Leave one of your children with me, who speaks the alien tongue.'

Ying returned to his grand palanquin with its demon faces

and chanting priests. He ordered himself to be carried and set down beside the Dowager Empress's moon palanquin on the hill. Saffron banners fluttered. Ying liked this lookout point; from here they had a view of the sea spread out below them like an arena. He had the Roman planted behind them in his cage, swinging in the wind. He might be useful.

'Good afternoon, Mother,' he called, but she was asleep.

Scouts rode in from the north. An armoured unit had been seen escorting Prince Zhang along the north shore. 'Hmm,' Ying said.

'Destroy them!' ordered King Punu, and Huns galloped away northward.

'I know Quistus,' Stigmus croaked. The Gold Head translated from the Greek, hissing softly, its pointed teeth close to Ying's ear. 'He's the worst man I know, you can't trust anything he does, there's always a trick.'

Ying thought for a moment. 'Roman, if you give me information that wins me this battle I shall give you your life, your freedom and as much silver as you can carry.'

'Quistus is decoying you. It's a shell game.'

Ying half-turned. 'What will he really do?'

'What you least expect,' Stigmus groaned bitterly. 'He's a complete bastard. I should know, he's done it to me before.'

'Does he know Manas is just a sacrificial pawn? Is he as clever as that?'

Stigmus gaped.

'I thought not. Quistus doesn't know who he's up against.' Ying smiled. 'He doesn't even know the name of his enemy. The one who told Golden Turtle everything, all along.'

'Then victory is ours,' Stigmus said, relieved.

Ying ordered, 'Give him one cup of water.'

The Dowager Empress woke. 'Tea?' she said.

'I name this boat *Son of Heaven*, and call on the blessing of the great god Neptune for fair winds and good fortune.' Quistus's voice echoed off the deserted quays and warehouses. The soldiers manning the oars cheered.

The last boat to leave the river was also the fastest. *Son of Heaven* was the only new vessel, of fresh-cut green wood, its decks still slippery with sap, leaky as a sieve, and it wouldn't last a week. The keel was braced by taut ropes for strength and lightness, the hull built long for speed, very narrow and a little like a trireme, with the same proportions Quistus remembered from Nero's trireme *Apollo*, but the freeboard lowered to save weight because he didn't expect big seas. It had only a single bank of oars, and one of Yunyazi's rudders instead of a clumsy steering-oar. The rowers were Roman soldiers separated by a narrow gangway, protected by lathe screens. Instead of the bronze ram of a trireme, which was impossible to manufacture, from the bow a tree trunk stuck forward, ending in a heavy bulb wrapped in tarred silk.

Just before casting off Quistus brought Prince Zhang, gold-cloaked, from the warehouse where he'd been waiting, hidden, and hurried him aboard.

'I don't understand.' The boy asked Zhao, 'Where's Viridorix?'

'You'll see him soon.'

'Where's An? Where's Chong?'

She said, 'We must trust Quistus now.'

Quistus hauled on a rope. Zhao stopped Zhang's questions by sending him forward to help. As it happened the brisk wind blew on almost the right heading, and once the sail was raised the rowers rested, or baled out water.

After an hour or two the backs of slower sails appeared on the horizon, only one or two at first, a few masthead pennants. Quistus stood on the raised bow. One by one, or in groups of two or three, more sails rose into view. The fleet was well scattered across the horizon and he was pleased. Slowly the hulls of the nearer boats came closer, the beamier vessels splashing foam. In the mid-afternoon there was a squall and a few sails split, those boats falling back close to *Son of Heaven* until repairs could be made, or continuing under oars. Quistus waved to them. Yunyazi's boat was near enough to hail. The magician still sat incongruously on his cart, Little Pelican beside him. He shook his head in reply to Quistus's call. No one had seen the enemy. 'Perhaps, Quistus, they'll choose to keep their feet dry,' Yunyazi called, 'and all your plans will be useless.'

Quistus shook his head. In this good wind the slowest boat travelled faster than a man could run for long, or a horse trot, and they had the whole wide shore to choose from as a landing place. 'Ying has to meet us on the water,' he said. 'He has no choice.'

But still, he saw no sails coming towards them. No sign of the far shore yet, but he made out the high peaks rising beyond.

'There!' Zhang pointed, always keen-eyed. 'Look, a sail. That isn't one of ours.'

Quistus climbed the mast. Far ahead across the clear blue water, lit by the fanned rays of the sun behind him, masts and sails lifted one after the other from the horizon. Behind them he sensed the green haze of the eastern shore. The wind usually dropped for an hour or two in the evening.

He slid down, grinning to hide his nervousness.

'Looks like they can't wait to say hallo.'

Golden Turtle had himself winched to the masthead in a creaking basket. The coloured banner identifying his vessel fluttered by the pulley. Below, the two Gold Heads left to him drew swords to encourage the Huns to hold the rope tight.

Golden Turtle grunted. The sea to the west was silver, he stared into the sun. There they were, dark sails apparently rising one by one out of the sea, a line of shadows with the sun behind them. With luck the wind would blow them into his arms by evening.

They'd try and sneak by him in the dark. That wouldn't happen. Which one was the boy-Prince aboard? The boy was their figurehead, they'd make the most of him to stop their men losing heart. Gold cloak, gilded boat, definitely.

Golden Turtle looked back at the boats spreading across the water behind him, satisfied. Haihu was a considerable port, he had easily the more numerous fleet. The Hun crews were full of enthusiasm if not particularly skilful, but he knew they'd acquit themselves well in action by sheer force of numbers if nothing else. Even the moon was on his side, somewhere high in the blue overhead, hidden by sunlight. It wouldn't set until a few hours before dawn.

He had himself lowered to the deck. 'Excellent,' he told the *Qin* commander. 'Enemy in sight. Signal Prince Ying.' Huns had no use for signals – they just charged as soon as they saw the enemy – but the *Qin* used a banner system. The masthead banner dipped, replaced by one of a different shape and colour. The signal was acknowledged by shaped banners around the palanquins on the green hilltop, almost too far to see, and also from the masthead of Prince Ying's barge drawn up on the sand, its hastily-added gilding and gold ornamentation glittering in reflection of the sun.

'Excellent,' Golden Turtle repeated, gold silks flying from his belly and thighs in the evening wind.

Xireg. Still deserted, like all day. Good. No merchants, too afraid. No peasants, keeping their heads down. Plenty of empty buildings, empty spaces, places out of the light. No more burning sun.

Like blown smoke, a dark figure drifted from the shadows into the doorway of the Jade Horse inn. No one to see it, no sign of life in the square. It waited until the last of the sun left the rooftops, then the hilltops, then the mountain tops, then slid forward with strange twisting, hobbling steps, for it had no toes.

Movement. Footsteps, running, but slowly. It shrank back, hissing through its nose-hole. Watching from the shadows. Unblinking ash-grey eyes, waiting.

Manas ran into the square from the east. He ran with the steady, jogging, determined pace of a man who has run all day, and will continue his journey all night. Without looking around the giant stopped at the fountain by the shrine, drank from his cupped hands, and ran steadily from the western side of the square.

The dark figure watched until he was gone from sight. It touched the wall with its cindered hand, charcoal-black, without fingers or thumb, then smiled from its lipless mouth.

Good. It sniffed Manas's footprints, and followed the way he'd come.

The wind fell at dusk. 'Oars,' Quistus ordered. He waited until they were ready. 'Give way.'

The oars splashed, tugging at the calm water. The Romans rowed steadily. Quistus had decided against a drum and they took their rhythm from the men closest to him in the stern, backs swinging together. Zhang had begged to be allowed to steer and Quistus had agreed. Slowly, *Son of Heaven* caught up with the line of vessels scattered apparently higgledy-piggledy across the sea ahead, blending into the second wave a little to the left of centre.

Publius, aboard a gold-trimmed barge in the centre of the first wave, called to Quistus and pointed ahead. He thought

Ying's ships were being commanded by Golden Turtle. A mile away an enemy ship rowed into the lead, sail limp and coloured banner drooping at the masthead. Publius thought he saw Golden Turtle standing on the bow. Quistus nodded in agreement. 'Rest oars,' he ordered, throwing up his arm for the other captains to do the same. The fleet slowly lost way, finally hardly moving, standing in its reflection on the still waters in the last of the light.

The moon hung overhead, rippling slightly beneath the boats.

In the windless air they heard Publius give the order to row. The gold barge moved slowly ahead of the others. A boy stood on the bow, his gold cloak unmistakable. 'Where's Prince Ying's boat?' Quistus said. 'I'd hoped he'd want to capture Prince Zhang personally.' He'd banked on it.

'That person's not me,' Zhang said.

'Some of the girl soldiers are just your size,' Quistus said.

'You've dressed a *girl* as me?'

'No such thing as pride if you want to stay alive.'

'Can't see Prince Ying,' Zhang said after a while. Colour drained from the sea; everything turned to moonlight, silver and dark blue.

Zhao pointed to fires flickering ashore. 'Is he there?'

'You've been wearing your sand pouches,' Quistus said approvingly.

'I only need them to read.' Zhao sounded annoyed. 'Not for distance.' Flaming torches, a swarm of dim sparks, moved north along the shore. 'I think my brother's caused some trouble. Ying's sending reinforcements.'

'The more the better. That's what Ban Chao likes.'

Three of the enemy boats had turned towards Publius's barge. They could hear the Hun crews cheering, racing each other to the easy target. Obviously Quistus had made a big tactical error, or the captain of the barge was arrogantly foolhardy with his royal cargo.

'Golden Turtle's too far away,' Quistus said glumly. Grey-blue smoke drifted from Publius's barge, obviously a cooking-fire or somesuch out of control.

Yunyazi, his vessel close alongside *Son of Heaven*, stood on his cart seat. Little Pelican held the tiller while he chanted incantations. None of the words stopped the Huns. The Romans looked bitter as Quistus did nothing. Hun boats clustered round the bow of the barge now, coming alongside. Men leapt aboard, shouting. The gold cloak fluttered and dropped. Publius's rowers jumped into the water, swimming away. The girl who had been Prince Zhang ran aft and she and Publius dove from the stern together.

The Huns gave a roar of victory that travelled like a wave across the water. The ship was theirs. There was a bright flash.

The Dowager Empress smiled for the first time, making Ying pleased that his mother was happy. 'Look, look,' the old woman rasped, enchanted. '*Yanhuo*. Beautiful.' The sparkling green-gold, yellow-gold, blue-gold reflections rising from the sea shone in her rheumy eyes. 'My son, I'm so proud of you.'

The shockwave made the flags and banners and pennants give a single flap, like one harsh snap of snare drums. Ying stared. Flames, tiny with distance, continued to rise. The circle of light spread out, illuminating the boats like a battle painting. The roar of the explosion reached them. He could see three of his own boats burning. Three at least.

'But that's impossible,' he whispered. He turned to the Dowager Empress. '*Yanhuo* are *fun*.'

Golden Turtle tried to understand the anger of the spells, his sense of grievance almost personal. Spells, magic, the trans-mutations of alchemy, had always been his friends. Dangerous, yes, but controllable, even elegant. He understood them thor-oughly, they were all for the glory of Heaven. Now everything was turned over, changed. Boats were deadly shadows in the glimmering moonlight, oars pulled threatening silver lines. A barge turned towards him and his men rowed away frantically. No one wanted to attack a barge, or even come near one after such awful magic. Of course, that made it all the more likely that Prince Zhang was aboard one of the barges trying to sneak past.

An arrow thudded into the deck at his feet. Some of the barges, at least, had archers aboard. He ordered his own archers to fire, but there were so many ships milling about. He wasn't sure where the arrows were going; he could be hitting his own men.

'Cease fire!' he ordered.

Two Hun boats attacked a barge, one from each side. He saw

Romans jumping from the stern. That was a very alarming sign. 'Retreat!' he yelled to the attacking men. 'Get back, you fools!'

Yanhuo flared. Golden Turtle covered his ears at once. He'd learnt that much.

He ordered his men to row at full speed. There was wreckage in the water. Oars broke, the ship slewed round.

More arrows from the Roman ships. These trailed thin grey smoke. Fire arrows. Golden Turtle smiled. Two could play at that game.

But the arrows burst with sharp explosions as they struck, spreading flame. The flame sprayed, clinging to men and ships. A sail and mast burned with amazing brilliance, flames almost reaching the moon.

Smoke hung like fog over the water, stinking of burnt spells.

At last, a fishing boat, safe to attack. Arrows whickered into the smoke and sky. One struck Golden Turtle with an audible clang, making his men gasp. He broke it in his fist.

'You aren't the only magician with tricks, Yunyazi!' he shouted into the dark. He told his men, 'The fishing boats only have soldiers aboard. Pass the word. Attack.'

He saw a fishing boat, crewless, ram one of his own vessels. Both boats burst into flame, blinding in the dark.

And it *was* getting darker, the waters blackening as the moon set, the stars coming out.

The night wind blew, sails were hoisted, ships moved fast through the dark. He glimpsed a small skiff, only two men aboard. Golden Turtle pushed the heavy steering-oar round by himself, smiling at last. One of the men stood up, whirling a smoking ball on a string. He let go. There was a whistling noise.

Golden Turtle heard his men screaming. The ones on fire jumped overboard. He blinked, trying to see through the flame shapes printed on his eyes. The skiff had turned nimbly, gone. He ordered the fires put out.

'Pull back,' he ordered.

A *Qin* staff officer said, 'Sir?'

'Pull back,' Golden Turtle screamed. 'Regroup.'

The flagship turned, finding a patch of clear, dark water. Boats were burning all round, no pattern to it. 'Which one?' he murmured. 'Where is he?'

* * *

The Dowager Empress sat upright in her palanquin, her hands on the arms of her throne, the fires reflecting in her eyes. 'It isn't war.'

Ying looked back. 'Mother?'

'This isn't war. Where's the personal combat, the blood, the glory?'

He said, 'I'm going to my ship, now, Mother.'

Stigmus rattled the cage.

'Don't leave me here,' Stigmus called. 'Take me with you.'

Ying considered whether to have him silenced. 'Well, Roman, can I win?'

'Yes,' Stigmus said.

Ying nodded. 'Release him.'

The Dowager Empress called after them, 'If you lose, don't come back.' Ying stopped for a stride, then walked away.

The old woman settled back on her throne. 'Not war,' she muttered. 'It's just death.'

'Sir!' The staff officer pointed.

Golden Turtle turned wearily. Prince Ying's gilded ship was gliding across the grey dawn waters, black battle flags flying as the oars dipped and pulled. Prince Ying stood on the quarter-deck. On the rail behind him was a fragile-looking glass pot. He stared at Golden Turtle.

Golden Turtle got the message.

He swallowed. His ears rang from the thuds and bangs that had assaulted him in the night. He looked down at himself. His silks were torn, his beautiful gold flesh blackened here and there, chipped by flying debris.

He turned, seeing his Gold Heads behind him, darlings, faithful to the end. They'd never leave him. He was all they had. He smiled, and they stroked their peeling faces against his hard hands.

Prince Ying's rowers shipped oars. The gilded ship slid slowly to a stop, rolling gently.

Golden Turtle looked forward as the sun rose over the hill-tops, streaming past his depleted forces, illuminating the enemy fleet strung out. On each boat, every single one, stood a bright figure in a gold cloak. No way to tell which one was Prince Zhang. The one standing on the bow of the one decked out like a royal barge? Too obvious – but obviously he was meant to think that. Any of the several gold-cloaked figures standing aboard skiffs? The real Prince would never have agreed to such a menial setting . . . but he'd turned a one-room hut in Nirvana into a palace, hadn't he? Golden Turtle groaned aloud. Ten, fifteen princes on fishing boats, another in the stern of an oar-driven galley looking a little like a trireme, another sitting on horseback on a barge – more than one of those – yet another on a horse with Roman girl soldiers armed to the teeth, and any of them could be Zhang, or none.

Quistus had outwitted him.

Golden Turtle looked at Prince Ying's boat. Ying was standing with the Roman prisoner, Stigmus. The prisoner pointed.

Golden Turtle swung on his heel. A light flashed behind the galley, a mirror reflecting the rising sun. It flashed again, *tick-tick-tick*. No accident.

'Give way,' he ordered. 'Break your backs. Pull, you Hun bastards.' He pushed the steering-oar himself, turning the bow towards Quistus's ship.

'Golden Turtle,' Zhao said calmly. 'He's seen us.' She called to Yunyazi to get his vessel clear, then asked Quistus, 'Run for it?'

Quistus watched the boat turning towards them, picking up speed.

'We've got the legs of them,' Zhao said. 'Quistus? Orders?'

'No,' Quistus said. He turned to Zhang. 'This is your choice. You've been running away for as long as you can remember. Sooner or later, a Prince has to stop running. He has to stop and turn and fight, or keep running for ever. Up to you, son.'

The drum thudded. The Huns hauled at the oars, ugly faces pouring sweat. Their hands left blood on the oars. Still the other ship hadn't moved. Motionless in its reflection, oars hanging, helpless.

Sitting duck.

Suddenly its oars swung, bending, pulling. The galley began to move, picking up speed. Quistus had made a fatal mistake, he'd left it too late. Golden Turtle watched the galley passing ahead of his bow, speeding up, but not fast enough. Golden Turtle nodded for the Gold Heads to use the whips. Faster, now. Perfect target. He'd ram them broadside-on, roll them

under. He hauled on the steering-oar, made allowance for deflec-
tion. Just . . . *there*.

The galley turned so fast it almost stopped in the water.
There was no steering-oar, it just turned by magic, and suddenly
Golden Turtle was going much too fast, overrunning the other
boat, leaving his own flank exposed. The tree trunk on the bow
of the galley splintered his oars, struck into the side, wedged
between the beams. Not a killing blow. All right, good, come
round. Tear it out.

Sparks stuttered from the silk-wrapped bulb on the trunk.

Flash.

Blind. Deaf.

Sight, hearing.

Golden Turtle stared at his body. There was blood all over
him but it wasn't his. The vessel rolled and he slid. He dug his
hands into the deck, caught hold of a deck-beam. 'No,' he said.
His boat was going over, he could feel it coming up over him.
Noises. Oars swept above his head, still rowing, as Quistus's
boat, the standard-bearer holding aloft the banner and eagle of
V *Scythia*, mounted his overturning vessel. The sea came up
under Golden Turtle. He clung to the rail as Quistus's boat
balanced, sliding, tilting down into the water, the stern coming
up, the bow digging in, putting out the fire. Then the stern
splashed down through the smoke, sending out heavy waves.
Quistus's galley hauled round, the oars backing, twisting towards
Prince Ying's boat, but Golden Turtle couldn't see because of
the smoke, or hear for screams as his own boat rolled down.

He heaved himself up the hull as it rolled, smashing holes
with his fists to get a grip. Air gusted out, screams, then water.
He could feel his men beating on the planks below his belly.

Golden Turtle sat straddling the keel. The battle had moved
on. All he could see was smoke. He had a horror of going
down into the water. He supposed he could walk ashore along
the bottom. After all, he was *Zhenren*, *Waidan* and *Neidan*. He
hoped it wasn't too muddy.

The sea rose over his feet, then over his knees. He twisted,
seeing his Gold Heads crouched on the hull behind him. 'Help
me.' They scuttled forward obediently, then stopped.

'Find a boat!' he shouted.

Something in the water took hold of Golden Turtle's foot.

He looked around calmly. The smoke cleared for a moment

and he saw Quistus's galley alongside Prince Ying's, which lowered its flags. He chuckled and tried to pull his foot free. Prince Ying turned, sword in hand, and smashed the glass pot.

Golden Turtle shrieked.

Prince Ying handed his sword to Quistus. Surrender.

The sea rose over Golden Turtle's waist. He struggled and held out his arms for his Gold Heads to lift him, but the pressure on his foot was very hard now, though more like the squeezing of hands than the grip of fingers.

No one lifted him.

He looked round. His two Gold Heads were backing away. He'd never seen this look on their faces before.

Terror.

Golden Turtle stared down into the clear water. Some things were too ugly to come back to life. He opened his mouth to scream.

Blue sea, blue sky, green grass. The sun was warm all day and for once no one noticed the mosquitoes. Quistus stood on the deserted seashore wishing for one of Omba's coffee balls, elated and exhausted at the same time. Driftwood and fleece rolled in the waves, and the air still smelt of angry spells. The Hun camp was deserted, tents abandoned, campfires kicked over.

Yunyazi came ashore with Little Pelican. 'Our victory was inevitable,' he told her loudly. 'I foresaw it.'

'You're so wise, Yunyazi,' Little Pelican said. Fu gave a jealous bark and Yunyazi picked him up. 'Last night he was killed in an explosion you know. I brought him back to life. That's the second time. Naughty dog,' he scolded, pretending to be angry.

Little Pelican touched Quistus's hand. 'I never forgot the promise I made to you and Zhao. In the celebrations I'll dance for you tonight.'

Zhao overheard. 'It's a great honour, Quistus.'

Quistus bowed to the dancer. 'We'll be very honoured indeed.'

Ban Chao galloped along the shore with his men, pulling up at the last moment in a spray of sand. 'I rode like a typhoon, Quistus! Observe!' He pointed to the north, a long column of troops advancing in rapid order. 'I know, I said a week, but these are fine men, always seeking to impress me! A whole legion force-marching through the mountains to reach my side! Traitors all!' He saw Zhang coming ashore. Ban Chao's horse bent its forelegs while the general bowed extravagantly from its back.

'The Emperor will hear from me that you disobeyed orders,' Zhang said, then gave a small smile, 'and why.'

Ban Chao saluted, reared his horse, and galloped south after Hun stragglers. Zhang turned to Quistus. 'Must there be celebrations? I must reach Loyang quickly.'

'These men and women fought for you against enormous odds, lived when they thought they'd die, and won when they thought they'd lose. I'd say a celebration is in order, wouldn't you?'

Zhang watched a Hun body rolling in the surf. 'Obviously Roman military tactic number thirty-seven was successful, but what is it?'

'That information's covered by tactic number thirty-eight.'

'Thirty-eight?'

'Never reveal number thirty-seven.'

A boat grounded. Prince Ying was dragged ashore, in chains, by Stigmus. 'Don't worry, Quistus, my friend,' he called, jerking the chains. 'I know where to keep this one safe until justice can be done.'

Publius looked as weary as Quistus. 'A great victory, I suppose. One worthy of the Republic. Not a single man or woman lost.' He grinned with his teeth. 'On our side, that is! The Huns are moving west, Ban Chao snapping at their heels. Loyang is safe.' He moved away, talking to Zhang.

Quistus walked uphill to the palanquin of the so-called Dowager Empress. She sat bolt upright, her eyes reflecting the empty sea. She was quite dead, and did not look unhappy.

The drums beat slower, like a heartbeat, then faster again. The bonfire burned low, then as Yunyazi raised his arms the flames erupted into a great standing pillar of fire, illuminating the rapt circle of faces. The soldiers had spread out over the grassland, a natural amphitheatre. Little Pelican was not dressed as *long*, dragon, as before; she simply was. By her posture, stillness, her intense personal discipline and her training that filled every movement with subtle meaning, she became Dragon.

She stood motionless, her tiny figure throwing a tall dragon's tail of shadow.

At the front of the audience Quistus sat a little behind, and lower than, Prince Zhang. Zhao sat on the other side, her hands pressed together, yet wore no make-up. Zhang was dressed in his now famous gold cloak and a broad-brimmed gold hat, his face shadowed as the fire brightened.

Prince Ying gazed inscrutably from the bamboo cage, Stigmus standing with a drawn sword, old Shu ready with a spear if needed.

Yunyazi gave a warbling cry, throwing up his arms, and the flames curled into the shape of a dragon's head. Little Pelican began to move.

'Stop.'

Quistus walked forward.

'What?' Yunyazi asked.

'Didn't foresee that, did you?' Quistus said.

Yunyazi bowed. 'I know what Heaven allows me to know.'

'You're just a man,' Quistus said.

Yunyazi drew himself up. 'A person who dares disrespect a magician will find himself wriggling like a worm. I am *Zhenren, Waidan, Neidan*.'

'I don't doubt it.' Quistus raised his voice over the sound of the flames, talking to the circle of soldiers and the royal entourage as well as the magician. 'We all know Yunyazi has great power. We wouldn't have won our victory without him. I wouldn't be here without him, twice. He saved me from lead poisoning and from smallpox.' He faced Yunyazi. 'I'm for ever in your debt. But you aren't perfect. You're only a man.'

Quistus nodded at the dragon's head of flame. 'Put that noise out, will you.'

Yunyazi breathed in. The dragon's head fell silent but the flames remained, eerily writhing and curling. A sandpiper called across the marshes. Someone in the audience coughed.

'You see,' Quistus said, 'Manas didn't murder Cerberus. Manas was wholly honourable, not only to the Prince but also to his accomplice. He bit out his own tongue rather than reveal their name. Manas wasn't even the leader. The accomplice, the leader, the real traitor, murdered Cerberus. Murdered him ritually – why, I kept asking myself, why was that necessary? – then left the house to find Gold Heads while Manas disposed of the body. The traitor returned empty-handed, set off the *yanhuo* in a desperate attempt to attract attention to the Villa Paria—'

'I know all this,' An called.

'Naturally, I suspected An, because he kept trying to make me suspect Zhao, he didn't like her. Feared her. Feared her influence over the Prince growing greater than his own. An was conveniently out of the way with the silver when Duke Chen's men attacked. So was Chong. Neither fought in the battle, that was left to Wild Swan. Maybe it was *both* men on Ying's side.'

'Yes,' Ying called from the cage. 'Both of them.' Stigmus prodded him with the sword. He shut up.

'The traitor left clues for Golden Turtle to follow all the way to Rome. At the Villa Paria, Wild Swan showed signs of having suspicions and wanting to confide them to Zhao. She was infected with smallpox and drugged with opium, not to ease her despair, but to keep her quiet.'

'By Little Pelican!' Yunyazi pointed.

'Your opium,' Quistus said.

Little Pelican lost her poise. 'I loved Wild Swan.'

'I know. You were friends. I thought, maybe the traitor is Little Pelican, but that's ridiculous. How could she get extra opium to drug Captain Lo? Maybe she put small doses aside – but no, Yunyazi said he administered the drug to Wild Swan personally. How could Little Pelican know the spells for *yanhuo*, when only Yunyazi knows them? Would she really be prepared to murder her friend so horribly?

'So, ladies and gentlemen, I decided to look for someone innocent to lead me to the guilty person. Innocent but foolish. Flawed. But *Qin* manners, and such a different culture from Rome, made it easy for you to hide flaws of character from me. It wasn't until last winter that I realized that you could *all* have been used.'

'This really is ridiculous,' An said.

'I knew Omba was with child by Manas, but that was love. It'll be born by now. Lots of relationships had nothing to do with love. Genji didn't know if she was pregnant by Shu or by Chong. Fen didn't know whether the father of her child was An, or Yunyazi, or Shu. Lien's child is by Yunyazi.'

'She loves me,' Yunyazi complained. 'Of course I don't love her, mere Lien! The very thought!'

'Only two girls did *not* get pregnant, Zhao and Little Pelican. I'll vouch for Zhao. That leaves Little Pelican.'

The dancer twirled slowly, limp fingers dangling, a flower waiting for the sun to open its petals.

'I thought she had no lover because her feet were ugly. I was wrong. To *Qin*, her mutilated feet are the highest expression of beauty. Little Pelican could have any man she wanted, and did, as you all know from personal experience. But who did she *really* want, and why?'

'It was me,' Yunyazi said. The colour drained from his face. 'But she loves me. How could she not?'

'No.' Little Pelican twirled. 'Not loved you.'

'My body, my knowledge, my strength, gives her sexual ecstasy. There's a profound spiritual bond between us.'

'Never loved you, magician, not one little bit. Lied.'

'We'd make love in my room. She watched me work. I hid nothing from her.'

'You're a bad lover. Thoughtless, selfish, soft, ignorant.' Little Pelican twirled, spinning faster. Quistus stopped her. She stared up, her hair hanging almost to the ground, vermilion ribbons suddenly lifeless.

'I didn't catch smallpox from Zhao's clothes,' Quistus said. 'Little Pelican wiped towels on Wild Swan before she came to me.'

Stigmus pointed his sword. 'Yesterday she signalled Ying with a mirror, showing Prince Zhang's boat!'

'I'd say that pretty much confirms it,' Quistus said. 'Thank you, Stigmus.' He added, 'She wrote *OZTIO*. She knew Latin. She was sleeping with Cerberus.'

The girl called to Prince Ying, 'Save me, Father. Tell them!'

'It's true,' Ying said. 'She's my daughter by a woman . . . a woman even less than a consort. Little Pelican was brought up in secrecy in Chu. Of course she hates Zhao – Little Pelican should have been brought up a lady, like Zhao. Little Pelican knew who I was, knew I loved her mother. It was I who paid for her lotus feet, her schooling in dance, I who brought out her talent.' He said tenderly, 'My favoured one, I'd have made you more than a lady – my princess.'

Little Pelican reached into her hair, demon-faced. Before Quistus could stop her the knife flashed through the air, thudding through Prince Zhang's gold cloak into his chest.

Little Pelican stared, dishonoured – and failed.

'Ow,' said Viridorix. He pulled off the hat and cloak to reveal leather armour. 'Who's going to pull this out?'

Prince Zhang came from the crowd, dressed as Viridorix. He

pulled out the knife. He looked angry enough to use it on the girl. Instead he called for the Family Book. Little Pelican's name, her soul, would be erased by a stroke of the brush; she would never have existed.

Quistus crouched face-to-face. 'I know Cerberus's death wasn't a ritual killing, Little Pelican. You were simply too short to reach his throat. You started off in the place you most hated men, between his legs, and kept cutting as he fell. That was all.'

Little Pelican looked Quistus in the eyes.

She danced away from him. He didn't stop her. She danced around the dragon's head of silent fire, ribbons flashing, faster, until she danced into the mouth of the fire.

Epilogus

'You are in the presence of Emperor Liu Ming-Di of Loyang, Son of Heaven, ruler of all Earth under Heaven, direct descendant of God, Huang-Di, by whose mandate the Emperor rules the great family of Middle Earth. Bow down.'

The audience chamber of the Imperial Palace in Loyang was priceless green jade from roof to floor. Quistus knelt on jade, looked at himself in jade, his forehead icy cold from pressing against jade, his knees aching. The jade was polished to a mirror shine so perfect that the ranks of silent courtiers stood, from his point of view, upside down. No sound in the immense palace was louder than a whisper, and every whisper echoed, growing louder before it died away.

The Emperor sat high as Heaven on a throne of white marble, his robes carefully arranged down the steps, each fold deliberate and perfect. At least, so it seemed to Quistus, upside down, peeping out of the corners of his eyes. The Son of Heaven was so glorious that he could be viewed only from a distance, by his reflection.

A door boomed. Footsteps, running. Prince Zhang ran past,

echoing. 'Hallo, Quistus! Hallo, Zhao!' he called. Gasps – then heads quickly lowered – as the Emperor came down the steps, robes sliding after him as he took his son in his arms, lifted him, hugged him.

'My son!'

Publius made a face, trying to stretch his knee.

'Prince Ying.' The Emperor spoke in the soft, gentle tones of the utterly powerful. 'I should order you to commit suicide. It seems at once excessive yet insufficient. You are my father's son. It is my judgement that you are no longer Prince Ying. Your lands are mine. Get you to a monastery and study the works of the Buddha. Go.'

Prince Ying was carried away. Ban Gu, the historian, wrote the Emperor's judgment with a tiny brush.

'Ban Chao.' The Emperor clicked his fingernails. 'You flouted orders, exceeded your authority, betrayed my trust. Well done – this once. You will continue to pursue the Huns west. You will not return until they are gone for ever.'

The Emperor turned. 'Publius Crassus. You and your brave people are rewarded with the town of Lixian in Gansu Province, for ever, to live in peace.'

The satin-slippered feet moved silently past Quistus. 'Yuan An, I appoint you Grand Administrator of Chu. Wang Chong, you are District Secretary. Yunyazi the magician, you will return to the mountains to seek and find the Golden Elixir. Stigmus the Praetorian, your capture of once-Prince Ying earns the gratitude of all *Qin*. Viridorix the Gaul, you saved the Prince's life and will be his servant and friend. As for you, Shu, you shall have a woman to look after you in your old age as a man should be looked after – though I warn you, one younger than you, and possessing an ardent spirit.'

The slippered feet returned without a sound. 'Quistus.' A hand touched his shoulder. 'Walk with me to the window.'

Quistus was amazed that the Emperor was so short. They joined Zhang at the window. Except for Ban Gu, busy at his task, no one in the room dared look at them. 'Quistus the Roman, you've succeeding in returning a much-loved son to his eternally grateful father. Perhaps, too, you have saved my Empire from destruction. There is nothing whatsoever I can offer you in reward – gold, jewels, earthly pleasures – that would not be an insult to so great a service. In fact, I ask even more of you. I would know much more of Rome. We will talk.'

Quistus bowed.

'You will keep the deadly secret of *yanhuo*. Entertainments for the joy of Heaven shall not be used to cause death. Is it true you crossed the mountains that touch the face of Heaven?'

'Yes, we did.'

The Emperor touched Quistus's finger. 'You wear the dragon ring Zhang gave you. It is not without usefulness. However, Zhang tells me the Emperor of Rome also owed you a reward for a similarly great service that you performed for him.' Quistus looked wary. This was dangerous ground; it had landed him in Luca's tavern. 'What prize did you demand of your Emperor, Quistus?'

'Viridorix told me about the letter Nero gave you,' Zhang said quietly. 'The one with the seal, that you almost died retrieving from the Villa Marcia while Rome burnt.'

Quistus chuckled. 'It was a promise. Nero made me a promise.'

'The Emperor of Middle Earth will promise no less than the Emperor of Rome.'

Quistus whispered, 'Nero promised me "Whatever the Emperor least wishes to give."'

Ming-Di studied him. 'A powerful promise indeed. A dangerously powerful promise, perhaps.' He nodded to Ban Gu. 'It is written. Do not use it lightly, Quistus.'

'I hope,' said Quistus, 'never to need to use it at all.'

Post Scriptum

B itterly cold in Nirvana, the first snow falling, and Manas travelled faster than news from the East. He was wrapped in stolen rugs and blankets, holding a goat on a leash, and the sack on his back was full of goat's milk, yoghurt and cheese.

He tethered the goat a mile from the stockade, stashed the

sack under a rock, and came forward through the dark and snow. The guards never saw his blue eyes beneath the watch-towers, the wind never heard him, the snow never touched him.

He stopped at the window of the hut by the lake and peered through. A candle burned on the table in case the babies woke, or needed to be fed.

He rubbed grease from his fingers so the door hinges made no sound. A little snow came in with him. The women were all sleeping. Fen's baby whimpered softly. Genji muttered a dream. Lien had taken her baby with her into bed.

Omba, of course, slept on her back. She always slept on her back. She was snoring, too. Never stopped. Memories flooded back to Manas. He loved her, truly loved her. He knew he'd break her heart sooner or later.

Better sooner, then.

His son slept in the cradle by her bed, fists clenched, a birthmark just showing on one tiny palm.

Semetei, he thought, for he could not speak.

He picked up his sleeping son, wrapped him in blankets, and slipped them all together inside the rugs over his chest. He backed out, closed the door, and Omba turned in her sleep. Her hand touched the warm cradle. She smiled and slept.

They never saw him go. He was the wind and the snow.

Manas walked with long strides, the sack swinging, his baby tied to his front. From time to time he camped, made a fire, milked the goat. Semetei was a strong son. To the north, beyond the desert, Manas saw the great mountains grow a little clearer each day. Home.

Kyrgyz.